I WASN'T ALONE . . .

Adrenaline rushed through my body, urging me to flee, but I couldn't run.

My heart pounded as I remembered what Daryl Buckmeyer had looked like that night, battered and bloodied. I wondered if he'd died right away or whether he'd slowly bled to death while Frank was searching for me in the cornfield.

I thought of Molly. Who would take care of her if something happened to me? Who would teach her not to be afraid?

I stabbed at the lock, but my hands shook so badly I dropped my key ring. Somehow, I managed to stand. I fit the key into the lock, shoved the door open and stepped outside.

Right into the arms of a man . . .

CHARLOTTE HUGHES

AND AFTER THAT, THE DARK

AVON BOOKS ◆ NEW YORK

**VISIT OUR WEBSITE AT
http://AvonBooks.com**

This book is dedicated with love and admiration
to two wonderful writers,
Janet Evanovich and **Suzanne Forster**.

AND AFTER THAT, THE DARK is an original publication of Avon
Books. This work has never before appeared in book form. This work is
a novel. Any similarity to actual persons or events is purely coincidental.

AVON BOOKS
A division of
The Hearst Corporation
1350 Avenue of the Americas
New York, New York 10019

First Avon Books Printing: February 1997

AVON TRADEMARK REG. U.S. PAT. OFF. AND IN OTHER COUNTRIES, MARCA
REGISTRADA, HECHO EN U.S.A.

Printed in the U.S.A.

RA 10 9 8 7 6 5 4 3 2 1

Acknowledgments

I would like to acknowledge the support of two buddies, Alfie Thompson and Lois Walker. A big hug to my husband, Ken, for all the little things he takes care of so that I might sit in front of a computer day and night. A special word of thanks to Donna and Norm Schaefer for their wonderful proofreading skills, and to Courtney Henke for her brainstorming talents.

Much praise goes to the following people for their advice and expertise in the writing of this book: Dr. Marshall Jones, pathologist, Beaufort Memorial Hospital; Dr. Robert F. Deane, retired pathologist, San Diego County; Dr. Mary St. John Gay, psychiatrist, Beaufort, SC; Tracy Dingle, social worker, Burton, SC; and Officer Dana Chandler of the Butler Police Department, Butler, MO. Your time and energy in this project are much appreciated.

Lastly, I would like to thank Mrs. Mary DeRosa, who prayed to Saint Martha (the saint of good wealth) every Tuesday (which, I understand, is the only day this saint receives prayers) so that I might sell this work.

Prologue

I was fifteen the night Daryl Buckmeyer died. Until then, my life had been uneventful. I'd never traveled more than a hundred miles from home, never been kissed, never even attended a school dance, for that matter. I suppose you could say I'd lived a sheltered life. I was a tomboy and a bookworm and every inch a virgin. My older sister, Lurlene, named after our great-grandmother, was a different story. Buh-lieve-you-me, she knew her way around the backseat of a man's car.

I'm fairly certain our parents suspected, though, on account they'd send her to her room whenever a repairman was called to the house.

Even now I remember wondering what was the big deal over sex. After all, I'd been enjoying the same pleasures alone, since I was eleven. That's not to say I didn't feel guilty afterward; we were Southern Baptists, and fear and shame were instilled at an early age. I'd do the deed, then spend the rest of the night thinking of Reverend Parmalee's sermons—about how God sends pestilence to those whose flesh is weak. I just knew that come morning our crops would be destroyed by locusts, and we'd all go hungry because I'd had my hand down my britches again. I once shared my concerns with Lurlene, and she told me I was as crazy as our Aunt Bessie.

Aunt Bessie was the family lunatic who was carted off to a mental institution in Columbia, South Carolina, for

1

trying to drown herself at family picnics. She'd claimed it was a peaceful way to die; also claimed she heard Mozart during these near-drowning events. My father said Bessie wouldn't recognize Mozart if he walked up and slapped her in the face, since all she ever listened to was country and western. He didn't much care for Aunt Bessie; he was the one who usually got stuck going into the water after her.

I guess we all have somebody in our family we don't want to be like, sort of an *anti*–role model. I was cursed with two: Aunt Bessie and Lurlene.

Being a virgin didn't necessarily mean I was perfect, of course. Which explained my rather perilous position that night—me out in the middle of nowhere at one A.M. and my daddy's pickup truck parked down the road with an empty gas tank. Lurlene was spending the night with a friend, so I'd decided it was my turn to have a little fun for a change. I knew, though, that Daddy would beat me into next week if he found out I'd been joyriding in his truck. Afterward he'd have me digging fence post holes and hauling manure till my hands bled.

My parents were harder on me than they were on Lurlene. Sometimes I resented it since if anybody deserved to haul cow dung it was my sister. She'd already failed ninth grade twice, and here I'd been an honor student all through school. Even back then, I knew I wanted to be somebody— a teacher, perhaps, if I could maintain scholarship grades. But I suspected I wouldn't live to graduate high school if I couldn't get myself out of that jam.

Lucky for me, I had run out of gas within walking distance of Fludd's Service Station. Still, it was a miserable trek. The night was airless and hot, even for July in the Carolinas, and I was gritty and sweat-soaked, my sneakers covered in road dust by the time I arrived. I crossed the cracked, oil-splattered pavement. The station looked as deserted as a cemetery after nightfall. A naked 150-watt bulb created a half circle of light near the front door to the station; nearby, a thermometer hung on a partially rusted sign advertising Camel cigarettes. I fanned a sluggish, dust-colored moth aside as I tried to read the thin line of mercury.

Eighty-five degrees. It didn't matter that the sun had set hours ago; it was still hotter'n an oven at Thanksgiving, humidity thick as Karo syrup. Everything was still. The oak leaves and Spanish moss didn't so much as flutter. That was about to change, though. I sensed it as I watched heat lightning dance along the horizon and heard thunder rumble off in the distance. The drone of cicadas was shrill and unrelenting, a sure sign that something was about to happen.

There was no way I could have known what the night had in store for me, no way I could have prepared myself.

I pushed open the service station door and was hit by a blast of cold air; it coughed and sputtered from a tired old window unit that had seen one too many hot spells. Sixteen-year-old Daryl Buckmeyer sat at a battered metal desk reading a comic book. He was a stocky, square-faced teenager with oily hair and a chin speckled with acne. He smiled the minute he saw me. Both the smile and the overalls he wore looked goofy, and kids didn't mind bringing it to his attention every chance they got. But nobody knew cars like Daryl. He could hear an automobile traveling six blocks away, give you the make and model, and tell you what was under the hood. It was actually kind of spooky that he knew so much about cars, seeing as how he wasn't allowed to drive one and probably never would be. His older brother, Herschel, who'd practically raised him, had recently purchased a brand new ten-speed bike for Daryl, and that seemed to suit him just fine.

"Em-lee, what are you doing out this time of night?" he asked, speaking slowly, as though he had to stop and search for just the right word as he went.

"It's a long story, Daryl. You got a gas can around here?"

"Uh-huh." He glanced around. "Somewheres."

"Would you mind filling it up for me while I run to the rest room? I need to wash up." My mother had raised me to believe that it was bad manners to discuss bodily functions. I started for the bathroom as Daryl began to search for a gas can. As he opened the door to the garage in back, I caught a glimpse of the clutter: oil rags, twisted tire rims, discarded fan belts, and Daryl gazing at it all as if wondering where he should start looking. I shook my head sadly and closed the bathroom door.

The room smelled of pine cleaner and urine, and it was painted the same mossy green as the rest of the station. I figured Mr. Fludd, the owner, must have found a bargain on that particular shade. No one in his right mind would choose that color on purpose. I peed and flushed the toilet, then washed my hands and face at the small sink. The porcelain finish had eroded over the years, leaving a dull, sandpapery surface that had absorbed a multitude of stains. I pressed a wad of wet paper towels to the back of my neck and wished I had stayed in my bed.

I was about to cut the light and open the door when another door slammed. Someone shouted angrily and it puzzled me, because I couldn't remember Daryl ever raising his voice about anything. Had he made a mistake, put the wrong kind of gasoline in a customer's car?

I cracked the door and peeked out. Daryl and another man stood nose to nose in the garage, just inches from the door. I didn't recognize the man because at the moment he had his back to me. I thought he looked familiar, though: tall and rangy, dressed in ragged jeans and a dirty white T-shirt. Probably one of Lurlene's rejects. My heart gave a start when I saw the tire iron in his hand.

"Stop jerking me around, retard," the man said, "and tell me where the money is."

I knew that voice. Frank Gillespie. If there was trouble in town, it usually had his name all over it.

"I don't got no money, Fwank," Daryl said.

"You're lying. Everybody in town knows Old Man Fludd keeps his wad stashed in a safe here."

I suddenly realized I was witnessing a robbery, and my knees immediately went loose as banana pudding. I swallowed, though with great difficulty; it felt like I was trying to get one of those tire rims down my throat. Even in my state of panic, I couldn't help but wonder why Frank was forced to rob when his family was the richest in town. Drugs, no doubt. Frank had been in more treatment centers than most movie stars. Rumor had it his daddy had cut off his allowance because he'd gotten tired of watching the money go up Frank's nose.

I had to do something, but I knew I was no match for Frank. I searched for a weapon in the tiny bathroom; all I could find was a plastic toilet brush. I grabbed it anyway.

Daryl was crying. He reached into a pocket and brought out a fistful of bills. "All's I got on me is a buncha ones, Fwank. To make change. Mr. Fludd don't let me have more'n that. I'm not so good at keepin' up with money."

"And why is that, dumb ass?" Frank demanded. "Is it 'cause you got shit for brains? And 'cause you're a fucking gimp?"

Daryl looked away shamefully.

"Answer me, stupid."

"Yeah."

"Yeah, what?"

"I got shit for brains."

"Well, I'm fixin' to find out if they're made of shit or not."

Without warning, Frank raised the tire iron and brought it down in one swift, crushing blow. Daryl didn't even have time to try and block it. Blood spurted and sprayed the walls. Daryl went down. Down, down, down, like a lifeless slab of meat. I dropped the toilet brush and clamped my hands over my mouth to keep from crying out. Too late. A small, whimpering-puppy-dog sound had escaped. Frank turned a split second before I slammed the door.

I fumbled with the lock, my hands made clumsy by fear, and there was pressure from the other side. The next thing I knew, Frank's fingers were wriggling through the crack like fat white worms. How had he managed to move so quickly? I wondered. I pushed the door harder; he cussed.

I slammed my body against it; he howled like a madman. Nevertheless, I could feel myself losing ground, feel the door inching open. Suddenly, he grabbed a handful of my hair and jerked. My head hit the door with a crushing blow. Light danced before my eyes, and I felt sick to my stomach.

"You're not going to get away from me, girlie," he muttered through the crack of the door. "I'm going to slice you up like summer sausage before we're through." He gave a menacing laugh. "Your hair smells good, you know that? Like strawberries. We might have some fun before I kill you."

Drawing from what little strength and courage was left in my body, I wrenched my head around and clamped my teeth down, as hard as I could, on his fingers. His scream was agonizing, but I didn't let that stop me. I refused to let go, even when I thought my jaw would crumble from the effort, even when I tasted blood. My stomach pitched, but I knew I had no choice. This man was going to kill me.

Somehow Frank managed to free himself, and when he did, I slid the lock home.

"You goddamn fucking bitch," he said from the other side of the door, kicking it several times in the process. "I'm going to break this door down and wring your neck. Just like a fucking chicken."

I heard his voice grow distant, heard various sounds like metal scraping the floor, something falling. I imagined Frank kicking items around in the garage as he searched for something to break in with. I cussed under my breath, realizing that when my back was against the wall, I knew more four-letter words than Lurlene.

I spied the small window and wondered if I would fit through it. I had to try; it was my only hope. I could probably reach it if I stood on the large metal trash can. I grabbed it and turned it over, dumping what looked like a month's worth of paper towels and sanitary napkins. All I could do was hope and pray the window hadn't been painted shut.

Luck was on my side. The window slid open almost

effortlessly, and I wondered if my good fortune had any-thing to do with my saving myself for marriage. Something slammed loudly against the door, splintering wood, and I glanced back long enough to see an ax blade sticking through. I thought my heart would leap right out of my chest. Frank pulled the ax out and swung it against the door once more as I popped the screen from the window and heaved myself up, scratching both elbows as I went. I just barely made it, thanks to the fact that I had almost no boobs or butt to speak of.

The door seemed to explode, and I knew Frank had made his way into the bathroom. I propelled myself through the opening and dropped to the ground on the other side. The good news was that I landed on my feet; the bad news, I twisted my ankle as a result. Pain radiated all the way up my calf, bringing tears to my eyes. I wondered how I would explain it to my parents, then realized I might not have to worry about it.

I stood there a second, eyes darting this way and that for any sign of life. Darkness everywhere, not even a headlight on the highway. I wasn't surprised. Nobody in Mossy Oaks stayed out later than nine o'clock. Those who did were Hell-bound, according to the Baptists.

I heard the station's front door open, and I knew Frank was coming after me. I also knew that the nearest house was a quarter of a mile away, through a massive cornfield. I took off at a fast hobble and disappeared into the field. Finally I was able to buy a little time while Frank searched the shadows around the gas station. I heard the rustle of dried cornstalks and knew he had followed me in. I realized I'd never manage to outrun him with an injured ankle; the only thing I could do was stop running and try to hide among the tall stalks.

Frank ran for a bit, almost in circles before he must've realized the futility of it. I huddled near the ground, trying to control my heavy breathing and the urge to scream. I wondered if Daryl was dead.

"Okay, girlie," Frank called out. "The game is over. I

just want to talk to you. I'm not going to hurt you."

Like hell you won't, I thought, listening as his footsteps came closer. I closed my eyes and tried to make myself as small as possible. I realized then that Frank had called me "girlie" a couple of times. He obviously hadn't gotten a good look at me, didn't know who I was. Maybe.

"Look, I ain't got all night," he said, as though realizing someone could pull into the station at any moment and find Daryl. Frank's car was parked right out front. Anybody who passed by would spot the bright red Trans-Am with the license tag that read C MIST, which stood for Canadian Mist, Frank's beverage of choice.

He continued to walk through the rows. Had there been a full moon, he would have seen me. Luckily, the moon was waning and was partially obscured by clouds. Even the stars had tucked themselves inside a blanket of cloud cover.

"You listening to me?" he asked, sounding doubtful. At this point, he might think I'd managed to get away. At least I hoped as much. "I just want to say how sorry I am you had to see that mess back there with Daryl," he said. "I wouldn't have hurt him if he'd just given me the damn money. Besides," he added, as though talking to himself, "Daryl didn't have much of a life anyway. We all know what he was."

I saw him glance across the cornfield and sigh as though it was useless, as though he couldn't believe I'd managed to get away. I could almost hear his thoughts. He could search all night and never find me; in the meantime, Fludd's Service Station might have a customer. He was taking a big chance by hanging around.

"I'll make a deal with you," he said after a minute. "You keep your mouth shut about what you saw, and I won't lay a finger on you. You got that, girlie? But if you so much as breathe a word of it, I'm coming after you. You *and* your family." He paused, and then his voice was lower. "Don't think for one minute I don't know where to find you."

Some minutes later, I heard the slam of a car door and

the roar of an engine, loud at first but eventually fading into the night. Frank had given up; I'd been spared.

I waited, marking off the minutes by the sound of approaching thunder. How long I remained huddled in a tight ball in that cornfield, I wasn't sure, but a fine drizzle was falling by the time I limped out. Surprisingly enough, I found a gas can just inside the front door of the service station and almost wept from relief, since it meant that I wouldn't have to pass by Daryl's dead body to find one. I filled it and took off.

The can would have been heavy under normal circumstances, but I was obviously in shock because I didn't really notice. I reached my daddy's truck and poured the gas into the tank, then tossed the can into a swampy area where it wouldn't be found for a while.

Back home in my bedroom, I stripped off my clothes and listened as the sky opened up outside. I threw up in the small trash can beside my desk until there was nothing left in my stomach but the awful taste of bile.

Two days later, the *Mossy Oaks Gazette* carried the story of Daryl Buckmeyer's murder as well as reports of the storm that had dumped eight inches of rain in twenty-four hours. The water had eventually gone down, but Sheriff Ben Hix hadn't come close to solving Daryl's murder. Herschel Buckmeyer, Daryl's older brother, was taking it hard, they said.

On Sunday, my daddy gave a grunt over the morning paper. "It's getting to where it ain't safe to go out anymore."

My mother looked up. "What is it, dear?"

He shoved his wire-rimmed glasses high on his nose. "That Gillespie boy robbed a liquor store last night and shot the clerk in the chest. The man's in critical condition."

Startled, I dropped my fork. It clattered against my plate, drawing looks from my parents. I'd been unusually clumsy these last couple of days, thanks to raw nerves and lack of sleep. My mother claimed it was puberty turning me into such an awkward, bungling girl, causing me to topple from my bed in the middle of the night and sprain my ankle. "You mean *Frank* Gillespie?" I asked, trying not to appear overly interested.

My father nodded. "Sheriff Hix supposedly questioned him about Daryl Buckmeyer's murder, but Frank claimed he was home in bed, and his father backed him up. Don't matter. Armed robbery and attempted murder carry a stiff sentence. Frank's going to be an old man by the time he gets out of prison."

My mother looked sad. "All this sin and violence," she moaned, and I knew we were about to receive a lesson from the Good Book whether we wanted it or not. "When our Savior returns, we shall be delivered from the bondage of corruption. Romans eight, verse twenty," she added.

I wasn't listening, and it was hard to pretend indifference to what I had just learned about Frank. Tears gathered behind my eyes, and I asked to be excused from the table so I could get dressed for church. My parents no longer forced Lurlene to attend; she wore provocative clothing and flirted outrageously with the men.

In my room, I finally allowed myself to react, and I was certain my sigh of relief could be heard down at the courthouse square. Frank Gillespie was going to prison. It was over.

But I was only fifteen then and didn't realize that nothing lasts forever.

I hadn't been asleep long that night when I heard it: someone moving stealthily about the house, causing the ancient wood floors to creak and groan like an old shrimp boat on choppy water. I tensed. I didn't like noises in the night. Even though I was now an adult, I hated dark hallways and shadowy corners because some childish part of me feared lurking figures, awful things that might reach out and hurt me. Shadow people, I called them. I'd always had an active imagination.

Suddenly I thought of Molly and wondered if the sounds might be coming from her room. My niece had threatened to split on more than one occasion.

I kicked off the covers and climbed out of the bed, moving swiftly but silently to the hall where a single night-light cast a soft glow to guide Molly, should she make a bathroom run during the night. I listened. Silence. It was eerie.

Finally, I couldn't stand it anymore. "Molly?" I whispered. "Is that you?"

No answer, only the steady beating of my heart and the rumble of my stomach. I'd been too upset at dinner to eat. Molly and I had argued again, this time because I refused to let her ride with a group of high school kids to a rock concert in Charleston, two hours away.

I wanted to get along with the girl, but after eight months of living under the same roof, we were still butting heads like two billy goats tangled up in a clothesline. These were the times I most resented my sister for committing suicide. And blamed myself.

I crossed the hall to the girl's door and peeked in. Thankfully, she was asleep in her bed, her face illuminated by the small lamp on her night table. People said we looked alike: same light brown hair, green eyes and slender build. Those who didn't know us mistook us for mother and daughter.

I remembered the first time I'd seen her, a bony three-year-old with stringy hair and a runny nose. I'd just completed my junior year in college and was home for the summer. After a four year absence, Lurlene had blown into town like a bad wind and claimed she was divorcing Molly's father. We hadn't even heard she'd married.

At three, the child was still in diapers and taking a night bottle. My mother and I would clean her up for bed, then watch in mixed fascination and disbelief as Molly rinsed her bottle and filled it with cold milk from the refrigerator. So while Lurlene, busy as a one-armed paperhanger, was trying to find a new man, my mother and I were trying to convince Molly to use the new musical potty-chair and take milk from a Bugs Bunny cup. We'd just about succeeded when Lurlene met a trucker from Tennessee. Quick as a flash, they were gone, without so much as a fare-thee-well. I had often wondered if I'd ever see my niece again.

The next time I saw Molly, she was ten years old and still scrawny. Lurlene reminded me of a crumpled and faded prom corsage; she claimed that her truck driver had beaten her regularly. She and Molly moved into my parents' house, and I was thankful I had my own place. Lurlene worked as a cocktail waitress at a place called the Thirsty Gullet until she met and married DeWayne Tompkins, an ambitious medical supplies salesman who drove a Town Car. We were thrilled with the match. DeWayne obviously thought Lurlene was the best thing since indoor plumbing, and he was the closest thing Molly'd ever had to a father.

They bought an old house, a turn-of-the-century low-country home with verandahs and six fireplaces and a large attic that smelled like mothballs and rat turds. They set about fixing it up, and we were confident it would work out. But Lurlene had a hard time sitting home nights while her husband traveled. It wasn't long before DeWayne caught her with another man—Harvey Freeman, who owned Budget Cars, a used-car dealership across the street from the Piggly Wiggly. Next thing we knew, DeWayne had packed his bags and moved out, and Lurlene, hard as she tried, couldn't convince him to forgive her and come back home.

Lurlene then went on a partying spree that took her as far as Charleston and Savannah. My niece was left to fend for herself, and no matter how hard I tried to convince my sister that she was ruining their lives, she ignored me. That's when I filed a report with the Department of Social Services. In the meantime, DeWayne hired a lawyer and had Lurlene served with divorce papers. I suppose it was too much. Several days later, my sister hanged herself in that smelly attic.

Unfortunately, Molly had found her.

As I gazed down at my niece now, I remembered the three-year-old who'd captured my heart all those years ago. I had so many dreams for her, but right now the two of us didn't seem to agree on much of anything. Despite our differences, though, we did have one thing in common: our fear of the dark, which explained the night-lights in every room and the lamp beside Molly's bed which was left to burn all night.

The child was indeed a contradiction to herself. While she could debate with the best of them the nonexistence of God, she never failed to leave the house without tucking the small crucifix my mother had given her into her pocket. Whether she believed or not was a mystery to us all, but I suppose after the life she'd had she wasn't taking any chances.

Sometimes I ached for Molly, for the fact that she'd

never had much of a childhood. I specifically remembered the night my own childhood had come to a screeching halt. I often wondered what she had seen even before she'd gazed upon her mother's lifeless body hanging from a rafter. I also wondered if I would ever know. Months of therapy hadn't provided me with any clues.

I spoiled Molly because I wanted to make up for the past hurts.

I closed the door and headed for the kitchen and the coffee pot. At the door, I found the light switch easily enough, thanks to the bulb always left burning over the stove. The wood floor was cold. Fall had arrived in Mossy Oaks, and the wee hours of the mornings were chilly.

The kitchen was my favorite room, papered in yellow gingham and decorated with baskets purchased from garage sales and flea markets. Most of my furniture was old and battered, having come from my parents' attic where it had been stored probably since before South Carolina had seceded from the Union and then gone to war over it. I'd painted or stained most of the pieces, and they resembled that expensive stuff the Spiegel catalog refers to as "distressed" furniture. I'm always amused at what it costs to buy furniture that looks like it's been in a house fire.

I bought my house three summers ago, a simple but cheap frame cottage that was built in the early sixties and had suffered neglect when it became rental property in the eighties. Mine was an old neighborhood, inhabited mostly by retirees who kept to themselves and ventured out only to collect the mail or water their shrubbery. The streets were lined with massive live oaks whose gnarled roots had grown right through the sidewalks, causing them to crack and buckle, making walking hazardous for the seniors. The branches would have formed a canopy over the street if the city hadn't cut them back on a regular basis so they wouldn't interfere with the power lines. In spring, the air was sweetened with magnolia and gardenia—our trees and shrubs were mature but hardy—and for a few short weeks the azaleas gave a festive look to the otherwise somber neighborhood.

The area was within walking distance of the post office and library, not to mention the elementary school where I taught and the middle school Molly attended. I considered this a plus since my old Toyota spent much of its time at Omar's Garage.

My place had been the only thing I could afford on a teacher's salary. I didn't mind pinching pennies now and then; I couldn't remember a time when I didn't want to teach. I suppose it had something to do with my own unlimited zest for learning. *Any* kind of learning. Hell, you could capture my rapt attention by describing the mating rituals of bullfrogs. Sad but true. That explained why I never met interesting men at parties. While everyone else mingled and made conversation, I was the one sitting off in some remote corner arguing with the most uninteresting man in the place about toxic waste or the thinning ozone. Some people become witty after a glass of wine; I become argumentative.

I groaned aloud when I saw the clock over the stove. Not even five o'clock yet. My fanny would be dragging by the time school let out at three. I needed to start taking vitamins. I pondered buying a bottle of Geritol on my next grocery run, then decided it'd be cheaper and easier if I drank more caffeine instead.

I turned for the automatic coffeemaker and was surprised by what I saw. The coffee was already made, and a cup had been poured in my favorite mug. I frowned. Molly? Of course, Molly; who else? But why? She never lifted a finger to do anything unless there was something in it for her. "The concert," I muttered in realization.

Molly was really sucking up, I decided.

That evening, I waited until Molly and I were seated at the dinner table before I told her about my wonderful idea.

"Tomorrow's Friday," I said. "Suppose we drive to Savannah and spend the night." It wasn't Charleston and it wasn't the concert, but it was a last-ditch effort to bring peace to our household.

Something flickered in her eyes. Interest? She stopped playing with her KFC mashed potatoes. "In a hotel?" she asked.

"Nothing fancy, of course. We'll eat dinner at one of those restaurants on the river and spend Saturday at the mall."

She was warming to the idea; the corners of her mouth weren't as droopy now. "Can we get a place with pay TV?"

I shrugged. "Sure. We can watch as many movies as you like. Except for the X-rated, of course. I don't want you to see anything like that until we've had our little talk about the birds and bees."

"Yeah, right," she said, her eyes rolling back once more. She seemed to ponder the idea. "I can take my birthday money, right?"

"It's your money."

She smiled. *Smiled!* I thought I understood how earthquake victims must feel when the trembling stops. "So, what do you say?" I asked.

She pushed her chair from the table and started for the hall. "I'm going to pack my clothes now so I'll be ready the minute you get home from work tomorrow."

I watched her go, confident that the concert was forgotten for now and life could return to normal. Or as normal as it could be with an adolescent living in the house.

Savannah was less than an hour away, but the drive seemed longer with the two of us taking turns adjusting the volume knob on the radio. The scenery was breathtaking; the marsh seared golden and swaying in the breeze, bordered by lush green woodlands. Quaint drawbridges spanned shimmering water, and the horizon was dotted with fishing boats. We entered one eerie stretch where the highway cut through swampland; trees and vegetation grew so thick they blocked the sunlight. Vines hung as though suspended in air, wrapped tightly around the cypress and tupelo and red gums as though loving them to death.

Mossy Oaks is situated in the low country and is every bit as beautiful as nearby Charleston, Hilton Head and, of course, Savannah. Fortunately, it has not been discovered by the tourists, and the locals plan to keep it that way. That's why we have only a couple of motels in town, despite wealthy Augustus Gillespie's wanting to build something grand that would draw visitors. So far he hasn't even come close to getting the votes he needs to begin such a project. It's nice to know that money and power can't buy everything.

By the time we pulled into a modestly priced hotel, my head was splitting. Molly is not content just to listen to music at its loudest; she has to adjust the bass so that each beat is felt at the back of the skull, just above the spinal column.

"This is where we're staying?" Molly asked, trying to talk above the racket and losing some of her former enthusiasm at the sight of the simple two-story brick building. She glanced across the street at the elegant-looking Hyatt, where flashy doormen struggled with luggage and golf bags.

"It's the best I can afford," I told her, "but it has pay TV and a restaurant. What more do we need?"

She brightened. By the time we'd registered and carried our bags into a spotless room decorated in navy and mauve, she was excited again.

It was a peaceful afternoon, still light at that point, but the breeze had an edge to it when we left the room a few minutes later with Molly's birthday money making itchy work of the pockets in her jeans.

A narrow cobblestone street separated the restaurants and shops from the river and was within walking distance of our hotel. Molly ducked into one interesting-looking shop, and I followed. The goods ranged from expensive gold necklaces to cheap ashtrays and coffee mugs with the words *I Love Savannah* painted on them.

While Molly perused the jewelry section, I read an assortment of greeting cards and laughed out loud over the inscriptions. I found one with a picture of a woman standing on a bathroom scale with a pistol in her hand and decided to buy it for my friend Lilly, who'd agonized over every pound she'd gained during her two pregnancies. I heard Molly make a purchase, but she tucked the small plastic bag into her purse before I could see what it was.

"Are you ready to eat?" I inquired as soon as I'd paid for the card.

She nodded, and we made our way out of the store. Ten minutes later we were sipping drinks beside a picture window and watching a diminutive tugboat push a loaded barge slowly up the river. In the distance, the setting sun resembled a giant egg yolk. Passersby stopped to watch the scene, obviously fascinated with the boats as well as the sunset. I felt more relaxed than I had in months, and I decided Molly and I needed to get away more often. We couldn't afford a real vacation, but we could at least take a brief trip somewhere close now and then.

"Should you be drinking?" she asked after a moment.

I offered her a blank look, then glanced down at the scotch and water I'd ordered. "I'm old enough. Besides, I'm not driving." Even as I said it, I wondered why I was explaining myself to a thirteen-year-old. What did it matter if I had an occasional drink? It's not like I did it routinely; I drank about as often as I had sex these days.

"What if DSS finds out?"

So that was it. "I hardly think the Department of Social Services is going to care if I have a drink once in a while."

"Then how come they took me away from Lurlene?"

I still thought it strange that Molly referred to her dead mother by her first name. "You know why you were taken away from your mother," I said, wishing we could avoid that subject when we were supposed to be having fun.

"Aren't you scared they'll take me away from you?"

"Nope."

"Maybe that's what you're hoping."

I sighed. The girl was playing mind games, something she did well because she was so much smarter than other people, including most adults. Her IQ was staggering, and her standardized test scores the previous year were impressive. She'd scored in the ninety-something percentile in all subjects. "She's smart enough to be dangerous," Lilly had laughingly remarked when she'd seen Molly's test results. I was shocked by the scores, of course, since Molly habitually earned Cs and Ds on her report card.

"Why would I go through so much trouble to give you a home if I didn't want you to stay?" I asked her after a moment.

"Maybe you're doing it because you feel guilty."

I took a sip of my drink. Molly could read me so well. I did feel guilty, but that's not the reason I wanted her with me. "Sometimes you act like you don't want it to work out," I said. "I think you're scared."

She looked wary. "Of what?"

"I think you want to feel safe and loved, but you're afraid to admit it because someone might snatch it away if you do." I reached for her hand and she automatically stiffened, but I refused to let go. "I'm always going to be here for you, Molly. DSS is not going to take you away. Not as long as I have anything to say about it."

She pulled her hand free and looked out the window as though afraid to meet my gaze. Her eyes were unusually bright, and I wondered if she was crying. I wouldn't ask. I didn't know what kind of demons Molly was fighting, simply because she'd shared so little of her past with me.

"I bought you a present," she said at last. She pulled the bag from her purse and handed it to me.

I stared at her in open amazement. "You spent your birthday money on me?" I asked.

She still refused to look at me. "Open it."

I reached inside the sack and pulled out a pair of onyx earrings and a matching necklace. "Oh, Molly," I said, knowing they hadn't been cheap. "You shouldn't have spent so much."

"They were half price," the girl said, tucking her hair behind her ears. "I wanted to give you something to sort of make up for the way I've been acting."

I feared I might cry, and I knew that would only embarrass her. "I don't think I've ever owned anything so beautiful," I managed.

"Don't make a big deal out of it, Aunt Em," she said, poised to flee.

I sat there for a moment, trying to compose myself. For the first time in eight months, I felt that my niece and I were making progress.

Unfortunately, by the end of the trip we were back to square one. My fault. I should have known better than to let Molly drag me into the mall's pet shop the following day.

"I'm not going to argue with you about this," I said, using the voice I used whenever I caught two second graders locked in the same bathroom stall at school. The snickering always gave them away. "Number one, I absolutely can*not* afford a puppy at this price. Number two, I said I'd think about it, and that's the bottom line. Now, it's getting late. We need to head back."

The ride home was much quieter than the one coming down. There was no music, no talking, nothing. I wondered when I'd started sounding so much like my mother.

My earrings were nowhere to be found, nor was the matching necklace. I searched my jewelry box carefully before admitting to myself that they were gone. I decided to look once more, this time with the aid of light. I flipped the light switch just as I remembered the bulb was burned out. Much to my surprise, the light came on. Molly must've changed it when she'd made my bed and dusted.

For two days, ever since I'd refused to buy a puppy for her, she'd barely spoken a word to me, but she was keeping the house in tip-top condition. I decided it was her way of punishing me for not buying the puppy while, at the same time, proving she could handle the responsibility of a pet.

When I knocked, I found her sitting cross-legged on her bed reading a Stephen King novel. This is the same girl who'd suffered hellish nightmares on a regular basis when she'd first moved in with me. Could it be she missed waking up in a cold sweat with her stomach churning in terror? I decided we could take it up when we discussed the garish midnight-blue mascara she was wearing, which made her look like a child prostitute.

"Have you seen my onyx earrings and necklace?" I asked. "The ones you gave me in Savannah?"

"Can't say that I have," Molly said without looking up. "Don't tell me you lost them already."

Yep, she was still mad as a mule with a mouthful of bumblebees, I thought. Lucky for her I was a patient woman. "I didn't lose them. I wore them yesterday, and I specifically remember putting them back in my jewelry box."

The girl looked up. "I haven't seen them," she said, impatience seeping into her voice.

"I thought maybe while you were straightening my room this afternoon you might have—" I paused at the look she gave me. "Why are you staring at me as though my hair is on fire?"

"I haven't *been* in your room or *touched* your jewelry. We had an agreement, remember? I don't go through your stuff, and you don't go through mine." She turned the page in her book. "At least I keep *my* end of the bargain."

"What's that supposed to mean?"

She peered at me from over the book. "I can tell when you've been snooping around, Aunt Em."

"I haven't gone through your things."

"Yeah, right. And you didn't sneak in and unplug my lamp in the middle of the night. If you're so worried about the power bill—"

"Why are you blaming me?" I asked. "The bulb is probably just burned out."

"How can it be burned out when I just changed it last

----

week?'' she said. ''Besides, the lamp came right back on once I plugged it in.''

Back in my bedroom, I sat on the edge of the bed and tried to make sense of the whole thing. Was I getting senile? Perhaps I'd taken off the jewelry at school and put it in my desk drawer or something. But I would have remembered changing the lightbulb and making my bed.

It bothered me that Molly suspected I'd been searching her room, and all I could do was chalk it up to teenage paranoia. But what about the lamp she claimed someone had unplugged? The only answer I could come up with was that she'd gotten up during the night to go to the bathroom and, in her sleep, tripped over the cord and pulled the plug from the outlet.

I continued to sit there as my frustration grew. My life had been simple before Molly had come into it—except for those brief periods when I felt sorry for myself for not marrying and having a house full of kids like my high school friends. I usually got over it as soon as I went down my mental list of eligible men in town—some of whom were second cousins, sadly enough—and I realized I was better off single. Besides, I could never love a man named Bubba or Junior or Billy-Bob, or a man who kept a wad of chewing tobacco tucked in one cheek.

But that had nothing to do with the problem at hand, and no matter how taxing life with my niece was, I couldn't give up on her. Not only that, but I couldn't imagine anyone else who'd want to take her with all her problems. Suddenly, a thought occurred. While I'd been sitting there bemoaning the fact that most of the men I knew resembled old *Hee Haw* characters, my subconscious had kicked in and tossed out a possibility that just might solve the riddle I'd been turning over in my mind a moment before.

What if Molly had been lying about the missing jewelry and the lamp just to scare me? It made perfect sense. She might very well be pulling these pranks so I'd feel uneasy and agree to buy a dog for protection. Why hadn't I thought of that sooner?

2

I sat on the edge of the bed and tried to shrug off the last vestiges of sleep. I'd had a fitful night, filled with strange dreams and images that I couldn't remember but that had left me feeling odd and out of sorts with the world. I attributed my mood to Molly's odd behavior and decided that a cup of coffee couldn't hurt. It might not solve my woes, but it would go a long way toward helping me gain a better perspective on the situation.

I stretched and rolled out of bed, forcing a bounce I didn't feel into my step. I smelled fresh coffee even before I entered the kitchen.

As I stared at the freshly brewed pot and my favorite cup already prepared, I shook my head in bewilderment. Let the games begin, I thought.

I should probably rethink the pet issue, I told myself as I sipped my first cup. I tried to calculate in my mind what it would cost to keep a dog in Chunks and Nibbles after I paid for rabies and distemper shots and had the animal spayed or neutered. I still wasn't certain Molly could handle the responsibility, but how would I ever know unless I gave her a chance? As I ruminated, I tried not to think of my parakeets, lifeless figures at the bottom of a cage that had become Molly's chore to clean when she'd first come to live with me.

It had been bitterly cold that day. Molly had awoken sick and feverish, and I'd agreed to let her stay home. I'd even moved her covers to the couch so she could watch TV. Although I worried about leaving her alone while I worked, I checked on her several times throughout the day. She complained that the birds kept her awake.

"I hate those birds," she said. "They're loud, and all they do is kick seed all over the carpet."

The parakeets were a source of irritation to me as well, what with their constant chirping and the mess they made, but they'd been a birthday present from my parents, so what was I to do? I arrived home shortly before four o'clock and found the house freezing and oddly quiet. Molly, who claimed she'd gotten too hot, had opened the windows, then huddled beneath the blankets and fallen asleep.

I'd found the birds frozen and lifeless on their corncob liner. That had been eight months ago, shortly after Molly had come to live with me, and even though I thought I'd put it to rest in my mind, it still nagged me from time to time.

As I finished my first cup of coffee, I gazed out the back window at a squirrel perched on the railing of my deck, munching an acorn. My Bradford pear looked bleak without its blooms, and I decided that it matched my mood perfectly. Sooner or later, I would have to come to a decision about a pet, something warm and cuddly that Molly could throw her arms around and latch onto. I sensed that the girl had a lot of love inside just waiting to be tapped.

Besides, it was obvious she wasn't going to take no for an answer.

I smiled as I pulled into my driveway the following afternoon and found a blue compact car parked out front. I let myself into the house a moment later and walked into the kitchen, where Molly and her social worker were playing cards, a cup of coffee beside each of them. Molly had been drinking coffee since she was four, and I still permitted it as long as it was decaf.

Susan Blake was a dark-skinned beauty who'd attended Mossy Oaks High at the same time I had and had been our first black homecoming queen. Like me, she had gone to college on a full scholarship and had chosen a career in social work—specifically, the Department of Social Services. She'd been assigned to Molly's case shortly after I filed papers to have my sister's parental rights terminated, so it was no surprise when Susan asked DSS and the judge to give me temporary custody instead of putting Molly in a foster home while they did their investigation. I had since been appointed her legal guardian and planned to adopt her as soon as I could afford the legal costs.

Although Susan and I had lost touch once we'd gone off to our respective colleges, we'd rekindled our relationship these past months. I held her partially responsible for the fact that I still had my sanity after all this time with my niece.

"Hi, guys," I said. "What are you playing?"

Susan pursed her lips, trying to affect a stern look. She failed miserably. She was about as stern-looking as an elf in new pointed hat and shoes. "Poker," she said. "Imagine my surprise when I asked Molly if she had a deck of Old Maid cards and she informed me that she only plays five card stud."

"Don't look at me; I didn't teach her."

"Grandpa taught me," Molly said, a toothpick pressed between her lips. "Are you going to show me what you got, Susan, or am I supposed to pretend I'm psychic?"

Susan laid down her hand. "Is this good?" she asked, displaying her cards.

The girl shrugged. "It's okay." She laid down her own cards. "But it doesn't beat a royal flush."

Susan exchanged looks with me. "She's already won all my toothpicks. I think she cheats."

I nodded. "I've played cards with her. I *know* she cheats."

We were quiet as Molly picked up the cards and slid them into their box. The girl looked up. "I told Susan how you accused me of taking your jewelry," she said matter-of-factly.

"I never accused you. I simply asked if you'd seen it."

"Sounded like an accusation to me," the girl mumbled.

Susan looked at me, and I sensed that she wanted to be alone with me. I turned to my niece. "What does your room look like?" I asked, in hopes of getting rid of her for a moment.

The girl shrugged. "Like somebody trashed it while I was at school today."

"Please go straighten it."

Molly got up and shoved in her chair. "If you wanted to be alone with Susan, all you had to do was tell me."

I didn't say anything until I heard my niece's bedroom door close rather loudly. "I'm sorry," I told the other woman. "She's showing off because she likes you. Usually she just sits around and sulks."

"Things are no better?"

"We have our good moments," I said. "There are times when I feel very hopeful. Then, when I least expect it, she withdraws, and I feel like we've made absolutely no progress."

"She's still seeing a therapist?"

I nodded. "She sees Cordia once a week, rain or shine." I sighed heavily. "For whatever *that's* worth."

Susan reached across the table and took my hand. "I know how hard you've worked with the girl. I'm sure it's frustrating at times."

"I keep thinking there's something I'm not doing right." I told her about our trip to Savannah and the puppy Molly wanted so desperately. Then I confessed my suspicions about the birds. I'd never told Susan I suspected Molly of killing them on purpose, and I could see that the whole thing disturbed her. "I can't bring an innocent pet into the house if there's a chance she'll hurt it."

"Why don't you get Cordia's opinion? That's what she's being paid for."

"I will."

Susan leaned closer. "Do you think she took your jewelry?"

"I don't know. I've looked everywhere for it. I've noticed that other things have just disappeared. See that rack of keys beside the door? That's where I keep my spares. I think one or two might be missing, but I couldn't swear to it. I'm not the most organized person in the world, you know."

"Does Molly have a house key?"

I nodded. "I was thinking that maybe she lost hers and was afraid I'd get upset over it, so she took another one without telling me."

"That's probably it," Susan said, getting up and carrying her coffee cup to the sink. "Let me know how things progress."

I promised to keep Susan apprised of the situation as I walked her to the front door. I watched her drive away, then made my way down the hall to Molly's room. I knocked lightly. When I opened the door, I found her lying on her bed, staring at the ceiling. There was no music playing, nothing.

"Is something wrong?" I asked.

She shrugged. I walked over to the bed and sat on the edge. "You look down in the dumps."

Another shrug. "I've got a lot on my mind is all."

"A boy?"

"Maybe."

"What's his name?"

"Henry Dean. But he's just a friend, so I don't want you making a big deal out of it, okay? He's new in school, and I'm just trying to make him feel welcome since the other kids don't have much to do with him."

"Okay," I said, feeling honored that she'd shared as much as she had. She seldom opened up, and I'd learned not to ask too many questions.

"I think it's great you're trying to make him feel at home in his new school. When do I get to meet him?" I asked as nonchalantly as I could.

"Tonight. He's coming over after dinner so we can do homework together."

I tried not to show my surprise. Molly was one of those kids who thought she shouldn't have to open a book once school let out for the day. I hoped having a homework buddy would teach her better study habits. "That's nice," I said.

"I don't want you to embarrass him by making a fuss. Just pretend he's not here."

I did not realize at the time what she was asking of me.

At seven o'clock, the doorbell rang and Molly went to answer it. I'd had visions of what this Henry Dean looked like: thin and awkward, with red or blond hair and a mouthful of braces. What I saw didn't even come close.

The boy was tall and gangly, and his clothes looked as though they'd been plucked from a Salvation Army bin. His ratty jeans and sneakers gave new meaning to grunge, but his hair was cut military-style.

"Aunt Em, this is Henry," Molly said.

I opened my mouth, heard myself mumble a greeting.

"Nice to meet'cha." The boy nodded, dragged a chair away from the table and sank into it. I noticed then that he was wearing a *swastika* on his left hand and some kind of spiky dog collar around his throat.

"Is there anything I can get you, Henry?" I asked. A leash, maybe, I thought.

"A cold beer would hit the spot."

Molly must've seen the horrified expression on my face. "He's only kidding, Aunt Em. If we get thirsty, I'll grab us a soft drink from the refrigerator."

I made my way on rubbery legs to my bedroom, where I closed the door and called Lilly. "You won't believe what Molly just brought into this house," I whispered. I described Henry to my friend.

"What if he's a skinhead?" I whispered. "One of those white supremacists who hate Jews and blacks."

"Well, you and Molly are Caucasian Baptists, so you don't have a thing to worry about."

"He'll probably grow up to be an Uzi salesman," I muttered. "Why does Molly insist on picking her friends from the bottom of the barrel?"

"Low self-esteem. It'll pass," Lilly said, "as long as you don't make a big deal out of it. Trust me on this one."

It was after nine o'clock by the time Henry left. Molly stacked her schoolbooks on the table, and I could feel her watching me. "So what'd you think of Henry?"

"Nice boy," I said as I went about setting up the coffee pot and wiping down cabinets. "You'll have to bring him around more often."

"For real?"

I looked at her. "Sure, why not? You should invite him to church with us Sunday. Afterward, he can have dinner with Grandma and Grandpa." I knew it sounded ridiculous even to suggest it, but I suppose I was trying to show my niece how different her friend was from the rest of us.

"Henry doesn't believe in God."

"I see." I was determined not to get rattled. "Oh, well, you can't hold that against him. I've met my share of nice atheists."

I can honestly say Molly went to bed a very confused girl that night, and I applauded myself for being such a good actress. Lilly would have been proud.

Nevertheless, I doubted I'd seen the last of Henry Dean.

The following Monday, we drove to the Mental Health Center for Molly's weekly appointment with her counselor. Cordia Bowers was an older woman who wore little makeup and had allowed her hair to go gray while most of her contemporaries were hounding their hairdressers for blue rinse. She'd studied child psychology back before the public even knew there was a need; she now practiced child and family counseling in Mossy Oaks and neighboring centers.

The first time I met her, I wasn't sure she was qualified to help Molly. Maybe it was the frilly peasant blouses and full, ankle-length skirts she wore that made her look like a refugee from a gypsy camp.

I still wondered from time to time if Cordia was right for Molly, but since she was *the* family therapist in our town and had an excellent reputation, I saw that Molly never missed an appointment. As she sat quietly and listened to Molly bemoan the fact that I was much too strict and couldn't be convinced to buy a pet no matter what, I wondered what the woman was thinking.

"Why do you suppose your aunt doesn't want you to have a dog?" Cordia asked after my niece had run out of things to complain about. The woman's Southern drawl made me think of mint-flavored iced tea and cool verandahs. When Molly shrugged her answer, Cordia looked at me. She made a production of it as though she were seeing me for the first time.

I felt myself squirm. I never knew exactly who was in analysis here. I'm always afraid Cordia is going to ask me if I masturbated as a child or if I ever fantasized about seeing my father naked. I know that if she ever does, I'll head straight for the lake like my Aunt Bessie.

"Your aunt looks like a woman who would naturally love animals," Cordia said after a moment. "Surely she's given you some reason for her reluctance." Cordia knew the answer to that, of course, but I suspected she wanted to hear it from Molly.

My niece glared at me. She had been pouting since I'd asked if she'd lost her house key, accusing me of not trusting her and of blaming her for everything that went wrong.

"You know why she won't get me a dog," Molly mumbled. "She thinks I killed her stupid parakeets."

"Did you?"

The girl sighed and did her eye-rolling bit. "No."

Cordia looked thoughtful. "I'm sure you can understand why your aunt is confused about how the birds died. If I remember correctly, you told her you hated them and wished they were dead."

"That's 'cause I got tired of cleaning up after them," Molly replied. "But I didn't kill them. I'd have let them go first. Before I did something dumb like *kill them*."

Cordia seemed to ponder this as I held my breath. "Yes, but if you *had* let them go, then your aunt would have known you'd done it on purpose."

Molly's cheeks were unnaturally pink; she was angry now. "So you think I opened the windows so I could make it look like an accident, right?"

"I'm not accusing you of anything; I'm merely asking what happened," Cordia said gently.

The girl's eyes watered, but I knew she'd carve her heart out before she'd let us see her cry. "I've already told you, I didn't kill those birds," she said loudly. She looked at me. "At least not on purpose. And I'm sick and tired of people thinking everything is my fault."

I could feel myself getting emotional, and I was glad when Cordia sent Molly into the waiting room. She didn't say anything right away; instead, she reached for a tissue and handed it to me. "Are you okay?" she asked.

I nodded, not trusting myself to speak at the moment. Finally, I cleared my throat. "Do you think she did it?"

Cordia shrugged. "I don't know. I'd like to believe the child was burning up with fever and wasn't thinking when she opened the windows on those birds. If she did kill them and is feeling absolutely no remorse, I would say there's cause for alarm." She paused as though to gather her thoughts. "How are her grades so far, these nine weeks?"

"Her midterm report wasn't good. She promised to do better on her report card."

"Has she been stealing?"

I hesitated. Molly had been known to take money from my purse, but I'd put a stop to it by keeping my pocketbook with me at all times. I seldom left loose change lying around the house in order to keep temptation at a minimum. "I'm not sure," I said. Cordia looked at me, and I explained the missing jewelry. Then I told her about Henry Dean.

Once again, she was quiet. I wondered at it.

"You know, Emily, there's a place not far from here that might be able to help Molly."

"What kind of place?"

"It's sort of like a therapeutic group home. The staff consists of trained counselors; it's very structured. They only allow five or six girls in at a time. You'd have to apply for Medicaid to afford it, but—"

"You're suggesting I send Molly away?" I interrupted, the thought making my heart beat faster. "After what she's been through?"

Cordia gave me a kindly smile, but I could see the concern in her eyes. "It's because of what she's been through that I'm making this suggestion. What we're seeing here is a clear indication of Conduct Disorder and Oppositional Defiance Syndrome, maybe even antisocial behavior. Failing in school, refusing to conform. Lying and stealing. Rebellious behavior. I'd certainly keep my eye on this boy she's spending time with, if he makes you uncomfortable."

"All kids go through a rebellious stage. It's part of growing up."

"Children who kill animals sometimes grow up to be adults who kill."

The thought terrified me, but I wouldn't allow myself to believe it. "We don't have proof of anything."

Cordia clasped her fingers together, not an easy task considering the number of rings she wore. "We may never have proof. We may have to go on gut instinct. We also have to consider the fact that there's a history of mental illness in the family. First, an aunt who tried to commit suicide by drowning, then Molly's own mother."

"Lurlene wasn't mental." I said it convincingly, as though I'd never had any reason to suspect otherwise. "She just . . . her problems caught up with her." Still, I'd privately wondered if she'd inherited some freaky gene from Aunt Bessie. It would have lessened my own guilt if that were the case.

"Something caused her to put that noose around her neck," Cordia said, obviously unaware of the guilt I'd shouldered for so long. I couldn't bring myself to share with her my fears that I could have been instrumental in

Lurlene's death by reporting her to DSS. "Suicide runs in families, you know," Cordia went on. "Molly might very well—"

I held my hand up to stop her from saying anything more. "You're not going to convince me to send Molly away," I said. I stood and discovered that my knees were trembling. Only then did I realize how badly her suggestion had upset me. "I'm all she has left. No matter what, I have to stick by her."

Cordia looked sympathetic. "What can I do to help, Emily?"

I shook my head. She looked so sincere, so kind, it was all I could do to keep my voice steady when I spoke. "I don't know. I need time to think." I let myself out without another word.

3

"Molly, don't make him an ugly pumpkin," I said a few days later as we prepared for Halloween.

Molly paused in her work, the paring knife poised in midair. "He's supposed to be ugly."

"You'll scare the little kids away."

She shrugged. "I don't like kids anyway. All they do is whine and carry on. Lurlene used to say—" She paused suddenly as though she had been close to saying something she shouldn't.

I pulled an errant strand of brown hair from her face and tucked it behind her ear. "What did Lurlene used to say?" I prodded gently.

Her bottom lip quivered. As tough as Molly pretended she was, I still caught glimpses of the scared and vulnerable child I knew her to be. "She used to say children were for couples who couldn't afford abortions."

I didn't say anything at first. The thought that my sister would say such a thing in front of her child left me feeling cold and angry. There were times I wished I'd throttled Lurlene when she was alive, but I'm not sure it would have mattered. For as long as I could remember, she'd been self-centered and uncaring when it came to other people's feelings.

"Some people go to great lengths to have children," I said. "They feel their lives are incomplete without them."

Molly went back to carving a set of wicked-looking

teeth. "Have you ever thought of having children?" she asked.

I nodded. "Sure, I want children. But I haven't met a man I'd want to father them."

"Grandma says—"

"I know what Grandma says," I replied dully. "My ovaries are going to dry up and blow away like road dust if I don't find a man soon. Back in Grandma's day, most couples married and started their families before they were eighteen. I'm an old maid in her book."

"Do you like it?"

"What? Being an old maid?" I thought about it. "Fact is, I don't mind being on my own." I smiled. "But then I'm not really alone anymore now that I have you."

I pretty much came to terms with being single when I was twenty-eight and a long-term relationship crumbled. Bill Price had been our gym teacher, and for two years I imagined myself in love with him. I'm almost embarrassed to admit that he was the first man I slept with, even more ashamed to admit he was the one and only. We'd come very close to marriage, but I realized at the last minute I didn't love him enough to spend the rest of my life with him. My only regret is that I'd waited until after the wedding announcements had been mailed to call it off. For that, my mother never forgave me.

A fine mist had begun to fall by the time we carried the pumpkin out and placed it on the front porch. Molly had put a candle inside, and the angry-looking orange globe seemed to scowl at the world. As the children scurried up the front walk in damp costumes, I saw them pause as though half afraid the pumpkin would pounce on them.

"Molly, that's downright mean of you," I said, noting how grisly she appeared with latex and fake blood caked on her face and arms. She was supposed to be a car accident victim. She'd succeeded. Looking at her, one would've thought she'd run head-on into a Mack truck while doing sixty in a golf cart. "Next year we'll have a happy pumpkin or none at all."

Molly wasn't listening. She was peering through the curtain. "If you think that pumpkin's scary, you ought to get a load of the man across the street. He just stands there staring at our house like he's frozen in place."

I joined her at the window. Even though it was dark, I could clearly make out the man standing directly beneath the streetlight in a haze created by the dampness. He was dressed in jeans and a plaid shirt but wore a cartoonish Ronald Reagan mask. Something about him made me pause and try to think if and where I'd seen him before. I couldn't place my finger on it; it was like tasting a new recipe and trying to figure out which ingredient was missing.

"How long has he been out there?" I asked.

"A while," Molly said. "I thought he was with that first group of kids we had. All of the little ones have had their parents with them. But he hasn't budged in fifteen or twenty minutes."

Several youngsters hurried up our walk, and I dropped the curtain. When the doorbell rang, Molly grabbed the bowl of goodies and answered it. I could hear her exclaiming how scary everyone looked, and I decided she didn't hate kids as much as she claimed to.

I wondered about the man across the street. What was he doing there? Watching the children? Waiting for the perfect child to come across my lawn without a parent? I shuddered at the thought. On the other hand, he could have been a neighbor from down the street, simply taking a walk and watching the trick-or-treaters. Still, why was he wearing that mask?

I knew I had to report him, even if he had a perfectly reasonable explanation for being there. I started for the phone, then retraced my steps to the window, wanting to get a second look at him so I could give an accurate description to the police. I lifted the curtain and found that, to my relief, he was gone.

It was a perfect fall day, the air refreshingly nippy after what had been an unusually hot summer. I sat on a wooden bench, chuckling to myself as I watched my students attack the playground equipment with gusto. Mine was the only class left in the school yard; the other teachers had herded their students inside for lessons. I had chosen to remain, simply because I wasn't ready to give up the fresh air and sunshine. Surely that was just as important as rehashing addition and subtraction problems.

I considered myself a fairly good teacher even if I didn't always follow the rules. I tried to make learning fun instead of the drudgery some of my colleagues felt was a necessary part of education. This meant I was always pestering Principal Higginbotham for field trips and guest speakers and a computer lab for our older students. I also tried to give of myself to my pupils, to let them get to know the *real* me. Kids are quick to notice when you're hiding something.

I leaned back and closed my eyes briefly, letting the sun warm my face and the childish laughter warm my heart. I needed this time to myself; the past week or so had done a number on my nervous system.

In a short time, Henry Dean had become a permanent fixture in our lives, eating me out of house and home and going through soft drinks like a group of football players at halftime. What bothered me most was his habit of taking little things with him on his way out each night. I had no proof, of course, but who else would steal a worthless toothpick holder made of plastic? I'd decided to keep quiet, but it irked me every time the kid walked through the front door with a toothpick in his mouth.

I was also missing the tacky alligator ashtray my parents had bought in a souvenir shop in Florida while vacationing one year. Not that I needed an ashtray, mind you, but that still didn't give Henry the right to just take the danged thing. I knew it was him because I'd smelled smoke in the kitchen once or twice after he'd left, and I knew he'd fired up a cigarette while he was there.

Molly seemed to be waiting for me to say something, but I kept quiet and hoped she'd tire of him sooner or later. This was the closest thirteen-year-old Molly had ever come to having a boyfriend, and I hated to spoil it for her, even though I disapproved of Henry. I went through this spiel each day in my mind because I had no idea if I was doing the right thing by letting him visit. Where my niece was concerned, I'd learned to take one day at a time and hope for the best.

Nevertheless, I made a habit of searching the house after Henry's visits, just waiting for the night he'd walk out with my color TV set.

I pushed thoughts of the boy aside and pondered instead the mums I would buy at the nursery on my way home and put in the ground before it got dark. This year I'd done the smart thing and waited until after Halloween to plant. Eager trick-or-treaters didn't think twice about running through someone's flower bed to get to that bowl of candy at the front door.

I didn't hear the footsteps; I suppose they were muffled by the grass on the other side of the fence. I sensed a presence, sensed that I was being watched. I bolted upright and opened my eyes, and there he was after all these years: Frank Gillespie in the flesh.

He wore sunglasses and an Atlanta Braves baseball cap, both of which looked brand-new. It didn't matter that fifteen years had passed between us, or that I could only see part of his face; I would have known Frank anywhere.

"Hello, Emily."

My spine tingled. His voice hadn't changed a bit, and it dredged up all the nightmarish memories I'd tried so hard to put behind me. I stared back at him in silence. I was suddenly excruciatingly aware that I was the only adult on the playground.

He removed his sunglasses, and when I saw his eyes I wished he'd kept them on. They were empty eyes, *dead* eyes. It was like looking into the window of a vacant house. A shudder rose up from the small of my back to my shoulders.

"My, my," he said softly, almost sadly. "Miss Emily Wilkop all grown up. And quite pretty, too."

"Hello, Frank." My voice didn't sound like my own. "What are *you* doing here?" The last time I'd seen him, two deputies were hauling him off in handcuffs and leg irons to begin serving a twenty-five-year sentence for robbery and attempted murder of the owner of the liquor store. I'd made a point to be in court the day of his sentencing. I did a quick calculation in my mind and realized he'd only served fifteen. The only thing I could imagine was that he'd managed to escape and that my second graders might be in danger.

"I've been paroled," he said. "I reckon that's bad news to most folks, ain't it? They probably hoped someone would lock me up and throw away the key."

"I see," I said, not knowing how else to respond. I considered sending my class inside, but I suspected that Frank was not a stable man, and the least little thing might set him off. So, despite my fear, I remained seated.

"It feels good to be out," he said after a moment. "Different, but good."

I forced myself to look at him. Standing on the other side of the fence, he appeared to be looking at me through prison bars. Incarceration had left an indelible impression on his face, carving deep lines on either side of his mouth and painting bluish-gray smudges below his eyes. His cheekbones were prominent against a sunken face. He had the gaunt, hollow-eyed look of a holocaust survivor.

"What are you doing here, Frank?" I asked again.

He glanced from me to the children and finally back to me. The look in his eyes unnerved me. He obviously knew I'd been the one hiding in the cornfield that night; otherwise, why would he be there?

"My father sent me. He has it in his head that I should try to speak to young people about crime and prison life. He hopes I'll be able to prevent somebody from going through what I did." He paused and sighed. "Do you realize I was only nineteen when I went in? Fresh meat, they

----

called me. I attracted the attention of a man who'd used a meat cleaver on his family."

I could feel the blood drain from my face. "I don't want to hear this, Frank." I stood on rubbery legs.

"I just hope folks will see that I've changed," he said insistently. "I found the Lord while I was inside, Emily." He's forgiven my sins. Now I want the townspeople to forgive me."

Looking into his eyes, I had a hard time getting a fix on him. Did he or did he not know I was the one who'd seen him kill Daryl Buckmeyer? If so, why didn't he just say something? Maybe he wasn't sure. Maybe he was waiting for me to say something. "I have to go now."

He reached through the bars and grabbed my sweater. I tried not to overreact. "Listen, I've only been out a little more than a week. Maybe you and I can get together. Talk about old times. You know, I always thought you were the prettier sister."

A little more than a week. About the same time since I'd begun to notice that things in my house were not as they should be.

I stood there staring at him, wondering if the air had suddenly turned colder or if it was me. I could feel icy fingers caressing the back of my neck. I pulled away, and he let go of my sweater. "I'm seeing someone," I lied. "We sort of have an understanding."

"Oh, well." He looked sad, and if it had been possible to feel sorry for Frank, I would have chosen that moment. He started to turn. "By the way, I heard about your sister," he said. "Heard your mother went to pieces over it." He shook his head sadly. "I reckon she'd go right over the edge if something happened to you."

I gazed back at him stupidly. What did that mean? I didn't have time to ask; someone tugged at my skirt.

"Mith Wilkop?"

I glanced down and saw one of my students standing beside me with a runny nose. Maribeth Bradshaw had more allergies than the rest of my class put together. I reached into my pocket for a tissue. "Here you go, honey," I said, handing it to the little girl. "Be sure to throw it in the trash can when you're finished with it."

She nodded and walked away, and I turned back to the fence, determined to get rid of Frank. But he was already gone. Somehow he had slipped away without my hearing him. A cold chill ran through me as I wondered where else he may have slipped in and out undetected.

The police department was an old red brick building that sat catty-cornered to the courthouse. It had been renovated in recent years, not because folks fretted over the comforts of law enforcement, but because one local church group had put up a fuss over how the prisoners were forced to live in ratty jail cells. Those cells now resembled something out of *Better Homes and Gardens*, a fact that peeved me greatly since we couldn't afford air conditioning at Mossy Oaks Elementary. It wasn't easy trying to teach a child to subtract in ninety-degree weather when the only thing coming through the windows was hot air.

As I approached the front desk, I was greeted by the smell of fried onions and burnt coffee, no doubt coming from the tiny kitchen at the end of the hall. Myrtle Freeman, the dispatcher, greeted me, said the chief could see me right away and pointed me in the direction of his office. I found him playing gin rummy with a young, pimply faced officer wearing a Marine-type haircut.

Chief Ben Hix was in his early sixties, tall and angular with thinning, battleship-gray hair. He limped due to an injury he'd received years before in the line of duty. At least, that's the story he'd given folks. Everybody knew he'd shot himself in the foot while cleaning his gun during a Super Bowl game on TV. He should have retired long ago—*would* have, had his wife not died of an aneurysm a couple of years back, quashing the plans they'd made for a cross-country trip in their motor home and leaving their modest house a lonely place to come home to at the end of the day.

"Hard day at the office, huh?" I asked, peering through the open doorway.

The old chief looked embarrassed. "This is when I do my best thinking." He dismissed the younger man. "Go see if Myrtle needs you for anything," he said, then motioned me in. "These gawl-derned rookies. I feel like a baby-sitter." He tucked a dead cigar into the corner of his mouth and propped his feet on the desk. "Sit down and tell me what's on your mind."

I sat in a hard plastic chair and regarded him matter-of-factly. "What, pray tell, is Frank Gillespie doing out of prison?"

The chief's eyebrows rose almost to the top of his head. "What d'you mean why's he out? He was paroled."

"You still didn't answer my question."

He shrugged as if he had no idea what I wanted to hear. "That's the way the system works. Course, the parole board has to be convinced the prisoner has changed his ways and all." He chewed on his cigar. "Now, don't go getting that pinched look with *me*, 'cause I'm not the one who came up with the idea."

"How long's he been out?"

" 'Bout a week. Maybe ten days."

"What a coincidence. That's when I first noticed that somebody's been sneaking into my house and taking things."

The chief looked annoyed. "And you're sure as tootin' it's Frank, right?" He chewed on his cigar another minute as he regarded me. "I haven't seen anything on it come across my desk. Did you file a missing items report?"

I glanced down at my shoes. "No, I kept hoping they'd turn up."

He shook his head and opened his desk drawer, from which he pulled out a form. "Okay, what are you missing?"

"Just little things. An ashtray in the shape of an alligator, a ceramic vase, a toothpick holder—"

He stopped writing. "And you're here to file a report over something like that?" he asked in disbelief.

"That's not all. I'm missing jewelry as well."

"How much would you say it was worth?"

"I don't know. It was a gift from Molly."

He studied me. "So you think ol' Frank's going to risk another stint in prison over small change?"

I had no answer. Not unless I was willing to confess the reason for my fears. "It makes sense to me."

"Way I heard it, Frank and Jesus are like bosom buddies now. I also heard Frank didn't fare well in the big house. I don't think he's going to take a chance on getting sent back. Maybe you just misplaced the items."

"I know somebody's coming into my house, Chief. I get up in the morning, and I can sense it. I go into the kitchen and find my coffee poured for me and the newspaper already on the kitchen table. Someone's going through my personal belongings."

"Have you considered Molly?"

"She was the first person I asked, but she swears she has nothing to do with it."

He pulled his legs from under the desk and sat upright. "Kids always lie when they think they're going to get into trouble. Maybe one of her friends took them. Have you thought of that?"

I stood. "I've thought of everything. But if her friends did it, why didn't they take something worth money? Like my camera or the VCR? Somebody is playing games with me. Have you seen Frank lately, Chief? His eyes? He's crazy."

"If I had to lock folks up just because they were crazy, I'd have to arrest half the people in this town. Besides, Gillespie ain't got no cause to mess with you."

"Tell me something," I said. "Why would anybody let someone as dangerous as Frank out of prison?"

He lit a match, put the flame to his cigar and puffed heartily. Smoke bellowed from his mouth like from an open furnace. "I'm afraid I don't have the answer to that. Like I said, that's up to the parole board. Just between you and me, I suspect Augustus greased a few palms. Wouldn't be the first time."

4

The Probation and Parole Office was tucked into the basement of the courthouse and, understandably, reeked of mildew. A network of cracks along the regulation-gray walls made me question the soundness of the building. Of course, those cracks had been there since I was a kid, so I decided I wasn't in immediate danger of having the entire building collapse on me.

As I walked into the front office, I looked for a secretary. The room was empty, save for a number of battered metal desks and matching file cabinets. Not a soul in sight.

I started down the hall and paused at the first door. A dark-haired man, his back to me, was talking on the phone. I waited politely, hoping he would sense my presence and look around.

"What d'you mean the press is still calling every day?" he demanded of the listener. "Haven't they done enough damage to my career, for God's sake? You know what they're doing, don't you? They're trying to turn this thing into another Rodney King incident. It's not enough that I quit my job and left town. They want my fucking scalp."

I backed away, certain the man didn't want me privy to his conversation. Still, I was curious and reasoned that as long as he didn't know I was listening, it was okay. That way neither of us would have cause to be embarrassed when it was all over. It really wasn't my finest reasoning, but it was the best I could come up with on such short notice. I just hoped the secretary didn't come through the front door and catch me eavesdropping. Having been raised Baptist, I was certain it was up there with the seven deadly sins.

The man listened to the person on the other end of the line for a while, then spoke again. "This town sucks, man. If you were trying to hide me, you succeeded. Do you realize the only culture to speak of is a strip shopping center and an ancient theater? I've seen the same Arnold Schwarzenegger movie three times in two weeks." He sighed heavily. "But all is not lost," he said, sarcasm slipping into his voice. "There's talk of cable TV coming to town. That's all these hillbillies can talk about."

I felt myself frown. The guy was starting to annoy me.

"Oh, and let me tell you about my secretary," he went on. "She's about three hundred pounds and perpetually smells like a Big Mac. I made the mistake of grabbing one of her Cheetos last week, and I thought all hell would break loose."

I glanced at the nameplate on his desk. Clinton Ward, Parole Officer. Should have read Clinton Ward, Resident Jackass. Deciding I could be as rude as he was, I banged on the open door and had the pleasure of seeing him jump. He whirled around in his chair, giving me an undistorted view of his scowling face. His eyes were brownish-black, his jaw unshaven. He wore a black Harley-Davidson T-shirt that had obviously shrunk from spending too much time in coin-operated dryers while he stood outside making drug deals. Still, he was physically fit; the shirt enhanced chest and arm muscles that would have been the envy of most bouncers.

"I'll call you back," he told the person on the line, then hung up. He regarded me silently.

"*You're* the parole officer?" I asked in amazement and disbelief. I could imagine him hot-wiring my car or holding up a liquor store, but counseling troubled parolees?

"You got a problem with that?"

"Uh, no," I stammered. I'm not easily intimidated, and

I don't usually put up with verbal abuse—I figure I get enough of that in the classroom—but I needed something from this man, and I desperately wanted him to be on my side where the matter of Frank Gillespie was concerned. For the moment, I decided to be polite. If things didn't work out, I could always gouge holes in his tires with my nail file when I reached the parking lot.

"My name is Emily Wilkop," I said, giving him my best smile, "and I have an urgent matter to discuss with you. I hope I'm not interrupting anything."

He clasped his hands behind his head and leaned back in his chair. "I was just about to stick my revolver in my mouth, but I suppose it can wait."

My smile faltered. Sometimes people had reasons for being jerks, I'd discovered over the years. A death in the family, financial problems, a divorce. Personal tragedy could sour an attitude, turn even the nicest person into a miserable louse or make them say things totally off the wall. Though we'd only just met, I felt that was not the case here. Simply put, this man was a jerk.

"Then perhaps I should leave and let you get on with it."

He almost smiled. "What's so important you had to come barging into my office?" he asked. "I thought you Southerners prided yourselves on good manners."

I stepped inside, deciding I could very well be an old woman by the time he invited me to enter. "What happened to the man who had this job before you? Allen Springer?"

"Retired. How can I help you, Miss Wilkop?"

I heard the impatience in his voice. "I want to know why Frank Gillespie was released from prison after serving little more than half his sentence."

"Gillespie?" His dark eyes narrowed briefly, and it was obvious he was trying to place the name.

"Served time in Georgia for robbing a liquor store. Almost killed the owner," I said.

He nodded suddenly. "Oh, yeah, I've seen the file. He

was released last week, I believe. What's this case got to do with you?''

''I've come to protest.''

''Too late for that. The bugger's already out.'' He picked up the phone; I suppose it was his way of letting me know I was dismissed.

''Is there someone else I can talk to?''

''Not unless you got plane fare to Bermuda. The guy who works with me is on vacation.''

I tried to imagine him at a cocktail party, at his wittiest, and couldn't. ''Somebody has been breaking into my house at night. There's no doubt in my mind that it's Frank Gillespie.''

I had the satisfaction of taking him by surprise. He hung up the phone. ''You actually saw him?''

''He's too smart for that.''

''What makes you so certain it's Frank?''

''He's crazy. I would think that's reason enough.''

''Look, Miss Wilkop,'' Clinton said. ''Mr. Springer performed the parole investigation in this case. I don't even know that much about it, other than what I've learned from glancing at the file. But I understand Frank Gillespie's behavior in prison was exemplary.''

''They probably refused to let him keep weapons in his cell,'' I said. He answered me with a shrug. ''You're not going to do anything, are you?'' I asked dully.

''It's out of my hands. The parole board felt Frank was ready to be integrated back into society, and they have the final word. As for your suspicions, I can't do anything without proof.'' He stood and escorted me to the door, as if to say the conversation was over. ''Sorry.''

He didn't look a damn bit sorry to me. As he led me out, I knew I was going to have to find help elsewhere.

DeWayne Tompkins was still handsome, despite drinking as though he feared that Prohibition would be reinstated any day. I suspected it was the only way he knew how to deal with my sister's death; worse, I knew he felt as responsible for her suicide as I did. Nothing I said seemed to make any difference, and each time I saw him, his blond hair seemed to have more gray in it.

"Em, what are you doing here?" he asked, finding me at his door that same afternoon.

He and Molly were the only ones who called me Em. I kind of liked it. "Hello, DeWayne," I said. "May I come in?" I glanced around anxiously as I spoke. The Orange Grove Motel sat on the edge of a two-lane highway, tucked between a junkyard and a juke joint. If somebody in town got stabbed or shot, the police immediately made tracks for this area. I'd never figured out why they called it the Orange Grove; there wasn't a citrus tree within five hundred miles, and never had been.

"Sure, come in," he said, backing from the doorway so I could step through. "I have to warn you, though, the place is a mess. I've been on the road two weeks straight. Just got in last night, as a matter of fact."

He hadn't been lying about the mess, I noted as I stepped inside a small efficiency unit. The bedroom/kitchen combination smelled of booze and spoiled food. I remembered a time when he'd been compulsively neat. I remembered a time when I thought that if anyone could change my sister, it would be DeWayne.

He grabbed a full laundry basket from one of the twin beds. He was obviously embarrassed. "Sit here," he said. "Don't worry; they just sprayed for fleas." I must've looked alarmed, for he chuckled. "Just kidding, Em, just kidding. Lord, I haven't seen you in a coon's age." The light went out of his eyes. "How're your folks doing?"

"My mother still has bad days." We were quiet for a moment, each of us remembering what it had been like after Lurlene's death, the awfulness of it all. I remembered how DeWayne had looked the day of her funeral, like a big blow-up doll that'd had all its air sucked out. I remembered the mourners who'd filled my parents' small house afterward, the smell of fried chicken and sweaty bodies and cloying perfume. DeWayne had grabbed my hand.

"Let's get the hell out of here," he'd said, pulling me out the back door. We'd driven to the nearest bar and gotten drunk. DeWayne had told me his life's story; I'd told him mine, including the part about Frank Gillespie. It'd been the first and only time I'd shared my story. That night we'd formed a strong bond, which I'd hoped would start our healing processes. Unfortunately, DeWayne was still not coping well, and I suspected it was the alcohol.

"So what brings you to this part of town?" DeWayne asked, drawing me back to the present. "Need a contract put out on somebody?"

"I wish you'd move," I blurted. "You've got a perfectly fine house on the edge of town." He hadn't sold the house he'd shared with Lurlene and Molly, but he refused to go within a mile of it. He paid someone to look after the lawn and surrounding acreage. He even refused to rent the place out so he could cover the mortgage payment.

DeWayne glanced around the room. "I don't mind this place. It's cheap and serves its purpose. Course, they switched my territory, and I won't be traveling as much, so I might not feel that way for long." He paused, then changed the subject abruptly. "So, how are you and Molly getting along?"

DeWayne knew we had our problems. "We're still trying to iron out the kinks."

"I haven't been much help. I promise I'll try harder in the future."

I didn't say anything. I wasn't certain DeWayne, with his drinking, would be a good influence on Molly. Before he and my sister had separated, before her death, he'd set a fine example for my niece and treated her like his own daughter. But those days were past, and if Molly had felt any sort of security during that time, it'd been destroyed the day DeWayne walked out. Finding her mother's body had more or less sent her over the edge emotionally. I liked to think she was getting better after all these months, but the truth was, I wouldn't have blamed her if she never trusted another adult as long as she lived.

"You look troubled, Em. What's on your mind?"

DeWayne could always tell when something was bothering me. From the beginning he'd been like the big brother I'd never had, and I'd often reminded Lurlene how smart she was for snatching him up when a number of women would've been glad to have him. Lurlene had found the whole thing amusing and teased DeWayne about marrying the wrong sister. But DeWayne had worshipped her, and how could he not? Lurlene had been strikingly beautiful. Most women, including myself, had felt mousy beside her.

It had come as a crushing blow to me when DeWayne walked out on her, but he assured me it would not affect our friendship or his love for Molly. Maybe I'd come to depend on him too much, I thought. I suppose that's why I'd told him about that night at Fludd's Service Station. That and three frozen margaritas. I'd also told him about my nightmares, my fear of the dark, of Frank stepping out of the shadows and doing to me what he'd done to Daryl.

DeWayne had confessed his own childhood nightmares, a result of living with an abusive, alcoholic mother and a grandmother who'd turned deaf ears. He had moved away from his family as soon as he was of age, eventually putting himself through college and landing a good job. I had to respect him for that. Some people sit around waiting for things to happen; DeWayne made them happen. But he'd seemed hell-bent on destroying it with booze.

"I need a favor," I said at last. "I want you to teach me how to shoot a gun."

He laughed, then sobered instantly when he saw I was serious. "I thought you hated guns."

"Things change."

"What things?"

"Frank Gillespie's out of prison."

His eyes widened. "You're not serious."

I nodded. "Been back a week now, which is how long I've been noticing things aren't as they should be at home." I went on to explain what had been going on. "He even dropped by the school. I sort of got the impression he has a few more loose screws than when he went in.''

"Shit, that could make him more dangerous than before.'' DeWayne got up from the bed and walked into the
kitchenette, where he reached into a miniature refrigerator
for a beer. He twisted off the cap and took a swig. Finally,
he regarded me. ''Did he threaten you?''

"Not in so many words.'' I repeated what Frank had
said about how my mother might go over the edge if something happened to me.

DeWayne looked angry. ''Why don't I move into your
guest room for a while? Just until I get a fix on the bastard.
I'll blow his goddamn brains out if he comes anywhere near
you or Molly.''

I would have been tempted to take him up on the offer
if it hadn't been for his drinking. I suspected I was in way
over my head trying to deal single-handedly with a man
like Frank Gillespie. But, much as I loved DeWayne, I
didn't want to subject Molly to his lifestyle. I had worked
too hard all these months, undoing some of the damage
Lurlene's death had caused.

"I have to do this on my own, DeWayne,'' I said. ''If
Frank is really out to hurt me, I have to convince him that
I'm not afraid and that I can take care of myself.''

He looked sad. Finally, he nodded. ''Okay, Em. If you
won't let me protect you, then I suppose the best I can do
is teach you to protect yourself. I only hope I don't live to
regret it.''

I was glad I'd come to him. DeWayne had never let me
down when I needed help. ''When can we start?''

"As soon as you like. In the meantime, I should probably
have a look at the locks on your door.''

"Don't worry about it,'' I said, knowing DeWayne
wasn't very handy when it came to that sort of thing. ''I'm
going to ask the school janitor to install dead bolts.'' Herschel Buckmeyer, Daryl's brother, had done small tasks for
me before, and I repaid him by baking his favorite cookies.

"Won't do a damn bit of good if you don't use them,''

he said. "I can't believe some folks around here still go to bed without locking their doors."

"I lock my doors," I said defensively. But I knew there were people who didn't and bragged about it. "Before Frank killed Daryl, people felt safe in their beds at night."

"Yeah, well, now that Frank's out of prison, I have a feeling we're in for a few surprises."

5

The telephone was ringing when Molly and I came through the front door the following day. Molly snatched it before the answering machine had time to pick up. She listened a minute, then offered the phone to me, her look bewildered. "It's for you. A *man*," she added as though she found it hard to believe someone of the opposite sex would be calling me.

"Try not to look so shocked," I muttered irritably as I took the phone. I'd had plenty of dates in the past few years, before Molly came to live with me, despite the fact that I hadn't met anybody who made me want to rush out and take cooking lessons or knit afghans. Lately I'd been so caught up in trying to get the girl on the right track that I didn't even have time for a social life. I spoke into the phone as Molly sat nearby and listened.

"Emily Wilkop? This is Clinton Ward from the parole office. I was wondering if you'd meet me for coffee."

I had a mental picture of scowling eyes framed by longish dark hair. "Why would I want to do that?" I asked, thinking it sounded about as appealing as a root canal without Novocain. I couldn't think of one reason to bother with him after the way he'd acted.

"I'd like to talk to you about Frank Gillespie."

Okay, so maybe there was *one* good reason. And if Clinton Ward wanted to see me, it could very well mean he'd come to his senses regarding Frank. "When?"

"As soon as it's convenient. You name the place."

I hesitated, my gaze automatically shifting to my niece. We'd already had dinner. "Do you know where the strip shopping center is?" I asked, trying to come up with a place that was close by. "It's called Oaks Plaza; it's right next to the theater playing that Arnold Schwarzenegger movie you like so well." I couldn't resist the dig.

A brief pause. "Yeah, I've seen it."

"There's a little coffee shop called the Sip Shoppe. I can meet you in ten minutes." I hung up the phone and turned to my niece. "Let's go."

Molly gaped at me. "You want *me* to go with you on a date?"

"It's not a date." I grabbed my purse and made for the door.

"Why can't I just stay here?"

"Because," I said, unable to think of a good reason. I didn't want Molly alone in the house, given what was going on. "There's a bookstore next to the Sip Shoppe. You can pick up a couple of magazines."

The drive to the shopping center took less than five minutes, during which time Molly grumbled nonstop. The last thing she wanted to do was kill time in a boring bookstore. Her idea of a fun evening was raiding the refrigerator and talking on the phone. She was still protesting how unfair it was when I turned into the shopping center and began to search for a parking place.

In its early days, Oaks Plaza—which had been built of cinder block—consisted of a grocery store, a medium-sized department store and various hardware, auto and alterations shops. Boring as all get-out, even for the most devoted shopper, and one by one, the stores had gone under.

Finally, Augustus Gillespie, who'd already made a name for himself in the textile business, had bought the place, enlarged it and then had the building stuccoed and the roof tiled so that it resembled what you might find in California. The new specialty shops offered something for everyone. Someone like Clinton Ward, who had sounded like he hailed from a larger town, might not think much of it, but folks in Mossy Oaks were happier than a pig in warm mud.

There was even talk of Augustus's buying up the now-abandoned stores downtown, closing some of the streets and building a mall of sorts with outdoor cafes. Poor Augustus. He wanted so desperately to make something of the town. Progress, he claimed, was the only hope we had of keeping our young people from moving away. I agreed with him in theory, but I still considered him a bully.

The parking lot was crowded, a sign that the shopping center was doing well. Augustus was probably rolling naked in all his cash. Too bad he didn't use some of it to build a padded cell for his crazy son, I thought. Surprisingly enough, I was able to find a parking place right in front of the coffee shop.

"I'm only going to be a few minutes," I told Molly. "Don't leave the bookstore until I come for you."

She wasn't listening. Her eyes were fixed on the man standing at the door to the Sip Shoppe. "Awesome!" she said. "Is that him?"

I glanced up and, to my surprise, saw Clinton Ward already waiting beside the door to the coffee shop. He was wearing faded denims and a long-sleeved flannel shirt that looked as though it had come from someone's dirty-clothes hamper.

"Yes, that's Mr. Ward," I said, climbing out of the car and waiting for my niece to join me on the sidewalk. "Come on; I'll walk you to the door of the bookstore."

Molly looked at me, and it was obvious that she wasn't happy. "Why do you always have to embarrass me? You think I can't walk twenty feet by myself without being kidnapped by some child pornography ring?"

"I wasn't trying to embarrass you."

"You do it all the time, Aunt Em. You're so overprotective. It sucks."

"Molly, your language!"

"I want to know why you feel you have to treat me like a four-year-old. Are you afraid I can't think for myself?"

I closed my eyes, trying to remain calm. "Could we discuss this later?" I asked. "Must we stand here cater-wauling on the sidewalk like a couple of mountain women?"

"There won't be any discussion," the girl muttered. "You always think you're right." She walked away without another word.

"Is that your daughter?" Clinton asked as I approached.

I noticed that he still hadn't gone anywhere near a razor or a barber. "Niece," I said.

"Cute."

"Sometimes, but not always. You must live close by to have beat me here."

He nodded. "My apartment is less than a mile away. Shall we go in?"

We stepped inside the coffee shop, and I selected a table near the front window where I could see Molly if she came out of the bookstore. The place smelled of fresh-brewed coffee and pastry. A slender waitress in a pink uniform took our order and left to fill it.

"So what did you want to see me about?" I asked.

"I interviewed Frank Gillespie today."

My stomach did a little flip-flop at the mention of Frank's name. "And?"

"He seemed very sincere about wanting to make a fresh start. He's already found a job."

"That couldn't have been too difficult; his daddy owns most of the town."

"He plans to go into the schools and tell kids what prison life was like, so they'll think twice before committing a crime. His father is even talking about building a youth center."

The waitress arrived with our coffee, and we waited to resume our conversation. I stirred cream and sugar into my cup and wondered what Clinton was up to. "Why are you telling me this?"

"So you'll stop worrying. If Frank acts a bit strange or

---

disoriented, it's because he's not used to having his freedom back. He's not out to hurt anyone."

"You say he's disoriented? Well, I say he's a raving lunatic who just happens to have a stomach for violence as well. I'm afraid to close my eyes at night knowing he's on the loose."

Clinton took a sip of his coffee. "Nobody wants to see a convict let out of prison, Miss Wilkop. Except for maybe his immediate family. But it's a fact of life: we can't afford to keep every single prisoner incarcerated. Like I said earlier, Frank's prison record was impressive."

"I don't care about any of this," I said, shoving my cup aside. I started to get up, but he stopped me, placing a restraining hand on mine. I stared at it so hard he finally moved it.

"He was savagely and *inhumanely* abused by the other prisoners," Clinton said, lowering his voice so the girl behind the counter wouldn't hear. "Not once or twice, but almost every day for fifteen years. I don't know why it was allowed to go on—probably because Frank knew he'd get a knife in his back if he said anything. So he said nothing."

"Which means he's probably more dangerous than ever," I said, voicing the same words DeWayne had.

"Aunt Em?"

I snapped my head up and found Molly standing a couple of feet away. "What are you doing here?" I demanded.

"The lady at the bookstore made me leave," she replied. "Said if I wanted to read something, then I was going to have to buy it first. You forgot to give me money." Molly looked at Clinton. "Who are you?"

Clinton stood and introduced himself. "You resemble your aunt."

I had the distinct pleasure of watching all the color drain from Molly's face. I stood as well. "It's time we left."

"You must be new in town," Molly said.

"Yes."

"Married?"

Clinton looked amused as he tossed a couple of bills on

the table. "No, I'm not married," he said. "Why do you ask? You wouldn't happen to know of any pretty ladies you could set me up with?"

Molly shook her head. "Pretty ladies? Not in *this* town. But my aunt is single, if you're interested."

I felt my face grow hot. I wasn't a raving beauty, but I certainly wasn't unattractive by any means, and I didn't need my niece trying to fix me up when I had a mother who was more than capable. I knew that Molly, usually quiet and withdrawn around strangers, was simply getting even with me for embarrassing her earlier.

"Could we go now?" I asked, giving her a stiff smile.

She shrugged. "Sure." But the look she tossed me told me she'd settled the score between us.

Clinton followed us out and paused beside my car. He looked thoughtful. "Maybe I should take your niece's advice and ask you out. You could do worse than me, you know."

I was tempted to tell him I'd have to look under every rock in town to prove that statement true. I felt my left eye twitch. It sometimes happens when I'm in a tight spot and don't know how to get out of it. Like the time, right after Lurlene's death, when I went to my family doctor because of lower stomach pains, and he set me up for a barium enema at our hospital. I tried to tell him it was stress, but he refused to believe it wasn't cancer until he'd stuck that thingamajig up my rectum so he could take X rays and have a look for himself.

"What d'you say?" Clinton asked when I still hadn't answered.

"Yeah, I'll go out with you, Mr. Ward," I said, then started for the parking lot. I glanced over my shoulder and tossed him a parting shot. "When pigs fly." I heard him laugh as I paused to unlock the door of my car.

The noise was deafening, and each time I fired the revolver, it kicked and sent shock waves up my arm. My feet slightly apart, I fired off the remaining rounds as DeWayne had taught me, completely missing the tin cans he'd placed on a bale of hay some distance away. We were standing in a field on the edge of town, having reached it by way of washed-out roads that ran through the area like arteries. The field was flanked by tall pines and red maples, thick with underbrush. I'd seen one or two deer as I'd followed DeWayne out to the site, and I prayed I wouldn't hit one with a stray bullet.

DeWayne drained the rest of his beer and dropped the empty can into a paper sack holding five others just like it. He shook his head sadly as I brought my arm down, lowering the .38 Smith & Wesson. "I believe you're the worst shot I've ever seen, kid. Maybe I should teach you to throw a knife."

I regarded him. He was drunk, having polished off an entire six-pack in little more than an hour. "That's not funny, DeWayne. Besides, it's not entirely my fault. This gun feels . . . I don't know . . . clumsy."

"It's the lightest thing I've got. You'll just have to get used to it."

"You think it's powerful enough?"

"Blow somebody to kingdom come. Thing is, you got to hit 'em first."

"Okay, so I need more practice."

"The offer is still open, you know. I could move in for a couple of weeks. Gillespie wouldn't stand a chance. I can shoot a cow tick off a dog's ear at fifty paces."

"I appreciate the offer, DeWayne," I said, trying to sound sincere, "but I've sorta got my hands full with Molly right now. And to tell you the truth, I don't want to have to explain your presence to the Department of Social Services. If they suspected Molly was in any danger—" I paused. "I'm not sure what they'd do."

"I understand," he said. Still, he looked hurt. "I admire what you're doing for the girl. We both know Lurlene and I should have been better parents."

"You did your best," I said, although secretly I wondered why he couldn't pull himself together now for Molly's sake. As for my sister, I didn't want to think about her because doing so always made me feel guilty. I knew Lurlene would still be alive today if I hadn't filed those papers with the court to have Molly removed from her home.

I had debated long and hard about contacting DSS, but when I'd learned my sister was leaving Molly alone nights, I'd had no choice but to act. Perhaps I should have turned to DeWayne, but at the time he seemed so miserable over their split. Besides, Molly wasn't his biological daughter.

How was I to know Lurlene would kill herself over it? I tried to convince myself that maybe Cordia was right, that my sister had been unstable to begin with, that maybe she *had* inherited some of Aunt Bessie's bad genes. But deep down, I knew it was my fault. I was as guilty as if I'd put that noose around her neck myself.

Somehow, some way, I was going to have to live with that knowledge for the rest of my life.

"I only have one question," DeWayne said, interrupting my thoughts. "Do you think you're going to be able to pull the trigger if and when the time comes? It doesn't matter how good your aim is if you can't fire at someone."

I knew I had to be honest with myself. The thought of putting a bullet in a man, even one as dangerous as Frank Gillespie, terrified me. Guns were for hoodlums and crack addicts and cold-blooded killers. Civilized people settled their differences without weapons. At least, that's what I'd always thought. Now here I was going against everything I'd ever believed. Could I actually shoot someone? I wondered.

"I don't know, DeWayne," I said after a moment. "I just don't know."

The following Friday found me sitting next to Ellen Gouge, our music director, in our antiquated auditorium, waiting for our faculty meeting to begin. I would normally have selected a chair next to Lilly, but I insisted that she leave early since her disk in her back was giving her trouble. One of the library assistants had been only too happy

----

to take over her class for the rest of the afternoon.

As Ellen told me of her plans for the Christmas program, I found myself eagerly looking forward to the holiday season. It would be the first for Molly and me. I was still nodding and smiling at her ideas when Augustus and Frank Gillespie followed Principal Higginbotham onto the stage.

Suddenly, it was as if all the oxygen had left the room. I felt breathless and dizzy, as though I'd just run ten miles uphill on open desert.

"Did you know the Gillespies were going to be here?" Ellen whispered.

I shook my head while trying to regain my equilibrium. I was only vaguely aware of our principal standing before the microphone, making announcements and discussing how much Christmas wrapping paper we'd have to sell to afford a new roof for the school. All the while, Augustus and Frank, wearing ultraconservative dark suits, stiff white dress shirts and bright ties, smiled at the crowd like a couple of politicians on a campaign tour.

Then, out of the blue, Principal Higginbotham started talking about crime and its causes. I blinked several times, wondering if I'd lost my place in his speech, wondering how we'd managed to jump so quickly from roofing estimates to the rising crime rate. It occurred to me that our principal might be as surprised with the change in our program as the rest of us.

"Today we are fortunate to have with us a young man who has seen prison bars from both sides," he read from an index card. "Frank Edward Gillespie started a life of crime after becoming addicted to cocaine at the age of seventeen. It was an addiction so strong that he was forced to steal to support his habit. At eighteen, he almost killed a man while robbing his place of business." He paused and waited for the crowd to grasp the enormousness of Frank's crime.

"Today, however, Frank Gillespie is a new man, having

spent fifteen years behind bars and suffering unspeakable horrors," the principal continued. "Thanks to a prison psychologist who believed in him and a chaplain who saw the goodness in his heart, Frank was able to turn his life around. He not only licked his drug addiction; he turned his soul over to the Lord."

There was mild applause. Principal Higginbotham invited Frank to the lectern, and I watched closely. Even in his expensive suit, Frank looked wretched.

He cleared his throat and leaned close to the mike. "Ladies and gentlemen," he began, "I've never been much of a public speaker, but what I have to say to you doesn't take a bunch of fancy words. My father and I have been before the school board, and they recently approved our idea for me to come into the schools and speak to your children about drugs and crime. Unfortunately, I am very knowledgeable on the subject.

"I can't begin to account the terrible things that happened to me in prison, but I would like to think my suffering had a purpose. I believe that purpose is to try to prevent as many youngsters as possible from following in my footsteps. I hope I can count on your support. Thank you for your attention."

He smiled and nodded, and this time the applause was louder. As he approached his chair, Augustus Gillespie stood and crossed the stage. He was a big man, at least six feet six, and weighed somewhere between 250 and 275. Even from where I sat, he looked imposing.

"Thank you for being here today," he said in a voice that commanded attention. He glanced at Frank, and he seemed to swell with pride. "When my son told me what he wanted to do for his community, I cried like a little baby." He paused as though to give the crowd time to imagine what an emotional moment it had been for him, but I personally had trouble believing Augustus had ever shed a tear in his life.

"Just like the rest of you, I wanted the best for my child," he said, smiling to the crowd and receiving nods in return. "I wanted him to have the things I didn't have when I was growing up. Since I came from a poor family, that pretty much covered everything." He paused and smiled, and the faculty members chuckled in return. This was Augustus Gillespie at his best, I thought: a simple man, raised in poverty, who'd built a dynasty for himself in the South. He looked so earnest as he spoke that it was easy to forget the way he threw his weight around. "I suppose I spoiled Frank," he said at last, "and paid the price dearly.

"In the fifteen years of Frank's incarceration, I asked myself over and over again, where did I go wrong? Did I love him *too* much, or were there circumstances beyond my control?" Once again he paused, as though he were considering it even now.

"I believe in my heart that both answers are true. I loved my boy so much that I was willing to do anything to make him happy. He had money and fast cars and everything else his old man could give him. I let Frank set his own rules because I didn't want him to dislike me. "That—" another pause, and he held up a finger, "was my biggest mistake. Children need rules and limits."

Several people on the first row clapped, one of them our school guidance counselor.

Augustus took a deep breath and gazed out at his audience. "When was the last time any of you drove by the old Stop and Shop on Harper Street?" A few grumbles rose from the row behind me, and I knew where Augustus was going with this speech. "Lord, that store's been closed down for five years, but every night the parking lot is full of teenagers doing God knows what. And speaking of being in a dark parking lot, has anybody kept up with the rising number of teenage pregnancies in our town?"

Several people in the crowd shook their heads. Others muttered under their breath that the rate was indeed growing. "Now, I don't have a degree in law enforcement or child psychology, and I'm not up here pretending I have all the answers, but I can tell you one thing for sure: That parking lot, and every single one in town like it, needs to be roped off. Our children and teenagers need a place to go that's free from drugs and alcohol and sex.''

More applause.

''And because of this need, Frank and I are going to sit down with an architect next week and design such a place and situate it near our most troubled neighborhoods. It will be a place for kids to go when they have no place else but the street. It will be run by counselors and will house an Olympic-size swimming pool, tennis courts, arcade, and everything else a growing kid needs in order to have a little fun in his life.'' He added in a softer voice, ''We will employ a minister as well, to meet the inner needs of our youth.''

This time the applause was loud. Once it died, Augustus invited Frank to join him at the microphone. ''This facility will be called the Frank E. Gillespie Civic Center, and it is our great hope that we can make a difference in the lives of some of our youth.''

When the applause started this time, there was a couple of whistles as well.

I didn't join in the fanfare; in fact, I was suspicious over the dog and pony show I'd just witnessed. Either Frank and Augustus had had a major soul-cleansing miracle, or they were playing us all for fools.

6

Molly and I usually met my parents for church on Sunday, then went home with them for an enormous dinner afterward. We had missed the previous Sunday, what with Molly being in such a nasty mood after our trip to Savannah, so I'd decided to make up for it by bringing a bucket of fried chicken over for dinner on Friday.

I was beginning to regret having made plans with them as I left the faculty meeting. Seeing Frank and Augustus had left me feeling out of sorts, and I knew that would only complicate the evening with Percy and Claire Wilkop, my beloved parents.

I really do love my folks to death, but at times they can be overly generous with their advice on how I should raise Molly. Not only that, I suppose I still hold a grudge against my mother for trying to set me up with every single man between the ages of twenty-one and fifty, outside of our immediate family.

As we sat on the front porch sipping lemonade before dinner, my father started on me. "Molly don't need no child psychologist," he said. "What she needs is a good kick in the behind." Luckily, Molly was in the bathroom.

My father's face was lined and weathered from years of farming and working with the Highway Department. He was officially retired now; he and my mother lived off Social Security and a respectable tomato-growing business which they often failed to report to the IRS.

Both of my parents were firm believers in spanking, and their weapon of choice when Lurlene and I were children had been a green hickory switch that left red welts on our legs for days. All God-fearing Baptists knew the importance of having a hickory switch in the house; otherwise, how was a child expected to escape the Devil's lures?

It seemed as if I'd spent most of my childhood fearing the Lord and ducking sin and temptation—not because I was the goody-goody Lurlene claimed I was, but because I trembled at the thought of Judgment Day. I worried that my mother would try to pass some of her beliefs on to Molly, and I'd cautioned her against it. The kid was already scared enough, I'd insisted, so my mother held her tongue.

"My papa woulda used a strap on us if we'd acted like kids today," my mother volunteered. Her hair was gray, but her skin and figure were youthful thanks to a diet of fresh vegetables that she grew in her very own garden and shared with family and friends. I may not have a slice of bread or a drop of milk in the house, but I have a pantry overflowing with canned green beans, cucumber pickles and stewed tomatoes.

I kept promising myself I'd prepare wholesome meals for Molly, but somehow we always ended up at the drive-through window of one of those places that considers lard to be the fifth essential food group on the pyramid.

I could feel my thoughts moving elsewhere as they continued. As tough as they talked, they'd never laid a hand on Molly, and the girl got away with murder when she visited.

I was glad now that I'd come; it felt good to sit there in the crisp country air and relax for the first time that day.

My parents' house was a simple, cream-colored raised ranch, the bottom section surrounded by latticework upon which grew my mother's Boston ivy. It had turned red once cool weather set in, and it gave the place a festive look.

Behind the barn and outbuildings, their property backed up to a tidal creek, which is why the house had been built a good eighteen inches off the ground to begin with. I'd known the creek to flood the fields once or twice when various hurricanes blew through, but it'd never reached the house.

"So how're things in town?" my father asked. "Me and your mama don't get in much."

Town was only fifteen minutes away, but to hear them talk you'd think they had to go by way of Atlanta to get there. "Same as always," I replied, knowing my parents loved gossip. They might be Southern Baptists, but my father still played poker and had an occasional nip from somebody's jug, and my mother read *True Confessions* and dished dirt with the best of them. "With one exception," I added. "Frank Gillespie's been paroled."

"That's terrible! How can something like this happen?" my mother asked, turning to my father for answers. "He almost killed a man."

He gave a sound of disgust. "I'm not a bit surprised," he said. "You see it every day, where people are getting out of prison early. They blame overcrowding, naturally, and the fact that it costs so much to hold 'em. I say we need to stop treating 'em so danged good. Who says they have to have three squares a day and a gymnasium? And how come it costs more to keep 'em in jail than it would to put 'em in some highfalutin country club?"

My mother took a moment to compose herself, then shook her head sadly and made a *tsk*ing sound with her tongue. I remembered her making that same sound when she'd discovered Lurlene wearing a push-up bra at fourteen.

"Times certainly have changed since I was a kid," she said. "I hear about all this crime, and it just makes me sick that Molly's going to have to grow up in a world such as ours. You ask me, I think it's high time the Lord came for His people and left the sinners in this place of torment."

I was tempted to tell her I wasn't quite ready for that, since I still had dreams of maybe falling in love one day and having my own family. Even if the Lord *did* take me with Him, I wasn't ready to just sit around with a bunch of people in white robes listening to harp music and eating grapes. But I suspected my mother would have gone into cardiac arrest if I'd shared this with her.

"I worry about you living in town," my father told me after a moment.

I was amused. They made it sound like I lived in Manhattan or Philadelphia or maybe Trenton. I knew my parents worried about Molly and me. They'd become even more protective since Lurlene's death, which was why I felt bad telling them about Frank's release and why I wasn't about to mention the suspicions I'd taken to Chief Hix and Clinton Ward.

"You and Molly should move back home," my mother said.

"Molly and I already have a home," I replied gently. "Besides, I'm not afraid of Frank. I understand he's found the Lord and changed his ways. The school board just appointed him as our new crime prevention spokesman."

They stared at me as if I'd just given them the whole spiel in gibberish. "Look, I just report the news as I get it. You're entitled to check elsewhere for confirmation."

"You should get a dog," my father said after a moment. "A big, mean-lookin' one like they got over at Bo-Bo's Junk Yard."

"Or an alarm system," my mother said. "I know they cost a lot, but you can make monthly payments. If you were married—"

"Stop worrying," I interrupted, knowing I didn't want her to get started on the subject of my single status or the fact that I'd come very close to getting married once, only to back out at the last minute and humiliate her so that she couldn't hold up her head in church for months afterward.

"I recently had Herschel Buckmeyer install new dead bolts," I told them.

"I would have done it for you," my father said, obviously hurt that I hadn't asked him first.

"I know. But DeWayne offered to do it, so I figured I'd better get Herschel out to the house fast. Otherwise I might end up buying new doors. You know how DeWayne is

----

when it comes to fixing things." I noted my parents' sudden silence and wished I hadn't brought up DeWayne's name. They gaped at me as if I'd just confessed to giving up my Baptist beliefs for one of those snake-handling religions.

"*Our* DeWayne?" my mother said, looking anxious. She exchanged looks with my father. "Don't tell me you're seeing *him*."

Now we were getting to the other reason I sometimes skipped church and made excuses not to drop by for days at a time. Along with all the advice they offered regarding Molly, and the fact that my mother begrudged me for not being married and having at least three times the national average of children, both parents tended to overreact to everything I said.

"Of course I'm not *seeing* him," I said. "I ran into him at the grocery store the other day, and we just started talking, that's all." I'd discovered it was better to lie at times like this.

That seemed to satisfy them.

"Is he still drinking heavily?" my father asked.

I nodded sadly. " 'Fraid so."

"How awful," my mother said. "I don't think he'll ever get over it."

It, of course, was my sister's suicide, a topic we still skirted around or avoided completely if at all possible.

It was still early when I left my parents' house, having agreed to let Molly spend the night so she could play cards with my father and watch the late shows afterward. My mother had stopped watching prime-time television when she heard an actress use the word *orgasm*. Now she only watched old black-and-white movies featuring stars like Fred Astaire, Ginger Rogers, Deborah Kerr and Humphrey Bogart.

As I drove home, I decided I would make a pot of coffee and grade the two weeks' worth of papers scattered across my backseat. But when I parked in my driveway and began scooping them into a single pile, I realized I didn't have my grade book.

"Damn." I could pick it up tomorrow, of course, but I was anxious to get caught up, not only the grading, but recording the scores as well. Dropping the papers into their untidy mess once more, I climbed back into the car and started off. Mossy Oaks Elementary was less than five minutes away; I could be there and back in no time.

I pulled into the deserted parking lot a few minutes later and parked close to the entrance. The playground looked eerie; bathed in shadows, the still equipment reminded me of giant Tinkertoy constructions. I unlocked the front door a moment later, then locked it behind me once I was inside.

The hall was darker than I'd have preferred because Principal Higginbotham was on a campaign to cut utility costs. Still, I was able to find my way. I passed a row of lockers and turned right, then made my way down another hall and climbed the massive staircase to the second floor.

Lurlene and I had used these stairs as children. "Have you ever been fingered?" she'd asked me on these same steps, when I was in fifth grade and she in sixth. At the time I suppose I was trying to appear sophisticated and knowledgeable in her eyes, so I told her I had indeed been fingered—several times, in fact. I hadn't actually found out what the word meant until I was thirteen years old, and I was so shocked I bit my tongue.

I reached my classroom. I'd spent a lot of time pulling it together, working hard to create a vivid atmosphere for discovery and learning. My students and I were in the process of changing the bulletin board from its present Halloween motif to Thanksgiving. Ghosts and goblins were being replaced by Pilgrims in shiny black boots and tall hats.

I'd taught my class to draw a turkey the same way I'd been taught, by tracing my hand on a sheet of paper. The thumb, of course, was the turkey's head, and the fingers made up his feathers. They thought it was most clever, so I naturally allowed them to think it was my idea to begin with. I wove my way through the maze of small desks to where my own larger one stood at the opposite end of the room.

The grade book was right where I'd left it, beside a stack of spelling papers I'd completely forgotten about. I picked them up and turned to leave. Out of the corner of my eye, I saw the envelope lying on my desk. It had my name on it, *Miss Emily Wilkop*, printed in neat, block-style letters. Too neat, I thought. The letters had been stenciled.

My curiosity piqued, I set down the grade book and papers and reached for the envelope. I tore it open and pulled out a single sheet of paper with black letters stenciled on it.

It's been fifteen years since I fucked a woman. When I'm finished with you, I'm going to have the girl.

I stood there for several seconds as rage and terror gripped me. I crushed the note in my fist, glancing around the room as I did so. Everything was as I'd left it, each work center tidied, folders and workbooks stacked in neat rows.

How had he gotten in? The school was too lax in security, I told myself. A teacher could get a key to the front door simply by asking. How hard would it be for someone as smart as Frank Gillespie to get his hands on one?

Or maybe he'd simply dropped it off after the faculty meeting.

Hands trembling, I stuffed the letter into my purse and grabbed what I'd come for. I was a fool for letting Clinton Ward almost convince me that Frank had changed. And to think, both Gillespie men had stood in our auditorium and pretended to care about crime and the community.

I suddenly felt nauseated. Frank might fool some people, but I knew him for the cold-blooded murderer he was. Not only that, he was sick, so sick he was playing mind games with me. He was just waiting for that moment when I would be most vulnerable.

Like now.

I let myself out without bothering to lock the classroom door behind me. The hall seemed darker as I stepped out, the shadows dense and ominous looking. I wished I hadn't come, and I cursed Frank Gillespie for making me afraid in my own home and workplace. I cursed Augustus for giving Frank a voice in our town and making us feel like we were beholden to him simply because we wanted a safe place for our children to play. Then I cursed Chief Hix for not believing me. I would take great pleasure in shoving the note in his face the first chance I got. Perhaps *then* he'd believe me. But would he take action? Probably not. That's what all of this was really about; he didn't want to stir the waters around the mighty Gillespie clan. Or maybe Augustus had paid him off.

I was at the top of the stairs when I heard it, a creaking sound on the wood floor that couldn't have been made by me, since I'd paused to grab the banister and get a better hold on the papers in my arms. The hair stood up on the back of my neck.

I wasn't alone.

Adrenaline rushed through my body, urging me to flee, but I couldn't run without risking a nasty fall on the dark stairs. My heart pounded as I remembered what Daryl Buckmeyer had looked like that night, battered and bloodied. I wondered whether he'd died right away or slowly bled to death while Frank was searching for me in that cornfield. I felt terrible about my silence.

I thought of Molly. Who would take care of her if something happened to me? Who would keep chipping away at the hard shell that surrounded her, that shut her off from the rest of the world? Who would teach her not to be afraid?

I was crying by the time I reached the bottom of the stairs. I turned down the main hall and caught sight of the two metal doors that led out. A sob caught in my throat. So far away. I picked up my pace. All at once, I was running. Papers shifted in my arms and scattered to the floor. They no longer mattered. I dropped the whole lot and fled.

Fear hit me in the face like a wet blanket when I realized I'd locked myself in. I reached into my purse, frantically groping and fumbling for my keys. Precious seconds ticked by, wasted, lost forever as surely as my life was about to be lost. I glanced over my shoulder. Once again, I felt someone watching me from the shadows, just like in my dreams. Why was he hiding? Why didn't the bastard just kill me and be done with it?

I stabbed at the lock, but my hands shook so badly I dropped my key ring. I heard the keys hit the floor in a jangled clump, and I scrambled to find them in the murky light. Thankfully, I didn't have to search long. Somehow I managed to stand, although at that moment I would have sworn my knees were made of bread dough. I fit the key into the lock, shoved the door open and stepped out. Right into the arms of a man.

I closed my eyes and screamed so loud it hurt my throat.

"Calm down, Miss Wilkop," a voice said. I felt someone shaking me. "Calm down; I ain't gonna hurt you."

I opened my eyes and found myself looking into Herschel Buckmeyer's concerned face. In the dim light, he resembled his younger brother. "What are you doing here?" I demanded, made angry by fear.

"I work here, remember?"

I relaxed slightly. Of course he did; he was the custodian. "Do you always work this late?"

He shook his head. "I left early today 'cause I was feelin' bad. I'm better now. I figured I'd come empty the trash and pick up a bit. You sure you're gonna be okay? I could maybe call somebody for you."

"How long have you been here?" I asked.

"I pulled up just this minute," he said, motioning to his pickup truck, which he'd parked behind a Dumpster. From where I'd parked, I doubt I would have noticed it even if it had been there all along.

"Here, let me walk you to your car," he said, putting his hand beneath one elbow and prodding me forward.

"No, I'm fine. You go on with your work."

"Are you sure? You know, you shouldn't come here by yourself this time of night. It ain't safe."

In my present state of mind, I didn't know if he was trying to warn me or threaten me. Then I told myself I was being ridiculous. Herschel, of all people, had no reason to harm me.

7

I frowned when I saw the dark Buick parked in front of my house a few minutes later, and I was tempted to keep going. I *would* have kept going had I not recognized Clinton Ward leaning against the car. He was just the man I wanted to see at the moment; I planned to give him an earful about his parolee. First, though, I had to make sure Molly was okay.

He caught up with me at the small front porch. "Hey, where's the fire?" he joked. His smile faded abruptly when I looked at him. "Jesus, what happened to *you*?"

I stepped inside the house and held the door for him to follow. I pulled the crumpled note from my purse. "Read it. I have to make a phone call." I left him standing there and hurried into the kitchen. I returned a few minutes later feeling calmer after the brief conversation with my mother. Molly and my father were playing poker and indulging in buttered popcorn and root beer.

When I peeked into the living room, Clinton was still standing where I'd left him. Once again, he didn't look like any parole officer I'd ever seen. His T-shirt advertised a tavern in Chicago. "You want a drink?" I asked. "All I have is scotch."

"Scotch is fine." He followed me into the kitchen, where I pulled a bottle from a shelf beneath the sink.

"I keep it hidden so Molly won't be tempted," I explained, knowing it was an odd place to keep liquor. "All I have to go with it is water."

"Water's okay."

I prepared the drinks and handed him one. "Sit down," I said, indicating a chair. "Unless you'd rather sit in the living room." Strangely enough, most people preferred my kitchen.

"This is good." He waited for me to sit, then joined me. He looked troubled. "Where'd you find this?" he asked, indicating the note.

I took a sip of my drink. I realized I was still trembling. "On my desk at school. I dropped by there tonight to pick up my grade book." I met his gaze. "I got the impression I wasn't alone."

"Did you see anybody?"

"No. At least not until I stepped outside and literally ran into the janitor who was on his way in." I leaned forward slightly and cupped my palm around my glass. "I didn't have to see anybody. I *know* someone was there."

Clinton studied the note. "Somebody went to a lot of trouble to disguise their handwriting."

"It's stencil," I told him. "I use it all the time."

"Have you reported it?"

"Who would I report it to?" I felt like laughing out loud at the suggestion. "I've already discussed my suspicions with you and Chief Hix. Neither one of you seems to believe me."

"I never said I didn't believe you, Emily. But if you don't have proof—" He paused. "Look, I'm just trying to do my job, okay? I don't have to like my parolees, but I do have to help them make the transition from prison to society." He glanced at the note once more. "It doesn't make sense. I can't imagine why Frank would do something like this, but if I catch him, I'll personally drag his ass back to prison."

I thought of the note. *When I'm finished with you, I'm going to have the girl.* I knew I couldn't count on Clinton or Chief Hix or anybody else to save us; they might wait until it was too late. It was up to me.

The following Friday, I managed to hit a couple of tin cans during my shooting practice, although I'm fairly certain it was by sheer accident. Sitting on a tree stump nearby, DeWayne cheered. One would have thought I was Nancy Kerrigan performing a triple toe loop, the way he carried on.

"There's hope for you yet, kid," DeWayne said, slurring his words badly. He took a slug from a tarnished silver flask. The more he drank, the more trouble he had arranging cohesive sentences.

I knew I had to get food into him; otherwise he'd pass out right on that stump, and I'd have to drag his unconscious body to my car. "What do you say we get something to eat?" I said. "It's getting too dark to see."

DeWayne stood unsteadily. "We can go to Clancy's. They have good burgers."

Clancy's also had a full bar, but DeWayne already knew that or he wouldn't have suggested it. "I'm driving," I told him in a matter-of-fact tone. "I'll bring you back later to pick up your car."

He looked surprised, then shrugged. "Whatever. Just give me a second to lock up."

We were on our way a few minutes later, after DeWayne tucked the .38 under the passenger's seat of my car. I had mixed feelings about its being there.

"Where's Molly tonight?" he asked.

I'd already told him once. "Spending the night with a friend."

"Nice girl?"

"What?" I glanced over at him.

"The girl Molly's staying with. Is she a nice girl?"

"Nice enough, I suppose. I haven't run a background check." I knew I wasn't being polite, but I had little patience with DeWayne when he was drunk.

"You can't be too careful these days. Kids get into all

kinds of trouble. You can't afford to be lax.''

I knew DeWayne was only trying to be helpful, but he came off sounding like my mother. I decided it was the booze. After all, I knew the Grady family well and felt that Molly was in good hands. We made the rest of the drive in silence. I pulled into Clancy's, parked and turned off the engine. DeWayne started to get out, then paused when he saw that I was still sitting there.

''What's wrong?''

I was glad we weren't going to a *nice* restaurant; I would have been embarrassed to be seen with him. His shirt was badly wrinkled, his slacks stained. I remembered a time when DeWayne had insisted that all his clothes, including casual, be sent to the dry cleaners, and the shirts given heavy starch. ''Why don't you get help, DeWayne?'' I asked.

He sighed heavily and leaned against the seat. At least he was sober enough to know where the conversation was going. ''Why are you bringing this up *now*?'' he asked. ''Can't you see I've got enough on my mind?''

''If you're waiting for the perfect time to stop drinking, there's never going to be one.''

''We've been through this before. Nothing's changed.''

''I keep hoping something I say will make a difference.''

''Well, it won't,'' he snapped, then immediately looked contrite. He shifted in his seat. ''Look, this is the only way I know how to cope with life, okay? I'm not like you, Em. Nothing ever gets to you.''

''Bull.''

''Well, you handle it better than the rest of us. You're so goddamn strong. It's like you don't need anyone—you get by on sheer grit and gristle.''

Boy, had he misread me. I didn't feel strong; in fact, there were times during the past week when I'd felt I would fly apart. I decided I must be putting up a good front. Then again, I had to appear capable for Molly's sake. ''You're strong, too, DeWayne, if you'd only believe it.''

He was quiet for a minute. "So I drink. So what? I don't hurt anybody."

"Except yourself."

"Are we going to sit out here all night, or are we going inside?"

We entered Clancy's and found a table easily enough, since it was too early for the dinner crowd. The bar was full, though, and there were half a dozen men in the back playing pinball and shooting pool. It was a *guy* place, paneled in rough-hewn wood with a drab vinyl floor that looked as though it hadn't been mopped since the country had put a Democrat in the Oval Office. The black vinyl booths were cracked and torn, spitting yellow stuffing. I wondered what the kitchen looked like, then decided I was better off not knowing.

As if to punish me for the talk I'd just given him, DeWayne ordered a double bourbon and proceeded to get completely soused. I was almost weak with relief when our burgers arrived, but DeWayne asked the waitress to put his in a to-go box, and he kept on drinking.

"You're disgusted with me, aren't you?" he asked.

I shook my head. "No." Actually, I pitied him.

"Lurlene was right. I married the wrong sister."

I glanced at him and saw him eyeing me steadily, as though waiting for my reaction. "As I recall, you and Lurlene were very happy in the beginning."

He dropped his gaze to his drink, stared at it as though it held the answer to some great riddle. "Yeah, but I was new in town and didn't know what she was."

I was appalled that he could speak ill of my sister now that she was in her grave. My expression must've showed it, because he immediately became remorseful.

"I'm sorry, Em. You're right; I've had too much to drink. If you'd be so kind as to ask our waitress for our check, I'd like to leave."

I did so. DeWayne insisted on paying, despite my best arguments. In the end, I realized we were creating a scene, so I shut up and helped him out the door and to the car.

He was in a semi-stupor when we arrived at his motel. As I looked at the place he called home, I found my sympathy for him growing. A garish neon sign blinked on and off, announcing to anyone who cared that there was still a vacancy at the Orange Grove. I almost shuddered at the thought of crawling between the sheets in such a place. When had DeWayne lost his desire to live?

I parked and he awoke, automatically reaching for the door handle. "Thanks, Em," he mumbled. "Don't turn off the engine; I can see my way inside."

"You going to be okay?" I asked.

"Why wouldn't I be? Now get outta here. You got no business being in this part of town at night."

I watched him stagger to his door and fumble with his keys for a minute but waited until he was inside before pulling away. Drunk as he was, he would have been a perfect target for a robbery. I suddenly realized I made a pretty good target myself, and I locked my door.

As I pulled out of the parking lot, I wondered if I shouldn't have helped DeWayne to bed. Finally, I convinced myself he'd be fine. After all, it wasn't the first time DeWayne Tompkins had gone to bed drunk.

I awoke the next morning feeling troubled and out of whack. I didn't know if it was because of the remark DeWayne had made about my sister or the fact that he was slowly killing himself. Probably both. I knew those weren't the only reasons. Someone was watching me. I felt it in my gut, and I was convinced it was Frank. Having DeWayne's .38 in my night table should have made me feel more secure, but it didn't.

DeWayne. I should probably call and arrange to drive him to his car. I climbed out of bed and moved sluggishly toward the kitchen, made coffee, then dialed his number while I waited for it to drip through. He answered on the first ring.

"How do you feel?" I asked, suspecting he was hurting this morning.

"Fine, why?"

"No headache?"

"I don't have a hangover, if that's what you mean. I seldom do."

I decided that was to his disadvantage. "I'll take you to get your car as soon as I'm dressed."

"I've already picked it up. Caught a ride with my neighbor on his way to work. Thanks anyway."

I looked at the clock. It wasn't even eight yet. "You must've gotten an early start."

"Yeah. Look, Em," he said, "I don't remember much about last night. I hope I wasn't out of line."

"Don't worry about it."

"You know how I feel about you. I thank God every day of my life that Molly has someone like you to look after her. I know I'm not a good influence on her; that's why I don't come around much. Anyway, I just wanted to say thank you and tell you I'm sorry if I said or did anything wrong last night." He paused. "I'm having a few problems with my job—nothing I can't handle. It just gets to me once in a while."

I wanted to ask him about the problems with his job, then wondered if it might just be another excuse for him to drink. Nevertheless, I was touched that he appreciated what a struggle it was raising Molly. "Thanks," I said.

"You've got the gun, right?"

"It's in my bedside table, hidden under my sweaters."

"Be careful, Em," he warned. "And call me if something comes up."

I promised I would. We talked another minute, then decided on a date for my next practice. I hung up and sipped my coffee in silence.

It was almost noon before I'd showered and dressed in jeans and sweatshirt. I put on minimal makeup, spent two minutes with a blow-dryer, then finger-combed my hair into place. I sat on the edge of my bed and stared at the .38 long and hard before tucking it into my purse. I was genuinely annoyed that I felt forced to pack a gun, especially since I hated all firearms to begin with. But what else could I do?

The fact that I'd noticed nothing out of place during the past couple of days made me wonder whether a weapon was necessary. There were even times when I wondered if I had misplaced the items myself, and I spent a lot of time digging through drawers and cabinets and checking under sofa cushions.

I also wondered if I'd just imagined someone following me that night in the school. It had seemed so real at the time, and it still gave me the heebie-jeebies to think about it. At the same time, I would have been thrilled to chalk it all up to an overactive imagination. That way I could return DeWayne's gun with a hearty "thanks but no thanks." But I was not convinced this was the case, and until I was, I couldn't let my guard down. There was more at stake than just me.

My mood had not improved by the time I left the house, and I decided it was up to me to do something about it.

Molly was not glad to see me when I arrived at the Grady house; in fact, she had planned to call and ask if she could spend another night with her friend Patty. "We have too much to do today," I told her, deliberately being vague.

She pouted through lunch at a fast food restaurant and continued to sulk in the car as I drove north through town. "Would you mind telling me where we're going?" she asked.

I shrugged. "No place special. I just thought it would be nice if we dropped by the animal shelter and had a look."

The girl's jaw dropped open. She closed her mouth. "You're going to let me have a dog?" she asked hopefully.

"I told you I'd think about it. I've come to the conclusion that you're mature enough to handle the responsibility."

"I am," she said eagerly. "I'll feed it and brush it and walk it. You won't have to do anything."

I knew this was the usual litany children fed their parents

when bargaining for a pet, but somehow I suspected Molly meant it.

Mossy Oaks Animal Shelter was a relatively new building with a smell of urine and dog doo that no amount of disinfectant could entirely cover. We chatted briefly with a female staff worker out front before making our way through a door that led to the cages.

The barking that erupted once we entered the holding area was like nothing I'd ever heard. Molly didn't seem to mind as she peered into each cage, an expectant look on her face. Dogs of all shapes and sizes beckoned with big, sad eyes and poked their noses through the openings in the cages, vying for affection. There was a female peek-a-poo nursing a litter of four curly haired puppies. Cute. I pointed them out to Molly.

"I don't want a puppy," she said. She must've noticed my surprise, and she was quick to explain. "Everybody loves puppies. They're easier to find homes for. It's the adult dogs that are hardest to place, and they have the greatest chance of being destroyed. I want a full-grown dog."

I can't be certain, but I believe this was the closest Molly had ever come to sharing her feelings, and it was indeed a proud moment for me. "It's your choice," I said, trying to suppress an urge to jump and click my heels together in delight. "Take as long as you need to decide."

We circled the cages once more.

"How am I supposed to choose?" Molly asked, having made several laps around the holding area with me on her heels. She'd studied each dog carefully and read what information existed about the animal. "I just know the one I don't pick will be put to sleep."

I touched her arm lightly. I had wanted this to be a pleasant experience for her, but I could see that was not the case. "I'm sure they hang onto the animals as long as they can," I told her. I had no idea, of course, but I didn't want Molly to shoulder the responsibility of what was in store for them.

It was easier for me to remain somewhat detached. I'd

been raised on a farm where it wasn't unusual to see my father twist a chicken's neck and send it inside for my mother to cook. When one of his hounds became so arthritic the animal couldn't stand, my father simply shot him in the head and buried him behind the barn. And I knew what happened to our hogs the minute they went to market, even those I'd made pets out of when they were babies. Some of the lessons were hard.

Twenty minutes later, Molly selected a scrawny, medium-sized dog with wiry black and gray hair, undoubtedly the homeliest creature I'd ever laid eyes on. His only redeeming features were a pair of sad, black eyes and a tail that wagged eagerly as Molly petted him.

"I'm going to name him Buster," she announced as the woman out front made arrangements for him to be neutered by a veterinarian of our choice. We also discussed shots and heartworm medication, and a special flea preventative that's often used on dogs in this part of the country because they develop an allergic dermatitis from flea bites.

"Can't we just buy him a flea collar?" I asked, my eye beginning to twitch as I tried to calculate the cost of raising the animal.

"The flea preventative is best. It doesn't kill the fleas, but it sterilizes them and prevents more from hatching."

I nodded at her dumbly while I entertained thoughts of some sort of chemical agent going down deep into the dog's fur and performing vasectomies and tubal ligations on all the fleas. As I signed the paperwork, I noticed that the dog had been there for some time, and I wondered if that had been the deciding factor for Molly. "Let's just go with the neutering, shots and heartworm medicine for now," I said. "I'll do the rest once I've talked with my lending company."

The woman didn't seem to find my remark at all humorous.

As we left the animal shelter, planning what we needed to buy before Buster came to live with us in two days, I decided that the experience had been a good one after all, even though I could probably have bought a good used car with what it was going to cost to own a pet. In my day, if you wanted a dog, you just waited until some stray wandered up. After you fed him for two or three days, he was yours forever.

It had been worth it, though, to view my niece at her most unselfish. Eight and a half months ago, she might not have been capable of caring as deeply about the plight of a few stray animals. The shell she'd climbed inside had been just that impenetrable.

It didn't take a smart person to figure out that she used the shell to protect herself from more pain, but Molly hadn't realized that as the shell prevented scary feelings from coming in, it also kept the good ones out. Although I was glad to see the shell beginning to crack, I knew Molly was going to have to make a decision. Once she decided to care again, she would have to risk a few fears and hurts.

I sensed that something wasn't right the minute Molly and I walked through the front door of the house that evening, after running numerous errands and stopping by the grocery store. It was just a feeling, but the skin at the back of my neck prickled because of it.

Shifting grocery sacks in my arms, I paused at the entrance and took in the cozy living room with its braided rugs and Shaker-style furniture and my prized collection of Andrew Wyeth prints. I glanced at Molly. "Put your sacks down and go outside," I said.

"Huh?" The girl looked at me as though I'd just rattled off something in Hebrew.

"Just do it," I told her in a tone that left no room for debate. "And if I tell you to run, I want you to run like hell next door and call the police."

Hesitating only a second, Molly set the bags on the floor with a loud thud. She stepped outside, then pressed her face against the screen door so she could see what was happening on the other side.

I could feel the adrenaline pumping through my body as

I made my way to the kitchen. The wood floor creaked despite my best efforts to move quietly. I turned on the light. The room was the same as I'd left it that morning, neat and uncluttered with the exception of my coffee cup and newspaper. I relaxed slightly. Only then did I realize I'd been holding my breath.

I checked the bedrooms next. Mine was reasonably tidy; Molly's looked as though a strong wind had come through in our absence. I imagined a couple of hoodlums going into my niece's room with the intent to rob, then backing out once they saw the mess.

I closed the door and leaned against it. Was I going to act like this every time I came home at the end of the day? Was I going to turn into a paranoid old woman who hid behind locked doors and slept with all the lights on?

I was jolted from my thoughts as Molly called out to me. "Can I come in now?" she asked.

I made my way down the hall toward the living room, feeling ridiculous for acting like such a fraidy-cat. "Yes, come on in," I told her. "Your aunt has a serious case of the jitters tonight; that's all." I passed the bathroom and, deciding to take a quick look inside, retraced my steps. I flipped the light switch and froze at the sight.

"Oh, my God."

A startled Molly came to a skidding halt at the front of the hall. "What's wrong?"

Shock and disbelief rendered me immobile for a moment. I simply stared at the sight before me: makeup and toiletries strewn across the bathroom, the shower curtain ripped to shreds with something sharp. My tampons had been torn open and pulled from their individual cardboard cylinders. Scrawled on the bathroom mirror in my own lipstick were the words YOU'RE DEAD, BITCH!

Molly joined me at the door and tried to nudge me aside so she could see. "What is it?"

I almost jumped out of my skin at the sound of her voice. I grabbed the girl's hand and made for the front door with haste. "We have to go next door and call the police. We've had an intruder."

"Why can't we call from here?" Molly asked as the screen door slammed behind us.

"He may still be in the house."

8

Chief Hix arrived ten minutes later; on his heels was the young officer he'd been playing cards with that day in his office. His badge read "Duffy." They checked the house while Molly and I waited on the front porch. When he was certain the villain wasn't lurking inside, the chief called us in.

I immediately went to the phone and called Clinton. I wanted him to see Frank's handiwork for himself. He answered on the second ring, assured me he was on his way and hung up. I found the chief standing at the bathroom door, studying the mess and holding a plastic bag with a tube of my lipstick inside.

"You say you found it this way when you returned from the grocery store?" he asked without looking up.

"Yes, not more than twenty minutes ago."

"You've been gone most of the day?"

"Since shortly before lunchtime. Molly and I went by the animal shelter, ran a few errands and bought groceries." I wasn't sure why I was going into such detail, but he seemed intensely interested in what I had to say.

"Anybody else got a key to your house?" Hix asked.

"My parents. And Molly, of course. I have new dead bolts on the doors. They're supposed to be the best." He took a moment to inspect both the front and back doors, then checked to see that all my windows were locked.

Officer Duffy came in through the front door with a

flashlight. It had started getting dark earlier these days. "I checked all the windows from the outside," he said. "No sign of forcible entry. The lady next door didn't see anything."

Hix seemed to ponder it, then glanced at me. "You got any fresh coffee for a tired old man?" he asked. When I told him I would be glad to make some, he looked at Duffy. "I'd like to talk to Miss Wilkop alone. You wait out front. Watch TV with the girl or something."

He shook his head the minute the young man disappeared. "These young kids they send me . . . you'd think after months of training they'd know somethin'. He's so wet behind the ears, I could plant a turnip patch."

I smiled sympathetically, but I suspected he enjoyed having someone like Duffy to jump at his beck and call. Besides, the old chief looked lonely. I could see it in his eyes.

He took a small notebook and pencil from his shirt pocket. "Now then," he said, pausing to lick the tip of his pencil. "You got any idea who mighta done this?"

"I've already made my suspicions crystal clear, Chief," I said.

"And I plan to check it out, but I want to cover all my bases, so to speak." He started doodling on the pad. "Tell me about Molly's friends."

"What do you want to know?"

"Who's she hanging around these days?"

I shrugged. "She spends a lot of time with Patty Grady."

"Any boyfriends?"

I thought of Henry Dean, then decided that as weird as he was, he wasn't capable of getting past my dead bolts. "Molly's too young for that," I said after a moment.

He closed his notebook. "Okay, I'll do some checking. In the meantime, I'd like to hang onto this tube of lipstick. See if we can get prints."

I heard the sound of a car out front, and a few seconds later someone tapped lightly on the kitchen door. I saw Clinton through the small panes of glass and let him in.

"You okay?" he asked, squeezing my hand briefly.

I nodded and introduced Clinton to Chief Hix. "We've met," Hix said, standing up to shake his hand anyway. "We see each other in court now and then. What's your interest in this?" Hix asked. "I thought you gave up law enforcement."

I looked at Clinton. "You used to be a cop?"

"A detective."

"One of Chicago's finest," Hix replied in such a way that I couldn't tell if he was showing approval or being sarcastic.

"I'm here because Miss Wilkop called me," Clinton said. "She believes Frank Gillespie is somehow responsible for the break-ins. As his parole officer, I feel I should check out her suspicions."

"You're free to have a look-see," Hix replied with a shrug.

We sipped our coffee in silence while Clinton took a look at the bathroom. He was frowning when he returned. "Some mess, huh?" he said, looking at me. "I'll help you clean it up, if you like."

"I can do it," I replied, feeling a blush creep up my neck as I thought of my tampons scattered on the floor for all the world to see.

"Have you talked to the neighbors?" Clinton asked Hix, taking a chair at the table and turning down my offer of coffee.

"Zilch. Most of these people are retired and spend their days in front of the talk shows. You could probably hold a Macy's parade down this street and they wouldn't know it."

It irritated me that Chief Hix felt as he did about my neighbors. After all, he was no spring chicken himself. "I have very nice neighbors, Chief," I replied coolly.

He winked as though he found humor in the fact that he'd riled me. He pulled a cigar from his pocket, unwrapped it and stuck it in the corner of his mouth.

Finally, he looked at Clinton. "This don't look like the

crime scene of a violent offender like Frank Gillespie," he said. "I'm willing to bet my last box of El Productos that some kid did this."

He glanced at me. "I reckon you heard old Henry Dean from down the road just got kicked out of that expensive military school in Charleston. You know, the one that was supposed to straighten him out? You ask me, his parents woulda put that twenty grand to better use if they'd flushed it down the toilet. This sort of thing is right down Henry's alley. Wouldn't surprise me if he was one of those Satanists you see on TV."

If I'd been upset before, it was nothing compared to how I felt knowing that Molly had befriended the boy. "Henry Dean?" I asked meekly. "A Satanist?"

"He was caught spray-painting a pentagram in the boys' bathroom at school last year. If that ain't Satanism, I don't know what is. I'm sure you've heard of him. He's Marge and Benny Dean's kid."

My mouth had gone dry. "He's in some of Molly's classes, I believe."

"Well, make sure she stays clear of the fellow. He's nothing but trouble." Hix stood and pushed his chair under the table. "Matter of fact, I might just take a run over there and see how Henry spent the afternoon. In the meantime, I'll make sure the area is patrolled on a regular basis."

He started for the door, only to run into Molly on her way into the kitchen. She looked very serious for a thirteen-year-old, and I wondered if she'd overheard our conversation. "Did you find out who broke into our house?" she asked him.

He smiled. "Still working on it, as a matter of fact. You got any clues?"

The girl shook her head. Still, I could see she looked troubled.

"I'm sure we'll find the person responsible 'fore long." He glanced at me. "I'll give you a call if something turns up."

I showed Hix and his sidekick out and returned to the

kitchen, where I found Clinton helping himself to a cup of coffee. "Where's Molly?" I asked.

He looked up. "I think she went to her room."

"I'd better check on her. Make yourself at home; I'll be right back."

I hurried down the hall and knocked on my niece's door. I heard her mumble something, so I opened it and saw her sitting on the edge of the bed, staring pensively at the posters on the wall before her. I closed the door and sat down beside her. "You okay?"

"He thinks Henry did it, doesn't he?" she asked.

So she *had* listened to part of our conversation. "He's not the only suspect."

"People always blame Henry for everything that goes wrong. Just because he made a few mistakes in the past." She looked at me. "He's trying to change. Why do you think he asked me to help him with his homework? He doesn't want to get sent away again."

"That's just the way people are," I said. "They often judge others by the way they dress. I guess I'm guilty of the same thing at times."

"Does this mean you want me to stop hanging around him?"

Frankly, I had no idea how to answer that question. Molly had only just recently started opening up to me. I was afraid I would lose her trust if I suddenly began choosing her friends. I would simply have to show her the same trust she'd shown me.

"I'm proud of you for trying to help Henry," I said after a moment. It was true. I couldn't help but wonder if maybe it would help her as well, take her mind off her own problems. That didn't mean I was totally confident with their relationship, but I had to believe in her.

She smiled. "That sounds like something you'd say."

"It does?"

"I know you tried to help Lurlene, but she didn't want it. And I know you would never have reported her to DSS if you hadn't been afraid for me."

"How do you know about that?" I asked, surprised.

"I heard the two of you arguing when you thought I was asleep. Later, after the funeral, I heard Grandma crying in her bedroom about the fact that suicide is an unforgivable sin. I heard her tell Grandpa that Lurlene was in Hell."

I felt my heart break. I wanted to reach out to her, but I was afraid she would withdraw. It had already cost her to admit what she had.

"Grandma sometimes gets carried away with her beliefs," I said. "I like to think your mother has found peace after all the trouble she knew here on earth." I could feel a lump growing in my throat as I thought of my dead sister.

Molly was quiet for a time; then, once again, her green eyes sought mine. "Bobby Furman says DSS pays you money for letting me stay here. He lives in a foster home and says they get big bucks for having him there." She met my gaze, and her eyes pleaded with me to say it wasn't true.

"Which explains why we live like royalty," I said. I sniffed. The child had no idea how I struggled at times to support the two of us. "DSS hasn't paid me one dime," I told her. "I took you in because I love you and because I hoped to give you a better life."

She seemed to ponder it. "So how long am I supposed to stay?"

"How long do you want to stay?" I held my breath.

She shrugged. "I don't know. I'll have to think about it."

Oh, but she was a cautious one. She'd rather die than confess she needed me and wanted to make her home here. Nevertheless, I felt we'd made progress. "Take your time," I said. "I'm not going anywhere."

I found Clinton still sitting at the table where I'd left him. He'd finished his coffee. "Everything okay?"

I nodded and took the chair opposite him. "I just wanted to make sure she wasn't scared."

"Are *you* scared?"

"At first I was. Now I feel numb." I raised my eyes to

his. "I guess you heard Frank was approved by the school board to go into our schools and tell kids what prison life was like."

"Maybe he can help somebody, Emily. If he prevents just one youngster from turning into a hood, it'll all be worth it."

"Yes, well, you know where I stand on the subject of Frank Gillespie, so we might as well drop it."

"Look, I could stay here tonight if you're uneasy. Sleep on the sofa, if you like."

I saw that he was sincere in his offer. "I doubt we'll have any more trouble tonight. Chief Hix promised to keep a patrolman nearby, so I feel safer knowing that."

He stood. "You know where to reach me if you need me." I nodded tiredly, not even bothering to walk him to the door. "By the way," he said. "I have every intention of questioning Frank Gillespie."

Which is all I wanted to hear at the moment. "Thank you."

"Don't forget to lock up."

I nodded. Like he needed to remind me.

9

Molly and I joined my parents for church the following morning and listened to a sermon on how we should count our blessings no matter how small they were. Hope Baptist was a sprawling, white frame structure with a simple wooden steeple. The concrete and brick verandah along the front didn't especially blend in with the basic architecture but was necessary for the handshaking and backslapping that went on after the service.

The church had been added on to over the years to accommodate a growing membership; we now boasted a small kitchen and dining area and several new Sunday school rooms. The building was surrounded by Japanese boxwood hedges, and the grounds were shaded by live oak, sycamore and pine. A massive fir, at least forty feet tall, stood at the front of the property. We decorated it each Christmas with the help of the local fire department.

It seemed like yesterday that Lurlene and I had sat under those same trees in our Sunday best, eating fried chicken at the annual picnic and trying not to make a mess of our clothes. I remember the women's eyes darting toward the parking lot where the men smoked and took sips from a bottle and the good Reverend Parmalee pretended not to notice. I can still recall my mother fussing at Lurlene for not keeping her legs together.

"My stars and garters!" my mother had exclaimed. "You want everybody here to see what color drawers you got on?'' Lurlene had closed her legs, but it wasn't long before my mother had to remind her all over again. I wondered now if God had been trying to send us a sign of things to come.

About halfway through the sermon, the topic turned to money. The congregation wasn't doing their part, wasn't pulling their weight as far as Reverend Haskin was concerned, and the church desperately needed a new furnace. He advised everyone to pray on the subject, then dig deep into their pockets when the collection plate was passed around.

Nobody much cared for Reverend Haskin; they still referred to him as ''that new preacher from Greenville,'' even though he'd been at Hope Baptist eight years. I sometimes felt he expected too much from his simple parishioners. I knew it cost money to operate a church, and I knew we needed that furnace before cold weather set in, but I suspected most folks in the community gave all they could. Nevertheless, I put in twice as much as I usually did when the plate came around.

With the service over, Molly and I joined the congregation on the front lawn and visited. My friend Lilly, who'd attended Hope Baptist all her life, waddled up to me, her six-year-old twin girls on either side. Lilly's hair, more red than blond, was cut in a pixie, much like her daughters' hair. The girls had inherited their mother's freckles and turned-up nose. I smiled, patted Lilly's protruding belly and wondered how the poor woman managed to get around these days.

Lilly had pulled me through the bad times following Lurlene's funeral; without her, I don't know how I would have made it. It seemed, at the time, that I had to be strong for so many people: my parents, DeWayne, Molly. I wasn't able to grieve for my own loss until weeks afterward.

''How're you feeling?'' I asked, recalling how uncomfortable she'd been on Friday.

''Like I swallowed a cement truck, only worse.''

I laughed as her husband, Stoney, joined us and slung

an arm around his wife's shoulders. He was an average-looking guy of medium height, with brown hair. Nothing to write home over, but Lilly adored him, and he was just as crazy about her. His real name was Walter; his parents had nicknamed him "Stoney" because he was conceived on their honeymoon at Stone Mountain, Georgia. I'd heard them tell the story many times.

"How can anything feel worse than swallowing a cement truck?" I asked, nodding a hello to the man beside her. Stoney owned the hardware store in town, and his conversations were limited to wrenches, plumbing fixtures and toggle bolts. Molly and I'd had dinner at their house only a month ago, and he'd spent much of the evening comparing wire screen to fiberglass until Lilly had cried, "Enough already!"

"Cement trucks don't kick you out of bed in the middle of the night," Lilly replied. She sighed a sound of pure misery. "So, did I miss anything at the faculty meeting Friday?"

I had thought a couple of times of calling her with the news, but Molly had been on the phone each time. As I gave her the details of the meeting, which included the speech Frank Gillespie had given, I watched her eyes grow big and round. "So Frank is our official crime expert, and his daddy will be building a youth center in his name."

"No shit!" Lilly slapped her hand over her mouth the minute she said it, then glanced around quickly to make sure no one had heard.

"In return, we're supposed to forgive and forget all the terrible things he did in his youth." I knew I would never forget what Frank had done to poor Daryl. But, close as I was to Lilly, I'd never shared my experience with her.

"I heard ol' Frank's got religion," Stoney said. "Heard he got up and confessed his sins right in front of everybody at Grace Church of Christ. They say his mother speaks in tongues," he went on in a whisper. "I'd like to see that."

"Not me," Lilly replied, giving a shudder.

I laughed at the two of them. They may have grown up,

but they were still as crazy as they'd been in high school. I remembered all those double dates we'd shared. I was seventeen before I was allowed to get into a car with a man, and then only if there was another couple present, preferably including Lilly Ross, whose reputation was as unblemished as a new rose.

My parents would have died had they known that Lilly and Stoney had been *doing it* since eleventh grade, and that my dates and I spent much of our time trying to make ourselves scarce while my friend and her steady got laid in the backseat of Stoney's old Ford.

"So, did you tell your doctor about your backache?" I asked Lilly. I had been trying to convince her to stop teaching weeks ago, but she claimed the time would pass quicker if she worked.

"He told me I still have another two weeks to go," she said, giving another sigh. "I'm ready for it to be over. The nursery is prepared, I've put away all my baby-shower gifts and the house is clean. It's time."

I squeezed her hand. "It'll be here before you know it. You won't forget to call me?"

"Stoney has the list of people to call in his wallet." She leaned close. "It's right next to the condom I'm forcing him to carry from now on. No more babies for us."

It struck me as odd that most of my friends had finished with their families, while I hadn't even begun. By now, I was getting used to being the only single female at church and family gatherings. Nevertheless, that didn't make it any easier when one of my aunts would blurt out something like, "Why ain't you married yet?" They'd look me up and down as though they half expected to find something terribly wrong with me, some grossly deformed body part that kept men at bay. I'd always tell them I was waiting for just the right man, but I suspected they'd begun to think I was a lesbian.

The twins had become restless. "Why don't you drop by the house after you've had dinner with your folks," Lilly suggested. "We never get a chance to talk anymore."

That much was true. "Maybe I will," I told her. "But only if Stoney promises to make you take a nap in the meantime." She looked tired.

"Don't worry," he said. "I'm putting her to bed as soon as we get home."

I promised to call later, then joined my parents, who were already at their car. Molly and I followed them the short distance home, passing corn and soybean fields that had been harvested that summer and sat waiting for the process to begin all over again. Here and there were farmhouses and double-wide mobile homes, as well as a few run-down shacks where aged and rusted cars had found their final resting places on cinder blocks.

We pulled into the gravel drive that ran alongside the house I'd grown up in and entered through the back door. A pale blue kitchen greeted us. It was hospital-clean and looked like something out of a Donna Reed show with its frilly white curtains, rag rugs and the framed counted cross-stitch that adorned the walls. The wood floor shone like a new appliance and smelled of Murphy's Oil Soap. Molly, more hungry than timid at the moment, peeked into the oven where a fat, stuffed hen was baking on a timer.

My mother chuckled. "It won't be long, honey," she told her granddaughter. "Here, why don't we slice up some cheese," she suggested, reaching into the refrigerator. "Oh, and I bought a box of those crackers you like so well."

I knew which crackers my mother spoke of. They were of gourmet quality and cost more than most retirees should spend on crackers. For Molly, though, they were only too happy to buy them. When I teased my mother about spoiling the girl, she simply shrugged and reminded me that, after all, Molly was her only grandchild. Why *shouldn't* she spoil her?

Lucky for me, I no longer let remarks like that put me on a guilt trip.

As usual, my mother's cooking was superb. Dinner consisted of the stuffed hen, squash casserole, green beans and potatoes, stewed tomatoes and my mother's own mouthwatering biscuits. Molly ate twice as much as anyone else. Afterward, she dove into the pecan pie with a gusto that was almost embarrassing. I promised myself I'd start cooking more and spending less time at fast-food restaurants.

My mother had just poured coffee when we heard a vehicle pull up outside. We went on talking and sipping our coffee at the table, knowing whoever it was would ring the doorbell eventually. It wasn't unusual to receive visitors on Sunday, since that's the only day most folks had off; but people often waited until early evening, after the supper dishes were done and it was time to relax on the front porch.

Suddenly, we heard the sound of a lawn mower. Frowning, all four of us got up from our seats and made our way to the window. A man dressed in jeans, T-shirt and baseball cap guided a riding mower across the backyard, taking great care not to hit my mother's azalea bushes. He looked familiar, but from a distance I couldn't place him.

"Who the Sam Hill is *that*?" my father asked.

"You mean you don't know?" my mother replied.

"I've never seen him before in my life."

I looked from one parent to the other. "Did either of you hire someone to cut the grass?" They hesitated, looking as baffled as my second graders did when I asked if anyone needed to go to the bathroom after lunch. Not a hard question: You either did or you didn't.

Finally, my father shook his head. "I don't know nothing about it."

"Then I'd better get out there and stop him," I said, pushing the back door open. They started to follow. "Better let me take care of this," I said. I don't know why I felt so strongly about handling the situation myself, except that I feared someone was trying to take advantage of a couple of elderly people. The man could be a con artist, showing up uninvited to do a job and then charging a great deal of money afterward. It seemed I'd heard about something along those lines on *Prime Time* or *20/20*.

I marched out to the backyard so stiffly one would have

sworn I had too much starch in my petticoat. I called out. With the man's back to me and the loud roar of the mower, it took a minute for him to hear me. When he finally did look my way, I almost tripped on my own two feet. Frank Gillespie nodded, reached for the switch on the riding mower and cut the motor.

"Hi, Emily," he said, as though it were an everyday occurrence for him to be mowing my parents' grass.

I stared back at him for a long moment. My legs felt weak; the meal I'd just eaten began to churn in my stomach. I refused to let him see that I was afraid. "Frank, what in blazes are you doing here?" I demanded, sounding much braver than I felt.

He looked startled by my reaction. "Just helping out," he said. "I joined this group at church. We try to assist the seniors any way we can. I drove by the other day and noticed how high the grass was, so I—"

"Did my father *ask* you to cut his grass?" I said sharply.

"No, I just thought—"

He looked so innocent, so caring about his fellow man, but I knew better. I had seen what he was capable of. He might fool everybody else by saying he was a changed man, but he didn't fool me for an instant.

"I'd appreciate it if you'd just leave," I said, forcing into my voice a calmness I didn't feel. "I'll cut the grass myself, if I have to." I realized I was shaking, realized I suddenly had to pee.

Frank stood. He was tall. I remembered how he'd towered over Daryl's body that night. "What's wrong with you, Emily?" He stepped closer, holding his hands out, palms up, an act of surrender. I had seen those same hands beat a man's brains out. He would have gladly killed me, too, that night, had I not escaped.

"I would think you'd welcome my help, what with your having to work full time and raise Lurlene's kid to boot. Your folks are getting too old to take care of themselves." He paused. "Don't you worry about them living way out here? Why, if something happened to them, it might be days before anyone found out.''

I was suddenly sick to my stomach. "Is that a threat, Frank?'' I asked.

He looked surprised and a bit startled. "Why would I threaten *you*, of all people?''

Was he playing games with me? He looked so bewildered that for a minute I thought he was sincere. Then I remembered the show he'd put on for the school. "I'm quite capable of taking care of my parents, Frank," I said at last. "I don't want to see you around here anymore." I thought of threatening him with the police but I didn't, afraid I might push him over the edge. I suspected he was very near that point as it was.

His eyes bored into me, hollow and glassy. They reminded me of the time I'd come upon a dead dog in the road and had pulled my car to the side to move him. The animal had been stiff, his eyes fixed forever in that empty expression.

"Okay, Emily, I'll leave," he said.

I walked away, heard the mower's engine and glanced around to make sure Frank wasn't aiming it in my direction. The old Frank would have just mowed me down right there in my parents' backyard. Oddly enough, it gave little solace that he drove the mower to his pickup truck and guided it up a metal ramp instead. I knew what to expect from the old Frank; the new Frank scared the hell out of me.

"What's going on?" my father asked, once I joined them inside the house.

"That was Frank Gillespie," I told them. "He claims he's doing volunteer work for his church. He's crazy; I don't want him here. If you see him on your property again, I want you to call the police.''

My mother nodded dutifully, but the look on my father's face told me he wasn't ready to take orders from me. I reached for my purse and found Clinton's business card. I was annoyed to see that my hands were trembling.

"Why don't y'all want that man cutting your grass?''

Molly asked, having come into the room when she sensed a problem.

"He's dangerous, hon," my father said. "Just got out of prison for robbing and almost killing a man." He glared at me. "Next time, you don't order me to stay in the house like I'm a child. I'm perfectly capable of handling a man like that."

"I'm sorry, Daddy. I was scared at the time." I went to the phone and dialed Clinton's number. It rang several times. I was just about to hang up when he answered.

"It's me, Clinton. Emily Wilkop." I told him about Frank's visit.

"Did he threaten you in any way?" he asked.

"Hard to say," I replied, remembering the comment he'd made about my parents being all alone and something happening to them. I didn't want to repeat it with Molly standing there, so I remained quiet.

"Is someone listening?" he asked, as though sensing the reason I wasn't talking.

"Yes."

"Okay, look, I'll drive over to Frank's and find out what's on his mind. You going to be home later tonight?"

"As far as I know."

"I'll either call or drop by."

I hung up and faced my family. I could see the questions in their eyes. "That was Frank's parole officer. He'll take care of it."

My father hitched up his britches. His feathers were still ruffled. "If that hoodlum comes back on this property, I'll pull out my twenty-two."

I realized I had probably embarrassed him by asking him to stay in the house, but I felt that this whole thing was between Frank and me. I did not want innocent people involved. "He's not worth the powder it would take, Daddy," I said. "Just call the police."

I helped my mother clean up the dinner dishes. From the living room came the sounds of Molly questioning my father about Frank, and I hoped he was being careful with his answers. Molly's nightmares, a regular occurrence after Lurlene's death, were less frequent now. I wanted to keep it that way.

"I'm so glad you decided to get a dog," my mother said as she rinsed a glass and set it on a towel to drain. I was in the process of scrubbing the stove where gravy had slopped over the skillet and crusted the burner and drip pan. My mother was a wonderful cook, but the kitchen resembled a disaster area afterward. It took a good half hour to restore order.

"Let's sit in the backyard for a while," she said, once we'd finished cleaning. She reached for two sweaters that hung on a rack beside the door. "Might want to bring these in case we get too cool."

The sun was still high in the sky, but the air was pleasantly nippy as we left the back steps and started for the swing my father had built shortly after his retirement from the Highway Department. My mother had planted mock orange on either side; in June, the white flowers gave off a scent that was similar to the smell of orange blossoms. I noticed the sheets and towels on the clothesline and offered to take them down for her.

"Oh, no, not now," she said, taking a seat in the swing. "I forgot to bring them in yesterday. Now it'll have to wait till tomorrow."

"You'll have to wash them again."

"Can't be helped. It's the Sabbath."

I sat down beside her. "I don't believe you," I told her. "Do you think the Lord is going to send you to Hell for bringing in your laundry on Sunday?" I shook my head. "Don't you know He has enough on His mind, what with drug lords and child molesters and serial killers running loose?"

My mother looked at me as though I'd lost my mind. She folded her arms over her breasts, pursed her lips and sniffed. "Let's not argue, Emily. You know how I feel."

"But you and I just cleaned the kitchen."

"That's different. We *have* to eat, and if we don't clean

up, it'll bring roaches. Remember, cleanliness is next to godliness. We don't *have* to bring in the clothes. Besides, it's just my linens, and I don't need them right now anyway.'' Another brief sniff. ''This has taught me a good lesson; next time I won't forget to bring in the clothes when I'm supposed to.''

I stared back at her, and it was impossible to believe I had once nestled within her womb. At times I felt we were from different planets. I still remembered the time she'd caught me ironing a school dress on Sunday night. You'd have thought I'd committed some incestuous act the way she'd carried on about how the Devil was going to iron my eyes out once I reached Hell. Her lecture hadn't stopped me from ironing my clothes on the Sabbath, but I'd learned to be more careful about getting caught.

My mind suddenly switched directions. If Frank Gillespie was as religious as everybody believed he was, why had he been out cutting grass on the Lord's day? It was something to think about.

''Your cousin Twyla is getting married,'' my mother said, interrupting my thoughts and letting me know that the subject of the wash was officially closed. ''She and her fiancé went down to Busbee's Jewelers just last week to choose their rings.''

I suspected my mother had been waiting all afternoon to shower me with this news. ''That's nice,'' I said. ''How many is that for her? Three? Four?'' I hated the part of me that can be petty at times such as these. I liked Twyla, and I didn't care if she married a gazillion times, but each time she found a new husband, she put *me* on the spot.

My mother looked indignant at my remark. ''What's *that* supposed to mean?''

''Just that I think Twyla ought not to rush into marriage every time she meets a man.'' Petty, petty, petty, I thought.

''I'm sure she's thinking of the children. They need a father.''

I didn't reply. I wasn't crazy about the previous husbands Twyla had selected, but that was her business, not mine.

Maybe this marriage would fare better than the others. "I'm very happy for her," I said after a minute. My mother shot me a sideways glance, perhaps to see if I was sincere. "Why don't we go in together on a wedding gift?"

"I know she could use a new mixer. But I'm going to wait until the last minute to buy it. Girls are so fickle these days. She might change her mind; then my sister would have to live through the humiliation of returning all those gifts." She sighed heavily, wearily.

I held my breath, knowing what was to come.

"Like what *I* went through."

I waited.

"With you."

10

It was coming up to four o'clock when I pulled up in front of the Dunseath house, a cute Victorian that Lilly and Stoney had spent an inordinate amount of time and money fixing up over the years. Stoney had complained when his wife had insisted they paint the outside a pale pink, but the look was both charming and cozy. As I parked, Molly complained bitterly that she wanted to go home.

"We won't stay long," I promised. "I just want to visit Lilly for a few minutes."

"What am I supposed to do in the meantime? Sit in the car?"

I was really getting annoyed with my niece. She'd spent the last hour at my folks talking on the phone with Patty Grady, ignoring my father's invitation to play cards. It amazed me, knowing her constant mood swings, that she had a friend to call in the first place. "You're certainly welcome to sit in the car," I said. "But if you come inside, I'll expect you to be polite."

Stoney met us at the front door. "Mama's had her nap, so she's in a pretty good mood. For a change," he added.

I smiled. "You're a good husband, Stoney. Lilly better be nice to you, or I'm taking you home with me." I pinched his cheek as I passed him. Truth of the matter was, I couldn't imagine myself married to a man who often quoted nail sizes and prices in his sleep. Lilly claimed she sometimes had to move to the spare bedroom once he got started.

I found my friend in the den, sitting in a comfortable-looking recliner with her legs up and a pillow at her back. "Don't expect me to get up," she muttered.

"Hmmm." I regarded her. "Stoney said you were in a good mood. Was he mistaken?"

"Lilly, could I use your phone?" Molly blurted.

The woman smiled. "Sure, honey. Use the one in my bedroom. Close the door so you'll have privacy."

Molly hurried away, a relieved look on her face. I took a seat on the sofa and hadn't even had a chance to make myself comfortable when Stoney carried in two iced teas. "My, but you've trained him well," I told my friend. He grinned and offered me a glass. "Thanks, Stoney."

"I'm going to take the girls for a walk," he told Lilly, then glanced at me. "I won't go far. If she blows, just holler."

I gave a snort. "If she goes into labor, I'm outta here."

Lilly took a sip of her tea, set her glass down with a thunk and sighed. "I hate myself. I'm bigger than a damn football field."

I set my own glass down and gazed back at her. I knew I should say something, *anything* to comfort her, but I didn't have a clue what it was. I'd never been pregnant, and after seeing how miserable my friend was during the past few weeks, I wasn't sure I ever *wanted* to be. The only way I could relate to what she was going through was to remind myself how yucky I felt right before my period. "I guess you're feeling a little bloated, huh?" I said, giving her my most sympathetic look.

She looked at me. Actually, she glared. "Bloated?" she replied in a tone that suggested I'd just asked the all-time stupid question. Suddenly, she looked like she might cry. "I can't even wear normal shoes anymore," she said, pointing to the house slippers I'd seen her in at church. "I feel like a big ol' sea cow, for heaven's sake! It wouldn't surprise me if Stoney packed his bags and left me."

"Stoney wouldn't leave you. The man is still smitten after ten years of marriage."

She looked unsure. "You think so?"

"I know so. And you know something else? I've heard husbands think their wives are prettier when they're pregnant."

She looked skeptical. "All I've done the last couple of days is cry. I'm always tired, and my feet hurt. I just wish I could lie down and have Stoney give me a foot rub like he used to when I was pregnant before. But he's got his hands full with the girls and trying to keep the house straight and help with the cooking."

"Is there something I can do while I'm here?" I asked. "Put clothes in the washer? Fold laundry?" I noticed that the offer didn't shock her as much as it had my mother.

She shook her head. "Stoney did it while I was napping, can you believe it?" She sighed. "I have no right to complain. The man has been an absolute jewel. Even the girls have been a big help, running after what I need so I don't have to get up. I'm just bitchy today." She chuckled. "I'll bet you wish you hadn't stopped by."

"Don't worry about it. You've certainly seen me at my worst." I remembered how hard it had been for me to get started in the morning after my sister's death, the days I hadn't wanted to get out of bed or face a new day. Once I'd seen to the details of my sister's burial and there was nothing left to do, I just wanted to be alone—close the drapes, pull the covers over my head, that sort of thing. Molly had made it easy for me because she was wrapped up in her own misery.

"You're not just hurting yourself, you know," Lilly had said when she found me sleeping at two o'clock one afternoon. I couldn't seem to find the energy to do the things that needed to be done. The house hadn't been cleaned since I'd gotten *the* call, and the only edible food in my pantry had been vanilla wafers, peanut butter and instant oatmeal.

"There's a little girl in the next room who needs you very much," Lilly had insisted at the time. "You're all she has. Now, get out of this damn bed and *do* something with yourself.''

I'd gotten through the next two or three weeks by focusing on my niece. If it hadn't been for Molly's needing me so much, I'm not sure how I would have pulled through.

Now Lilly held her hand out. ''Help me up,'' she said, interrupting my sad memories. ''I want to show you the nursery, since it's finished.''

I pulled her from the chair and followed her into the room where the newest member of the Dunseath family would sleep once he or she arrived. Although I'd had a peek in the early stages, I had not seen it since Lilly had put the finishing touches on it. The dominant colors were mint green and pale yellow. It was purposefully neutral; Lilly's doctor knew the sex of the baby, but both parents had insisted on waiting until the delivery to find out.

Once I'd viewed every single outfit in the dresser—including the matching booties, most of which were also yellow and mint—I led Lilly back to her chair and insisted that she sit.

''I don't think I'm going to be able to work anymore until after the baby comes,'' she said. ''I thought I'd call the school tomorrow. Stoney says if I don't, he will.'' She closed her eyes, and when she didn't open them right away, I was afraid she'd dozed off.

I was still sitting there wondering what to do when Stoney opened the front door and ushered the twins, Beth and Maryjane, inside. He saw the uncertain look on my face. ''What's wrong?''

''She's tired,'' I said. ''I think what she needs right now is a little TLC.'' I saw Stoney's eyes soften as he looked at his wife.

He knelt beside her, and the look on his face was so tender it almost took my breath away. It was hard to imagine that he spent his days selling barbed wire and fence posts. ''You okay, hon?'' he asked gently.

Lilly's eyes fluttered open. She looked embarrassed. ''I

----

must've drifted off." She glanced at me. "Some hostess, huh?"

I swallowed. Now I knew why I'd stayed single all these years. I was waiting for a man to look at me the same way Stoney looked at Lilly. "Hey, I've got an idea," I said. "Why don't I take the girls home with me tonight? I can get them up for school in the morning, since we're all going to the same place. It'll give Lilly a break."

Stoney looked as eager as the twins. He regarded his wife. "What do you think?"

She hesitated. "I don't know, Emily. They get awfully rambunctious at times."

"I teach second grade," I reminded her.

"Are you sure you don't mind?" Lilly asked.

Stoney got up and headed for the bedrooms. "I'm going to start packing before she changes her mind." He motioned for the girls. "Beth, Maryjane, come help me."

"You're sweet," Lilly said once we were alone. "Stoney and I haven't spent an evening alone in ages."

"Well, you'd better make the most of it because there's going to be *three* little ones before long," I told her. I wondered how she did it. I had my hands full with just Molly.

Stoney reappeared a moment later, twins in tow, each carrying a small Lion King suitcase and a book bag. "Give Mommy a kiss," he told the girls and waited until they gave their mother a perfunctory peck on the cheek. He led them to the door, giving them the rundown on how they were to act at Aunt Emily's house.

"Go ahead and put them in the car," I told him, "while I wrestle the telephone from Molly's hands." I knocked on Lilly's bedroom door and peeked in. Molly, telephone in one hand, was rifling through the top drawer of my friend's nightstand. She closed it when she saw me. I stepped inside the room and closed the door behind me. "What do you think you're doing?"

"Trying to find a pencil and paper. So I can jot down a phone number."

"You have no business going through Lilly's things," I said, trying to make my voice low so my friend wouldn't hear.

"I was just looking for a message pad or something," Molly said. "Don't make a big deal out of it, okay?"

"Tell the person on the other end that you have to hang up now."

She shot me a dirty look. "My aunt says I have to go now," she blurted into the phone and slammed it down without another word.

I was determined not to lose my temper. "When you are in someone else's house, you *ask* to borrow something. You do not go through their personal belongings without permission."

She bounced off the bed. "Why are you being so paranoid?" she said. "Why do you have to make a big case over nothing?"

"Those are the rules," I said. I started for the door. "Oh, and the twins are coming home with us."

She looked about as excited at that prospect as she would about bathing in cold bacon grease. "Why?"

"Because Lilly needs a break."

"I hope you don't expect *me* to baby-sit."

"Don't be silly. I wouldn't dare think of asking you to do something nice for me or anybody else."

I offered Lilly a brief hug and assured her that everything would be fine. "I expect you to rest," I said as I headed for the door.

When I arrived at my car, Stoney had already buckled the girls into the backseat and put their belongings on the floor in front of them. "Be good," he warned them.

I motioned him over and gave him a stern look. "I expect you to give your wife a good foot rub and see that she rests." I shot him a stern look. "Don't make me come after you, Dunseath."

He grinned. "It's a done deal."

The twins chatted easily as we drove. In the front seat, Molly remained silent as a tree stump. We pulled into the driveway, and I hadn't even had time to cut the engine before she climbed out of the car and slammed the door.

"What's wrong with Molly?" Beth asked.

"Nothing really," I said. "This is just the way girls act when they're thirteen. I'll bet you guys can't wait."

"She probably misses her mommy," Maryjane replied.

"You could be right," I said, wondering how much they knew about my sister's death, at the same time knowing that Lilly would never give them the lurid details. "Why don't we try to cheer her up?" I suggested and was met with enthusiastic smiles. "We could bake cookies."

They looked at one another and nodded eagerly, and I wondered if Molly had ever been that agreeable. Perhaps at one time. Then life had dumped on her and left her withdrawn and frightened and distrustful.

Inside the house, I led the twins to the guest bedroom, a narrow room next to Molly's that held a full-sized bed, a battered dresser and a chest of drawers that looked as though it had been plucked from someone's curb on trash day. In one corner stood an old Boston rocker, the one my mother had rocked Lurlene and me to sleep in when we were babies. She'd given it to me and said she hoped I'd find use for it. I had. It was piled high with ironing.

Both girls stared at the room as if wondering what to make of it.

"I know it's not much," I said, remembering their adorable room at home with its frilly bedspreads and curtains and enough stuffed animals to fill an orphanage. "I just haven't had time to work on it." Besides, I seldom had guests, and I liked it that way, which meant I was probably lacking in the Southern hospitality department.

"This is nice," Beth said, putting her small suitcase on the bed and setting her book bag by the door. It was obvious that the girl was merely being polite. Maryjane mumbled a few pleasantries about the room as well, and I suspected Lilly would have been proud of her daughters' manners.

"What kind of cookies would you like to bake?" I

asked. The girls shrugged, and I decided they were too shy to choose. "How about Toll House, since that's the only kind I ever bake?"

They nodded. So easy, I thought.

"It's unanimous, then." I told them to wash their hands while I gathered the ingredients, hoping as I did so that I had all of what I needed. Since I didn't cook or bake on a regular basis, I kept most of my perishables frozen, which explained why my brown sugar and butter and chocolate chips were hard as a slab of concrete. But I owned a cheap, no-frills microwave, so I knew I could thaw everything in no time. I searched for walnuts. It didn't look promising. The closest thing I had to crunchy was a can of French's French Fried Real Onions.

The doorbell rang, and I wondered if it was just Henry Dean with his homework. When Molly didn't come out of her room to answer it, I hurried into the living room and opened the door. I froze at the sight of the man glaring at me through the screen.

If I'd thought Augustus Gillespie looked imposing on stage, it was nothing compared to coming face to face with him at my front door. I had to look straight up to meet his gaze. His eyes were hard as stone and glittery with anger.

"You and I need to talk," he said without preamble.

I regarded him silently. Although his hair was completely gray and his face heavily lined, he was still attractive in a rugged sort of way. His suit, an expensive charcoal-colored wool, had not come off any rack in Mossy Oaks. I'd heard his clothes were tailor-made in New York City. "What do you want?" I asked, willing myself to remain calm.

"I want to know why in the hell you insist on making my boy miserable after all he's been through."

"I wasn't aware that's what I was doing," I said coolly.

"Then how come his goddamn parole officer showed up at my front door this afternoon and ruined Sunday dinner?" He put his finger up, and it would have been right in my face had the screen door not separated us. "I know what you're doing, little lady," he said. "You're trying to turn

Mr. Ward and everybody else in this town against Frank.''

"Your son had absolutely no business at my parents' house this afternoon," I said.

"He was trying to be neighborly."

"I don't want his help. And if I see him out there again, I'll report him just like I did today."

"Oh, he ain't coming back out there," Augustus said. "I'll see to that. And you'll stop harassing him if you know what's good for you."

"Are you threatening me?"

His eyes bored right through me. He had intimidation down to an art. "Don't fuck with me, Emily Wilkop."

I slammed the door in his face and locked it, then leaned against it and listened to his retreating footsteps.

11

I waited until I heard Augustus's car pull away before I allowed myself to breathe a sigh of relief. The phone rang. I hurried into the kitchen where the twins were sitting at the table and staring at it as though wondering if they should answer. I hoped they hadn't heard Augustus. I snatched the phone up and spoke into the receiver. My voice trembled.

Clinton Ward spoke from the other end. "You okay?" he asked.

"I've never been better," I said angrily.

There was a moment of silence. "I was just calling to let you know I spoke with Frank."

"Augustus just informed me of that fact."

"He's there?"

"*Was*. I just slammed the door in his face."

"Good for you. Mind if I come over?"

"Do you have any chopped walnuts?"

"Not on me."

"Would you mind picking up a package on your way over?"

"Any particular brand?"

"Just don't buy black walnuts. They have a bitter taste."

"You got it."

By the time Clinton arrived, bearing a small brown sack containing the desperately needed walnuts, the girls and I

----

had finished making the cookies and were waiting for that last ingredient.

He refused to let me pay him for the nuts, saying he would collect his due in milk and cookies. I introduced him to the twins, who simply stared at the rough-hewn man with their mouths open.

"You look like Paul Bunyan," Maryjane said. "Do you chop down trees?"

Clinton chuckled, and it took some of the severity out of his face. "No, but if you could find me a nice money tree, I might chop it down."

Both girls giggled.

"Why don't the two of you watch TV in the living room," I suggested. "I'll call you when the cookies are ready."

"Where's Molly?" Clinton asked once we were alone.

"Sulking. It's what she does best. Help yourself to a cup of coffee."

He filled a cup, then sipped it slowly as he watched me drop teaspoonfuls of cookie batter onto a Teflon-coated baking sheet. He plucked a chocolate chip from one doughy mound, and I smacked his hand.

"So what did Augustus have to say?"

"That I was making his boy's life miserable and trying to turn his parole officer against him."

"Sounds like the version I got, except he threatened to have me fired as well. I told him not to do me any favors." He paused. "That's some house they live in. Looks like a museum."

"Yeah, they've got more money than the Kennedys. Did Frank deny that he was at my parents' place?"

"No. In fact, he had a perfectly reasonable explanation for being there."

"Spare me; I've heard it. Just because he had an explanation to be there doesn't mean he had a right. He never okayed it with my parents."

"That's true. But you'll have a heck of a time convincing Chief Hix to lock him up over it. Frank shares his father's belief that you're trying to turn me against him. Says he feels persecuted and wants a new parole officer.''

"What'd you tell him?"

"It's a small town. I'm all he's got."

"What about the other guy that works with you?"

"He handles mostly probation. I could probably pass Frank off to him, but I don't want to give Augustus the satisfaction. Anyway, the long and the short of it is, I told Frank to stay the hell away from you. *And* your family. He's not to come near your house or the school; he's not to write or call or even send smoke signals in your direction. Otherwise, I'll drag his ass to court and have his parole reversed."

"Thanks, Clinton." I felt a calm settle over me. Frank had been warned. That's all I cared about.

He watched me quietly for a moment. "Look, Emily, you've got every right to feel uneasy after what's been going on lately."

I waited. "But?"

"I just don't think Frank's your man. He spends most of his time in church these days."

He looked and sounded sad, as though he knew those weren't the words I wanted to hear. "He has a lot to repent for," I said evenly, although I was secretly annoyed that Frank had managed to convince Clinton he was innocent of any wrongdoing. I knew what the man was capable of.

"If Frank's as clean as he claims, then he has nothing to worry about," I said. "But if I catch him around here I'm going to—" I paused. What *was* I going to do, *shoot* him? Even if I had the guts to go through with it, I couldn't tell Clinton something like that. Besides, he'd probably feel it his duty to report me if he knew I was carrying a concealed weapon without a license. "I'll think of something," I said at last.

"Don't go doing something crazy, Emily. Let the police handle it."

I studied him as he sipped his coffee. He would have been handsome had he shaved off the stubby black- and grizzle-colored beard that made him look like he belonged on an FBI Most Wanted poster. The fact that his hair fell well below his collar convinced me he hadn't yet found a barber to his liking.

"Sometimes I can't help but wonder if Chief Hix is competent," I said. "He's changed since his wife died. It's like he's lost interest in everything. People are starting to doubt his abilities. I often wonder why the mayor hasn't already asked him to step down." I sighed. "Perhaps I should start a Neighborhood Watch on this street."

Clinton nodded. "Now, that's the best idea you've come up with yet. I could help."

"How?"

"I've set up a few in my day."

I paused and studied him curiously. "Why didn't you tell me you used to be a cop?"

"It never came up."

"Rough place, Chicago?" I asked.

He nodded. "Can be, at times. Especially when you've spent fifteen years in homicide."

I almost winced. "So why are you here working as a parole officer?"

"I quit the force. Difference of opinions, you might say. It was time to get out. Anyway, my supervisor knew a guy who knew a guy who got me this job."

"Do you like it?"

"It beats standing in the unemployment line." He shrugged after a moment. "It's different from what I'm used to. My father was a cop, two uncles were cops, I've got a slew of cousins on the force. It's a way of life." He paused briefly. "I'll be glad to help you with your Neighborhood Watch Program, if you like. Arrange a time and place, and I'll be there."

I was curious about why he'd quit the force after all those years, but I didn't pry. I slid the cookie sheet into the oven and pulled the other one out. The cookies were slightly brown around the edges, perfect. "Okay, just tell me what I need to do to get started."

We discussed it for a few minutes, and I was impressed at how knowledgeable he was. "I'll try to talk with my neighbors this week. I'll even arrange to hold it here so I don't put anyone to a lot of trouble. Is there a night that would be most convenient for you to speak to them?"

He shrugged. "I'm free most evenings, but I still haven't seen that new Clint Eastwood movie, so you might want to give me a day's notice." He smiled and drained his coffee. "I'm ready for that cookie now."

"Keep your pants on; they have to cool first. Is it true that police have the highest divorce rate?" I don't know why I asked.

He set his cup down and regarded me. "Yes. We also excel in alcoholism and suicide. Why do you ask? You thinking about going out with me after all?"

I couldn't help but smile. "Actually, I'm considering signing up. After teaching second grade, I figure I can handle anything." We were quiet for a moment. "It's because of all the bad things you see, isn't it? That some of you turn to alcohol or suicide."

He nodded. "Most of us become callused over a period of time. You have to. But the bad stuff still gets inside of you now and then."

"Does counseling help?"

"Sometimes. It's not always easy to get a cop to agree that he needs help. Not when he's used to having people come to him for it."

I sat down at the table and leaned close. "Okay, you've seen a lot of awful stuff out there," I said softly. "What if a child were to see something especially bad? Do you think he or she could ever fully recover?"

He met my gaze. His smile was gone, and I found myself looking into the face of a seasoned detective. Despite his swarthy appearance, he inspired confidence. I knew if I were in a jam, I'd want him on my side.

"This is about Molly, isn't it?" he asked, his voice low enough not to be overheard.

I glanced toward the door to make sure my niece wasn't

nearby. ''Her mother hanged herself nine months ago. Molly was the one who found her.''

''Jesus!'' He shook his head and wiped one hand across his face. ''Why do people insist on screwing up their kids?''

''She's in counseling, but I don't know if it's doing any good.''

''It may take time. What was her life like before her mother killed herself?''

''Not so great. Very little stability.''

''At least she has that now. Is her therapist any good?''

''Supposed to be the best.''

''Do you see progress?''

I sighed. ''It's hard to say. Our relationship flips back and forth. Sometimes she acts like she thinks I'm okay; other times she's withdrawn and I can't get anything out of her. And then she acts frightened, like she's waiting for the world to cave in on her. Her counselor recommended a group home. But I can't send her away. I'd feel like I was abandoning her. The kid has already been to hell and back. I'm no child psychologist, but I think what she needs now is a lot of love and reassurance that I'm going to stand by her no matter what.''

''She's lucky to have you.''

I felt my face grow warm under his bold appraisal. He was giving me too much credit. ''Just because I think I know what she needs doesn't mean I always go about it the right way,'' I said. I started to add something more, then heard a noise. I glanced up and found the twins standing in the doorway.

''Are the cookies ready yet?'' Beth asked.

I smiled, knowing they'd been patient as long as they could. ''They're ready,'' I said. ''Go call Molly while I put them on a plate.''

The girls hurried down the hall, yelling for Molly as loudly as they could. ''I hope I haven't made a mistake by inviting them to spend the night,'' I whispered to Clinton. ''You know, with what's been going on around here.'' I told him about Lilly. "The poor woman needed some time to herself."

"You should be okay," Clinton said. "Just make sure you keep the doors locked at all times. You've got my number; I'm less than ten minutes away."

The girls hurried into the kitchen with Molly right behind them. I loaded a plate of cookies and poured glasses of milk for everyone. I was amazed at how much the twins ate. Even Clinton seemed awed by the amount of cookies they put away.

"This is the best dinner I've ever had," Maryjane said. "No vegetables."

I offered her a blank look. "Didn't you eat anything after church today?"

"Daddy made us a peanut butter and jelly sandwich. He said it should hold us till dinner time."

I stared at the girl, mouth agape. Molly and I always ate so much at my parents' house on Sunday that we either skipped dinner completely or had a small snack if we got hungry. I'd just assumed it had been that way for the Dunseath household, then realized Lilly wouldn't be up to cooking a big spread.

"Just consider this a celebration dinner," I told the girls, "since you're staying with your Aunt Emily. But next time I'll have to prepare something a bit healthier, and you girls have to promise to eat it."

"Okay," Beth said easily.

"Oh, and don't mention this to your mother. It'll just be our secret."

I saw Clinton grin, and I shot him a dirty look. "Stay out of this."

When we had all eaten our fill of Toll House cookies, Clinton announced that it was time for him to go. I offered to walk him out. We exited the kitchen door and made our way toward the front of the house. The night was cool and star-filled. It felt good after being in the hot kitchen. "I appreciate your talking to Frank," I said once we reached his car.

''No problem. And I plan to keep my eye on him from here on out.''

I nodded. Finally, there didn't seem to be anything left to say.

He leaned against the door of his car. ''What would you say if I asked you out one night?'' he said.

I looked down at my feet. This is when I feel most uncomfortable with the opposite sex. I handle friendship well, but the minute it moves to a boy-girl thing, I get flustered and tongue-tied and say the dumbest things.

''I don't know. I haven't had much luck with men lately. I'd sort of given up on them.'' Dumb, dumb, dumb.

''You haven't gone out with *me* yet.''

''True. But don't you think it would be awkward for us? I mean, after all, your client is stalking me.'' Now I was being serious again.

''We don't have proof of that.''

''I've got all the proof I need, thank you very much.''

''Don't you think a person is capable of changing?''

''Maybe most people. But not Frank. Also, Augustus is always there to clean up after him.''

''What's Frank's mother like?''

''I don't know her personally, but I understand she's very devout in her religious beliefs. I'm sure living with Augustus would make anyone look forward to an afterlife.''

He seemed to ponder it all, then crossed his arms. ''Okay, let's get back to the part where you've given up on men,'' he said, obviously ready to change the subject. ''If that's true, then who was that guy I saw you with at Clancy's the other night?''

''You were *spying* on me?'' I asked, rather indignantly.

''No, I wasn't spying. I was pulling into the parking lot as you were pulling out. I happen to eat at Clancy's a lot.''

I felt ridiculous for being suspicious, but I had plenty of reason to be wary these days. ''The man you saw was my brother-in-law. At least he was before my sister died. He's not weathering it well.'' I paused and took in Clinton's grungy clothes. "As for you and me, I'm not sure we'd be compatible."

He seemed to get my meaning right away and grinned. "So I've let myself go just a tad. I think I'm having my midlife crisis. But I clean up well, so don't sweat it."

I wanted to ask him more about his crisis but didn't. "Okay, you talked me into it. When?"

"Friday night?"

"Only if I can get Molly to spend the night with one of her friends. I don't want to leave her here by herself."

"I'll call you."

As I watched him get into his car, I could imagine he'd used that line before with other women and hadn't called. Instinct told me he would follow through this time.

12

We picked up Buster from the vet's office the following afternoon, once school had let out. I drove while Molly tried to calm him down, but it was obvious Buster hadn't spent much time riding around in the backseat of a Toyota Celica. He paced and slobbered, then hiked his leg as though he had every intention of taking a leak right on my upholstery. Molly screamed so loud I almost ran off the road.

Once we arrived home, my niece led him through the gate in the backyard and showed him where his new sixty-five-dollar doghouse sat. Next to it were twin dog dishes containing food and water, and a massive rawhide bone.

The whole business had set me back almost two hundred dollars, but seeing the expression on Molly's face made it all worthwhile. I could only hope Molly would still be wearing that look when we were forced to eat Beenie-Weenies for a week.

I watched for several minutes as Molly tossed a ball and Buster ran for it, then, instead of bringing it back, headed in the opposite direction. He was a bit on the skinny side, but I decided we'd fatten him up in no time.

"Looks like you got your work cut out for you," I said, chuckling at her attempts to get the dog to retrieve the ball. The next time Molly threw it, Buster simply stood there as if to say he was bored with the game.

Molly stamped her feet in frustration and shoved him

hard. "Go get it, stupid!" she yelled. The dog cowered down before her as though he expected a beating.

I felt myself frown. "That's no way to train a dog, Molly," I reprimanded gently. "He doesn't know what you want."

"I shouldn't have chosen this one," she said. "I should have gotten the German shepherd. Everybody knows they're smart. That's why the police use them." She swiped her eyes angrily; I suddenly realized she was crying. "The only reason I got this ugly mutt was because he'd been there the longest, and I figured they'd kill him first. I should have let 'em have him."

I didn't know what to say. One part of me wanted to take her in my arms and offer comfort, but the animal cowering in front of her stopped me. I thought of my parakeets. Then I told myself that, since Lurlene had been known to knock Molly around at times when she was angriest, the girl probably had no idea how to discipline.

"Why is it so important for you to have him trained in one day?" I asked. "Why can't you just enjoy his company? Why don't you just play with him? Or take him for a walk."

She sighed. The tears were still streaming down her face. "He probably doesn't even know how to walk on a leash."

"I'm not going to let you keep him if you're going to mistreat him," I said.

She snapped her head up and regarded me. The look on my face must've told her I meant it. "I lost my temper with him, that's all. I'm not going to hurt him. It's just—" She paused. "I've never had a pet, and I don't know how to train one."

"Then hold off until we find a book." She nodded and walked over to the dog. He raised his head up and looked at her, the expression in his eyes unsure.

"I'm sorry, Buster," she said, sitting down on the ground next to him. He stood and licked her cheek, and his tail wagged frantically as though he'd just found his best friend. She hugged him.

I hadn't realized how tense I was until I felt my shoulder muscles relax. Still, I wouldn't let myself feel relieved until I was certain Molly would be good to the dog. I promised myself I'd be watching closely over the next few days.

I left them sitting there and went inside to start dinner, yet found myself checking on my niece every few minutes to see that everything was going okay.

When she came in, her cheeks were pink from running with the dog, her light brown hair flying every which way. "What's for dinner?" she asked.

"Spam casserole."

"Yuck."

I chuckled. "Have you already forgotten how much I spent on that dog? You'd think the animal was planning a vacation in the Far East with as many shots as he had to have."

The phone rang. "That's probably Henry," Molly said. "I can't wait for him to see Buster." She raced to her room to answer it.

I felt myself frown as I opened a can of Spam and began slicing it thinly. Henry Dean was the thorn in my side that I felt couldn't be removed without hurting Molly. Besides, since our neighborhood consisted mostly of retirees, there was nobody else close by for her to do homework with. Still, I monitored the friendship closely.

I poured oil into a skillet and let it get hot while I coated the Spam with flour. Some people don't like the stuff, but I was raised on it. I suppose that's why I buy it now and then. It reminds me of the meals I had as a child, and that reminds me of how secure life had been at one time.

That was before *that night,* before I realized how cruel people could be to one another, before I realized that my sense of security had been an illusion.

Molly and I chatted easily during dinner, and I found myself hoping our newfound camaraderie wasn't just temporary. "So what are your plans for the weekend?" I asked.

Molly shrugged. "How should I know? This is only Monday."

I hesitated with my next question. "I was just wondering if you were planning to spend the night at the Gradys' house again."

She looked at me. "It's Patty's turn to come over here. Remember how you're always saying we have to take turns in order to be fair."

I'd suggested it after Patty had spent three weekends in a row at our place. "I know. But I sort of made plans for Friday."

She leaned back in her chair. "You're going out with Clinton."

"I was thinking of it, yes." I wondered why I sounded defensive.

Molly watched me as she chewed a mouthful of Spam. "You think he likes you or something?"

"You sound surprised."

This time she shrugged. "He's just different from other men you've gone out with. He looks kinda . . . reckless. What does he do for a living?"

"He's a parole officer."

Her eyes widened. "So he works with criminals? How did you meet him?"

I looked at her. "You realize you're grilling me, don't you?"

"So I'm curious."

I took a sip of my iced tea. It was a stall tactic, of course. "The Board of Education has decided to send one of Clinton's parolees into the schools to speak on crime." Molly nodded as though it made complete sense, and I was glad I hadn't been forced to go into more detail and lie to her.

"I'll do the dishes tonight," she said, once she'd finished eating. "You can relax, take a hot bath or something."

"Thanks." I tried to make my voice sound natural, as though it was an everyday occurrence for my niece to volunteer to work. I sat at the table and watched her clear it.

"Should I feed these scraps to Buster?" she asked.

I shook my head. "Let's just keep him on dog food. We can't afford for him to become finicky on us."

She scraped the plates into the garbage. The house lacked both dishwasher and garbage disposal. "I really appreciate your letting me have him, Aunt Em," Molly said. "I've never really had anything that belonged to just me. Lurlene was allergic to animal fur, you know. At least that's what she said. But DeWayne bought her a rabbit jacket shortly after they got married, and she didn't seem to have any problem wearing it. I just think she didn't want to have to take care of a pet."

I didn't say anything, but I knew darn well Lurlene hadn't been allergic to fur. Otherwise she would never have made it growing up with cats and dogs and a slew of farm animals. I suspected that my sister hadn't wanted to complicate her life with pets because she had a habit of picking up and leaving at a moment's notice. Once again I felt sorry for Molly, who'd paid such a high price for being born to Lurlene.

I only hoped I'd heard the worst of it. I could deal with what my niece had told me thus far, the neglect and abuse my sister had doled out from time to time. But what if there was more? What if Molly was keeping secrets, the kind of secrets Cordia was most concerned with? Those were the questions that nagged the darkest corners of my mind.

"Aunt Em, are you okay?"

I blinked, suddenly realizing I'd gotten caught up in my thoughts. I smiled. "Just clearing the cobwebs," I said, remembering the old saying my mother had used when she'd been caught daydreaming.

"You're thinking about Clinton, aren't you?" she said.

We were back to that. I shook my head. "No, not really. I'm not sure Clinton and I would get on very well. Besides, I haven't had much luck with men." I winced as I said the words. Lord, they were beginning to sound like my slogan.

"Oh, guess what I heard," Molly said, changing the subject. "Marmee Fischer said she saw DeWayne's car at our old house."

I was surprised to hear it. DeWayne had sworn never to set foot in it again after Lurlene's suicide. "Was she sure it was DeWayne's car?'' I asked, knowing how the trees and shrubbery blocked the long drive.

"Said it sure looked like it to her. Maybe he's thinking of moving back. Maybe he's even thinking of getting married again.''

"Could be,'' I said, hoping DeWayne was finally coming to terms with my sister's death. Maybe now he would put the house on the market instead of letting it sit empty.

"I wish he'd come around more,'' Molly said.

I noted her wistful look. "You really care for DeWayne, don't you?''

"He was going to adopt me. I heard him talking to Lurlene about it once. Then she had to go and screw it up.'' The girl looked angry for a minute. "She was always screwing up. I still remember when DeWayne caught her with that man. He was so cool about it. He could have beat her up like I'd seen other men do, but DeWayne just packed his clothes and left.''

She turned hurtful eyes to me. "The only thing I couldn't understand is why he didn't take me with him. I mean, if he loved me as much as he said he did.''

I wanted to reach out to her, but I knew that would draw attention to her having just opened up to me and might perhaps cause her to back off. I had no way of knowing for certain, of course. I had very little background in psychology and had had absolutely no experience dealing with an emotionally troubled adolescent until my niece moved in.

"I'm sure DeWayne loves you as much today as he did before,'' I said. "It's just—'' I paused and tried to come up with the right words. "Your mother's death hit him so hard. I don't know if he'll ever get over it.''

She turned away, and I wondered if she was fighting tears. Molly had not cried when she found her mother's body, nor had she shed a tear at the funeral. Even Cordia, who'd poked and prodded during their frequent sessions, had not been able to get past that tough exterior and reach the frightened girl inside.

I felt like I was walking on eggshells at times, waiting for the moment my niece would crumble. I didn't know what to expect. If and when the walls come down, would they do so sporadically, or would they collapse in a torrent of tears and rage? I hadn't a clue. So I waited and hoped I'd be prepared.

On Friday, I dropped Molly off at the Gradys' house, returned home and got ready for my date with Clinton. Since I had no idea where we were going, I wore winter white wool slacks, a salmon-colored blouse and a dark gray blazer. With time to spare, I called Lilly, who'd seen her doctor that day and discovered she had dilated one centimeter. Although it looked promising, he warned her that the process could take time.

Clinton arrived, and I was surprised to find him cleanly shaved and wearing something other than faded jeans. I prepared us a drink, and we sat in the living room talking and snacking on cheese and crackers, killing time mostly because Clinton had been unable to get reservations at the restaurant until nine o'clock. We only have a couple of really nice restaurants in town, so there's usually a wait on weekends.

We were just about to walk out the door when the phone rang. I debated on answering it, then decided I should in case it was Molly or Lilly. Chief Hix greeted me from the other end.

"You seen Clinton Ward?" he asked. "I been calling his place for an hour."

"Hold on, Chief," I said, extending the phone to Clinton, who looked surprised to be receiving a call at my place. He answered, then listened for a minute. "Where'd it happen?" he asked. Finally, he checked his wristwatch. "Okay, we're on our way to dinner, but I can swing by if you like."

He hung up. "You mind if we make a brief detour on our way to the restaurant?"

I shrugged. "I don't mind. What's up?"

He sighed and wiped his hand down his face. "They've found a body. A woman in some trailer park who committed suicide this evening. Chief Hix asked me to take a look."

13

I was still in a daze over the suicide when Clinton helped me into his car, but I wrinkled my nose when I smelled something rotten. "What is that terrible odor?" I asked.

His look was sheepish. "Damned if I know. I took it in to have it washed and asked them to spray it with a deodorizer. It didn't start to smell bad until I was on my way to your place, so I drove with the windows open. I was hoping it had aired out by now."

I rolled my window down, deciding I'd rather be cold than enclosed with the stench. "We can take my car if you like," I told him, although I knew he'd probably be uncomfortable in such a small automobile.

He reached into his glove compartment and brought out a small metal cylinder. "That's okay. I'll just keep spraying this stuff until the smell dies down." He sprayed the car thoroughly until we were cloaked with a citrus scent. "Better?" he asked.

"Much."

The Tall Oaks Trailer Park was located on the edge of town near the now-defunct drive-in theater where, I suspected, Stoney had stolen Lilly's virginity in the backseat of his old Ford Thunderbird while I'd waited with my date on the mosquito-infested playground.

The mobile homes varied in size and general condition; you could pretty much tell who took pride in their place and who didn't by the amount of clutter on their patios and the number of junk cars in their yards. Clinton pulled up beside a trailer that fell somewhere in the middle. It was small—no more than one or two bedrooms—and was surrounded by two patrol cars, an ambulance and a Volvo station wagon that I knew belonged to the coroner.

Grim-faced neighbors in various stages of dress were clustered together beside a tall utility pole bearing a single light. Off to one side, Officer Duffy questioned an elderly woman in her bathrobe and took notes on a small spiral pad. I thought the woman looked much too frail to be outside without a coat.

Chief Hix and another officer stood on the front patio beneath a metal awning. Several lawn chairs with torn webbing sat beside a cheap plastic table bearing a dead potted plant that nobody had thought to throw out.

"Why don't you just wait in the car?" Clinton asked. "This shouldn't take long."

"Fine with me," I mumbled, having no desire to see a dead body. "Just leave the windows down." I let Clinton think I wanted to air the car out, but curiosity was my guiding force. I could hear every word being said.

Hix, in the process of talking to a group of men, glanced up the moment Clinton closed his door. "This here's the guy I was telling you about: Clinton Ward from Chicago," Hix said. "He's spent a lot of years in homicide. I thought maybe we could use a second opinion." The men nodded. One officer, who looked to be in his mid-twenties, held out his hand.

"Jim Conners," he said. "I was the responding officer on this case."

"Nice to meet you," Clinton said. They shook hands. "Whatcha got?"

"Call came in 'bout an hour ago," Conners said. "Her parents found her in the bathtub with both wrists slit. Name's Cindy Brown. Twenty-two years old, cocktail waitress at PJ's. Rough place, PJ's," he added. "I've broken up more fights than you could shake a stick at in that joint.

"Anyway, seems Cindy has quite a reputation with the

men; least that's what her neighbors said. It's not unusual for her to bring someone home with her at the end of her shift. I guess it's her way of supplementing her tips, if you get my drift."

"So she was a working girl," Clinton said.

"Right. Anyway, PJ's was having a slow night, so her boss let her leave early."

"Did anyone leave with her?"

"If he did, nobody saw him. The boss swears his girls are clean. You ask me, I think he's pimping 'em. He negotiates a price with the johns, and the players meet up in the parking lot. God knows there's enough sleaze motels in the area where they can go."

Clinton nodded. "Where are Cindy's parents now?"

"I had someone run 'em home," Hix said. "The victim has a four-year-old kid. Her parents were baby-sitting for her; that's why they came by tonight in the first place—to drop off the little girl. They were pretty upset. I figured we could question them later." He paused. "If y'all don't mind, I'd rather not go in there," Hix added. "I've known this girl since she was a baby. Her daddy's an old friend of mine."

Clinton nodded. "Is anyone with the body now?"

"The coroner and our chief pathologist."

"I assume one of them did a rectal exam?" Clinton asked.

Conners nodded. "Yeah. She'd been dead less than two hours when they checked her. I reckon it's coming up to three now."

"Okay, I'll have a look."

Clinton disappeared inside the trailer with Conners while the others remained on the patio. I settled back in the seat and waited and thought about the little girl who'd lost her mother to suicide. I thought of Molly, who'd lost her own mother that way, and I wondered what drove people to such desperate acts. I wondered how the little girl would handle it, wondered if she'd have as many problems as Molly had. I prayed that her grandparents were patient and loving.

Clinton and Conners stepped out of the trailer a few minutes later. I searched their faces for some sign of distress but found none. I didn't know about the other officer, but I suspected Clinton had seen his share of Cindys in his line of work.

"What d'you think?" Hix asked.

Clinton didn't hesitate. "I think somebody went to a great deal of trouble to make it look like a suicide. I asked Dr. Wade to bag her hands so nothing gets lost on the way to the morgue, but I don't think we're going to find skin under her fingernails."

"Tell me why you don't think her injuries were self-inflicted," Hix said, "when there are no defense wounds on her hands and fingers and little possibility of finding anything under her nails."

Clinton didn't hesitate. "Most suicides who use knives or blades leave hesitation marks—start and stop, start and stop, that sort of thing. They don't just slice themselves wide open without testing the level of pain first."

"This was a clean job, Chief," Conners added. "One deep slice per wrist—so deep, in fact, that the knife made contact with the bone."

I shuddered and wished I'd rolled up my window.

Clinton nodded. "Which leads me to think the victim was already unconscious when it happened."

The chief sniffed. "I hope that's the case," he said. "I don't care what the poor girl did for a living; I'd hate knowing she was aware of everything that was going on. What'd Dr. Wade say?"

"He agreed."

Officer Duffy joined them, looking important with his note pad. "I just talked to the lady that lives across the street, Chief," he said. "She saw a man enter the victim's trailer earlier. His name's Randy, and he lives on the other side of the trailer park."

"You got a last name?" Hix asked.

"Not yet. But she said she'd ride over with me in the squad car and point out his place."

''Good. I want him brought in. Conners, you go with Duffy in case this guy gives y'all any problems.''

The officers nodded and hurried away.

A thin, balding man with a Groucho Marx nose and eyebrows stepped out of the trailer. He looked weary. The black medical bag he held told me he was the doctor.

''We're finished here,'' he said.

''Where will she go now?'' Clinton asked.

Dr. Wade glanced at him. ''Well, the coroner and I agree it looks suspicious. It's routine to send such cases to Charleston for an autopsy.'' He lowered his voice. ''If she's as popular with the men as they say she is, I don't want to touch her anyway. She could be HIV positive.''

Something flickered across Clinton's face. I couldn't quite identify it, but I knew he wasn't entertaining friendly thoughts about the man. ''I hadn't thought of that, Doctor,'' he said smoothly. ''I suppose I was more concerned about finding her killer.''

''It's something to think about,'' the man replied, obviously unaware that he'd struck a sour chord with Clinton. He glanced around as the coroner strode down the hall in jeans and flannel shirt, carrying a battered attaché case. I recognized Earl Gibbons; he'd sung in our church choir for years.

''I'm all finished,'' he told Hix. ''You'll have my report first thing tomorrow. If it's all the same to y'all, I'd just as soon let them take her away so I can go home and climb into my nice, comfortable bed.''

Hix regarded Clinton. ''Would you mind stopping by the station?'' he asked. ''If they pick up this Randy whoever-he-is, I'd like you to have a look at him, maybe even interview him if you don't mind.''

''Can I do that?'' Clinton asked. ''I mean, legally?''

''Anything's possible. I'll have to ask you to resign your other job temporarily so I can deputize you. We have ways of getting around the rules down here.''

Clinton sighed. ''I don't know, Chief. I really have no desire to—''

"It's just for a couple of days. After that you can go back to that fancy office job of yours."

Clinton was obviously still considering it when a black, dust-coated Jeep pulled up next to his car and parked. Albert Turner from the *Mossy Oaks Gazette* climbed out, camera in one hand and Styrofoam cup in the other. He reminded me of the actor Ned Beatty: tubby and slack-jawed, with stumpy legs and a propensity to sweat. He closed his car door and started for the patio, just as the paramedics struggled to get the stretcher carrying Cindy Brown's body through the narrow doorway of the trailer. Turner paused and snapped several pictures.

"Cut that out, Turner," Hix growled. "Don't you have no respect for the dead?"

Turner looked hurt. "Course I do, Chief. But my readers have a right to know what's going on in their town. What's the deal here?"

"Woman slashed her wrists in the bathtub. End of story."

The reporter pulled out a pad. "Name?" He was poised to write.

"I'm not giving you her name till we've notified all her kin."

"You suspect foul play?"

Hix looked annoyed. "I just told you it was a gawl-derned suicide. Now, that's all I got to say."

"She on her way to the morgue?"

"We're taking her to Charleston," one of the paramedics replied over his shoulder.

"Aw, shit!" Hix grumbled. "Ain't you boys got nothin' better to do than stand here giving out free information?"

Turner grinned as he regarded the chief. "So you're sending her to Charleston, huh?" He eyed Hix as he took a sip from his cup. "You think I been selling vegetables on the side of a road all my life, Chief? I know folks don't get hauled off to Charleston unless something looks suspicious."

Clinton stepped forward. "If I might speak for the chief,

I think what he hopes to ascertain from Charleston is whether or not the victim injested drugs or alcohol before she took her life.''

The reporter studied Clinton. ''Who are you?''

''Clinton Ward. I'm assisting the chief in this investigation. I'll personally see to it that you are briefed once we have the facts.''

''Hey, I've seen you in court,'' Turner said. ''Aren't you the new parole officer?''

''He used to be,'' Hix said. ''But I'm short on manpower and need his help. Now, it's too late for you to get this into tomorrow's edition anyway, so leave me alone and let me do my work.''

''Mind if I talk to the neighbors?''

''Would it matter?'' Hix replied.

Turner shrugged and walked away.

''He probably won't get much out of the neighbors,'' Clinton said. ''They look like a mean bunch to me.''

Hix gave a snort. ''Don't bet on it. Folks'll spill their guts to get their names in the paper. Before we know it, everybody will be in a state of panic.'' He started for his patrol car. ''I'll see you at the station.''

When Clinton joined me in the car, he looked resigned. ''I'm afraid we have to make another stop,'' he said.

''I heard. Don't worry; I couldn't eat anything right now even if somebody tried to force me at gunpoint.''

He sniffed. ''Is it my imagination, or is the smell getting worse?''

''It's getting worse. I even sprayed some cologne I keep in my purse, but it didn't help.''

We drove to the police station with the windows open. Clinton parked the car near the front entrance and helped me out, then grabbed a flashlight from his glove compartment and shined it on the floors and seat. He felt under my seat. ''What the hell?'' He pulled out some kind of bundle, something wrapped in newspaper that looked soggy.

''What is it?'' I asked.

''Damned if I know.'' He set it down on the asphalt and

pulled the newspaper away, exposing a dead chicken.

"Oh, God!" I turned my head, but not before I got a good look at it. It was stiff and grotesque-looking, its feathers plucked, neck completely broken. The smell hit me like a punch in the face; it had been dead for a while. I couldn't even begin to imagine why someone had put it in Clinton's car. "You don't think the guys at the car wash put it there, do you? As some kind of practical joke?"

"If they did, I'm going to ask for my tip back. Check that trash can and see if you can find something else for me to wrap it in. This is all wet."

I did as he asked. As I was rummaging through the trash can, I couldn't help but wonder if I'd gotten more than I'd bargained for by going on a date with Clinton Ward: first a suicide/possible murder, and now a dead chicken stuffed under the car seat. I found a couple of sheets of newspaper and carried them to him.

"What are you going to do with it?" I asked, watching him wrap the bird.

"Show it to the chief and see if he can make sense of it."

We walked into the police station, where an older gentleman was acting as dispatcher. He frowned when he saw what Clinton was carrying. The chicken's legs were hanging out of the newspaper.

"You Clinton Ward?" he asked, though his gaze remained fixed on the chicken. "The chief is waiting for you in the break room. Last door on the right."

We found Hix and Conners sipping coffee in a small kitchen area, staring at a man through a glass window. Hix looked at Clinton, caught a glance at the chicken and almost spilled his coffee. "Where in tarnation did you get *that*?"

Clinton dropped it unceremoniously onto the table, and the wrapping fell away. "Someone stuffed it under the seat in my car."

"Jesus." Conners came out of his seat. "You got any enemies in this town?"

"Obviously somebody isn't too crazy about me," Clinton said.

Hix yelled for Duffy, who came running. He spied the chicken on the table and gasped. "Take that gawl-derned thing out of here," Hix ordered. "My stomach's already churning just thinking about Cindy Brown."

"Yes, Chief," Duffy said, wrapping the bird and giving a small shudder as he started for the door. He paused. "Where should I put it?"

"I don't care where you take it. Just get it out of this building." He looked at Clinton. "Who had access to your car today?"

"It was parked outside the courthouse most of the day. Unlocked," he added. "I didn't think folks around here bothered to lock their doors." He paused. "Actually, it could be a number of people. I've discovered that being a parole officer isn't the most popular job you can have."

"I'll bet Frank did it," I said, drawing looks from all three men.

"What is *she* doing here?" Hix asked Clinton.

"She's with me," he said. "We were on our way to dinner when we got sidetracked."

"That's right," I said, trying to sound flip when my insides were still jangling over what I'd seen and heard this evening. "Now that you've ruined our dinner plans, you could at least offer us a cup of coffee."

Conners nodded. "I'll get, it, Chief."

Hix grumbled under his breath as Conners got up and poured everyone a cup. I grabbed a bottle of glass cleaner from near the sink and sprayed the table, then wiped it down with paper towels. I had no desire to sip coffee at a table where a dead bird had lain only moments before.

Conners handed me a cup and the fixings to go with it. My hands were trembling so badly that I decided not to set it down until I was more composed.

"Does this mean the two of you are officially dating?" Hix asked me as we joined him at the table.

I couldn't believe he was interested in my love life at a

time like this. "This was supposed to be our first," I said. "Till you botched it up. You know how scarce men are in this town."

"You going to be okay?" Clinton asked me. "Maybe you should wait in the chief's office."

I glanced at him. I might fool the rest of them with my glib reply, but he knew my insides were a mess. "I'm okay. I'd rather wait here, if you don't mind."

Clinton turned his gaze to the window. "Is this the suspect?"

"Yeah, that's the scumbag," Conners said. "He's a bit lickered up. Maybe he'll talk."

I looked as well. The man was slouched in a hard plastic chair, his head propped on one fist, eyes closed. His hair was long, his jaw unshaven. He looked like he'd slept in his clothes. Another officer stood just inside the door guarding him.

"Name's Randy Dempsey," Hix said. "Claims he's from Galveston, Texas. We're running a criminal history on him now, should have it in a few minutes." He regarded me once more. "You're not supposed to be in here," he said. "But I'll let it slide this time since I ruined your evening. I don't have to remind you that everything you hear is confidential."

I pretended to lock my lips and throw away the key. Hix merely shook his head.

He pulled a notebook from his pocket and handed it to Clinton. "Just so nobody can come back on us, I want you to write a phony resignation so I can deputize you."

"Why don't you and Conners do the interview?" Clinton said. "I can watch and give pointers."

Hix hesitated. "Naw, I'd rather you and Conners work on him. This guy looks cagey to me."

It was the first time I'd seen the chief wear a look of uncertainty, and I suddenly felt sorry for him. Some folks— most, actually—said he should have retired long ago. They said he couldn't cut the mustard anymore; maybe he was beginning to believe it.

Clinton shrugged and scribbled a couple of lines on the notebook while Hix reached into his shirt pocket for a badge. He muttered a few lines of mumbo-jumbo, handed Clinton the badge and declared him deputized. "You need a gun?"

Clinton shook his head. "I got my own."

The dispatcher hurried in with a sheaf of papers. "Here's the history on the suspect, Chief," he said.

Hix took the readout, and Clinton leaned close so they could go through it together. Conners stood behind and read over their shoulders. Finally, Hix gave a snort. "Just what we need," he muttered. "One of *those*."

Clinton glanced up at Conners. "You got any ideas how you want to handle the interview? You're the one who collared him."

Conners grinned. "I think I'd like to see the way they do it in Chicago. I'll just follow your lead."

Clinton and Conners left. Hix regarded me. "So, are you and Clinton an item?"

I wondered why Hix was so curious about our relationship but decided that the less he knew, the better. I shook my head. "He's not my type. I probably won't even see him after tonight."

"That's too bad. I'd like to see him hang around, and you might be just the person to convince him to stay."

14

The door to the next room opened, and Clinton stepped through with Conners on his heels. They relieved the officer from his post and closed the door behind him.

"Evenin', Mr. Dempsey," Conners said, as Clinton took a seat directly across from the man and regarded him silently. "You need anything? A cup of coffee? Soft drink? An aspirin?"

Dempsey glanced at Conners. His shoulders seemed to relax a bit. "I'm fine."

"Mind if I call you Randy?" Clinton asked, his expression unreadable.

A shrug. "Yeah, okay."

Clinton glanced at the papers in his hand. "I assume you've been advised of your rights?"

"Yeah."

"And you waived your right to a lawyer?"

"I'm innocent. I don't need no lawyer."

I noticed the satisfied glint in Clinton's eyes. "Great. We can get started. Why don't we just cut to the chase, and you tell me how well you knew the victim, Cindy Brown."

Randy clasped his hands together in front of him. Even from where I was sitting, I could see that his nails were dirty. "I live in the same trailer park. I didn't see her often since she worked nights. Usually by the time I got home from the garage, she was gone."

"You're an auto mechanic?"

"Yeah."

"How long have you been living in Mossy Oaks?"

" 'Bout a year."

"And you're from Texas, it says here."

The man nodded. I saw what looked like a flicker of anxiety in his eyes. "That's right."

"Why'd you leave?"

He hesitated. "I wanted a change of scenery. No law against that, is there?"

"Certainly not." Clinton took a pen from his pocket and scribbled something on one of the papers. As he did, his jacket pulled away slightly, giving Randy Dempsey a clear view of his holster. I wondered if it was intentional. "So, how'd you meet Miss Brown?"

Randy dropped his hands to his lap and began to fidget with them. "She was taking a nap one day and her kid, Annabel, slipped out. I found her clear on the other side of the trailer park, crying, saying she was lost. I helped her find her trailer. Cindy had woke up in the meantime and was in a panic. She gave me a cold beer for finding the girl. After that, we sort of became friends."

"What do you mean by 'sort of'?" Clinton asked. When Randy didn't reply, he went on. "You were lovers, too, weren't you?" He looked at the papers in his hand as he said it, and I wondered if that was in the report.

Randy didn't hesitate. "No."

"Would you have liked to have been?"

Randy shifted in his chair. "I told you: We were just friends."

"You didn't answer my last question," Clinton said. "Would you have preferred a more intimate relationship with Miss Brown?"

Randy crossed his arms in a defensive gesture. "You saw her; what do you think? Thing is, one of the reasons she liked me was I didn't come on to her like most men. We just drank a few beers together now and then."

"Did you ever get high together?"

"Maybe some weed every now and then. I don't use the hard stuff."

Clinton looked up. "You sure about that? You sure you and Cindy weren't using some kind of hallucinogen tonight, just before she was murdered? Maybe things got out of control?"

"I told you: I don't use that shit. As for what she was doing tonight, I couldn't tell you. Cindy had an active social life."

"Meaning?"

"She usually had a date when she got off work."

"Do you know who she was seeing?"

"I didn't ask, and she didn't say."

Clinton merely looked at him. From where I was sitting on the other side of the window, I felt the silence stretch out between them. "Did you think Cindy was a good mother, Randy?"

He shrugged. "I reckon she coulda been better. She left Annabel with her parents a lot, but I didn't figure it was any of my business."

"You baby-sat for her a few times, didn't you?"

Randy began to fidget. "Once or twice, when Cindy's parents were busy."

"And you liked Annabel?"

I wondered where Clinton was going with his questioning. I glanced at Hix, but he was caught up with what was happening in the other room.

Randy glanced at Conners, who was leaning against the wall. He seemed to be asking for help. Conners looked sympathetic. "Just answer the question, pal," he prodded gently. "We already know most of it anyway."

Finally, Randy nodded. "Yeah, sure, I like Annabel. She's a good kid. I thought she deserved better."

Clinton put his notes down and gazed at the man. "You ever been arrested?"

The other man hesitated. "I've had a couple of DUIs."

"That all?"

"Yeah."

"You sure about that?" Clinton leaned back in his chair and crossed his legs as though he had all the time in the world. "We've had you checked out, Randy. You've got more than a couple of DUIs on your record, don't you? The good folks in Texas say you like to fondle children. They say you've got a bad habit of pulling your weenie out in front of little kids."

Randy's face flamed. He sank lower in his chair. "That was a long time ago."

"You ain't one of those pedophiles, now, are you, Randy?"

"Fuck you, man," he said. Randy covered his face with his hands. Even from where I sat, I could see that he was trembling. So was I.

Clinton didn't so much as flinch. In fact, he looked very calm as he pulled his revolver from his holster and handed it to Conners.

Hix turned to me. "You shouldn't be listening to this."

"I'm a teacher. I'm used to this kind of language."

"Very funny."

All at once, Clinton stood up so fast that his chair toppled over. He rounded the table, grabbed Randy's shirt and pulled him to his feet so that their faces were an inch apart. He bared his teeth. At that point, I wouldn't have been surprised if he'd growled. I clenched my fists in my lap. "Can he do that?" I asked Hix breathlessly.

He shrugged. "He can do any danged thing he wants as far as I'm concerned."

Clinton released the man with force, and he literally fell back into his chair. "I have to tell you, Randy. I have a real hard time dealing with child molesters. Last time somebody left me alone with one, I almost beat him to death. You think we could talk Conners here into taking a walk so we can settle this man to man?"

Conners walked over, patted Clinton on the back. "Chill out, man. I don't have to remind you what happened last time you lost it." He tossed Randy a warning look. "Don't piss him off."

Randy leaned as far back in his chair as he could. He was visibly shaken. "I don't got those problems anymore. I went to counseling. I'm cured."

Clinton looked at Conners. "You think people like Randy here can be cured?"

He shrugged. "Anything's possible."

Clinton seemed to consider it, then shook his head. "Know what I think, Randy?" he said. "I think you were doing the kid. I think her mother found out about it and was planning to blow the whistle on you, so you killed her. All that's left for us to do is figure out how you got her to be still long enough that you could slice her up. Was it drugs? Poison?"

"Won't take long to find out," Conners said. "Soon as they do the autopsy. No need to try and beat it out of him, Clinton."

"You could make it easy on all of us, Randy, by cooperating," Clinton said smoothly. "You tell us what really happened; maybe we can help you. I don't want to see you end up on death row with a bunch of freakin' animals. And that's all they are, Randy. Animals."

Randy was quiet for a moment. I turned to Chief Hix. "They're good." He nodded as though he wasn't surprised.

Randy looked more than a little upset. "I ain't goin' to confess to something I didn't do," he said. "I never laid a hand on that kid. I swear to God." He looked like he might cry. "I loved Cindy. I even asked her to marry me, but she said she wasn't marrying some auto mechanic without a pot to pee in."

Clinton regarded him. "I'll bet that pissed you off."

"I got over it."

"Did you?" He smiled nastily into Randy's face and backed away. "You know, even if you manage to get out of this mess, we're going to have to warn folks that we've got a known baby rapist living among us. We're going to have to have posters printed up with your picture, and me and Conners are going to plaster them all over town."

Randy clasped his hands tightly together and squeezed

his eyes shut. Finally, he opened them. "Look, I left Texas because I wanted to make a fresh start. I paid for my crimes, and I saw a shrink like they told me to. I'm working hard to make a new life for myself. I plan to open my own garage one day."

"It won't be easy if folks have to worry about you diddling their kiddies between lube jobs," Clinton said.

"What do you want from me?"

Clinton didn't hesitate. "I want you to stop bullshitting me and tell the truth."

"I *have* told the truth."

"You've been lying through your teeth since you got here," Clinton shouted, "and I'm fixin' to book your ass for murder."

"I would never kill Cindy. I loved her."

Clinton gave a grunt and began to pace. "I got an eye witness that puts you at the victim's trailer shortly before her parents arrived and found her floating in bloody bath water."

Randy continued to look down at his hands. I could see the tears streaming down his face. "I didn't do it, man. I swear to Christ."

Clinton turned and banged his hand down on the table, hard. On the other side of the mirror, I jumped. "Then what the hell were you doing at her place?" he demanded.

Randy wiped his eyes and looked toward the ceiling. "Oh, Jesus."

"You'd better call Jesus, boy, 'cause you're going to fry like sausage over this one. Or maybe you'll just get life. By the time the big boys get finished with you, you're going to wish you'd never been born with an asshole."

On the other side of the mirror, I cringed and wished I'd gone to the chief's office as Clinton had suggested. This was a side of him I wasn't ready to see and maybe never would be.

"I was there, okay?" Randy blurted loudly. "But I didn't kill her. She was already dead." He began to sob.

"She was already gone, and there wasn't a damn thing I could do for her."

"What time were you there?"

"Seven-thirty, eight o'clock. I saw her lights on and decided to walk over. I knocked and called out, but there was no answer. I thought maybe she was asleep, so I went in and headed down the hall to the back bedroom. I took one look at her, saw she was dead and ran out. Got sick in her backyard."

"Then what?"

"I went inside my trailer, turned the lights off and started drinking. Wasn't long before I heard the sirens."

"Did you touch anything while you were in the bathroom?"

"I don't think so . . . maybe the doorjamb, but I don't remember. I just walked in, saw the body and freaked. Next thing I know, I'm outside puking my guts out." He looked up. His face was wet. "I ain't never seen nothing like that in my whole sorry-ass life."

"Why didn't you call the police yourself? Why'd you let the girl's family walk in on something like that?"

"Because of my record. I knew it'd look bad."

"It *does* look bad."

Randy tried to talk around his sobs. Finally, he got control. "I swear to God, I didn't kill her. She was the only real friend I had."

"Not good enough, Randy."

"Look, I don't know for sure, but I think she was seeing someone."

"Who?"

"I don't know. Like I said, we didn't talk about the other guys in her life, but I think she was seeing someone regularly because she spent the night away once in a while. Also, he was sending her gifts."

"What kind of gifts?"

Randy's sentences became jerky. "Oh, I don't know . . . flowers and candy . . . that kind of stuff. One night when I was over there . . . I had to go to the bathroom, and I no-

ticed a new washer and dryer. You know . . . the kind that
stack up and take less room.''

"How do you know she didn't buy it?''

" 'Cause I asked. She said a friend bought it for her.
That's all I know.''

Clinton shook his head and walked to the door. Conners
followed.

"Hey, where are you guys going?'' Randy called. "Are
you just going to leave me here?''

"Only till your ass grows to that chair,'' Clinton said.
"You're going to have to do a better job of convincing me
you didn't kill that woman, if you want to stay out of jail,''
he added. He opened the door and walked out with Conners
right behind him. A moment later, the other officer resumed
his post just inside.

Nobody spoke when the men first reentered the break
room. Conners was grinning. "You played him like a fid-
dle, man.''

"You didn't do so bad yourself,'' Clinton said. His gaze
found mine and lingered. I glanced away, unsure about
what to make of this new side of him. I only hoped I never
found myself in Randy Dempsey's shoes, with a man like
Clinton sitting across from me.

"So what do you think?'' Hix asked after a moment.

Clinton didn't hesitate. "Tell the grandparents to have a
doctor check the little girl as soon as possible. We can only
hold this guy for twenty hours unless we find something
else. Have you got someone searching Randy's trailer?''

Hix nodded. "And Cindy's, too.''

Clinton looked thoughtful. "Frankly, I don't think this
guy did it.''

"What makes you say that?'' Hix asked.

"I don't think he's capable. The man we're looking for
is a whole lot smarter and much more dangerous.''

15

I awoke the next morning with a headache. My dreams had been horrible: images of a lovely young woman bleeding to death in her bathtub while her little girl tried to wake her. It made me think of Molly when she'd found Lurlene. Toward dawn, I'd closed my eyes and fallen into a heavy sleep that left me feeling as though I'd just recovered from some illness. I suspected the stress was getting to me. I should have agreed to let Clinton sleep in the spare room as he'd offered.

I stared at the full pot of coffee. I thought of Molly, then realized with a sinking feeling the girl was still at the Gradys' house. I tried to think. Could I have awakened in the midst of one of my bad dreams and turned on the coffeemaker myself? I closed my eyes and pressed my hands flat against the kitchen counter, willing myself to remember.

Was I losing my mind?

I poured a cup of coffee and drank it while I watched Buster chase a squirrel to a tree. He stood there, front paws resting on the trunk, wagging his tail as if to ask the little creature to come down and play. I smiled despite the heaviness in my chest. I wondered if my parents had heard about the murder, and I wished there was something I could do to keep it from them.

Deciding to take a hot shower, I set my empty cup in the sink and turned for the hall. Out of the corner of one eye, I spied a napkin-draped basket on the table. I blinked, too astonished to do much else. *What in heaven's name?* I felt myself being pulled in that direction as though I suddenly had no control over my body. I lifted the napkin, then froze and felt my body recoil in horror. I screamed, dropping the napkin into place, and backed away from the table.

As a child growing up in the country, I'd seen my share of field mice, they'd infiltrated our house each winter, searching for a warm place to nest. You could always tell when they started coming in. The very minute Lurlene spotted one, she went into what my father claimed was a conniption fit, and we were just certain that all the screaming and hollering would break the crystal goblets my mother had acquired with her S & H Green Stamps. Finally, we took in a stray tomcat, and the problem disappeared.

This was not a simple field mouse. This was an ugly brown rat with oily fur and vicious-looking teeth, lying stiff on a bed of fresh donuts. Even from where I stood, I could see that his neck lay at an odd angle, as though someone had twisted it.

"Oh, God," I mumbled. I glanced around frantically, wondering if someone was in the house, wondering if he was standing just in the next room listening to the pitiful sounds I made. Trying to remain calm, I checked both doors and found them locked tight. I moved from one window to the next, finding them locked as well, then looked under the beds and in the closets. Back in the kitchen, I dialed the police department.

Shortly afterward, I watched Chief Hix climb out of his patrol car and make his way up my driveway. He looked tired, and I wondered if he'd managed to get any sleep the night before. It would probably have been better to call Clinton, but I still considered him the parole officer of Frank Gillespie, who was my main suspect.

"Good morning, Chief," I said as I opened the door. I had thrown on a robe, but my teeth were still chattering from the chill and all I'd seen in the past twelve hours. "Thank you for coming so quickly."

"Show me what you found this morning," he said.

I led him into the kitchen and pointed to the basket. "Under that napkin."

One gray brow lifted as he raised the napkin and caught sight of the rat. "Nasty-looking fellow, ain't he?"

I folded my arms in front of me, letting my gaze rest on the nearby wall calendar that advertised Stoney's hardware store. "You'll notice that his neck is broken," I added, knowing I'd see it every time I closed my eyes.

"Uh-huh. If you'll get me a garbage bag, I'll dispose of him."

I chanced a look in his direction. He'd tucked a cigar into one corner of his mouth and seemed to be chewing on it. I was thankful that he'd dropped the napkin back into place. "You're not going to take pictures or dust for fingerprints?" I asked.

He chuckled. "You been watching too many cop shows, Emily."

I reddened. "Then how do you expect to find out who did it?"

"I already know who did it. Kids."

"How can you be sure?"

"I've been doing some checking, that's all. I understand Molly's good friends with Henry Dean."

I felt my face grow warm. Hix had already warned me about the boy, but I hadn't heeded his advice. "They do homework together."

"I told you what I thought of that boy to begin with. If you insist on letting Molly hang around with him, you can expect more of this."

"How'd he get in, Chief?" I asked tightly. "Everything was locked up tight. I've got the best dead bolts money can buy."

"Wouldn't be the first lock ol' Henry's picked."

I was becoming annoyed with him. I had spent a lot of money on those locks, and Herschel had insisted they were foolproof. When I'd suggested chains as well, he hadn't felt they were necessary, unless I wanted them just for my own peace of mind.

"Believe me, Miss Wilkop," he'd said. "This place is as tight as Fort Knox now."

"You know what I think, Chief?" I said. "I think you're using Henry Dean as your scapegoat so you don't have to question Frank and risk upsetting the mighty Augustus."

I could tell I'd angered him. He gazed back at me a long moment, his face red. "You've got Molly in counseling, don't you?"

I hesitated. One of the drawbacks of living in a small town was the fact that everybody knew everybody else's business: who drank too much, who was cheating on whom, whose kid stayed in the most trouble. There were times when I longed for the anonymity of a big city. "Why do you ask?"

"I was just thinking—" He paused and shifted in his chair. "Have you considered the possibility that Molly's the one pulling these oddball stunts?"

I was indignant, and it showed. If I had suspected Molly of trying to scare me in the beginning, I was now convinced of her innocence. "Molly wouldn't do something like this. Besides," I added, taking great joy in doing so, "she's not even here. She's spending the night with Patty Grady." He looked more than a little surprised; stupefied would have been a better word. Until that moment, I'd not realized that Molly was at the top of his list of suspects.

"I think you'd better look elsewhere for our villain, Chief," I said. "Try the Gillespie mansion."

Cindy Brown's picture was plastered across the front page of the newspaper when Molly carried it in from the front yard the following morning. I'd barely had time to look at it when my mother called.

"Have you seen the paper?" she asked.

"Just now," I told her.

"Do you believe what this world is coming to? And to

think there was a time when we didn't even worry about locking our doors. People don't believe me when I say we're living in the last days, but this is all the proof I need.''

I sank onto the stool next to the phone and listened while my mother predicted yet another doomsday. I wasn't sure why she looked forward to meeting her Maker when she made Him sound so formidable. I knew she'd carry on most of the day over the murder, and I was in no mood to listen. Nor did I want Molly to hear any of it.

"I was just about to call you, Mom," I said. "Molly and I can't make it for church today."

There was silence on the other end. "I've already prepared a pork roast."

"I'm not feeling well," I said, telling myself it wasn't really a lie because I was exhausted after all that'd gone on.

"What's wrong? Are you having your monthly?"

"No, just a sore throat. And a few body aches." *Now* I was lying.

"Your father and I can come by after church. I've got soup in the freezer. Won't take no time to thaw in the microwave."

"No, that won't be necessary. I have plenty of soup on hand."

"I'll bet it's canned," she said in such a way that one would have thought all the nutrients had been sucked out in the process. "That's what's wrong with you, Emily; you don't eat right. It's a wonder you and Molly don't get sick more often than you do."

"Mom, what I really want to do is go to bed and rest. Hopefully, it's just a twenty-four-hour bug."

She sniffed. "Well, if you change your mind about the soup . . ."

I hung up, turned and saw Molly standing there, arms crossed, giving me a smug look. She'd caught me. "Okay, so I fibbed. I was actually doing both of us a big favor."

*   *   *

The next few days passed without incident, although I continued to stay on edge, like Chicken Little waiting for the sky to fall. Of course, I didn't breathe a word about the rat to Molly, and I had every intention of keeping it from her for good.

I bought Molly a book on dog training, and in a couple of days' time, we had taught Buster to sit and lie down. Although I was fond of the dog, I did not particularly like the way he smelled. Molly had mentioned once or twice that he farted a lot, but it was not something I spent a lot of time thinking about.

"Don't you think it's time we gave him a bath?" I suggested when we arrived home on Wednesday. I was determined to get rid of the smell once and for all.

"I thought you wanted to wait until he got used to us," she said.

"That was just an excuse I used for putting it off."

We called Buster into the house, and he spent the first few minutes checking the place out, sniffing here and there, snooping under beds and in closets. I ran a tub of warm water, grabbed a bottle of dish detergent and coaxed him into the bathroom.

"Okay, here goes nothing," I said, lifting him into the tub. The poor animal immediately tried to scramble out; his toenails sounded like castanets against the old porcelain tub. He farted three times. "You try to hold him still while I wash," I told Molly, trying not to gag.

If I had considered Buster homely before, it was nothing compared to the wet and shivering animal that stared back at me so pitifully now. As I soaped him quickly from head to toe, Molly talked to him gently. Before long, he'd calmed down enough to sit, although I suspected he would have leaped from the tub had we not been holding him securely.

Once I'd scrubbed him thoroughly, I let the water out of the tub, grabbed a large plastic cup and began to rinse him, taking care not to get soap in his eyes. Something about the animal—maybe the downtrodden look he wore—suggested that he had not always been treated well. Just as I was beginning to feel sorry for him, he farted again.

"Eee . . . yuck!" Molly cried as the animal wagged his tail happily.

Drying him was not an easy task; it took several towels and a whole lot of patience, not to mention prayers on my part that he wouldn't break wind again. When he was pronounced ready, we released him, and he pounced out of the tub and shook, spraying Molly and me both. I opened the bathroom door, and he shot out, headed straight for the back door.

"He can't go out right now, can he?" Molly asked. "It's cold out there. He'll get sick."

"We'll wait till he dries," I said, reaching into a cabinet for his treats. "Here, give him a biscuit for being so good."

Buster saw the biscuit and stood on his hind legs, doing something of a balancing act that had both of us laughing. Molly offered it to him, and he grabbed it and scurried beneath the table to eat it. I wondered if he was used to losing his food to other dogs. That would explain why he was so skinny. I pondered for a moment how Molly and her pet had both been abused and neglected in the past.

"What are we going to do when it gets to be winter, Aunt Em?" she asked. "He won't be able to sleep outside."

"His doghouse will keep him warm." She continued to look worried. "I might ask Herschel to install some kind of heating device." There was no way she was going to convince me to let him become a house dog, with his problems. "I think I should call the vet," I said, noting the time. If I hurried, I might catch them before they left for the day.

The doctor was already gone when I called, but his assistant was more than happy to listen to my woes.

"Sounds like a problem with his anal glands," she said. "I'm surprised we didn't notice it when he came in. He probably just needs to have them expressed."

"Expressed?"

"Yes, to release the odor. You see, dogs have these little sacks on either side of their rectum and they fill up—"

"I think I understand," I said weakly. "Is there somebody I can pay to do this?" I pictured a man wearing a gas mask and a special suit. I figured we'd have to drive Buster to one of those nuclear waste sites where the odor could be locked into airtight containers once it was released.

"Oh, we can do it," the woman said. "Won't take a minute. Just drop by in the next day or two. You don't even need an appointment."

By the time we sat down for dinner, Buster was dry, but Molly was having so much fun with him that I hated to put him out.

"Why don't you put him in your room?" I suggested, knowing I'd never get through a meal with him sitting beneath the kitchen table *expressing* himself. Once we finished dinner, she let him out, and he followed her back and forth across the room while she cleared the table. Afterward, she called him into her bedroom once more. I washed the dishes and straightened up the rest of the kitchen, then made my way to Molly's room. I found Buster curled up at the foot of her bed.

"Let him stay in just for tonight," Molly pleaded, peering at me over her English book. "He's clean, and I think he's passed all the gas he's going to for the night."

I hedged. I really wanted Buster outside, where he could warn us if someone came into the yard, but Molly looked so hopeful that I hated to say no. "Just for tonight," I said. "Tomorrow he goes back out." I started for my room. "Isn't Henry coming by to study?"

She shook her head. "He's grounded."

I felt my hope surge. "How come?"

She gave me the look that told me I was intruding. "I didn't ask."

I knew she was lying, and if I pressed her, she would just continue to do so. "Well, I guess I'll go grade papers or something. Or maybe I should tackle the ironing."

"Boy, you must be desperate for something to do," she mumbled without looking up.

The phone rang. Buster raised his head as though annoyed by the noise. Molly snatched it up and answered. "It's for you," she said. "Clinton."

"I'll take it in my bedroom," I said, hurrying across the hall. I picked it up. "Hi," I said. "I was wondering when you'd call." Already I was irritated with myself for thinking it was him each time the phone rang, then being disappointed when it wasn't. That's the problem with having a man in your life, I'd decided since our so-called date. You're always waiting for the phone or the doorbell to ring.

"I've been tied up at the police station," he said. "Hix just charged Randy Dempsey with the murder of Cindy Brown."

I was silent for a moment. "Have you changed your mind about his innocence?" I asked at last.

"I don't know what the hell to think. The good news is, the doctor found absolutely no physical evidence that Cindy's little girl has been molested."

I heard my own sigh of relief. "So what happens now?" I asked.

"They plan to hold his arraignment first thing tomorrow. Bond will be set. I doubt Randy will be able to bail himself out of a murder charge."

"What kind of evidence do they have?"

"Randy's fingerprints were all over the place, even the bathroom. And the neighbor saw him run out of Cindy's trailer shortly before her parents arrived. She said he was agitated, saw him stop once to throw up. As far as Hix is concerned, it's enough to charge him."

I heard the weariness in his voice. "We don't have to talk about it, if you don't want to."

"Good. So, how're things going on your end?" he asked, changing the subject.

"Nothing new to report, thank goodness."

"I wish you'd called me instead of Hix when you found

----

the rat," he said, not for the first time. "I worry about you, Emily."

"I'm not going to let something like that send me over the edge," I told him. "Do you know if Hix followed up on it?"

"I know he took it seriously, if that's what you're asking. He's got a man watching Frank, and he sent Duffy out to question a few people, including your neighbors. He and I have been tied up with this other stuff."

I suspected that Henry Dean was one of the people Duffy had questioned. Perhaps that's why Henry was grounded. I decided not to push Clinton for more information. Instead I invited him to dinner Friday night, figuring I could pick up a pizza on the way home.

"You don't know how good that sounds," he said. "I've been living off burgers and pizza for weeks. I'd love to have a home-cooked meal."

I paled at the thought of trying to put together a full dinner. "Yes, well, how does seven o'clock sound?" I asked, knowing I had to meet DeWayne after school for my shooting practice. I wondered how I'd find time to put a full meal on the table.

"I'll be there," he said.

16

Stoney called me first thing Friday morning to let me know that Lilly had gone into labor during the night and had just birthed a baby boy, Daniel Adam Dunseath.

"Eight pounds, five ounces," he said proudly. "Both mother and son are doing well. Lilly's sleeping now; she had to push for two hours to get the little sucker out." He paused to catch his breath. I had never heard him sound so hyper. "Listen, Emily, we've sort of run into a hitch. Lilly's mother fell and broke her ankle while racing down the stairs to catch a taxi for the airport."

"What are you going to do?" I asked, knowing Lilly would need help during the first few days.

"My mom's driving up, but she can't get here until tomorrow. I was wondering if you could keep the twins tonight."

"I'd be glad to," I told him, then reminded myself I'd have to cancel my lesson with DeWayne. And Clinton was coming for dinner. Oh, well, he probably wouldn't mind having kids around. "Where are they now?" I asked.

"I dropped them off at the neighbors' house on the way to the hospital. They said they'd get the girls off to school for us this morning. You know where we keep the spare key. I figured you could go in and pack what the girls need once school lets out. Lilly says all their clothes are clean. That's all she's done for a week: wash and iron and clean and remind me how much she hates being pregnant."

"Don't worry about a thing," I said. "And tell Lilly to call me when she's up to it."

"Thanks, Emily, we owe you. Let me go now. I'm going to try and reach the twins before they leave for school, so I can tell them the good news."

I hung up the phone, then immediately called DeWayne. He wasn't home, but his message machine picked up. "Hi, DeWayne, it's me," I said hurriedly. "I can't make our lesson; something's come up. I'll call you later."

I knew I probably sounded frantic. I had planned to go by the grocery store and find something relatively easy to cook for dinner that night. Now I wondered where I'd find the time.

Beth and Maryjane were waiting outside my classroom when school let out. "Did you hear we have a new baby brother?" Beth said. "His name is Daniel, but Daddy says we'll probably end up calling him Danny."

I gave them my best smile. "Yes, I heard. Congratulations!"

"When can we see him?" Maryjane asked.

"I'm not sure. Your mom's pretty tired right now. But I'll drive you to the hospital as soon as she says it's okay." We climbed into my car, and I drove to the middle school. Molly was waiting out front. She didn't look surprised to see the twins in the car.

"Did Lilly have her baby?" she asked as she climbed in.

"Uh-huh. A little boy. I have to go by their house to pick up some clothes."

Molly didn't look excited at the thought of driving out to the Dunseath house. "Could you drop me off at home first?"

I hated to say no and have her pout all the way. Besides, the last few days had been quiet, and I felt hopeful that Chief Hix had taken care of the matter. "Okay," I said at last, knowing I didn't plan to be gone long. "But only if you promise to lock up."

Molly shook her head sadly. "You're so paranoid."

I dropped her off, then drove to the Dunseaths' house in record time. I was so rushed I didn't have time to be happy for Lilly. Maybe later. Right now I just wanted to grab what the girls needed and return home.

"I thought Grandma was coming," Maryjane said as we climbed out of the car. I ushered them up the front walk as fast as their short legs would carry them.

"Something came up at the last minute," I said. "Grandma Dunseath is coming instead, but she won't arrive until tomorrow." Both girls looked disappointed but didn't say anything. I figured Grandma Dunseath was probably big on vegetables.

I found the house key wedged behind the porch light. "How do you know where we keep our key?" Beth asked, looking both surprised and a little suspicious.

I grinned at her. "Your mommy and I have been sharing secrets for a long time, sweetie."

Inside, the house felt desolate without Lilly's smiling face and Stoney's ramblings about lumber prices. We packed a couple of days' worth of clothes and toiletry items, just in case something happened and the twins ended up staying longer than planned.

They seemed to take forever to find what they needed; I thought of Molly all alone at home and wished I'd made her come with me. Finally their bags were packed and ready to go.

I herded the girls out to the car and put their suitcases in the trunk. I could feel myself rushing; I checked my watch and noted we'd been gone half an hour.

"Do you think we can see our baby tomorrow?" Maryjane asked as I pulled out of the driveway.

I knew I'd have to give the girls an answer soon or risk hearing the question again in fifteen minutes. "I'll call the hospital when I get home and ask your daddy."

"You know where babies come out from, don't you?" Beth asked me.

I offered her a vague smile in my rearview mirror as I

inched my Toyota over the speed limit. "I've never had a baby, but I think I have a fair idea."

"They come out of your butt," the girl replied matter-of-factly.

Maryjane groaned in disgust. "They do not!"

"That's what Sylvia White told me today, and she should know 'cause she's in fourth grade. Don't they come out your butt, Aunt Emily?" Beth asked.

"No, I can definitely say they don't come out of your butt," I told her. "But I think you need to take this up with your mother. After all, she's the expert."

I reached town and pulled into a chicken place, muttering under my breath when I saw how long the line was. I wanted to kick myself for letting Molly stay home alone. Fifteen minutes later, I pulled away with a bucket of chicken and all the fixings.

On the road again, I drove faster than usual, noting I'd been gone well over an hour. I pulled into my driveway ten minutes later and was relieved to find my house standing just as I'd left it. Molly was right, I decided. I was just being paranoid.

The girls grabbed their book bags, and I carried the food and my purse. I paused at the kitchen door and knocked. No answer. I tried the doorknob. Molly had locked the dead bolt as I'd told her. I could hear music blaring from her room, which explained why she couldn't hear me. That's the only reason I could think of for her not answering.

"Let's go around back," I said, and the twins followed. Buster saw us and made a mad dash, jumping and pawing my clothes despite all my protests. The twins squealed when he tried to do the same to them. I figured they would have gone berserk if he'd still had his anal gland problem. Thankfully, I'd found time to run him to the vet the day before.

I banged on Molly's bedroom window and went weak with relief when she pulled the curtain aside. She looked surprised to see me. "What are you doing out there?" she asked.

"Please unlock the door," I told her, trying to remain calm. I could feel the beginnings of a headache. She dropped the curtain into place, and the twins and I hurried around to the kitchen door once more. I heard the rattle of the key in the dead bolt; a second later, Molly threw open the door. "Do you have to play your stereo so loud?" I asked, annoyed with her now that I knew she was safe.

"I got scared. Music helps me relax."

I set the food containers on the counter and faced her, trying to hide my anxiety. "Why were you scared?"

"I don't know. It was just a feeling I had. Probably because you made such a big deal about locking up. Can I go out and visit Buster now?"

"Yes. Take the twins with you so I can straighten the house. I've invited Clinton for dinner."

She didn't look happy at the idea of watching the girls for me, but she didn't argue. Instead, she grabbed a handful of Buster's dog biscuits and motioned the girls to follow her. "Y'all can watch me train him," she said. "But only if you're quiet and don't get in the way."

"We won't," they promised in unison.

They left through the kitchen door, and I immediately went to work polishing the furniture in the living room. Afterward, I vacuumed the area rug and plumped the pillows on the sofa. In the kitchen, I wiped down the counters, swept and mopped, then took my cleaning supplies into the guest bathroom. Every so often, I checked through the kitchen window and saw the twins watching in rapt attention as Molly tried to teach Buster to speak. She was making little progress; the dog simply wanted to play.

Lilly called at five-thirty and spent fifteen minutes telling me about her grueling labor, at which time I decided once again that I was better off single. I assured her that the twins were fine but desperately wanted to see their new brother, and she promised to get back to me. Right now she was more concerned with when her doctor was going to let her have a sitz bath, whatever that was.

I hung up, made a mad dash to the shower and tried to

----

scrub away the smell of pine cleaner. I emerged a few minutes later, toweled off and tried to decide what to do about my makeup.

My parents had never permitted Lurlene and me to wear makeup in high school, although Lurlene had worn it anyway. She would hit the girls' bathroom the moment our bus stopped in front of the school, slather it on, then scrub it off only minutes before she climbed back on the bus to go home. I had never learned all those clever eye shadow tricks that my sister'd had down to an art by the time she was twelve.

Once I'd brushed a little mauve shadow on my lids, I tried to draw a straight line with eyeliner but failed miserably. I smudged it up a bit like I'd seen other women do, then gave a once-over with my mascara. Not bad. I put gel in my hair, raked my fingers through it and decided to let it dry naturally instead of melting the natural curl with my hair dryer.

"You look nice," Molly said as I stepped into the kitchen a few minutes later, wearing my nicest jeans and a lightweight sweater. "You should wear makeup more often."

"I do wear makeup," I told her. "I just don't wear that much."

"What time is Clinton supposed to be here?"

"Seven."

"You haven't even started cooking."

I motioned to the cardboard containers on the counter. "I stopped by the chicken place. All I have to do is stick a few things in the microwave and put them in serving dishes."

She peeked into one of the sacks. "Why don't we just eat it out of the box?"

"It'll look nicer the other way."

"Oh, I get it. You're going to make him think *you* cooked it."

"I didn't say that."

"What are you going to do with the big cardboard bucket and all these other containers?"

"You're going to carry them outside and put them in the trash can."

"That's cheating. But I don't blame you. You need to win him over fast, what with your biological clock ticking away."

I looked at her. She smiled to let me know she was joking. "Very funny," I said. "One day, thirty won't seem so ancient to you."

"Like when I'm eighty?" She started rummaging through the food. "So, what can I do to help?"

It was unlike Molly to offer her assistance, so I figured she must be starving. "You and the girls can set the table. Make sure it looks nice."

I went about emptying containers as the girls set the table, taking great care with the cloth napkins I used for special occasions. The doorbell rang precisely at seven, and I hurried to answer it, as did Molly and the twins. Clinton looked surprised to find me surrounded by children.

"Hi, ladies," he said, then glanced at me. "Dinner was for tonight, right?"

"Yes, come in." He tried to step inside, but it was crowded. "Girls, would you please put ice in the glasses for me?" I said. "We'll be right in." They reluctantly made their way to the kitchen. "I hope you don't mind the extra company," I said. "Beth and Maryjane's mother just had her baby. They're staying here tonight."

"No problem. I get along with kids okay."

I led him into the kitchen and found the twins emptying ice trays and Molly carrying the food to the table.

"Boy, that's quite a spread," Clinton said when he spied the platter of fried chicken. "I wish you hadn't gone to so much trouble."

"No trouble," I mumbled as Molly shot me an accusing glance. "I hope you don't mind if we eat now. I'm sure the girls are hungry."

"So am I," Clinton said. "I didn't have time for lunch

----

today, so I grabbed a pack of crackers out of a vending machine.''

"Everybody sit down," I told them once I'd filled the glasses with tea and poured two plastic cups of milk for the twins. I had already grabbed a folding chair from the hall closet so that everyone had a seat. "Clinton, why don't you take a piece of chicken and pass the platter to me so I can help the twins," I suggested. He did so, and I was informed by Maryjane and Beth that they ate only drumsticks. Once our plates were full, I prompted them to eat, but they seemed more interested in talking to Clinton, who was making a game out of trying to tell them apart.

"I forgot to tell you," I said, turning my attention to them once they'd given Clinton clues about their subtle differences. "Your mother called while you were outside. She and the baby are doing fine. We can visit tomorrow."

"Are we going to be able to hold the baby?" Maryjane asked.

"I'm not sure what the hospital rules are. We'll have to ask."

We chatted easily throughout the meal, and the girls—even Molly—were on their best behavior. Molly asked Clinton about his job and how many murderers he knew. When he told her he'd resigned temporarily to help Chief Hix investigate the murder of Cindy Brown, I thought her eyes would pop out of her head. It was obvious that she wanted all the gory details, but he immediately changed the subject.

The doorbell rang, and I glanced at Molly. "Are you expecting Henry?"

She shook her head. "He's still grounded. Probably just a salesman. You want me to get rid of him?"

"Only if you can do it in a nice way," I said.

She disappeared into the living room. I heard conversation, then footsteps. When I looked up, I saw DeWayne standing in the doorway with a large pizza box and Molly wearing a broad smile. "Look who's here," she said.

He glanced from me to Clinton and back to me again. I

could tell he was embarrassed. "I'm sorry to interrupt your dinner, Em," he said. "I got worried when you canceled our . . . uh . . . meeting."

I immediately rose to my feet, as did Clinton. I introduced the two, and they shook hands. "You're not interrupting, DeWayne," I insisted. "Please join us; there's plenty of chicken."

"I'll get another chair," Molly offered eagerly.

"No, please don't," he said as she started for the living room. "I have to be somewhere at seven-thirty. I just wanted to make sure my two favorite gals were eating right." He handed the flat box to Molly and winked. "Besides, I know how much you like pizza."

She smiled. Actually, she glowed. "Thanks, DeWayne."

I noted the look on my niece's face and tried once more to convince him to stay, but he was already backing out of the kitchen. "Maybe some other time," he said. "I can't miss my appointment."

I suspected there wasn't a place in the world that DeWayne had to be, but I wouldn't embarrass him further by insisting that he stay. "Let me walk you to the door," I suggested.

"I can find my way out," he insisted. "I'll call you later."

He hurried out, and I heard the front door close a moment later. "I should have made him take that pizza with him," I said. "I worry that he's not eating right."

Molly reclaimed her seat at the table. She was still beaming. "He's so considerate to think of me."

"Isn't that the man I saw you with at Clancy's?" Clinton asked.

Molly's smile faded abruptly. "You went to Clancy's with DeWayne?" she blurted. It came out sounding like an accusation.

"I saw him briefly," I said. "He just wanted to talk."

"You never told me."

"I guess it slipped my mind."

"He wanted to talk about Lurlene, right?" she asked

dully. "It's always Lurlene." She got up from her chair so fast that it almost toppled over. "I'm glad she's dead."

"Molly!" I jumped up as well, then felt Clinton's hand on my wrist. "Let her go, Emily. You didn't do anything wrong. She needs to work through this on her own."

I sat down and noticed Beth and Maryjane eyeing me nervously. I smiled. "This family is a little dysfunctional right now," I said. "But I have every reason to believe it's going to be uphill from here on out."

17

Clinton waited until the twins had eaten and carried their plates to the sink before he broached the topic that had upset Molly.

"Sorry for opening my big mouth," he said. "I didn't know it was supposed to be a secret."

"You had no way of knowing," I told him. "Molly's upset with DeWayne because he stopped having anything to do with her after her mother's death. She thinks it's her fault, but I suspect that DeWayne's embarrassed to have her see him when he's drinking. And to tell you the truth, I don't want her to see him like that, either." I was quiet for a moment. "I want to help him, but I don't know how."

"I think it's pretty much up to him."

"I know that. But I still feel bad for him. Life hasn't been kind to DeWayne. His mother drank and was quite abusive. Then he married my sister and . . . well, you know the rest." I glanced up suddenly and realized that Clinton was watching me. "I'm sorry, I didn't mean to get on such a depressing subject." I stood. "Would you like a cup of coffee?"

"Sure." He stood as well. "You make the coffee, and I'll clear the table."

I didn't protest. I liked men who knew their way around a kitchen. I put the coffee on while Clinton carried the plates and serving dishes to the counter. I ran a sink of hot, sudsy water, scraped our plates and set them in it.

Once I'd put away the leftovers, I poured our coffee and suggested that we drink it on the front porch, grabbing a jacket from the hall closet on my way out. The brisk night air felt good on my face. Clinton waited until I sat down in the rocking chair before taking the chair next to me.

"I meant to tell you—I like your hair like that," he said. "You look different . . . younger."

I touched my hair. It was soft, curling naturally around my face. "My mother complains that I've let myself go," I told him, "but I never was one for primping in front of a mirror all day. I used to think my sister was crazy for spending so much time on herself when there were so many other *fun* things to do."

"Lucky for you, you don't have to spend a lot of time in front of a mirror," he said. "I think you look just fine."

I felt something catch in my chest and wondered if it was the first stirrings of heartburn or my reaction to Clinton's complimenting my looks.

"Do you plan to stay in Mossy Oaks?" I asked, not knowing what else to say and doing an awkward job of changing the subject.

He chuckled. "You totally ignored what I just said about the way you look. Why is that?"

I knew the fluttering in my stomach was due to anxiety. "I didn't ignore it. I guess I'm feeling self-conscious. I'm out of practice where men are concerned."

"Why is that?"

I shrugged. "I was involved with someone for several years. Came close to marrying him, as a matter of fact, before I broke it off two years ago."

"Why'd you break it off?"

"I didn't think he was the right man for me. I couldn't imagine waking up beside him every morning for the rest of my life."

"What kind of man *do* you want to wake up beside?"

"I still haven't a clue. Maybe I'm better off single."

"Oh, yeah, I just remembered that you'd decided to give up men." He looked amused. "And I seriously doubt our date the other night did anything to change your mind.''

"That wasn't your fault. Actually, I was impressed with the way you handled yourself. I could tell Chief Hix was, too. I certainly wouldn't have wanted to be in Randy Dempsey's shoes that night.''

"Sometimes getting to the truth is more important than how you go about it.''

"Yes, well, it wouldn't surprise me if Hix offered you a job.'' I chuckled. "It wouldn't surprise me if the mayor offered you *Hix's* job.''

Clinton looked thoughtful. "I still don't think Randy did it, but you're not going to convince Hix of that. I'd hate to think he would arrest an innocent man just to save what's left of his career.''

"I think he's terrified of hanging up his badge and going back to that empty house of his.''

"Well, I'm still involved in the investigation,'' Clinton said. "Hopefully, I'll come across something soon. It would help if I could find Cindy's so-called washer and dryer friend.''

He set his coffee cup down, rose from the chair and leaned against the porch rail directly in front of me. He gazed at me a long moment. "As for your question about how long I plan to hang around, I don't know. I didn't think I'd miss being a cop when I resigned my job in Chicago, but I guess it's in my blood, because all I can think about is finding out who murdered Cindy Brown.''

I waited for him to go on, waited for him to tell me *why* he'd left Chicago in the first place, but he said nothing and I didn't push. I was so accustomed to backing off when Molly clammed up; now I was doing the same thing with Clinton.

"I should go,'' he said after a minute. He stood, and I rose from my seat as well, finding myself only inches from him. "Thanks for dinner,'' he said.

"You're welcome.''

There didn't seem to be anything left to say.

"You'll be sure to lock up tight?''

"Do you really think it's something I'm likely to forget?"

He smiled, then leaned his head close and brushed his
lips against mine. It was totally unexpected, but I realized
that a part of me had been waiting for him to do just that.

"Good night, Emily. Don't forget to call if you need
me."

I suspected I was already beginning to need him more
than I wanted to. He stepped away from me, and I watched
him walk to his car. He climbed in and drove off a few
minutes later. I waited for his taillights to disappear around
the corner before I went in, thinking to myself that it might
not be a bad thing to wake up next to a man like Clinton
Ward every morning.

It was coming up to nine by the time I cleaned the
kitchen and saw the twins bathed and in bed with their
favorite books. Molly was listening to music in her room;
she'd turned it low in consideration of the twins, and I was
proud that I hadn't had to remind her. Since it wasn't a
school night, I allowed her to stay up as late as she liked.

Once I was convinced that the twins were sleeping
soundly, I took a quick shower, put on a nightgown and
sat in the middle of my bed, grading papers and catching
up with other paperwork. It was after eleven when I finished. With that out of the way, I picked up the book from
my nightstand. I'd been reading it for some time, and now
I tried to get back into the story.

I must've fallen asleep; when the phone rang, it startled
me so badly that I jumped. I grabbed it on the second ring
and spoke softly into the receiver, so as not to wake Beth
and Maryjane across the hall.

"Emily?"

The voice sounded strange, muffled, as though the
speaker was talking through a face mask or something else
that might distort his voice. I didn't recognize it. "Who is
this?" I asked, gripping the phone tighter.

"I'm angry with you, Emily," the man said. "You're

trying to turn Mr. Ward against me. He's threatening to send me back to prison.''

I shook my head as if to clear it. Frank? It had to be. But why was he trying to disguise his voice? Was he afraid I was recording my calls?

"I told you to leave me alone, Frank," I said, my voice surprisingly stern. Inside, my guts were shaking. "I wouldn't have to call Mr. Ward if you'd only stay away from me."

"You're going to pay for this, Emily. I'm going to slice you up like summer sausage before it's over. You *and* the girl."

A chill ran through me. "Leave me alone," I said through gritted teeth. "And stay the hell away from Molly or I'll make you sorry they let you out of prison to begin with."

He laughed softly, and the sound sent shivers up my spine. "You can't stop me. Not you or Ward or that pathetic creature in the backyard. Some watchdog you've got, Emily. I'm afraid you're going to have to replace him."

He hung up. I was still holding the phone when the line went dead. I didn't want to believe what I was thinking, but I knew Frank Gillespie was capable of anything. As I grabbed my robe and stuffed both arms into it, I felt a sense of dread wash over me. I hurried into my closet and reached to the uppermost shelf for my gun.

In the kitchen, I grabbed a flashlight from beneath the sink. I must've been in shock; I stood at the back door for a full minute trying to decide what to do. I knew I should call Clinton or the police, let them handle it. But Chief Hix hadn't done anything so far, and I would look foolish if they arrived and found Buster perfectly okay.

I unlocked the dead bolt and cracked the door, peering out to see if anyone was there. The night air wafted through the opening. I whistled softly for Buster and waited. Nothing. I couldn't stand not knowing one way or the other.

I took a deep breath and stepped out onto the driveway. The concrete felt cold beneath my feet, but I was only vaguely aware of it because I was listening for the smallest sound. Once again I called Buster and waited for him to come running from his doghouse and prop his front paws on the gate.

The floodlights shone brightly but didn't quite reach Buster's doghouse or the outskirts of my backyard, where shrubs and trees created dense and looming shadows. I imagined Frank hiding among them, just waiting to jump out at me. I shuddered, then told myself I was being silly. I had just hung up with Frank. He wouldn't have had time yet to drive here from wherever he'd made the call. Quickly I unlatched the gate and slipped through it. I aimed the flashlight in one direction, then another, spotlighting the entire backyard. There was no sign of Buster.

Feeling as though my heart would surely explode in my chest, I approached the doghouse, shined the light on it and saw Buster inside, obviously sound asleep. Relief almost made me dizzy. Some watchdog, I thought. I knelt before him. "Buster, wake up, you sorry mongrel," I said gently. I reached inside.

His body was cool and stiff when I touched him, and I knew now why he hadn't come running the moment I'd called. I felt something wet and sticky, saw the blood at his throat and where it had pooled beneath him. "Oh, Buster," I cried.

18

Suddenly I realized how much danger I'd put myself and the girls in by coming outside, and I couldn't get inside the house fast enough. I could feel the tears streaming down my face; I fought the urge to scream. I locked the dead bolt and started for the phone. It rang before I could pick it up.

I snatched it up. I suspected it was Frank, calling to see if I'd discovered his handiwork. I waited for him to say something.

"Em, is that you?" It was DeWayne. He sounded drunk. "Hey, I'm sorry for barging in on you tonight. I should have called first."

I hadn't realized I was holding my breath. I exhaled. "Oh, Jesus, DeWayne, I thought you were somebody else." I tried to pull myself together, tried to choke back the sob. Instead, I burst into tears.

"What's wrong, Em? What the hell is the matter?"

I told him about Frank's call and about finding Buster in his doghouse with his throat slashed. I was crying uncontrollably by the time I got the whole story out.

"Calm down," he said, talking slowly, repeating it several times. I didn't know if he was doing it for my benefit or his. "Listen to me, Em. Where's the gun?"

"Right here. On the counter next to me."

"Did you lock the door when you came back in?"

His rapid-fire questions took a moment to sink into my

----

dazed brain. "Yes, I think so—" I glanced toward the door, saw that I had. "Yes."

"Where's the key to the dead bolt?"

"Uh, still in the lock."

He sighed. "Someone could break the window in the door and turn it. Put it on the key rack. Do it now while I hold."

I dropped the phone on the counter and did as he said, double-checking the lock to make sure I hadn't accidentally unlocked it in the process. "Okay," I said, once I'd picked up the phone.

"Now, I want you to hide the gun and try to pull yourself together. I'm going to hang up and call the police. Don't answer the door until you see a uniform. Do you understand?"

"Yes." I promised to follow his instructions and hung up the phone. I grabbed the gun, saw that it was sticky with blood but knew I didn't have time to clean it at the moment. I hid it, this time in a boot at the top of my closet. I checked the twins, found them sleeping soundly and prayed they'd continue to do so. I closed the door and turned, and my heart did a somersault in my chest when I saw Molly standing in the hall. Her eyes were red; she'd been crying. She knows, I thought.

"Buster's dead, isn't he?" she asked, eyeing my bathrobe.

I glanced down and saw blood smeared across the front. I hadn't realized I'd gotten it on me. "I'm sorry, honey," I said, stepping closer to her.

I reached for her, and she backed away. The look on her face frightened me. My tears felt hot on my cheeks. "Molly, I feel awful about this, too," I said.

"It's my fault," she said, her tone void of emotion. "I should have left him at the animal shelter."

Once more, I tried to get close. "Honey, it's not your fault. Why would you even think it?"

"Everything I get close to dies."

I shook my head. "You didn't have anything to do with

this." I wanted to tell her that I already knew who was responsible, but I could see her shutting me out.

"You don't know me," she said. "You think you do, but you don't. You don't know how happy I was when I found Lurlene swinging from that rope."

I cringed. "Molly, please—"

"It's true. She was a whore, and I hated her. I used to wish she would die. That way, me and DeWayne could be happy. But Grandma says that if you wish for bad things, the Lord will turn His wrath on you. The Lord has a mighty army, you know. And a lot of wrath."

I stood there, noting the fear in her eyes. The girl was terrified. "Your grandmother was wrong to say that, Molly. This isn't the Lord's work; this is the work of some evil person. You didn't cause this to happen." I could see that I wasn't getting through to her. "Why don't you go lie down?" I suggested. "Chief Hix will be here soon. We'll catch the person who did this—"

"Hix can't help us. Nobody can."

The thought sent a shudder through me, and I was thankful when the doorbell rang. Nevertheless, I could feel my anger rising against my mother, who I was certain had been filling Molly's head with her beliefs. Couldn't she see that the child had been through enough? "That's probably the chief," I said. "Why don't you go back to bed? I'll come in shortly to check on you."

She moved woodenly toward her room.

I watched her go, and I was afraid that irreparable damage had been done.

Chief Hix looked rumpled and out of sorts as he stepped inside with Officer Duffy. He did a double take at the sight of the blood on my robe. I was glad. Maybe now I could get some help.

"Where's the animal?" he asked.

"In his doghouse. It backs up to the house; you can't miss it." I wanted to give accurate directions, since I had no intention of going back out there.

They went out the kitchen door, moving quickly for two

lawmen who weren't used to much action. I dialed Clinton's number, but there was no answer. Surely he'd had time to get home, I thought. I left a quick message on his answering machine and hung up.

Chief Hix was coming through the door when I turned from the phone. "He's dead, all right," he said. "You got something we can wrap him in?"

I had to think for a minute. "There's a plastic drop cloth on a shelf at the back of the garage. It's got yellow paint on it, but I doubt Buster will care one way or the other." He stepped outside, spoke briefly with Duffy and returned. I switched on the automatic coffeemaker and continued to pace while the old chief asked questions and made notes at the kitchen table.

"Tell me exactly what the caller said."

I repeated the conversation word for word, including how Frank had threatened to slice me up like summer sausage. "And it wasn't just *any* caller. It was Frank Gillespie."

He eyed me steadily. "You're positive about that? There's absolutely no doubt in your mind it was Frank?"

I hesitated. "He tried to disguise his voice, but I recognized him anyway." I couldn't tell him how Frank had made the same threat fifteen years earlier. I suddenly realized how wrong I'd been not to come forward in the beginning. Would Molly and I pay for that mistake for the rest of our lives? And if I did decide to tell the truth, what proof did I have? Fludd's service station had been torn down years ago, and replaced with a convenience store. Where was my evidence? I was lost for answers.

The coffeepot sputtered, and I poured us a cup and joined Hix at the table. I thought of my niece in the next room, and my eyes teared. "I don't know how Molly's going to get over this," I said. "She loved that dog."

Hix put down his notepad and rubbed his eyes beneath his glasses. "What would you say to spending a few days at your folks' house, Emily?"

"I don't want to bring them into this. They don't know I've been having trouble."

The phone rang. I jumped up and grabbed it before it had a chance to ring a second time. Clinton spoke from the other end. I filled him in briefly. "Chief Hix is here now," I told him.

"I'm on my way." He hung up without another word.

I rejoined the chief at the table where he was back to making notes: time, date, nature of the crime. I watched him write. His hands trembled. I wondered if he was nervous or if he was just getting old.

Finally he looked up at me, his expression perplexed. "I have to tell you, this is one baffling case," he said. "Here you are swearin' it's got to be Frank, and I just can't find the proof. The boy's doing everything he can to show us how he's changed."

"I know all about it," I told him bluntly. "I know he's joined his mother's church and is setting the world on fire with his community service work. But I don't believe it for an instant.

Hix seemed to ponder this, but I didn't think he was convinced. He tapped his pencil against the notepad.

Officer Duffy stepped into the kitchen, and I offered him coffee, which he politely declined. "I wrapped the animal in plastic and put him behind the garage," he told me. "You'll want to bury him as soon as possible."

"Unless you want us to take him," the chief said.

I considered it. Although I didn't want Molly to see Buster like he was, I suspected it would be healthier for us to hold some kind of funeral for him. Even if Molly balked at the idea, I wanted to offer her the choice. "I'll see that he's buried," I said.

Hix looked at Duffy. "Get Patrolman Finley on the radio," he said. "I need to talk to him."

Duffy did as he was told, then passed Hix his handheld radio. Hix carried it into the living room, where I heard him mumbling softly to someone on the other end between short bursts of static that I hoped wouldn't wake the twins. He was still talking when I heard a car pull up. A moment later, Clinton tapped on the kitchen door. I opened it, and

----

he must've read my relief at having him there. "You okay?" he said, slipping his arm around me. I nodded but didn't trust myself to speak.

"If you weren't so upset, I'd have your ass for going out there alone tonight. Do you realize the danger you put yourself in?"

"I—I had to know, Clinton," I managed. "I couldn't stand not knowing whether Buster was—" Tears smarted in my eyes once more. "I tried to call you right after it happened, but you didn't answer."

He looked embarrassed. "I couldn't sleep, so I took a walk. Where's Buster now?"

"Behind the garage. Officer Duffy wrapped him in plastic."

Clinton thanked the officer, then looked at me. "I'll bury him in the morning, if you like. How's Molly?"

"Not good."

He led me to the table. "Sit down, babe; your knees are shaking." He waited until I was seated. "Tell me everything."

I repeated what I'd told Hix.

"And you didn't see or hear anything?"

"Nothing. No bark, not even a whimper."

Hix came into the room, handed Duffy the radio and regarded Clinton. "I'll bet your colleagues in Chicago would think this is silly, us making a big to-do over somebody killing a dog."

"Not at all."

Hix looked at me. "Frank Gillespie spent the evening at the movies. They were running a double feature tonight, and Frank's car never left the parking lot."

I wiped my eyes. "How do we know he didn't slip out the back exit and make his way here on foot?" I asked. "The theater's less than five minutes from here by car. He would have had plenty of time."

Hix looked at Clinton. "I'm sure the theater is closed by now, but we can question the manager first thing tomorrow. They run matinees on weekends, so he'll probably be in early." He paused. "You got any ideas?" he asked Clinton tiredly.

Clinton poured a cup of coffee and took the chair next to mine. "It doesn't take a genius to realize that somebody's got something personal against Emily."

"Or maybe this person has something against the kid," Hix replied. "Don't forget: He's threatened her twice."

I snapped my head up as he said it. "That's crazy," I said. "Molly's only thirteen years old. What could anyone possibly have against her?"

"Think about it, Emily," Hix said. "How much do you really know about your niece or the way she lived before your sister's death? We know Lurlene was buying nose candy out the kazoo." He glanced at Clinton. "Cocaine," he added, "in case you didn't know."

"Ah, yes." Clinton nodded, as though he'd somehow managed to escape the street talk during all his years with the Chicago police force.

"Could be Lurlene owed somebody a lot of money. Maybe that's why she killed herself. It wouldn't be the first time someone took that way out of their financial problems."

I listened. I'd known my sister was involved in drugs, so none of this was a surprise. That's why I'd called the Department of Social Services to begin with. "I don't see what any of this has to do with Molly," I said.

"Maybe the person or persons who sold your sister drugs knows Molly can identify him or her. Maybe these threats are really aimed at Molly."

I knew that wasn't the case. "I think you're looking in the wrong direction," I told him, not for the first time. "And I refuse to let you drag my niece into this. She's taking it hard enough as it is. Besides, if what you're saying is true, then why is this person waiting until now to come after her? You want me to answer that? Because the person responsible for this was in prison until just recently."

Both men were silent as they heard me out.

"You know what bothers me most?" Clinton asked after

a moment. "I was here for dinner tonight, and the dog barked several times. I remember thinking he was a pretty good watchdog. So why didn't he bark when this person slipped into the yard tonight?"

"Because he knew the person," Chief Hix said matter-of-factly.

Clinton nodded. He must've seen the horror on my face, because he went on quickly. "That doesn't mean it had to be someone close to you, of course. It could just mean that the person responsible for killing Buster made friends with him over the past few days. He could have dropped by now and then when he knew you weren't home, given Buster a couple of dog biscuits and split."

I was so caught up in the conversation that I was only vaguely aware of Duffy talking on the radio. He carried it outside, no doubt to keep the noise down and not wake the girls. A moment later, he called for the chief.

Hix got up, mumbled something under his breath and joined Duffy outside. When he reentered the kitchen, he wore a frown. "That was dispatch," he said. "Seems DeWayne Tompkins got lickered up tonight and decided to take the law into his own hands. He showed up at Frank Gillespie's house a few minutes ago with a double-barreled shotgun."

19

The news hit me hard, making me suddenly sick to my stomach. I knew DeWayne would never have done something so stupid if he hadn't wanted to protect Molly and me. I covered my face. "What else can go wrong?" I asked.

"DeWayne's lucky," Hix said. "If Augustus hadn't wrestled the gun from him, Conners would be booking him for murder right now. Seems DeWayne was so drunk he could barely stand."

I began to cry. Clinton put his arms around me.

Hix's tone softened. "Look, if it'll make you feel better, I'll see if I can get the judge and the prosecutor to come in tomorrow and arraign DeWayne so you can go ahead and bail him out."

"How much do you think it will cost?" I asked.

"That's up to the judge. But I'm going to have to book him with disorderly conduct and attempted assault with a deadly weapon. Could run as much as twenty grand. A bondsman would have to have about ten percent of that."

"I don't have that kind of money," I said.

Hix was quiet for a moment. "Well, DeWayne's never been in trouble before, not even for a DUI, surprisingly enough. And he's held a steady job for years. They might let him out on a signature bond. I'll call you as soon as I know something." He sighed. "In the meantime, I'm going to leave Duffy here with you, just in case."

I had about as much faith in Duffy as I had in DeWayne, who was probably passed out cold in a jail cell by now.

"I'll stay," Clinton said. "I was going to offer anyway."

Hix nodded. "It'd help me out. I don't have much of a staff. Not like they got in Chicago," he added in a voice that suggested he didn't much care for big-city police departments anyway. "I'll have a patrolman in the area." He looked at me. "You gonna be okay?"

I nodded but refused to look his way. I couldn't seem to stop the tears from flowing. Finally, Clinton showed them out.

"Where do you want me to sleep?" Clinton asked the moment we were alone.

"I'm afraid it'll have to be the couch." I suddenly remembered the girls. "Excuse me." I hurried out of the room and peeked into the guest room. A night-light illuminated the twins, who'd obviously slept through the whole thing. Deciding to check on Molly, I found her lying on her side, eyes wide open. I approached her bed.

"Molly?"

No answer.

"Molly, I'm really sorry about Buster. *Really* sorry," I added. "Do you feel like talking about it?"

She didn't respond; in fact, she didn't give any indication that she'd heard me. "Okay," I said. "We can wait until tomorrow." I left her staring straight ahead at nothing. I think that's what bothered me most. It would have been easier if she'd cried or railed at the unfairness of life, but she didn't.

I left the room and went to the linen closet, where I pulled out sheets and blankets. Clinton insisted on making up the couch himself. "Thanks for staying," I said, then worried about what I'd tell the twins when they found him there in the morning. He must've read my thoughts.

"I've already set the alarm on my watch. I'll be out of here before the girls wake up, and I'll take the dog with me."

"That would probably be best," I said, deciding that I

wouldn't put Molly through the trauma of a doggie funeral after all. It might have proved therapeutic for some children, but I suspected she'd dealt with enough death during the past year. "I appreciate all you've done, Clinton."

"I'm sorry about DeWayne."

There didn't seem to be anything left to say. I told him good-night and made my way to my own room, where I slipped out of my bloodstained gown, scrubbed, and pulled on a fresh one. I washed my face and brushed my teeth, then climbed into bed.

Silent tears streamed down my cheek, tears of sadness and fear and exhaustion. I didn't know how Molly and I could go on. I wished now that I hadn't canceled our last appointment with Cordia, because I was going to have to set up something with her as soon as I could.

Someone tapped lightly on my door, and I swiped at my wet cheeks and turned on my lamp. Maybe it was Molly wanting to talk after all. "Come in," I said softly.

Clinton peeked in. "I was just wondering if I could borrow a pillow. Hey, are you crying?"

I nodded and offered him a weak smile. " 'Fraid so."

"May I come in for a minute?"

I shrugged. "Might as well. I doubt I'm going to get much sleep tonight anyway."

He stepped in and closed the door behind him quietly. His eyes did a quick sweep of the room, and I wondered if it was habit that made him check his surroundings first or if he was just curious about what my bedroom looked like. He walked to the bed. I noticed that he'd taken off his shoes and unbuttoned his shirt, which offered a partial view of his chest and stomach. I would not have been female had I not looked—and noticed the dense black hair and muscle.

"Mind if I sit?" he asked.

Another shrug. I couldn't speak without crying, and I didn't want him to be nice and sympathetic because that's all it'd take to have me sobbing uncontrollably. So I just

----

sat there, refusing to speak or even meet the look in his eyes.

He sat on the edge of the bed, then took my hand. "Look, I know this is hard on you and Molly, but I've solved some pretty tough cases in my day. I'll find out who's doing this and put a stop to it if it's the last thing I do."

My eyes filled. The tears slid down my cheeks, and I didn't try to stop them. I felt broken inside. "Why would someone kill a poor, dumb mutt who never hurt anyone?" I asked.

Clinton shook his head. He looked sad. Finally he pulled me into his arms so that my head was resting against his chest. "I don't know why people do the things they do," he said. "I've seen enough cruelty and violence to last a lifetime, and I'm still appalled at what goes on. You'd think I'd get used to it."

"What happened to you in Chicago?" I asked, unable to contain my curiosity any longer.

He didn't answer for a long time; he simply sat there, holding me. I was comforted by the gentle rise and fall of his chest. I realized that it had been a long time since a man had held me or offered any form of comfort, and I wanted to make the most of it.

"The suspect was a repeat child molester who'd been out of prison less than six months when he raped an eight-year-old girl," he said. "He'd gone on the run, and I was the first to find him." Clinton paused and took a deep breath. His voice was flat; it sounded as though he'd told the story many times.

"The guy obviously had no intention of going back to prison; he was doing everything in his power to get me to shoot him. He taunted me, telling me how much pleasure he got from fucking little boys and girls. I lost it. Beat the shit out of him. Almost killed him, as a matter of fact.

"At the hearing, I was accused of using brutal and undue force. I was suspended without pay. I decided to do everybody a big favor and quit."

"I can't imagine someone siding with a child molester," I said.

"Maybe if the media hadn't gotten involved. They blew it all out of proportion. My lieutenant still has hopes that I'll return one day."

"You don't like working in parole, do you?"

He shrugged. "It grows on you. I still have to deal with sleazebags, but I can handle it."

"Suppose things die down in Chicago. Would you go back?"

"That's the question I keep asking myself. I was a pretty good detective."

We were quiet for a while. My tears had subsided. But I had another worry, this time concerning my feelings for Clinton. Wouldn't it be just my luck to fall madly in love with him in the meantime?

He lay back against a pillow, and I fell asleep in his arms, comforted by the knowledge that I didn't have to face the night alone. I didn't wake until I heard him get up shortly before dawn. I found him folding the bedclothes in the living room. Wordlessly, he stashed them in the closet, took my hand and led me toward the door. I felt his breath on my face before he pressed his lips against my forehead. "Lock up," he said.

A moment later, I heard his car pull away from the house and wondered at the empty feeling in my gut. I went back to bed and fell asleep until eight, when I heard the twins stirring about the kitchen, looking for something to eat. I decided to go all-out since I had company, and I brought out a brand-new box of Honey Nut Cheerios.

I checked on Molly and found her standing in front of her dresser, pulling her hair back. She wore her grungiest jeans and a paint-splattered T-shirt. I wondered what had happened to all the nice things I'd bought her in Savannah. I closed the door, not wanting the twins to overhear our conversation.

"Are you okay?"

The look she tossed my way was one of loathing. "What

----

do you care? While I was up half the night crying over Buster, you were in the next room fucking Clinton.''

I didn't realize I'd slapped her until it was too late. We looked at each other, both obviously in shock, neither of us knowing what to say. Molly's eyes glistened; I was instantly sorry. ''Oh, Molly, I didn't mean to—''

''You're no different from Lurlene,'' she blurted. ''You'll be punished just like she was.''

''Molly, listen to me—''

''Leave me alone!''

I decided that was best, with the twins just in the next room. I would try to talk to Molly later, when we were alone. I left her in her room and hurried into the kitchen, poured another cup of coffee and tried to pull myself together. Maryjane and Beth were watching me curiously; they'd obviously heard the commotion in Molly's room.

I smiled and tried to pretend everything was okay. ''So, I think the visit went pretty well, don't you? We'll have to do it again real soon.'' They ate their cereal and didn't say a word.

The phone rang at eight-thirty, and I snatched it up quickly. It was Clinton. ''How's it going? Were you able to go back to sleep once I left?''

''For a little while,'' I said. ''Listen, I need a favor. Would you look after the girls while I run into town?'' I asked, being deliberately vague. ''Shouldn't take long,'' I added.

''You going to see about bailing DeWayne out?''

''It's the least I can do.''

''I'll be there in half an hour.''

I left the girls to eat their breakfast while I grabbed a quick shower, put on minimal makeup and slipped into a pair of slacks and a starched white shirt. I called Myrtle at the police department, asked about DeWayne's charges and was told that Hix had already taken him before the judge and prosecutor and was on the phone trying to convince a local bondsman to issue DeWayne a signature bond. She would call me back when she knew something.

Clinton arrived looking freshly showered, dressed in jeans and a long-sleeved shirt. It was frightening how much I was beginning to depend on him. I told him what was going on as I poured us each a cup of coffee. Finally, Myrtle called back with good news. Hix had managed to get DeWayne released on the signature bond, and I could come for him. I grabbed my jacket and hurried out the door, promising to be back as soon as I could.

I drove the few short blocks to the police department, where Myrtle told me to wait while they finished up the paperwork. After what seemed like a very long time, DeWayne joined me in the lobby of the station room, shot me an apologetic look and followed me out to the car. I remained silent until we were both inside.

"I'm sorry, Em," he said. "I didn't mean to get you involved."

I looked at him. His eyes were bloodshot, his clothes wrinkled. He reeked of booze. "You look like shit, you know that?" He glanced away as though embarrassed. "Do you have any idea how much trouble you're in?"

"I did it because I love you," he said. "And because nobody else would help you. I would gladly have killed Frank for you."

I sighed and leaned against the steering wheel. "Oh, DeWayne." I didn't know what to say. I could feel him looking at me, studying me intently.

"What's going on between you and Clinton Ward?"

I raised my head. "Nothing." I could tell by the look he shot me that he didn't believe me.

"If he cared for you, he'd send Frank Gillespie back to prison, and we could go on with our lives. How do you know Augustus hasn't paid him off? What do you really know about this guy, anyway?"

I realized that I knew very little about Clinton personally. Professionally, I knew he'd left the Chicago Police Department under bad circumstances. Nevertheless, I didn't think Clinton was the type of man who could be bought. I started my engine. "He can't send Frank back to jail until we have proof."

"Yeah, well, it might be too late then."

I felt a shiver race up my spine at the thought. We made the short drive to his place in silence. I couldn't decide if the Orange Grove Motel was more offensive by day or by night. "I hear you've been out to the house," I said.

He looked at me. "Who told you that?"

"People talk."

"Yeah, right. A man can't take a piss in this town without everybody knowing."

"Are you considering moving back?" I asked hopefully, thinking it might restore DeWayne's sense of pride if he had something to work for.

"Why would I do that? So I can relive all those happy memories?"

I touched his arm lightly. "There were *some* happy ones."

He stared straight ahead. I saw his eyes glisten. "All I ever wanted was a family. Someone to come home to after a long week on the road. A *good* woman. I gave Lurlene everything. I treated Molly like my own. Then I realized that I'd married a woman just like my mother." He sighed and pinched the bridge of his nose. "I still have nightmares about that woman."

My heart ached for him. He looked like he was in so much pain. "You're going to destroy yourself if you continue to live in the past. Let it go, DeWayne. You've got to move on."

He shrugged. "That's why I went by the house. I thought that if I went back, I could sort of come to terms with it." He sighed. "I should probably sell it."

We sat there for a long moment, neither of us saying anything. I remembered that Clinton was with the girls, and I'd promised to take the twins to see their new baby brother. "I have to go," I said at last, although I hated to leave him like this. "Are you going to be all right?"

He nodded as he opened the door and climbed out. "I'm

fine. Look, I don't want you coming back out here. It's not safe.''

"Which is why I wish you'd move."

"Maybe I will. Now get going. I don't want to have to worry about a couple of druggies getting their hands on you.''

I pulled away feeling bad for DeWayne, feeling depressed that his life had been reduced to a bottle and a dumpy motel room. Still, what could I do? I wasn't his wife. I couldn't go before a judge and demand that he get help. Until DeWayne was ready to help himself, there was nothing much anyone could do.

20

The twins were dressed and watching cartoons when I returned home. Clinton sat at the kitchen table, reading the morning paper. He glanced up as I made my way into the kitchen.

"Is he out?"

I nodded and poured myself a cup of coffee. "Forget all the mean things I've said about Chief Hix. He went out of his way to help." I joined him at the table. "Has Molly come out of her room?"

"No. I assumed she was still asleep. So what's on the agenda for today?"

"We're supposed to go by the hospital to see the new baby. I'll have to call first and see what time."

"Want me to drive you over?"

"That won't be necessary. I don't think I'll have any trouble in broad daylight."

He looked thoughtful. "Okay, I need to run by the station for a while. You can call me there if something comes up. In the meantime, I want you to stay on the main roads wherever you go. Don't take shortcuts through alleys or back roads."

"Yes, boss."

"I'm serious, Emily." He glanced at his watch and stood. "I'd better go."

We stood there for a moment, looking at one another. I realized we'd reached that awkward stage in a relationship when partings can be uncomfortable. I sensed that Clinton felt it as well. We were more than friends, but we weren't lovers.

He took my hand and squeezed it. "I'll see you later."

I nodded. "Thanks. For everything."

I called Lilly at the hospital and discovered that we could visit anytime we liked. Her mother-in-law had just arrived in town, so I could pass the girls on to her when we arrived. I found Molly in her room, staring at a wall. Once again, her room was silent. Her CD player had been draped with a sheet, her phone unplugged. She'd straightened her room.

"What's going on, Molly?" I asked, suspecting that she was reacting to Buster's death.

"Nothing."

"We're going to the hospital."

"I suppose you want me to go, too."

"I can't leave you here by yourself."

She got up from the bed and moved to her closet, her expression sad and weary. I left her so I could help the twins get their things together. Molly emerged ten minutes later, wearing neat slacks and a pullover sweater.

"You look nice," I said, surprised that she'd changed of her own accord.

I packed Beth and Maryjane into the backseat of my car, tossed their belongings into the trunk and waited for Molly to join me in the front seat. She didn't reach for the radio as she normally did; instead, she stared straight ahead. The drive to Mossy Oaks Memorial took less than ten minutes. The old hospital was under constant renovation, and I wondered how the patients managed to get any rest with all the noise.

Stoney and his mother were standing at a window looking into the nursery when we stepped off the elevator into the maternity ward. Beth and Maryjane and I oohed and aahed over the newest member of the Dunseath family while Molly stood in the background and stared at her feet. Finally I told them I wanted to see Lilly. Molly followed.

When we stepped into the room, the new mother was

----

sitting up in bed reading a magazine. "My, you've lost weight," I said.

Lilly frowned. "Only twelve pounds—do you believe it?"

"The rest will come off easily enough."

Molly sat in a chair at the end of the bed and nodded when Lilly spoke to her.

"So, were the girls well behaved?" Lilly asked, once I explained that they were out at the nursery getting acquainted with their new brother.

"They were perfect," I said.

"Actually, they're lucky to be alive," Molly said sadly. I froze.

I saw the smile fade from Lilly's mouth. "What?"

Molly sat up straight in her chair. Her eyes were glazed. "Didn't Aunt Emily tell you what happened? Someone came into our backyard last night and slit my dog's throat."

Lilly gasped and looked at me. "Oh, how awful. Do you have any idea who it was?"

I was still stunned by Molly's outburst. "We didn't see or hear anything," I managed. "Chief Hix is looking into it."

"This isn't the first time things have happened," Molly said. "Someone's been breaking into our house for a couple of weeks now. He left a dead rat on our kitchen table." She looked pleased when she saw how thoroughly shocked I was that she knew about the rat.

Lilly turned to me, and there was accusation in her eyes. "You should have told me."

I stepped closer. I was still trying to figure out how Molly knew so much. "He'd stopped for a while, Lilly. I thought it was over. Believe me, I would never have invited the girls otherwise. A policeman spent the night at the house last night to make sure we were safe."

"He's not a policeman," Molly said hatefully. "He's your lover."

"Molly, that's enough," I said. I could feel the heat on my cheeks. Why was she doing this? Did she hate me that much? I turned to my friend and found her watching me, her expression hurt and confused.

"I can't believe you'd take such a chance with my children," she said.

"I'm sorry, Lilly. I was only trying to help."

"By putting Beth and Maryjane in danger?" She looked at me for a long moment. "Do you have any idea what it would do to me to lose them?" She paused. "No, you can't possibly know. You've never had children of your own."

I stood there, letting the hurt wash over me. Lilly had every right to be angry, of course. I'd been thoughtless, having her girls at my place with so much going on. But she and Stoney had been in a bind, and I'd just naturally agreed to help without thinking it through. I could see now how wrong I'd been. "I should probably go," I said at last. "I'll call you later, okay?"

There was no response. I started from the room with Molly following. In the hall, I turned to her. If I had expected her to look triumphant over what she'd done, I was wrong. She looked sad and disoriented. Nevertheless, I wanted to shake her. "I thought I had seen you at your worst," I said, "but I was wrong. I'd like to know just how in the hell you found out about that rat."

"I hear things."

"You've been listening to my phone conversations with Clinton, haven't you?"

She didn't answer. She didn't have to. "Can we go now?"

"Did Henry put that rat on the kitchen table?"

"Why would he do something like that?"

"I've no idea. Nothing makes sense anymore. But you need help, Molly. We have to call Cordia."

"Cordia can't help me. Nobody can."

I wondered the same thing as we walked out of the hospital.

There were several messages on my answering machine when I got home. One of them was Clinton, asking me to call as soon as I returned. My mother had called to make sure that Molly and I would be at church the following morning and told me to plan to come for dinner. The next message chilled me. I recognized the muffled voice from the previous night.

"I know where the dog is buried," he said. "Don't be surprised if I dig him up and put him on your doorstep."

I winced at hearing the cruel words. I imagined Molly and me leaving for school and finding Buster on the front porch, stiff and bloody. My hands shook as I dialed Clinton. When he answered, I repeated the message verbatim.

"Did you recognize the voice?" he asked.

"It was muffled like before." I sighed heavily. "I'm just so sick of this whole thing. If Frank wants to hurt me, why doesn't he just meet me face to face and get it over with? Why all these mind games?"

"I did some checking around this morning," Clinton said. "Frank *did* go to the movies last night, a double feature. Started at seven-thirty, lasted till eleven-thirty. He arrived home shortly before midnight and went straight to bed."

"And who told you that? Augustus? Don't think he wouldn't lie for Frank."

"I called the theater late this morning and talked with the manager. He remembered seeing Frank last night. He was sort of keeping an eye on him because of something he'd done in the past. Seems that Frank started a fire once when the theater was full and caused a big panic.

"Anyway, he said Frank took a bathroom break between movies, bought a box of popcorn and went back in for the second show. Didn't come out until after it was over."

"Clinton, you know darn well that he could have slipped out one of the exits without being seen. How long does it take to slit a dog's throat? He'd have had plenty of time to get back."

"I think you're grasping at straws here, Emily. If you want to consider Frank a suspect, that's fine. But keep an open mind. We might be staring the person right in the face and not know it.''

I wondered if he was hinting at Molly, then decided I was letting my imagination get the best of me. Molly'd loved Buster. She wasn't capable of killing him.

You don't know me. You think you do, but you don't. You don't know how happy I was when I found Lurlene swinging from that rope.

It was ridiculous that I would even consider such a thing. Besides, how would Molly have gotten out last night without my seeing her? Crawl out her window? That was highly unlikely, given that she would have had so much trouble getting back in. The house was raised at least a foot off the ground, making the window too high for her to climb back in. And how would she have made those calls?

No, it wasn't Molly, I told myself. Molly might be a lot of things, but she wasn't a killer, and she had no reason to hurt me. A thought nagged at me. I tried to push it away, but it refused to let go. What if Molly *knew* who was doing these things and was keeping secrets? No, I couldn't imagine her doing that, either.

''Are you still there?'' Clinton asked, rousing me from my disturbing thoughts.

''I'm sorry; my mind was elsewhere.''

''Anything you'd care to share?''

''I don't have any answers, if that's **what** you're asking. Only questions.''

''Do you have a grill?'' he asked.

I wondered what that could possibly have to do with anything. ''It's in the garage someplace. Why?''

''I thought I'd pick up some steaks later. Maybe one of us will come up with some ideas in the meantime.''

Despite all that was going on, I looked forward to seeing him again. ''Sure. I'll put together a salad and stick some potatoes in the oven to bake.''

''Six o'clock okay?''

''Fine.'' I knew I didn't sound enthusiastic. I wanted to

tell him how strange Molly was acting, but I couldn't. Not without heaping more suspicion on her.

"I'll be at the station if you need me," he said before hanging up.

Next I called the mental health center and got a recording saying that all the offices were closed. I was offered another number in case I was in crisis. I hung up. I looked up Cordia's home number and dialed. I was greeted with yet another answering machine. I slammed the phone down, feeling more frustrated by the minute.

I heard Molly's bedroom door open, and she came into the kitchen carrying a box filled with CDs. She dumped the box on the table. "I've decided not to listen to this stuff anymore," she said. "All they sing about is sex and getting high."

"Molly, I have something to ask you," I said. She paused but kept her back to me. "Turn around so I can see your face." She did so. I could tell she'd been crying. "I want to know if Grandma has been saying things to you. About her religion, I mean."

"I know we're living in the final days," she said. "I know that when the end comes, the bad people are going to suffer greatly. Those who aren't saved will be tortured and dismembered, their throats cut wide open like Buster's."

The words came out sounding like a litany. "Grandma didn't tell you this," I said, knowing my mother wouldn't go quite that far. I stepped closer, determined to get to the bottom of it. "Who told you this, Molly?"

She eyed me steadily. "I read about it."

"In the Bible?"

"Just some book. I don't remember the name of it."

"Do you still have it?"

She shook her head. "I don't know what happened to it."

"Who gave it to you?"

"I don't remember. Why are you asking all these questions?"

"Because you're starting to worry me. You're not yourself."

"Maybe it has something to do with the fact that my dog was murdered last night."

"We can get another dog," I said, knowing that wouldn't come close to solving the problem but not having any other ideas at the moment.

"Why, so he can get his throat cut, too?"

"Molly—" I reached for her.

She stepped away, avoiding my touch. "May I go to my room now?"

I knew we needed to talk, knew there was much more to be said, yet I had no idea how to go about it. "I don't want you reading that book anymore," I told her. "And if you find it, I want to see it."

She suddenly looked furious with me. "I told you that I don't know what happened to it. Why do you keep bringing it up?" She flounced out of the room angrily. A second later, her bedroom door slammed.

Clinton arrived promptly at six, carrying a large, brown sack. Just seeing him again lifted my spirits.

"I thought about you today," he said. "A lot."

"I thought about you, too. You want a drink?" I was already reaching beneath the sink for the bottle of scotch, and I realized I was looking forward to drinking it because I needed something to calm me down. I had already put the potatoes in to bake and prepared a tossed salad. Although I'd set the table for three, I wondered if Molly would come out of her room long enough to eat.

She hadn't budged all day. I'd heard her on the phone a couple of times and had decided that was a good sign. If she couldn't talk to me about what was bugging her, perhaps she could take her problems to her friends.

Clinton handed me a package of thick New York strips, and I put them in the refrigerator. "I bought a bag of charcoal and some lighter fluid, just in case," he said. "You say your grill is in the garage?"

"It was the last time I saw it."

He let himself out the side door. A moment later, I heard him dragging the grill into the backyard. He was dumping charcoal into it when I carried out the drinks. "Hold these a second," I said. "I'm going to grab a couple of folding chairs." I hurried into the garage, found the chairs and carried them out.

"What's Molly up to?" he asked as he squirted lighter fluid onto the charcoal.

"She's in her room. She's going through a bad time right now, what with losing Buster." I sighed. "I don't know how I can help her." I paused as I saw something through one of the azalea bushes, something that I hadn't noticed before. I set down my drink and walked over to it. Pulling the bush away, I found myself staring down at a wooden box that had once belonged to my father. He'd kept tools in it until I bought him a nice metal box for his birthday. I had brought the wooden box with me three years ago during my move, put it in the garage and forgotten about it.

"What is it?" Clinton asked, having followed me over.

"I'm not sure." The box was homemade, about three feet long and a good eighteen inches wide and deep, with rusted hinges along the back. A combination lock was affixed to the latch, the combination long forgotten. I would have to use a hacksaw to get it off, and I didn't own one, which was why the box had been sitting in my garage for so long. Now it was partially hidden behind the hedges, directly beneath Molly's window. Lying flat, it wasn't much help, but when I turned it up, it reached the window easily.

"Would you mind telling me what you're doing?" Clinton asked.

I stepped away from the window in case Molly was listening from her room. "I think Molly could have used this box to sneak in and out of her window."

He seemed to ponder it. "Well, it wouldn't be the first

time a kid sneaked out. Do you think she's meeting somebody?''

I could tell he didn't get it. "What if she sneaked out last night?''

"Are you suggesting she might have seen who killed Buster?'' When I merely looked at him, he went on. "Surely you don't think *she* did it?'' When I continued to stare at the box, he went on. "No way, Emily. The person who killed that dog knew what they were doing. The poor animal was almost decapitated.''

I shuddered at the thought of poor Buster, whose only sin was not knowing how to fetch a ball. I regretted bringing him home in the first place. "I saw Molly mistreat the dog a couple of times,'' I told him. "I'd even threatened to take him away if she continued.''

He motioned for me to follow him over to the grill so he could check the coals. A small fire was still burning. "Kids don't always have a lot of patience with animals, but that doesn't mean they're capable of killing them.''

"You're the one who suggested that this person was someone close to me.''

"Yeah, but not Molly.''

Naturally, my next thought was Henry.

Clinton was quiet for a moment. "Have you considered that it might be DeWayne?''

I felt my jaw drop open. I closed it. "Boy, you really don't like him, do you?''

"Whether I like him or not has nothing to do with it. I don't think you can rule him out entirely.''

"What possible reason would he have for trying to hurt me?''

Clinton shook his head. "I can't answer that; I don't know him as well as you do.''

I gazed back at Clinton, wondering if he was letting personal feelings get in the way of his professional judgment. "DeWayne and I have been friends for a long time,'' I said. "We sort of leaned on one another after my sister did what she did. He might be a drunk, but he's not a killer.

Besides, he wasn't even in town when all this started. I specifically remember him telling me he'd been on the road for two weeks.''

"He could have lied."

"And how about last night? Why would he show up at Frank Gillespie's house with a shotgun if he was the guilty one?"

Clinton held his hands out. "I'm just trying to offer possibilities. I didn't say DeWayne did it, but I want you to look at everyone as a suspect until we know otherwise."

I covered my face with my hands. "I don't know what to think anymore." I looked up. My insides were coming apart. "You're just trying to get me off Frank's tail, aren't you? You're using DeWayne as a diversionary tactic. Did you make some sort of deal with Augustus?" I didn't realize how loudly I was talking until I stopped.

Clinton put his hands on my shoulders. "Calm down, Emily. Here, sit down and take a sip of your drink." He waited until I sat, then knelt before me, placing his hands on my knees.

"First of all, I don't make deals, especially with bullies like Augustus Gillespie, and I *have* been checking Frank's whereabouts just in case. But I've been in the business long enough to know that you have to keep an open mind in these situations. I'm not trying to point a finger; I'm merely trying to get you to look at all the possibilities."

"I think I'm losing my mind."

"You're under a lot of stress." He was quiet for a moment. "Listen, I was thinking. Why don't I stay here for a while? Just until we find out who's behind this."

The thought pleased me greatly. At least I would be able to close my eyes at night without fear of someone coming in on us. Then I thought of my niece. "Molly's not real happy about the fact that you stayed here last night. She thinks . . . well, you can imagine."

"She thinks we're lovers?" I nodded. "It's not a *bad* idea," he said, giving me a smile, "but I think I'd prefer to make love to you when you don't have so much on your mind. You have a guest room, right?''

My stomach had taken a dive the minute he'd mentioned the possibilities of us going to bed together. ''I don't know, Clinton. What would my neighbors think? What if my parents found out? They don't know I'm having problems.''

''I'll be very discreet about it,'' he said. ''I can keep my car in your garage.''

''You've seen my garage.''

''What I meant to say was, I can keep my car in your garage as soon as I've cleaned it. I'll work on it tonight after dinner, then drive to my place for clothes. We'll talk to Molly together, explain why we think my being here is necessary. She'll probably welcome it after what happened to her dog.''

I considered it as I went inside for the steaks. I knew I'd feel better having Clinton around. Now all I had to do was break the news to Molly.

21

Thirty minutes later, Clinton, Molly and I sat down to a nice steak dinner. Although I'd managed to convince her to join us, she was quiet throughout the meal, and she picked at her food. She was scared. I could see it in her eyes, and I wanted to reassure her that everything was going to be okay. "Clinton has offered to stay with us for a while," I blurted, deciding just to lay it on the line.

She didn't bother to look up. "That's convenient."

"I think it's a good idea under the circumstances. Naturally, he'll sleep in the guest room."

She looked at him. "You think somebody's going to come in here and do the same thing to us that they did to Buster?" she asked.

Clinton shook his head. "No. I believe the person behind this is trying to scare you and your aunt, and nothing more. But it has gone on long enough, and I'm going to do everything in my power to catch him. It'll be easier with me in the house."

"Which is why we have to keep Clinton's presence a secret," I said. "He's going to hide his car in the garage. I don't want you talking about it at school, and I certainly don't want you mentioning it to Grandma and Grandpa tomorrow at church. Can I trust you to keep quiet?"

Molly seemed to need time to think about it. Finally she nodded. "I won't say anything." She looked directly at me.

"And I'm sorry for what I did at the hospital. I hope Lilly doesn't stay mad at you forever."

"So do I."

"Can I get up now?"

"One last thing," I said, feeling brave now that she'd opened up. "Did you drag Grandpa's old toolbox out of the garage?"

She looked from me to Clinton and back to me again. "Was I not supposed to?"

Her response told me she had. "What were you using it for?"

"I was teaching Buster to jump over it. I pushed it behind the bushes when I finished so it'd be out of the way. And so it wouldn't get wet if it rained." She must've sensed a problem. "You can ask Beth and Maryjane if you don't believe me."

It sounded plausible. I tried to hide my relief. "You can go ahead and get up," I said. "I'll clean the kitchen tonight."

Clinton shoved his chair out from the table and carried his plate to the sink. "I'll be in the garage."

"I'll come out and help as soon as I put the leftovers away."

"No need," he said. "It won't take me long."

By the time Clinton had made room for his car in the garage and gone home for his clothes, I had straightened the house and put in a couple of loads of laundry, which I was now folding in front of the eleven o'clock news. They ran a short segment on Cindy Brown and showed footage of Chief Hix and two of his men leading Randy Dempsey from the jail into the courtroom for his arraignment.

"Well, that should make the good citizens of Mossy Oaks rest easier tonight," Clinton said, sarcasm slipping into his voice. "Too bad they got the wrong man."

I was too tired to think about it. "I've put fresh sheets on your bed," I said. "You'll find spare towels in the bathroom off the hall."

"I'll be fine. Go to bed; you look exhausted."

I smiled. "I appreciate everything you've done. I'm sorry for all the bad things I thought about you in the beginning."

He looked amused. "What bad things?"

"You're probably better off not knowing. Good night, Clinton." I left him sitting on the sofa in front of the television set, then decided to check on Molly before I went to bed. To my relief, I found her asleep. No doubt the last couple of days had taken their toll on her.

I awoke the next morning feeling more rested than I had in days, and I knew it was because of Clinton. Sitting at the kitchen table with our first cup of coffee, he noticed the change in me right away.

"The dark circles are gone from under your eyes," he said.

"Thanks to you."

"So what're your plans for the day?"

"Well, Molly and I are meeting my parents for church. Afterward, we'll have dinner at their house. You're welcome to join us after services. My mother's a wonderful cook."

"Just give me directions, and I'll be there."

I took a sip of my coffee. "I feel that I should warn you, though. My mother will automatically assume we're serious about one another and will start making wedding plans. Please don't do or say anything to encourage her. It would be best if you'd just tell her you're gay. Better yet, I'll tell her you're already married, and this is just an affair."

He grinned. "She's pressuring you for grandchildren, right? Don't forget, I have a mother, too."

I was glad he could relate. "Have you ever been married?"

"Once, right after college. It lasted five years. She wasn't crazy about being married to a cop."

"I'm the only remaining unmarried woman in my family, except for cousin Racine, but nobody counts her, so I'm a great source of disappointment to my mother."

"What's the deal with cousin Racine?"

"She weighs three hundred pounds and doesn't shave her legs or bathe on a regular basis."

"Hmmm, and Molly said there were no pretty women in this town."

"I'll be sure to invite you to our next family reunion. Racine never misses them."

A subdued Molly and I left the house a little later. "I know you're very sad right now," I told her, "but I'd appreciate it if you'd try to act like everything's normal. At least until we have a better idea what's going on."

"Why are we being secretive?" she asked.

"You know how Grandma and Grandpa worry. They'll insist that we move in with them for a while." I pondered it for a moment. "You know, Molly, it might not be a bad idea if you stayed with them a few days."

"So you can be alone with Clinton?"

The girl could be so exasperating at times. "That's not it at all, and you know it."

"I don't want to stay with them. They treat me like a baby. I'll run away if you make me."

I looked at her. At this point, she probably *would* run away. "Okay," I said. "But I'll expect you to cooperate with Clinton while he's with us. He's very concerned about our safety."

We arrived at church with little time to spare and joined my parents in the third row from the front—*their* row, as they called it, and the only one they ever sat in. My mother reached across to smooth Molly's hair. It wouldn't have mattered if the girl had just walked out of an expensive salon; my mother would have been able to find a smudge or stray hair or something.

The minister preached about the Prodigal Son, a sermon I'd heard often while growing up. I found myself yawning more than once, capturing my mother's attention and subsequent frown. Afterward, she asked me if I'd slept at all the previous night, and I assured her that I had.

We exited the church, and I immediately thought of Lilly and wondered when her doctor would release her from the hospital. They didn't keep new mothers more than a couple of nights, she'd told me, unless there were problems. I wanted to call her; we'd never been mad at one another for more than a couple of days. Maybe if I apologized again . . .

I headed for my car, but not before I ran into a slew of aunts and uncles and enough cousins to start our own softball team. I visited briefly with each of them while Molly waited for me in the car. I knew better than to ask them what was new. Nothing was ever new. I wondered if my own life had been as dull and uneventful before Frank had gotten out of prison.

I followed my parents to their car and pulled my mother aside. "I hope you don't mind, but I've invited someone to have Sunday dinner with us."

"A man?" she asked, her eyes narrowing. I could see her mind at work.

"Just a friend. He's new in town."

"I wish you had said something earlier. I'm afraid I didn't go to a lot of trouble. But you never bring anyone home with you, so I just made something simple."

I was certain that whatever she'd made was not at all simple. I'd spent enough years with her to know that she went all out on Sunday because when the mood struck her, she'd invite half our relatives to join us. "Mom, it'll be fine," I said. "Are you sure you don't mind if Clinton joins us?"

"Clinton? What's his last name? Is he from around here?"

Once again I could see the calculating look. If Clinton had been from Mossy Oaks, she would already have been searching his family tree for signs of alcoholism, mental illness or birth defects.

"He's from Chicago," I said. "His last name is Ward. He's the new parole officer in town." I decided not to tell her that he was assisting the chief in his investigation of Cindy Brown's murder because I didn't want her asking him questions about the case in front of Molly.

"Hmmm. A Yankee. Well, that's okay, I suppose."

I shook my head. This was the same woman who would have encouraged me to run off with a cousin if it weren't against the law. "I'll call him when we get back to the house," I said.

As was usual, I followed my parents to their house and pulled into the drive behind them. I studied the place, wondering what Clinton would make of it. It was small, but I was proud of where I'd grown up. My parents kept the house and yard in mint condition.

Inside the spotless kitchen, I could smell a ham baking with just a hint of cloves. My mother had made her famous macaroni and cheese, a mouthwatering dish with eggs, three different cheeses and heavy cream. We didn't count fat grams when we ate it. I called Clinton, who promised to be there right away once I gave him directions.

The four of us sipped lemonade on the front porch while we waited for Clinton. My dad, who was used to eating the minute they returned from church, was a bit on the grouchy side, but I humored him and hoped Clinton didn't waste any time getting there.

"So where did you meet your young man?" my mother asked.

"He's not *my* young man," I said, but my mind was busy trying to come up with how we could have met without hinting at the problems I'd had. "We met at the Sip Shoppe," I told her. "I was sitting there having a cup of coffee while Molly was at the bookstore next door; anyway, we just struck up a conversation."

"That's an odd way to meet," she said. "When I was growing up, we met our boyfriends at church or school. We certainly didn't pick them up in some *coffee shop*. What do you know about his family?"

I wondered how my mother had managed to make a simple coffee shop sound like one of those places where tattooed women danced naked on the tables and men rode mechanical bulls in the back. "He's not my boyfriend," I said, wishing now that I'd told her we'd met at Clancy's and both of us had been drunk out of our minds at the time.

"I haven't asked him about his family," I added, "and I don't want you to ask him a bunch of questions, either."

"I've always made it my business to know who your friends are," she said.

"I'm thirty now; I'm officially relieving you of that duty."

"You act as though he has something to hide."

I gave her that look, and she finally changed the subject.

I saw Clinton's car turn the corner, and a moment later he pulled into the driveway. I suddenly wished I hadn't invited him. I got up from my chair and hurried across the yard to greet him, although I imagined that, to my mother's way of thinking, it was a very unladylike thing to do.

He climbed out of his car, closed the door and stood there looking at me. He'd dressed in nice slacks and a pale blue oxford shirt. I was relieved that he hadn't worn his Harley-Davidson T-shirt.

"Hi," he said, grinning broadly. "You're looking very pretty today. Is that your Sunday best?"

He knew perfectly well what I was wearing because he'd seen me when I left the house. But this wasn't something I was about to shout from the rooftops. "I shouldn't have invited you," I whispered. "My mother is making a big deal out of this."

"Don't worry. Most mothers don't approve of me. After today she'll probably stop hounding you to get hitched."

"Don't bet on it," I said between gritted teeth.

My mother had a strange, unreadable look on her face as I made the introductions. I decided that she was mentally trying to select a china pattern for us. She poured Clinton a glass of lemonade, then asked me to come inside and help put the finishing touches on dinner. We had no sooner reached the kitchen than she started.

"How long has this been going on?"

"*Nothing's* going on. Do you want me to set the table?" I asked, changing the subject.

"Use the good china. And your grandmother's silver. And don't forget the linen tablecloth."

"We never use that stuff anymore."

"This is different."

I did as I was told. It was my own fault for inviting Clinton, of course, but I wanted him to see the home where I'd grown up. My mistake. By the time I finished setting the table, you'd have thought the governor was coming.

As usual, my mother outdid herself and had cooked enough food for half the population of Mossy Oaks. Clinton raved about it, and I wanted to tell him he was treading on dangerous territory. My mother sat at her end of the table and accepted his praise, all puffed up like a hen on a cold morning.

I couldn't wait for it to be over. I only hoped she would not show him the fully stocked hope chests she'd started for me years ago, courtesy of S & H Green Stamps and the JCPenney white sales. If I ever do get married, I'll have enough sheet sets and towels to open my own motel.

Molly was quiet at dinner, which my parents would probably have noticed had they not been out to impress Clinton. Once the meal was over, she asked if she could lie down for a while.

"Are you ill?" my mother asked, placing an open palm against her forehead. "You barely touched a thing on your plate. And I made a big bowl of banana pudding, your favorite."

"I'm just tired," Molly said, then, in an obvious attempt not to worry her, smiled. "Maybe I'll feel like eating dessert after my nap."

My mother and I cleaned the kitchen while my father and Clinton watched some sports event on TV. "I need a favor," I said as I dried a plate.

"Sure, honey." She glanced at me.

"I don't want you discussing parts of the Bible with Molly anymore. Like Revelations."

My mother looked surprised. "What makes you think I have been, dear?"

"I think someone is scaring her, and I don't want Molly to live in fear."

The woman sniffed. "We should all fear the Lord."

"I think Molly's spent enough time being afraid, don't you?" I asked gently. "I'm going to stop taking her to church if it doesn't stop."

My mother looked hurt. "I don't know what I could possibly have said to make the child afraid. Could somebody else have said something?"

I thought of the book Molly'd claimed she'd read. "I'm not sure," I told her. "I just wanted to make you aware."

"Well, it's certainly not like her to lie around. She's usually bursting with energy."

This was true, and I suspected that my niece was depressed. Not that she didn't have every reason to be, but I had no intention of sharing this with my mother. I planned to call Cordia first chance I got in the morning. "I'm sure she'll be okay," I said. "She's just tired because she stayed up late watching TV last night." I found that it was getting easier and easier to lie.

Finally it was time to go. My parents walked us to our cars, and I could see that my mother wasn't finished with Clinton yet.

"Perhaps you'll join us for church next week," she suggested.

"You're Baptist, right?" he asked.

She lifted her head proudly. "Born and raised."

"I'm Catholic, myself."

I saw the disappointment in her face. He might as well have told her he was one of those Hare Krishnas who shaved their heads, wore white robes and sold flowers on the street. I could see her plans for my church wedding at Hope Baptist disintegrate.

"We have to go," I said. "I've got a ton of papers to grade."

My parents stood there, smiling and waving as we pulled away, though I could see that my mother's smile was forced. She would call the preacher first thing tomorrow and ask his advice.

I stopped for gas on the way home, and Clinton pulled

into the station as well. "Here, let me pump it for you," he said. He fit the nozzle into the opening of my tank, then gave me a quizzical look. "So what do you think?"

"You didn't win any Brownie points by telling her you're Catholic."

"I noticed that didn't go over so well."

"She'll try to convert you," I told him. "After she does a background check."

"She might not like what she finds." He finished pumping the gas, and I went in to pay. Back at the house, Clinton's car went into the garage. He moved a few more things to the guest room while I urged Molly to get started on her homework.

"I'll help you grade papers, if you like," Clinton said when he was finished unpacking. He had winced when he saw the stack in the middle of the table.

I smiled sheepishly. "Grading papers is not one of my most favorite things to do. I always wait until the kids start bugging me for their scores."

"You got any coffee?"

"I'll put on a pot."

For the next two hours we graded math and spelling tests, a *Weekly Reader* quiz and a question and answer sheet on President Lincoln. Molly finished her homework and said she was tired and wanted to go to bed early. I offered her a sandwich and asked if she wanted to watch TV first, but she declined both.

"Would you like a sandwich?" I asked Clinton. "I don't usually cook on Sunday night since we eat so much at my parents'."

"I'm still stuffed," he said.

The phone rang. It was DeWayne, checking to see if things were okay. "I drove by your house a couple of times earlier," he said. "You weren't home. Are you still mad at me?"

"I think 'disappointed' is a better word."

"Are we on for our lesson tomorrow?"

I hesitated. With Clinton in the house, I wasn't certain I

needed to know how to use a gun. Then I reminded myself that I shouldn't become too needy where he was concerned. Nevertheless, I would have to come up with a good reason to be out. Otherwise, he might want to go with me. I was torn about telling him I was taking shooting lessons. After all, he was involved in law enforcement, and I was carrying a loaded weapon without a permit.

"Emily, are you still there?" DeWayne asked when I hesitated.

"Yes, I'll be there. Same time?"

"Sure. And don't hesitate to call me if something happens tonight."

"I think we'll have a quiet night," I told him. "Last night was uneventful."

I hung up and found Clinton watching me. "Just DeWayne," I said. "Checking to make sure all is okay."

"You're meeting him somewhere tomorrow?"

I felt like I was being interrogated. "Just for coffee. I think he wants to apologize."

Clinton nodded, but he looked troubled. "Be careful, okay?" he said, although I was certain he wanted to say more.

"DeWayne is *not* a suspect," I said emphatically.

"*Everybody's* a suspect."

22

DeWayne and I met the following afternoon. He was dressed in nice slacks and a crisp, button-down shirt. Right away I noted how clear his eyes looked.

"I've given up the booze, Emily," he said. "I haven't had a drink since the night I showed up at the Gillespie place with my shotgun. I even joined AA."

Tears smarted in my eyes. I threw my arms around his neck and hugged him tight. "I'm so proud of you!" I cried.

He shrugged as if it were no big deal, but I knew it hadn't been easy for him to reach his decision. "I didn't want to tell you over the phone last night. I wanted to tell you in person."

"You can do this, DeWayne. It's going to be hard at first. You're going to have to change your whole lifestyle."

He nodded. "I know. Stay out of the bars. I was hoping me, you and Molly could get together once in a while. See a movie. Go roller-skating. I haven't done that in ages."

I had no problem with his spending time with my niece as long as he was sober. "Molly will be thrilled," I said, suspecting that this might be just what she needed to pull her out of her despair.

"And you?"

He'd caught me off guard. "I'm always happy to see you; don't be silly."

We began the lesson, and I managed to hit a respectable number of cans. Two or three times, DeWayne commented that I wasn't holding my arm straight. He stood behind me and showed me what I was doing wrong. After a moment, I realized that he was standing a little too close; I could feel the length of his body pressed against mine, feel his breath warm at the back of my neck. I wondered if I should say something, then told myself I was being ridiculous. He'd never been out of line before.

"Okay, I've got it," I said, moving forward slightly to break the body contact.

"So who's your new houseguest?" he asked when the lesson was over and we headed toward our cars.

I paused. "How'd you know I had a houseguest?"

"I drove by twice last night and noticed that the light was on in your guest room. I figured it was one of your neighbors staying with you." He looked apologetic. "I wasn't trying to snoop, but I wanted to make sure nothing was going on. The truth is, I try to keep myself busy if I can; otherwise I'll just sit home thinking about drinking. So when the urge hits, I hop in the car and take a ride. Sometimes I run to the store for candy and soda; other times I just drive around and think."

I hated to lie to DeWayne, but I knew his feelings would be hurt if he found out Clinton was staying with me—especially since DeWayne had offered twice to move in. I didn't want to do anything that might prompt him to drink. "Mrs. Ramsey from across the street is staying with me," I told him. "She's all alone, so she didn't mind moving in temporarily." I thought he looked relieved, and I wondered if he'd automatically assumed Clinton was there.

"Good idea," he said. "I doubt she'll be much help in an emergency, but if it puts your mind at ease, I'm all for it."

He walked me to my car, saw that the .38 was tucked safely in my purse and started away. "I'll call you about that movie," he said.

"Okay." I pulled away feeling guilty for deceiving him.

Clinton had already put beans into the oven to bake and was in the process of grilling hamburgers when I arrived home. He'd set the table and prepared a tossed salad, and I stared at it for a moment, thinking how great it was to have a domesticated man in the house.

"Grab a soft drink from the refrigerator and join me," he said, heading out the door to check the meat. "I hate to cook alone."

I opened the refrigerator and was amazed to find food inside: a fresh turkey breast, a couple of packs of hamburger meat, a small ham. I checked the cupboards and found them stocked as well. "You bought groceries," I accused him, once I'd joined him in the backyard.

He gave me a peck of a kiss on my forehead. "*Somebody* had to."

"We eat a lot of fast food around here."

"I'll bet your cholesterol level has more digits than my savings account."

"You're not one of those health freaks?" I asked dubiously.

"No, I just like good food. And I don't mind cooking it, if that's what it takes."

I sat down in one of the lawn chairs. "Okay, you cook; I'll clean up."

"Deal. So how'd it go with DeWayne?"

"He stopped drinking. Even started going to AA."

Clinton arched one brow. "I'm impressed. What d'you think made him give it up?"

I shrugged. "I think he felt pretty stupid for showing up at Frank's house with a shotgun, and for getting himself locked up as a result."

"Or maybe he hopes he'll have a chance with you."

I didn't say anything, but I thought of the way DeWayne had stood so close to me earlier. I wanted to think it was an accident, that he'd been so absorbed in what he was doing that he hadn't noticed, but I couldn't be sure. "DeWayne knows we're just friends," I assured him.

"Did you tell him I was staying here?"

"No." I went on to explain why. "I don't want to say or do anything to make him fall off the wagon," I said.

"He's going to find out sooner or later, you know."

I nodded, dreading that moment. I had no desire to hurt DeWayne or lose his friendship.

The following day dragged for me. During recess I scribbled a short note of apology to Lilly and sent it to the office, via one of my most trusted students, for mailing. Once again, I reminded myself that I had not acted wisely by offering to keep the twins at my place with all that was going on, but I had only wanted to help my best friend. It annoyed me beyond belief that my house was not the safe haven it had once been.

Herschel Buckmeyer came out the door and began to pull trash bags from the metal garbage cans. He nodded and walked over to me. He was not the friendly, talkative type, so I was surprised when he sat down on the bench next to me. "I hear you got problems at your place," he said, wearing that sad-sack expression that always made me want to cheer him up.

"News travels fast in this town," I replied.

"Heard someone killed your dog. Who do you reckon would do such a thing?"

Although Herschel and I seldom spoke, he had always gone out of his way to help me when I needed a strong back to carry things to my car or when something broke down in my classroom. I didn't imagine there was much he couldn't fix. "Chief Hix is still looking into it," I said, avoiding answering.

He was quiet for a moment, working his mouth as he often did when he was unsure about something. "Look, I don't like carryin' tales, but I think you should know, I heard Martha Gribble talking about Molly this morning in the teachers' lounge. Made me mad, the things she said."

I tensed. Martha Gribble was our school gossip, and if you wanted to keep something under wraps, you made sure Martha didn't get wind of it. I usually ignored what she said, but I was concerned since the talk was about my niece. "What'd she say?"

"Says she has a friend over at the middle school who claims Molly is going steady with that Henry Dean fellow. Says they can't keep their hands off one another. I don't know if you can believe anything that old biddy says, but I wanted to let you know all the same. Henry Dean's been in some pretty bad trouble for someone his age."

I could see the concern in Herschel's work-worn face, and I was touched that he cared so much. I was also frightened. Molly had convinced me that she and Henry were nothing more than homework buddies; now I had reason to believe there was more to it. Much more.

I was suddenly reminded of the box I'd spied at her bedroom window. Had Molly been slipping out with Henry? If so, there was no telling how far things had gone between them. Should I tell Cordia? Should I have Molly examined by a doctor? I was lost for answers.

"Thank you for coming to me, Herschel," I said. "I'll look into it right away."

My head swam with questions for the rest of the afternoon, and I watched the hands of the clock turn in slow motion toward three o'clock. I had decided that Molly and I were going to have a long talk when we got home. I was going to find out, once and for all, what was going on between Henry and her. I also planned to question her about Buster's death. If she had any ideas about who might have killed him, I was determined to find out.

Unfortunately, we never got the chance to have that talk. When I arrived home, I found Susan Blake and two others from the Department of Social Services waiting on my front porch. I offered Susan my best smile but wondered why she'd brought two staff members with her.

"Hi, Susan," I said. "Were we scheduled to meet today?" I would have been happy to see her under any other circumstances, but right now all I wanted to do was clear up a few matters with my niece.

The black woman didn't return my smile. In fact, she looked near tears. "Emily, these are my supervisors,

Charles Hamilton and Roberta White. We need to speak with you.''

I paused on my front steps. ''Is something wrong? Is Molly—?''

Susan touched my arm. ''Molly's fine. She answered the door but said she's not allowed to have anyone in the house without your permission.''

''Molly knows *you*. I can't believe she'd just leave you out here.''

''Why don't we go inside and talk,'' the man suggested.

I opened the door and motioned for them to come into the living room and sit down. I offered coffee, but they declined, and I was glad because I didn't want the visit to last that long. I had more important matters to tend to.

Susan looked at her supervisors, then back at me. They were a solemn bunch; you would have thought they were on their way to a relative's wake. ''Someone called the office this morning claiming that Molly's in danger,'' she said.

I felt my back stiffen. ''Who?''

''You know I can't divulge that information. But we checked with Chief Hix and discovered that the allegations were true. Naturally, it's our job to look into it, since Molly is still under the jurisdiction of DSS.''

I gazed back at her. This was not the Susan I knew, the smiling, fun-loving woman who'd eaten dinner at my house a number of times, who'd once wolfed down a pound of chocolate-covered nuts when a relationship had gone sour.

''I don't know what to say, Susan,'' I told her. ''We've had some problems, but I don't think Molly's in any danger.''

''Is it true that you suspect someone's coming into your house at night?'' Roberta White asked.

''I can't prove it.''

She glanced at the police report in her hand. ''You've had jewelry stolen and someone's gone through your personal belongings?''

I hesitated but realized if she had the report they probably knew the answer to that already. "Yes."

"Hix told me about the dead rat," Susan said, "and the note you found on your desk at school, which I took as a direct threat against you *and* Molly. He also told me about Molly's dog."

I shook my head. "I can't believe you actually called the police."

"Who do you think is behind this?" Hamilton asked me.

I looked at him. "Chief Hix seems to think it's just kids playing pranks," I said, deciding to play it down.

"You understand why we had to investigate," Susan said. She paused. "I went by the school earlier today and spoke with Molly's teachers. They say she's withdrawn and depressed. She's failing all her classes."

I knew I looked surprised. I remembered the nights Molly sat at the table doing homework with Henry. "I don't know how to explain her grades," I said. "I would think one of her teachers would have contacted me by now if she's doing that badly. As for her depression, she's just lost her dog. I've been trying to reach her therapist all day, but she's out of town on an emergency."

Everybody was quiet for a moment.

Hamilton finally spoke. "In light of all this, I'm sure you can understand why we feel that Molly would be better off in another environment," he said, pulling a sheet of paper from his briefcase. It looked like some kind of legal document. He offered it to me, but I refused to take it. "At least temporarily," he added, laying it on the coffee table.

It took a minute for his meaning to sink in. "What are you saying?" I asked, looking directly at Susan.

She refused to meet my gaze. "We have to take her, Emily."

I stared at the other woman, thinking that she couldn't be serious. "Are you out of your mind?" I blurted. "Do you have any idea what that would do to her?"

"We can't let her remain in the home if there's a chance she'll be hurt." Susan looked thoughtful. "Besides, you wouldn't have an armed detective living with you if you didn't think you and Molly were in danger.''

I could feel tears gathering behind my eyes. ''You can't do this, Susan. I've worked too hard trying to build a normal life for her.''

''Dead rats and dogs don't make for a normal life, Emily, and you know it. I'm sure Cordia Bowers would be in full agreement with us on this.''

The tears fell. ''Cordia advised me to send her away, to some kind of group home or institution. Is that what you want for Molly?''

''Perhaps Molly needs more help than you can give.''

''I thought you were my friend.''

Her own eyes misted. ''It's because I'm your friend that I'm taking action. You need to find out who's behind this, who's tormenting you. I'll see that Molly is placed in a safe location. Nobody will know where she is except you and DSS. If any of her friends call or try to visit, I want you to tell them she's sick and can't come to the phone.'' Her dark eyes implored me. ''It's only temporary, Emily.''

''Does Molly know?''

Susan shook her head. ''I thought it would be better if you told her.''

''Oh, thank you very much for bestowing that privilege on me,'' I said, sarcasm ringing loud in my voice. I sat there, trying to pull myself together. ''Will I be able to see her?''

''Yes. You can visit anytime.'' She leaned forward. ''Nobody's faulting you on how you're raising Molly, Emily. We just don't want her in this house right now.'' She paused. ''If something happened to her, DSS would be held accountable. We can't risk it. All we can do is hope that Chief Hix gets a fix on the situation soon.''

I was tempted to tell her we could all grow old waiting for that to happen. I wiped my eyes. ''I guess I'd better tell her then,'' I said, standing.

Susan stood as well. ''Do you want me to go in with you?''

I shook my head, afraid to even look her way for fear that I'd burst into tears. "You can all wait on the porch," I said in a voice I barely recognized. "You've already done enough."

23

Molly was lying on the bed, her legs tucked into a fetal position, her eyes staring straight ahead at nothing. She held a tattered Bible in one hand, and I recognized it as the one I'd used as a child. I wondered where she'd found it.

I gazed at her for a long moment, blaming myself for her state and hating the person responsible for making her afraid. I promised myself I would find him if it was the last thing I did.

"Molly, we need to talk," I said gently. I noted several crucifixes tacked to her wall. They'd been made of ice cream sticks glued together at the center, and they were placed near her window as though to keep bad things out. I crossed the room, sat on the edge of the bed and wondered how our lives had come to this.

Molly continued to lie there. "This is serious, honey," I said.

"I'm listening."

"Susan Blake feels that you might be in danger living here with all that's going on."

"They're taking me away, aren't they?" Her voice was flat, without emotion.

"Just for a little while. Until we catch the person who's doing these things."

She rose slowly. "What if I refuse to go?"

"I don't think we have a choice. It's better if we just play along and hope it blows over quickly."

She eyed me for a long moment. "You and Clinton can be alone now."

"This has nothing to do with Clinton." I knew the girl was striking out in the only way she knew; still, I could feel my heart breaking. "Molly, I never meant for any of this to happen. All I've done is try to give you a good home. But some lunatic has a grudge against me, and until he's caught, it probably won't be safe here."

"Then why can't we just go to Grandma and Grandpa's?"

"I don't want to put them in danger."

"It's easier just to send me away, right?" She got up from the bed, opened her closet and pulled out the battered suitcase that had belonged to her mother.

"You can use one of my bags," I told her.

"I'd rather not," she said, walking over to her dresser. She opened a drawer, scooped its contents into her arms and dropped them into the suitcase. She went on to the next drawer and did the same. Her bottom lip trembled, but she probably wouldn't let herself cry until she was alone—if then.

"I need to ask you something, Molly," I said as she closed the suitcase and started from the room. She paused and looked at me, and the look in her eyes almost took my breath away. I could not decide whether she was more angry than hurt, more confused than scared.

"What *now*?"

"Just how close are you and Henry Dean?"

"I've already told you. We're just friends."

"Has he been telling you things? Things that scare you?"

"Why would he want to scare me?"

"You and I both know he's been in a lot of trouble. It seems odd that we didn't start having problems until he came into the picture." Of course, the same could be said for Frank Gillespie, but I was looking at all the possibilities, just as Clinton had advised.

"Henry didn't kill Buster. Buster's death was a sign, and

you're too blind to see it." She started down the hall, and the big suitcase banged against the wall.

I followed her. "A sign from whom?" I said.

"If you can't see for yourself, then I'm not going to tell you."

"Molly, this is important," I said. She tried to turn the corner, and the suitcase wedged itself into the angle. "Here, let me help." I tried to take it from her.

She turned on me, and her eyes were wild. "I don't *want* your help!" she screamed. "It's all your fault this bad stuff is happening in the first place. Can't you see that? Just leave me alone!" She managed to free her suitcase. A moment later, she shoved through the front door, crossed the porch and made her way across the yard to where Susan and her supervisors waited.

I stood there, not knowing what to do or say next. I felt defeated as I watched Susan load Molly's suitcase into the trunk and help her into a dark sedan. I sniffed, determined not to break down in front of them. Susan paused and looked at me, and I couldn't stand the pity I saw in her gaze.

"I'll call you later," she said.

"Don't bother," I replied. I closed the door and locked it. Finally I allowed myself to cry.

I was awakened sometime later by the ringing of the doorbell. I opened my eyes and blinked, feeling groggy and disoriented. As soon as I realized I was in Molly's room, it all came rushing back to me. I had curled up on her bed and given in to the pain of losing her. The tears had been relentless. Now I felt old and broken.

The doorbell pealed again, followed by frantic knocking. I got up and made my way down the hall and into the living room, where somebody was doing his level best to break down my door. I peered through the curtain and saw Clinton.

Sighing my relief, I unlocked the door. He rushed inside. "Where the hell were you?"

"Sleeping."

"I thought something happened. I saw your car out there, and when you didn't come to the door—" He paused. "Jesus Christ, what happened to your eyes? Have you been crying?"

I raised my hands to my eyes. They were puffy and swollen; I wasn't surprised. I walked over to the couch and sat down. "They took Molly."

"Who?"

"The Department of Social Services. They were waiting for me when I got home."

He looked angry. "On what grounds?"

"They feel that she's not safe here." I paused, half afraid I would start crying again, then told myself that there couldn't possibly be any tears left in my body. "Somebody called them, told them all that's been going on."

He sat down beside me. "Who would do something like that?"

"I don't know. What does it matter? She's gone."

"Can they do that? Take her away, I mean?"

I shrugged. "I'm just her legal guardian. I haven't adopted her yet. I was planning to, but she has to be with me for a full year before I can start proceedings." I realized that my crying had given me a headache. "I don't know what to do anymore. Maybe the kid is better off without me."

"Did they give you any kind of legal notice?"

I wiped my face. "Right there," I said, pointing to the form on the coffee table. "I didn't even bother to look at it."

He snatched the paper from the table and read it quickly. "It says you have ten days to respond. You'll probably need a lawyer."

I gave a grunt of disgust. "Like I can afford it."

He continued to read. "It says you can have reasonable visitation. You can call first thing in the morning to arrange it. In the meantime, I'll find someone who can represent you."

I sighed. I had never felt so weary. "Molly doesn't want to see me, Clinton. She thinks I'm the cause of all these bad things." He looked confused. "I don't know what's gotten into her. It's like she's gone over the edge." I finally told him about some of the conversations we'd had. "At first I thought my mother was filling her head with a lot of stuff from the Bible, but she claims she hasn't said a word."

He looked confused. "What kind of stuff?"

"Passages from the Book of Revelations. It's pretty scary stuff, especially for a kid. Somebody's convinced Molly that we're living in the last days, that we're being judged even now. At first she thought it was her fault about Buster, but now she's shifted the blame to me. She's accused me of being like her mother." I shook my head, knowing it all sounded far-fetched.

"Who could be telling her these things?" Clinton asked.

"My mother would admit it if she were the one putting these ideas in Molly's head. She's quite proud of her beliefs." I tried to think. "I can't imagine her friends talking about it." I had a scary thought. "What if she's just making it up in her mind?"

"Do you think she's delusional?"

"I don't know. I'm ashamed to admit it, but I canceled our last appointment with her counselor after the woman suggested that I send Molly away."

"Do you think Molly knows who's behind all this?"

"I can't see her standing by and letting someone kill her dog, no matter how much she likes this person."

Clinton took my hand. "I worry about you, Emily. I wish I could convince you to go away for a while."

"It would only postpone the inevitable, because he'd know I was gone. He'd simply wait until I came back, and the games would start all over again." I paused. "It's weird how I keep using the word *he*, isn't it? Who says it's not a woman?"

"Most violent crimes are committed by men," Clinton said.

"So what now?" I asked out loud.

"For starters, I want you to calm down. You have ten days to prove yourself fit to raise your niece. I'll start making calls first thing in the morning. I've already met a couple of good lawyers in this town. In the meantime, we'll do everything necessary to catch this maniac." He checked his watch. "Right now I'm going to make myself a stiff drink and a sandwich. I'd like to take a nap, so I can sit up tonight. If something happens, I plan to be watching."

"I want to stay up with you," I told him. "But I don't think I'll be able to close my eyes in the meantime."

"Trust me. One stiff drink and a back rub, and I'll have you asleep in no time." He took my hand, pulled me up from the sofa and led me into the kitchen. "Sit down," he ordered, motioning toward the kitchen table.

I did so and watched him search under the sink for my bottle of scotch. He poured two drinks, added a little water and tossed in a couple of ice cubes. I tasted mine and shuddered because it was so strong. He took a sip of his and regarded me.

"Ham or turkey on your sandwich?" he asked.

"I don't care." I took another sip of the drink, shuddered again. The scotch burned a path down my throat and warmed my stomach. "I don't know what I'd do without you," I confessed, hoping I didn't sound weak and clinging.

"That's a good sign," he said, pulling sliced meat and cheese from my refrigerator. He made the sandwiches while I continued to nurse my drink.

"I'm not so sure it's good," I said. "There's still the question of where you'll be this time next year."

"Let's handle one crisis at a time, Emily." Several minutes later, he put a plate of sandwiches on the table and grabbed a bag of potato chips. I gazed down at the food doubtfully. "You need to eat," he said.

I was already feeling the scotch. I picked up a sandwich and nibbled at it. "Clinton?"

"Yeah?" He glanced up.

"Would you mind sleeping with me tonight?" He looked surprised. "I'm not looking for anything sexual. I just want you beside me."

His gaze softened. "Sure, babe. I'd consider it a pleasure."

Darkness had fallen by the time we climbed into my bed, although it was only six o'clock. Clinton set the clock for ten. He'd decided to keep his clothes on, just in case, but kicked off his shoes before he joined me beneath the quilt. I wore comfortable if not flattering sweats.

I suppose it was the stress I'd lived under during the past few weeks, or maybe the strong scotch and gentle back rub Clinton gave me, but I fell asleep almost as soon as my head hit the pillow, while his warm hands still massaged me under my shirt.

I was sleeping soundly when the loud ringing jolted me awake. At first I thought it was the alarm clock, then realized it was the phone. A sense of dread washed over me as I reached for it. Chief Hix spoke from the other end of the line.

"Is Clinton around?" he asked.

I handed the phone to Clinton, and he mumbled something into it. I noted from my alarm clock that it was just nine-thirty. I listened intently. Finally Clinton spoke. "Where?"

I rose up in bed and switched on the light. My first thoughts were of Molly. Had she run away from wherever Susan had taken her? I tried to be patient, tried not to panic as I waited for Clinton to get off the phone.

"Okay, I'll be there in fifteen minutes," he said, already climbing out of bed.

"What is it?" I said. "Is it Molly?"

He shook his head. "No, nothing to do with her."

"Then what?" I demanded. He seemed hesitant to tell me. "I have a right to know," I said.

He sighed and wiped his hand down his face. "They've found another body."

24

Clinton and I picked up the chief at the police station so the three of us could make the two-hour drive to Evansville, South Carolina.

"What's she doing here?" Hix asked Clinton as he climbed into the backseat.

"I have a name," I said. "I'd appreciate your using it."

"What burr climbed up your behind?"

I opened my mouth to respond, but Clinton cut me off. "I'm not leaving Emily alone with all that's going on. But if you two are going to rag on one another, you can take the trip without me."

"This is highly unorthodox," the chief mumbled. "I hope you're not planning to have a look at the body."

"I have no intention of going anywhere near the victim. I'm just along for the ride."

Suddenly the chief's voice softened. "Look, I heard about Molly, and I'm truly sorry."

I half turned in my seat, glancing at him over my shoulder. "Are you?"

He looked surprised at my tone. "Of course I am. I told them what a time you'd had with the girl, how you'd done everything you could to help her. It didn't seem to matter. They'd already made up their minds."

We rode in silence. I didn't want to think about my niece and start crying all over again. Still, I held the chief partially responsible for what had happened, even though I

235

knew even Hix could not be held accountable for not reporting something to DSS. He could have said something
to prevent DSS from taking her.

"Where's Conners?" Clinton asked.

"His mother-in-law had a stroke. Got the call an hour
ago. He and the missus are on their way to Atlanta. Perfect
timing," he muttered.

"What do you know about this victim?"

"Not much," Hix said. "They called us in because the
Evansville chief of police is recovering from bypass sur-
gery, and they didn't want to disturb him. Also, they heard
about our murder and wanted to see if there was a connec-
tion. This one's been dead a few days, so be prepared."

"How'd she die?"

"The actual *cause* of death was strychnine poisoning, if
you can believe it. I thought they'd outlawed that stuff a
long time ago. Anyhow, I guess a simple poisoning didn't
give our screwball the thrill he was looking for, because
the doc said he cut her up pretty bad afterwards."

"How did the doctor know it was strychnine?" Clinton
asked. "Does he already have lab results?"

"No, nothing yet. But this Dr. Hislop remembers seeing
another strychnine poisoning some fourteen or fifteen years
back, and he never forgot it."

"I've heard they can be gruesome," Clinton replied.

I couldn't help feeling intrigued by their conversation.
When I tried to fall asleep later, I'd probably be sorry for
asking, but right now my curiosity got the best of me.
"What's the deal with strychnine?" I asked.

"It causes violent convulsions," Hix said. "The victim
is usually found wearing an awful grimace. Least that's
what I hear. I've never had the misfortune to run into one."

"Historians say that Cleopatra experimented with that
poison when she decided to kill herself," Clinton said.
"She tested it on her slaves. Once she saw how awful the
victims looked afterward, her sense of vanity would not
permit her to take it, and she used an asp instead. Supposedly, an asp bite is quick and painless."

"In other words, you'd be a fool to use strychnine when there are so many fast and less-agonizing ways to kill yourself," Hix added.

I shuddered and decided not to ask any more questions.

The town of Evansville, South Carolina, was no bigger than Mossy Oaks and looked as though it had jumped out of a Norman Rockwell painting. The houses were dark now, of course—it was after midnight—but I could imagine how the families would look in the morning, sitting around their breakfast tables and eating steaming bowls of oatmeal.

Evansville General Hospital looked relatively new, a two-story brick building flanked by small gardens where wooden benches sat in clusters. A group of teenagers loitered in the lobby, looking as though they were ready for trouble, and near the closed gift shop, a woman held a squalling infant.

Clinton and I followed Chief Hix to the information desk, where a security guard sat reading a magazine.

"Excuse me there, young fellow," Hix said. "We're looking for Dr. Hislop. You know where we might find him?"

The security guard looked startled, then seemed to get a grip when he noted Hix's uniform. "His office is down next to the morgue. You got an appointment or something?"

Hix put his elbow on the counter and looked at the man. "Do you think I'd be out visiting the morgue this time of night if I didn't?"

The man looked embarrassed. "No, sir, of course not. I'd better draw you a map of how to get there. I'd take you myself, but I think I'd best keep my eye on these youngsters. They got a friend in ICU, and they refuse to leave until he's better. They done been kicked out of the upstairs lounge for being so loud." As he spoke, he tore a slip of paper from a pad and drew directions, then pointed to the elevator that would take us down. I could barely hear for the baby. The noise wouldn't have bothered me under normal circumstances, but right now my nerves were brittle.

Hix looked at me. "You want to wait up here in the lobby?"

I shook my head. "I'll ride down to the basement with you."

We made our way to the elevators, and Hix pushed the button for the basement. The elevator moved downward swiftly. A moment later the door swished open, and we found ourselves in the very belly of the hospital.

An Asian man was waiting for us. He was small and middle-aged, with an easy smile. "Chief Hix?" he asked, holding out a well-manicured hand.

Hix shook hands and introduced Clinton, then me. "Is there some place where our lady friend can wait?" he asked the doctor.

"She's welcome to sit in my office," he replied. "I just made fresh coffee." He showed me the way, and I thanked him.

"I'll show you where you can suit up first, gentlemen," the doctor said from the hall. "I think I mentioned that this one's been dead a good seventy-two hours."

Inside the doctor's neat little office was a battered desk, on top of which sat a massive microscope. I stepped closer and noted various slides arranged in neat stacks. Tissue samples, no doubt. I shuddered and searched for the coffeepot.

I had finished my coffee by the time the men returned, Hix and Clinton both wearing serious looks on their faces. They talked with the doctor several minutes more. "What's so sad about this case," Hislop said, "is that the victim left two small children behind. There's no family, to speak of. Who knows where they'll end up?"

"That's the saddest part of all," Clinton agreed as I joined them in the hall. The doctor ushered us to the elevator.

"Aren't you spooked, working down here all alone?" I asked Dr. Hislop.

He smiled. "I don't usually work these late hours, but

no, I'm not afraid. Dead people can't hurt you. It's the living you have to worry about." He smiled again as we got on the elevator and waited for the doors to close.

I was tired when we reached Clinton's car, and I offered to sit in the backseat so he and the chief could discuss the case while I slept. I must've dozed for a while; when I woke up, the men were whispering in the front, and it seemed like we'd been riding a long time.

"You think Randy Dempsey did both of them?" Hix asked softly, turning in the seat, obviously making sure I was still asleep.

I heard Clinton sigh. "I'm not convinced that Randy killed Cindy Brown. As for whether or not the same man did both killings, I'd agree that there are similarities."

"Hislop said she'd been dead several days. Randy could've easily done it," Hix added as though he hadn't heard Clinton.

"Randy also puked his guts out in Cindy's yard after he saw the body, Chief. Do you *really* think he's capable of watching a woman die so violently, then cutting her up?"

"Hard to say. He coulda been putting on an act. Right now he's the only lead we got. We already know he's got a history of fondling children. Maybe he hates women as well."

"Not just *any* woman," Clinton corrected. "Both victims were party girls, so to speak—a bit on the promiscuous side. Also, they had small children. Maybe the guy thought he was doing the kids a favor by killing off their mothers." He sighed. "It'd be nice if we had a weapon."

"Well, all we can do now is wait for the lab results. I could tell old slant-eyes was in a hurry to get rid of her; otherwise, he would'na stayed so late. I'll bet she's already in the meat wagon and on her way to Charleston. Wonder how long it'll take them to get that suicide note analyzed?"

"Why do we care?" Clinton asked, almost irritably. "Even if it is her handwriting, we know she wrote it at knifepoint. You saw what she looked like, Chief. A woman doesn't try to disembowel herself before she swallows poison.''

I felt something catch inside my chest. *Both women were party girls . . . promiscuous.*

Hix grunted. ''You got anybody in your files up at the parole office that might be capable of something like this?''

''You mean *other* than Frank Gillespie?''

''You think Frank coulda done it?''

Clinton was quiet for a moment. ''Frank's a lunatic—I'll be the first to admit it—but this is the work of a sociopath. Frank became violent when the man he was trying to rob for drug money reached for his weapon. Two completely different MOs.''

''What I don't get is, why would he try to make it look like a suicide, then cut her up like that?''

''He lost control,'' Clinton said. ''And if it's the same guy, you can bet the killings will get even more gruesome and happen more frequently.''

''Jesus Christ,'' Hix said. ''Just what we need.''

''There's no way to know for certain at this point,'' Clinton whispered, ''but he could very well be a serial killer. I've only run into one other in all my years in homicide, but he killed six women before we caught him.''

''So what do you suggest we do now?''

''Odds are, this guy has killed more than we know about, probably in different parts of the country. I'm no expert in the field, but I've studied it. What we need to do is establish a pattern, and the only way we can do that is to contact the FBI.''

''That's fine,'' Hix said. ''But I don't want you mentioning one word of this to anybody else. The last thing I need is for folks to get into a panic.''

I rose up from the backseat then, startling both men. ''I need a favor,'' I told Clinton, placing a hand on his shoulder.

He covered my hand with his. ''Name it.''

I hesitated. I wasn't certain why I suddenly felt as I did,

but I knew I would never forgive myself if I didn't ask. "I want you to look at my sister's file."

"Aw, shit," Hix said, obviously realizing that I'd heard the entire conversation.

It was after two A.M. when we pulled into headquarters. The chief, who'd remained quiet since my request, ushered us into his office and closed the door. "Have a seat," he said. He walked to a file, pulled open one of the drawers and thumbed through it. He pulled out a manila folder and tossed it onto his desk.

"I don't know what you're supposed to be looking for, but this is the file Emily asked you to look at."

Because I had no wish to view my dead sister's photos, I automatically moved to the vinyl sofa on the other side of the room. Clinton took a chair in front of Hix's desk, opened the file and studied what was inside. "Can you give me some specifics?" he asked the chief.

"Lurlene Tompkins, aged thirty-one at the time of her death. Beautiful girl, just beautiful. Had more suitors than you could shake a stick at."

I cleared my throat. "What Chief Hix is too embarrassed to say in front of me is that my sister was promiscuous, just as these other women were reputed to be. Before she married DeWayne, she slept around quite a bit. Molly spent most of her time with me or my parents."

Clinton looked at me. "Was DeWayne aware of this when he started going out with her?"

"I certainly wasn't going to tell him. He didn't hang out in bars like he does now, and he traveled a great deal, so I doubt he had the opportunity to run into her old boyfriends. Lurlene calmed down a bit after they were married, then started going out again when DeWayne's job took him on the road so much."

"How'd he react when he found out?"

"Molly claims he was a perfect gentleman. Packed his bags and moved out, but continued to pay the bills."

"And started drinking like there was no tomorrow," Hix added.

Clinton picked up one of the photos and studied it in the light. "You got a magnifying glass?" he asked Hix.

The chief pulled open a desk drawer and passed him one.

"Do you think DeWayne Tompkins is capable of murder?" Clinton asked Hix.

The other man looked thoughtful. "Hard to say. I'd have to see him sober first, and I ain't seen him that way since Lurlene died."

I stood. "Clinton, you can't possibly think that DeWayne had anything to do with my sister's death. He worshipped her. Why, he was inconsolable afterward. Still is."

Clinton looked at the photo. "Well, from what I can see in these pictures, I'd say *somebody* killed her."

25

At first there was only silence, and I felt my heart slam to my throat. "How do you figure?" Hix asked after a moment.

Clinton didn't hesitate. "The rope burns on her neck aren't consistent with a hanging. See that lateral line across her neck? That was made by someone standing directly behind her. She was strangled. That would explain the small bruise at the back. It's not perfectly clear, but you can make it out if you look closely. That's probably the killer's knuckles digging into her vertebra during strangulation."

"Well, I'll be danged," Hix said.

Clinton looked at me. My expression must've shown my horror. "You okay, Emily?"

I felt sick to my stomach, but I was determined to find out the truth. "So you're saying she was strangled, *then* hanged?" I asked weakly.

He nodded. "Looks that way." He handed the photo to Hix. "You could have an expert look at it, if you like."

"I think I already have," Hix said. He wiped his forehead and sat at his desk. He looked sad, and his coloring was gray. "I was so sure she'd done it herself," he said. "There was a chair beside her that'd been knocked over, which I figured she'd kicked out of her way. There was even a suicide note in her own handwriting." Hix looked at Clinton. "You know, back when I was appointed chief, we didn't have the knowledge y'all have today. We went on gut instinct.''

"You did the best you could,'' Clinton said.

I sank into the sofa, feeling as though I'd pass out from the implications. My sister hadn't killed herself after all. For months, I'd blamed myself for turning her in to DSS; now I realized, selfish as it was, that I was off the hook. At the same time, I knew a moment of pure anguish as I thought of someone forcing Lurlene to write her own suicide note.

"If Lurlene Tompkins was killed by the same man who killed these other two, then that pretty much rules out Frank Gillespie,'' Clinton said. "He was still in prison at the time.'' He paused and looked at me. "Do you know if she was seeing another man at the time of her death?''

I felt a sinking sensation in my stomach. "She was seeing several men. I think one of them may have given her a tennis bracelet, because when I showed it to DeWayne after cleaning out her things, he claimed he'd never seen it before. I kept meaning to have it appraised. I don't know if it's diamond or cubic zirconia.''

"Where is it now?'' Clinton asked.

"In a safety-deposit box with some of Lurlene's papers. I figured I'd give it to Molly on her wedding day. That is, if it's worth anything.''

Clinton looked thoughtful. "I'd like to see it.''

It was after three A.M. when we left the police department, and I could barely hold my eyes open. "I have to see my parents tomorrow,'' I said, once we'd arrived home and readied ourselves for bed. "And tell them about Molly and what's been going on.''

Still dressed in his jeans and socks, Clinton lay on his side of the bed and waited for me to set my alarm clock. He must've sensed that I didn't want to be alone because he made no move to go to the guest room. "Want me to come with you?'' he asked.

I envisioned my mother's reaction. I knew she wasn't

going to take the news well. "It'd help. I'm going to tell them you're an ex-cop and you're staying in my spare bedroom. Otherwise, they'll insist that I move back home. I don't want to put them in danger."

"I can take you after work tomorrow."

"I'll call her in the morning and tell her we're coming for dinner. She'll automatically suspect that we're going to announce our engagement, so be prepared."

He laughed softly. "I hardly think she feels I'm the man for you, since I told her I'm Catholic."

"She'll try to convert you."

"That won't be easy. I stopped practicing any form of religion long ago."

I lay down beside him, then rose up on my elbow and studied his face. He looked as tired as I felt. "You don't believe in God?"

He reached up and touched my cheek. "I've been at enough crime scenes to know that God isn't always available when you need Him most. But you and I don't need to get into a discussion about religion right now," he said. "It's late, and we both have to be up early." He paused and looked thoughtful.

"What?"

He glanced at me. "I was just thinking. Dr. Hislop mentioned another strychnine poisoning some years back."

"Yes, but it was fifteen years ago. What could that case possibly have to do with this one?"

"In all my years as a detective, I've never come across even one," he said. "Strychnine just isn't that popular, in homicides *or* suicides. And what makes this coincidence even more baffling is that it happened twice in a town of less than six thousand." He got out of bed.

"Where are you going?"

"I want to find out what Dr. Hislop remembers about the other case."

"Now?"

"Now."

Clinton disappeared into the kitchen, and I followed. I

----

didn't like being left alone these days, even if I was only in the next room. I pulled out a chair and sat down at the table while Clinton dialed information in Evansville.

"Could you give me the number for Dr. Hislop's residence?" he asked. He grabbed the pen I kept near the phone and scribbled the number on a pad of paper. He hung up and dialed once more, and it seemed that several minutes ticked by before he spoke.

"Dr. Hislop, this is Clinton Ward. Chief Hix and I met with you earlier. I'm very sorry for waking you up, but I just thought of something that may be important." He paused, and I wondered if the man on the other end had hung up on him.

Finally, Clinton spoke again. "You said there was another strychnine poisoning in your town fifteen years ago. What can you tell me about the victim?" he asked. "Anything you can remember will be helpful." He waited, obviously giving the man on the other end time to collect his thoughts. Once more, Clinton started making notes. I listened intently to the one-sided conversation but wasn't able to learn much. Clinton thanked the doctor, apologized once more for waking him and hung up.

"Well?" I asked.

"He couldn't remember exactly how many years it'd been, but he said the victim was an older woman and a pillar of the community. Minister's wife and all that. Nothing in the house was touched, so robbery was ruled out, but everybody thought it strange that a Christian like herself would take her own life."

"So they still don't know whether it was murder or suicide?"

He shook his head, then sighed. "Not that it means anything to us. I don't see any similarities."

I gazed back at him, wondering why I should feel weird about what he'd just told me. I could feel my memory being jogged, but it wouldn't spit out whatever was nagging at me. It was like trying to remember the punch line to an old joke. It reminded me of an old black-and-white movie I'd recently watched with my mother. Although I'd never remembered seeing it before, I realized about halfway through the plot that I knew exactly what was going to happen, precisely what the characters were going to say to one another. I decided I must've seen it as a child and forgotten. That's how I felt now.

We returned to the bedroom. "You want me to stay with you tonight?" he asked.

"I thought you'd never ask."

We both lay down on the bed, although Clinton didn't climb under the covers. "I may get up several times during the night, so if you wake up and I'm not here, don't worry." He leaned over and kissed me gently on the lips. "My friends at the force in Chicago would have a good laugh over this."

"Over what?"

"Us sleeping together but not having sex. I'll have to say it's a first for me."

"Do you want to?"

He looked at me curiously. "What? Have sex? Of course I do. But not with you about to jump out of your skin at the slightest noise."

I couldn't help but feel irritated that he could dismiss the idea so easily when my mind was running amuck with images of him taking me into his arms and kissing me senseless, or at least until I forgot my problems. But I knew the timing was off, so I didn't take offense. Okay, so maybe I did just a little bit. "Just so you'll know," I said, "we happen to call it *making love* in this part of the country, not *having sex*."

He grinned. "Yeah, but we both know it boils down to the same thing, don't we?" His look turned tender. "Good night, Emily."

I must've drifted off right away; the next thing I knew, the alarm was ringing, and Clinton was no longer beside me. I'd never heard him get up—never heard anything, for that matter—and I was thankful it hadn't been up to me to keep watch through the night. I shut off the alarm, then remembered the part about Molly being gone, and the pain returned.

I climbed out of bed, grabbed my bathrobe from a nearby chair and slipped it on. The floor felt cold beneath my bare feet. I tiptoed into the living room, where I found Clinton asleep on the sofa, a throw pillow tucked under his head and an old quilt at his feet. He still wore his jeans, and his gun lay on the coffee table beside him. It looked menacing and out of place next to a vase of dried flowers and small baskets of potpourri.

I decided to let him sleep while I grabbed a quick shower. When I returned to the living room ten minutes later, wearing a towel and bathrobe, I found him still asleep.

I walked over toward him, and the wood floor creaked beneath my feet. He bolted upright, startling me so badly that I jumped. ''Lord!'' I cried. ''You 'bout scared me to death.''

He saw that it was me, and the tension left his face. ''That makes both of us. Sorry. Occupational hazard. Did you sleep okay?''

''Fine. Did you sleep *at all*?''

''On and off. The night was uneventful.'' He eyed my bathrobe and towel. ''Are you naked under that thing?''

My stomach dipped at the question. ''What a thing to ask,'' I said, trying to brush it off lightly while the heat flooded my cheeks. I felt that our relationship had taken a sudden turn, and I hadn't seen the road signs leading to it. ''Would you like a cup of coffee?''

''Sounds good.'' He must've seen me blushing. He chuckled. ''Hey, I didn't mean to embarrass you, Emily. I'm sorry.''

I didn't think he looked a bit sorry as he followed me into the kitchen and waited until I'd poured us each a cup. We both noticed my trembling hands.

''I sometimes say things before I think them through,'' he confessed.

''And I sometimes overreact when I have a lot on my

mind," I admitted. "You want to use the shower? We're running a little late this morning."

He gulped his coffee and hurried away.

Clinton delivered me to school ten minutes late. Principal Higginbotham was standing outside the door of my class-room when I arrived, slightly out of breath.

"I'd like to talk to you. Do you have any free time this morning?"

I felt a sense of dread. Had he heard about DSS taking Molly? Was he planning to dismiss me over it? "My class has library at ten. I could drop by your office then."

"Good enough." He nodded and walked away.

The next hour dragged as I tried to concentrate on my math lesson for the day. I always started the day with math because that's when my students were most alert. We had advanced to borrowing in subtraction, something some of the children still had trouble understanding. If I waited until afternoon, probably none of them would grasp it.

With math out of the way, I rewarded them by passing out the *Weekly Reader*, and we focused on the animals that were in danger of becoming extinct. I found myself wishing that possums and raccoons were on the list. The only thing they seemed to be good at was getting themselves run over on back roads at night. If I'd had a dime for every one I'd seen flattened in my life, I could have afforded to buy the Gillespie mansion.

I selected several students to read the report—those in my top reading group who raised their hands eagerly when I asked for volunteers. I know teachers who go down the row systematically so each child can read a paragraph aloud, but I avoided doing so because I didn't want to embarrass the slower readers.

By the time we'd finished the reading part and had answered all the questions on the back, my class was ready for their milk and bathroom break.

Afterward, I had my class line up for their trip to the library. Holding hands, they scuffled along the ancient wood floor like a drunken caterpillar. I left them in the capable hands of Mrs. Rentz, our head librarian. For the next half hour she would mesmerize them with a story and, afterward, help them choose a book from the shelves.

Principal Higginbotham was dictating a letter to his secretary when I knocked on his door. He motioned me in and pointed to a chair in front of his desk, where I waited while they finished up. His office was gloomy, paneled in dark wood and carpeted in two-tone beige and brown. There was a picture of his three children on the credenza, but I knew they were now grown and scattered throughout the country. If I'd hoped to find a golf or tennis trophy, I was wrong. Higginbotham had no hobbies; he was devoted to his work.

"That'll be all, Mrs. Farmer," he told his secretary, an older, stern-faced woman who still wore her hair in a French twist. Her shoes were black tie-ups: very sensible, very ugly. She got up from her chair, nodded once in my direction and closed the door behind her as she left.

"I'll get right to the point," Higginbotham said. "I was contacted yesterday by the Department of Social Services regarding your niece."

I felt my stomach pitch. "What'd they want?"

"They asked about your work habits, whether I thought you were a good teacher, et cetera, et cetera. I told them I had no complaints. I tried to find you after school yesterday so I could relay the information, but you'd already left. Can you tell me what this is about?"

I swallowed. The last thing I needed to do was get emotional. "DSS took Molly away from me yesterday," I managed. I glanced at my feet. "I've had some problems at my house. Break-ins. Stolen items. Somebody killed Molly's dog."

"How awful. Did you report it to the police?"

I nodded. "They've been involved from the beginning. Anyway, somebody called DSS and told them Molly was in danger, so they came and got her. I have ten days to respond. I guess I'm going to have to hire a lawyer."

"Do the police have any idea who's breaking in?"

I shook my head. "Not a clue."

"Well, I want you to be careful. After hearing about that poor woman they found in the bathtub—well, I worry about my single teachers."

I wondered how he'd feel when he read about the latest victim. "I'm being very cautious," I told him.

"Do you need some time off?" he asked. "We can arrange for a substitute."

"I'm okay for now," I told him. "I might need time later."

"I just want you to know that you can count on me if you need some sort of character witness."

I was suddenly sorry for all the things I'd said about him. "Thank you."

Higginbotham stood, bringing the meeting to a close. "I'm sure you have to get back to your class. Let me know if I can do anything to help."

I thanked him again, then paused in the doorway. "Does anyone else know you got a call from DSS?" I asked.

He shook his head. "I didn't figure it was anybody's business."

"Thank you, sir."

I left Higginbotham's office and started for the library, then took a quick detour when I discovered I was crying. I hurried into Herschel Buckmeyer's office, which was no bigger than a closet, and found him baiting several mousetraps that were, no doubt, headed for our basement.

"Emily? What is it?" He stood quickly.

I closed the door behind me and leaned against it. "I'm just upset right now, Herschel, and I don't want to have to face my class. I just need a few minutes to . . . to compose myself."

"Here, sit down." He motioned to the chair he'd been sitting in a few seconds before. "Can I get you something?" he asked, once I was seated. "A drink of water?"

I sniffed. "No, I'll be okay in a second."

"I hope you're not crying because of what I told you yesterday," he said, concern ringing loud in his voice.

I wiped my eyes and tried to smile. "No, it's not that. I've just got a lot on my mind right now."

"You just sit there as long as you need to," he said. "I've got to run these down to the basement. Higginbotham saw a rat in the cafeteria today and is ready to take my head off. I'll be right back." He closed the door behind him as he left, giving me the privacy I needed.

I continued to cry, then glanced around for a box of tissues so I could blow my nose. I pulled open the middle drawer to Herschel's desk and didn't find one. Finally, after searching the others, I opened the bottom drawer and found what I was looking for. I picked up the box and pulled several tissues from it before setting it back into place. As I did, my eyes caught sight of something shiny. I looked closer. My onyx earrings and necklace had been tucked into one corner.

I started to reach for them, then heard a noise outside the door. I dropped the box of tissues and slid the drawer closed just as Herschel stepped inside once more. "Feeling better?" he asked.

I opened my mouth to speak, but the words wouldn't come. I simply nodded.

"You look white as a sheet," he said. "Maybe you're coming down with a bug."

"I—I'm okay," I managed, standing and wadding the tissues tightly in one fist. "I'd better get back to my class."

Clinton must've read the worry on my face when he picked me up. "What's wrong?"

I leaned back in the seat and told him about my visit with Principal Higginbotham and what I'd found in Herschel Buckmeyer's office.

"So what do you think it means?"

I shook my head. "I've no idea. I would never in a million years suspect Herschel of taking something that didn't belong to him."

"Would he have had the opportunity?"

I felt something heavy settle in my chest. "He put the

new dead bolts on my doors." I looked at Clinton for his reaction. He was staring out the windshield of the car, but I could see his mind working.

"Then he'd have less trouble breaking into your house than anybody else I can think of."

"And he could have left that rat on my table," I said, thinking of the trap Herschel had been setting when I'd barged in on him in the morning. Still, my mind refused to believe it. Herschel had never given me any reason to distrust him.

"It's all speculation at this point," Clinton said, "but it might be wise to keep our eyes open. Like I said before, everybody's a suspect."

We were late getting to my parents' because Clinton insisted on stopping by the bank so we could go through the contents of the safety-deposit box. "What do you think?" I asked as he studied the tennis bracelet in the light.

"Looks real to me," he said, dropping it into the pocket of his jacket. "Of course, even if it is real, we don't know if the diamonds are of good quality and worth a lot. I'll have it appraised tomorrow."

My mother was standing on the front porch waiting when we pulled into the driveway. "Hello, dear," she said, kissing me on the cheek when I joined her on the porch. "Where's Molly?"

"She didn't come with us this time," I said.

"Oh?"

"How are you, Mrs. Wilkop?" Clinton asked, obviously trying to change the subject for the time being.

"I'm fine, thank you. And you may call me Claire." She opened the door wide so we could pass through, but her gaze never left Clinton. "I hope you're good and hungry."

"And looking forward to a great meal," he said as though aiming a cupid's arrow straight toward her heart.

She couldn't mask her pleasure. "I made meat loaf with mashed potatoes," she said. "And green beans that I canned last summer."

"Nothing like home cooking," he told her.

"I thought maybe we'd have a little drink first," she said. "And chat."

I felt my brows rise clear to my hairline. I'd never known my mother to drink.

"My cousin brought me some muscadine wine the other day," she said, leading us to the sofa. A decanter sat on the coffee table, surrounded by small juice glasses. "I don't normally imbibe, but I thought just this once—"

She paused and smiled at me, and I knew she was expecting one hell of an announcement. It irked me something fierce that she thought I could meet a man, fall in love and plan to get married in just a couple of weeks.

My dad nodded at us from his recliner where he was watching the news. I walked over and kissed him on the forehead, and he and Clinton shook hands. "Good to see you again," he told Clinton as he pushed the chair upright and waited eagerly for his glass of wine. He didn't share my mother's belief in abstinence.

"Should we make a toast?" my mother asked once she'd poured about a tablespoon of wine into each of the glasses and passed them out.

I suddenly felt sorry for her. I was the only child she had left, and I was not putting forth grandchildren at breakneck speed. "I have something to tell you, Mom," I began, "but I'm afraid it's bad news."

The smile faded from her face by degrees. She glanced from me to Clinton and back to me, lowering her glass as she did so. I noticed that I had my dad's undivided attention as well. "What is it, dear?" she asked.

"They took Molly away from me."

She almost spilled her drink. She set the glass on the coffee table. "They? Who?"

"The Department of Social Services."

She merely gaped at me. My father got out of his chair and set his glass beside hers. "What are you talking about?" he demanded. I was suddenly reminded of the many nights he'd paced the floor waiting for Lurlene to come home from a date, a dark scowl on his face. He wore that look now.

"There's been some trouble at my place. Somebody has been breaking in and doing damage. Chief Hix thinks it's kids, but—"

"He didn't mention it when I ran into him at the feed store the other day," my father said.

"I asked him not to. I didn't want to worry you."

"Has someone been taking things?" my mother asked.

"I noticed a few things missing here and there, but that's not what concerned DSS." I hesitated. I really had no wish to cause them worry, but I knew they'd be furious with me if they found out from somebody else. "This person, whoever he is, killed Molly's dog."

My mother gasped. She looked stricken. "Someone killed Buster?" She and my father exchanged anxious looks.

"Yes. That's not all, but I'd rather not get into it. The bottom line is that DSS feels Molly might be in danger."

"What about you?" my mother insisted. "You could be in danger as well. You'll have to come home, Emily Anne. At once," she added in a voice that told me she was still my mother, and I shouldn't forget it.

"I can't come home, Mom," I said. "If I do, it'll put you and Daddy in danger."

"I don't give a damn about that," my father snapped. "I think I'm capable of taking care of my family. If you think I'm going to let you go back home by yourself—"

"I've been staying at your daughter's house, Mr. Wilkop," Clinton said.

"What!"

The color drained from my mother's face. "What do you mean, staying? *Sleeping* there?" Once again she looked at my father. He clenched one fist. I was half afraid he'd hit Clinton.

"Yes, what do you mean, you're staying there?" he echoed.

"Calm down, Daddy," I said, feeling fifteen again.

"I'm sleeping in her guest room," Clinton said.

I stood, trying to divert my father's attention so he would calm down. "Clinton used to be a detective for the Chicago Police Department, Daddy. He's offered to stay at my place until we catch this . . . this nut. In fact, Chief Hix deputized him."

"You got a gun?" my father asked him.

Clinton nodded. "And believe me, I won't hesitate to use it."

My mother got up and walked to the window. She stared out for a long moment, and I knew she was trying to get herself under control. I joined her. I saw the tears in her eyes and put my arm around her waist. We may not have always seen eye to eye on everything, but I couldn't stand to see her in pain. "I'm sorry about Molly," I said. "I have every intention of getting her back."

She sniffed. "I guess you heard another woman was killed less than two hours from here. They think it might be the same man who killed this Brown girl." She shook her head sadly. "Sometimes I think I'll go crazy worrying about you and Molly like I do. Especially after what happened to Lurlene. I know you think I try to interfere, but—" She merely shrugged.

I knew what it was like to love someone and worry about them, because I had done the same thing with Molly. How could I not love and admire this poor woman for feeling the same toward me? "Nothing is going to happen to me," I told her. "I have all the faith in the world in Clinton."

She turned to him, her eyes imploring. Clinton stood respectfully. "Please don't let anything happen to her," she said. "I've already buried one daughter."

"You have my word, Claire."

It was still early when we pulled into my driveway. I called Susan Blake and asked her when I could see Molly. She hesitated.

"I've already tried to make arrangements," she said.

"Unfortunately, Molly doesn't want to see you. She doesn't want to see *anybody*."

I was used to the pain by now. "So she blames me for her having been taken away?"

"I don't know. She isn't talking much, and the foster parent says she doesn't have much of an appetite. As far as I can tell, she's depressed."

"It's not like she doesn't have reason to be," I said, my tone accusing.

"We're watching her closely, Emily. She has an appointment with Cordia Bowers at four o'clock tomorrow. You're welcome to drop by, although I have no way of knowing how Molly will react."

"Why should I? I'm no longer her guardian." I realized I sounded childish, but I couldn't help it. Not only had I lost my niece, but I no longer considered Susan my friend.

"Emily, I'm only thinking of Molly's safety. It's my job. I'd like to think you and I can get through this without letting it affect our friendship."

"Go to Hell, Susan." I hung up.

Clinton was watching me when I turned around. "Do you think that was a good idea?" he asked.

"What does it matter at this point?" I walked over to the kitchen table, pulled out a chair and slumped in it. "You've no idea what Molly's already been through. This could destroy her."

Clinton walked up behind me and started massaging my shoulder muscles. "You're tense all over," he said. "Why don't I run you a hot bath?"

It sounded tempting, but I just wanted to wallow in my misery. "My life is shit."

He worked his way up my neck. "That's true. But your luck is likely to change any minute now."

I dropped my head forward. "I have something to tell you."

"Sounds serious."

I knew he was trying to lighten the mood, but I suspected nothing would help at this point. "I'm supposed to meet

DeWayne tomorrow,'' I said. He didn't reply. ''Don't you want to know why?''

''Only if you want to tell me.''

''He's giving me shooting lessons.''

He stopped rubbing my shoulders and walked away. ''How long has *this* been going on?''

''A few weeks.'' He looked angry. ''Try not to make a big deal out of it, okay?'' I said, sounding much like my niece.

''You could have told me.''

''I didn't tell you because—'' I paused. ''Well, because I'm carrying without a permit.''

He stepped in front of me. I could see the worry in his eyes. ''You have a gun?''

''It's just a thirty-eight.''

''*Just* a thirty-eight. Damn, Emily! Where are you keeping it?''

''My night table.'' He looked like he was about to freak out on me. I could see the cop in him coming out. I stood. ''I wanted to tell you sooner, but I was afraid you'd—'' I held my hands out. ''I was afraid you'd act just like this.''

''Oh, this is great,'' he said. ''Just great!'' He shook his head in disbelief. ''You've got a drunk teaching you how to shoot, and you've been keeping a gun in the house with an emotionally unstable thirteen-year-old. Great idea!''

I decided I didn't much care for his tone of voice. ''Well, forgive me if I acted irrationally, but it's not every day that I have somebody leaving dead rats and chickens wherever I go and slitting my dog's throat. You don't have to be such a jerk about it,'' I added.

''Sorry,'' he said, sarcasm ringing loud in his voice. ''It's just that I thought I was supposed to be protecting you, and I just realized I'm going to have to protect myself as well.''

I cocked my head to the side. ''What's the matter? You afraid I might shoot you?''

''It could happen,'' he said. ''You know I'm up and down during the night. What if you heard me and thought it was him? Of course I'm afraid you'll shoot me.''

"I'm not a complete imbecile."

"Oh, right. You went to an *expert* for your lessons. Did DeWayne sober up for the event, or was he drunk as a skunk when he taught you gun safety?"

I glared at him. "I don't have to listen to this." I turned and made my way to the living room. Clinton followed. I reached for the doorknob.

"Where the hell do you think you're going?"

"Out." He followed me onto the porch. "I'm going across the street to Mrs. Ramsey's house, okay? To talk to her about the Neighborhood Watch program. I'm not taking my gun with me, so you don't have to worry that I might trip and blow my head off."

He leaned against the door frame. "Aren't you going to put on a sweater?"

I wanted to tell him that he was beginning to sound like my mother, but I decided not to waste my breath. Without another word, I crossed the yard and street and made my way up Mrs. Ramsey's driveway. She had a small front porch—not much more than a stoop with a rail around it, actually. An iron pot sat on either side holding plastic Gerber daisies.

I rang the doorbell and waited. I could hear the television set blaring and wondered if she really liked it that loud or if she was feeling lonely. I heard her come to the door and pause, then realized she was checking her peephole. Finally she unlocked her door and opened it.

"Emily, what a nice surprise," she said, giving me a warm smile. "Come in, come in."

Iris Ramsey was a petite redhead who would probably have gone gray by now if not for her monthly visits to Iva Lee's Beauty Salon, where her reddish-orange locks were maintained and her nails were silk-wrapped on a regular basis. She'd lost her husband eight years ago to cancer, but it hadn't stopped her from living a full life. She bowled on Monday, took ballroom dancing on Thursday and volunteered at the hospital most weekends. What she didn't do was spend a lot of time on housework. Her place was always cluttered, and she had enough Elvis memorabilia to start her own Graceland.

I smelled freshly baked bread as I stepped inside. "I can only stay a minute," I told her.

"Come with me into the kitchen," she said, taking my hand and leading the way. "Here, sit down at the table, and I'll pour us a glass of wine. You drink wine, don't you?"

I saw that she was already getting out a wineglass. "Just pour me half," I said, knowing I had very little tolerance for the stuff. I sat there and watched her fill both glasses to the rim from a large bottle. She peeked into the oven, where several loaves of bread were baking, then carried the glasses to the table, sloshing wine over the sides as she walked. I suspected it wasn't her first drink of the evening.

"So to what do I owe this visit?" she asked, setting my glass before me. "I never see you anymore. Not since school started back."

It was true. During the summer we saw each other often as we worked in our yards. Both of us were flower lovers. I'd helped her in her garden a time or two, and she'd thanked me by leaving a nice plant on my doorstep. "Oh, I just wanted to tell you about an idea I had," I said. I took a sip of wine. It was so fruity it made my jaw muscles ache. "I thought it might be a good idea to start one of those Neighborhood Watch programs on our street."

"I knew something was going on," she said, snapping her fingers. "I've seen Chief Hix's police car over there several times, and another officer came by and asked me a whole slew of questions one day. Has something happened? I've been dying to ask you, but I didn't want to appear nosy, and that young policeman acted like everything was a big secret. Does this have anything to do with that girl they found in her bathtub?" She paused to catch her breath.

Her rapid-fire questions caught me off guard, and my first reaction was to lie and reassure her that everything in our neighborhood was fine. Then I told myself I would be defeating my purpose. "This doesn't have anything to do with that poor woman,'' I said, ''but I've had some problems with prowlers at my place, and I thought you should know.''

She looked anxious. ''What kind of problems?''

I started from the beginning and finished with the part about Molly being taken away. By the time I was finished, we had drained our glasses. Iris got up, grabbed the bottle from the refrigerator and refilled them. ''So what does the chief think?'' she asked.

It was a question I'd been asked several times. ''He thinks it's kids.''

''Must be an awfully smart kid to get away with it for this long. And to get past your new dead bolts.''

I thought of Henry Dean, our juvenile delinquent. Hix'd questioned him but had obviously discovered nothing or he would have told me. The boy was either innocent or conniving as hell. ''So there've been no break-ins here?'' I asked.

She shook her head. ''No, thank goodness. I used to be pretty lax about locking my doors, but after that nice policeman came by and warned me, I started being cautious.''

''You must've talked with Officer Duffy.''

''I don't remember his name, and he wasn't wearing a name tag. He was a detective, actually. Dressed in regular clothes.''

''You said he asked a lot of questions?''

''Yes. Mainly about you. He wanted to know if I'd seen anyone unusual hanging around your house, and I told him I try not to pay any attention to what my neighbors do because it's their own business. Then, when I realized you might be in danger, I felt bad for saying what I had.''

I wondered if Clinton had questioned her, but I wasn't aware that he'd discussed the break-ins with my neighbors. I realized Iris was still talking.

''. . . Pity, isn't it? You wouldn't think we'd have to be so careful in a small town. Why, I remember a time when we didn't even bother to lock the doors before we went to bed at night.''

"Things have certainly changed," I agreed, "and that's why I thought it would be a good idea to have a watch program. I'll even hold the meeting at my place, if we can get enough people interested. A good friend of mine is an ex-cop, and he's offered to help."

"Is that the man who's living with you?" I felt my mouth drop open, and she blushed. "I didn't mean to pry. I saw him hiding his car in the garage the other night, and I just figured . . . well, you know, this *is* the nineties, after all."

I thought it a bit strange that my neighbors might not notice some crackpot sneaking into my house at night or killing a dog in my backyard, but they knew the instant I brought a man into the house.

"We're not living together," I said. "Mr. Ward has been deputized by Chief Hix and is providing protection."

"Oh, I see."

I wasn't sure she did. I took a long gulp from my glass and set it down with a thump. "It's strictly business."

She nodded. "And he's agreed to help us with the program, you say?"

"Right. So what do you think?"

"I think we should have done it sooner. Maybe it would have prevented these terrible things from happening to you. How much area do you want to cover?"

"I'd like to concentrate just on our street for now," I told her. "We can always expand later."

She looked thoughtful. "Tell you what. I'll start knocking on doors tomorrow. I don't mind doing most of the legwork since I know how busy you are. We'll compare notes in a couple of days, see how many people are interested, then set up a date for the meeting."

"I'd like to shoot for the weekend," I said. "How does Sunday night sound?"

"Fine with me." She eyed me closely as she took another sip of wine. "So tell me more about this Mr. Ward. Is he married?"

I chuckled. "You know, you're beginning to sound an

awful lot like my mother." I glanced down at my wine-glass and was surprised to find that I'd already drunk most of it. As though acting on cue, Iris filled it.

"You used to tell me everything," she said, a teasing glint in her eyes.

"Really, Iris, there's nothing to tell." I raised my glass and sipped.

"Okay, whatever you say."

I wasn't sure, but I thought maybe she was beginning to slur her words. Or maybe it was me. "Besides, he's just here temporarily," I continued. "He has a job waiting for him in Chicago. He's a homicide detective, sort of on a leave of absence, you might say." As I continued to talk and sip, I noticed that Iris's face looked fuzzy, and I didn't feel so well. "I gotta go home."

"So soon? You didn't finish your wine."

I stood and made for the door. "I have to be up early tomorrow."

She was watching me from the table. "You want me to walk you home?"

I didn't think she'd be able to walk me to the door. "Naw, I'll be okay. See you, Iris." I opened the door and stepped out. I pulled the door closed behind me and started across the yard, trying to ignore the shadows that sprang up from bushes and trees. I wish I'd asked Iris to turn on her porch light. I stumbled, then felt someone's hands reach out for me. Big hands.

I opened my mouth to scream, but a hand covered my mouth and blocked all sound.

26

I must've struggled for a good five minutes before I realized that it was Clinton. Once I knew I was out of immediate danger, I wanted to kick him. "What were you trying to do?" I cried. "Give me a heart attack?"

"I was coming to get you. Lilly called. Wants you to call her right back. Sounded urgent."

"You came sneaking over here to tell me that?"

"I wasn't sneaking. God, you smell like . . . like drunk apples. What have you been drinking?"

"Wine." I started for the road once more. "I have to tell you, I don't handle it well."

"That's one I would never have figured out on my own," he mumbled. He helped me across the street, cupping my elbow in his hand. "So why'd you decide to get drunk?"

"I'm not drunk," I said irritably.

"Right."

"By the way, have you been questioning my neighbors?"

"No, why?"

"Mrs. Ramsey said somebody came by asking questions about me. Hix probably sent somebody from the department." I paused. "No, that's not it."

"What?"

"It was probably someone from DSS posing as a cop."

"I don't think they can do that. By law, they'd have to

264

state the reason for their visit. Hix said he was going to send a patrolman out to talk to the neighbors. That means he's finally doing something.''

We were on my front porch now. Clinton opened the door and I stepped in. I made my way to the kitchen, where I dialed Lilly's number. She answered on the first ring. ''It's me,'' I said. ''Emily.''

''I think I can recognize your voice after all these years,'' she replied.

I leaned against the wall, feeling dizzy. ''So, are you still mad at me?''

''That's why I'm calling. To apologize for overreacting. I know you would never intentionally put Beth and Maryjane in danger. Stoney accused me of acting like a horse's ass.''

''You just had a baby. You have a right to act any darn way you please.''

''Have you been drinking?'' she asked.

''A little wine.'' I sighed. ''Actually, a lot of wine.''

Lilly was quiet for a moment. ''I'm worried about you, Emily. First, a strange man answers your phone and tells me you're not home, then you call me back and you're plastered. What's going on? And who is this Clinton my girls have been telling me about?''

''It's a long story, Lilly.''

''I have the time.''

''Well, I don't. I need to throw up. S'pose we talk tomorrow?'' I hung up the phone, hurried to the bathroom and got sick. Sometime later I washed my face and brushed my teeth, but my breath still smelled as though I'd eaten an entire box of Froot Loops. I opened the door and found Clinton leaning against the wall in the hallway. I thought he looked vaguely amused.

''Feel better?''

''I have just one question. Now that I've thrown up, does that mean I won't have a hangover tomorrow?''

''I wouldn't count on it.''

''That's just great.'' I stumbled down the hall to my bed-

----

room, where I found my bed made and the covers pulled down neatly. "Thanks for making my bed," I mumbled, kicking my shoes off. "It's going to be hard getting used to squalor and junk food when you go back to Chicago."

"I didn't."

"Didn't what?"

"Make your bed."

I felt something icy touch the back of my neck. Fear? I looked at Clinton. "What do you mean you didn't make it?" I asked angrily. "Are you sure?"

"Of course I'm sure."

I stared back at him. Realization slapped me like a cruel hand. "He's been in my house again!" I shrieked. "That scumbag came in here today while we were gone!" I reached for the quilt and pulled it off my bed, half expecting to find coiled rattlesnakes beneath it. Next, I walked to the headboard and grabbed the pillows, tossing them to the floor. One landed on my vanity, scattering my makeup and knocking over perfume bottles.

"What the hell are you doing?" Clinton demanded.

I could barely think past my fury. "That bastard! He touched my things . . . he—" I reached for the lamp on my night table. All at once I felt Clinton's arms enfold me, pinning my own arms to my sides.

"Stop it!" he said. "This isn't going to solve anything."

I stopped struggling. Tears stung my eyes. "Why doesn't he just kill me and get it over with?"

"He's playing mind games with you, Emily. That's all he's doing."

I started to cry. "You're right," I said. "He *is* playing mind games with me. But that doesn't mean he isn't going to kill me when he gets tired of them." I shuddered as I thought of the possibilities. "He's going to kill me the same way he killed Buster."

"He's not going to get close enough. I don't care how many locks you've got on your doors; I'll put chains on first thing tomorrow, like I should have done in the beginning."

"That's not going to stop him from coming in when I'm not here. One day he'll be waiting for me when I get home and—"

"I *won't* leave you alone!"

"You can't be with me twenty-four hours a day, and I can't handle you guarding me constantly. I'll go crazy. We'll both go crazy."

Clinton raked his hands through his hair. I'd never seen him look so tired. "Maybe you really should think about going away for a few days. I could drive you to a motel somewhere."

I shook my head. "You know perfectly well I can't do that. I have to be here. To bait him." I buried my face in my hands. "Besides, he'll probably just follow me."

"I don't want you to stay if it's going to rip you apart like this, Emily. I could get you out of town without him knowing."

"I can't leave, Clinton. I can't take a chance on losing him. Oh, no!"

He looked alarmed. "What is it?"

"I have to throw up again." I hurried toward the bathroom.

By the time I had cleaned myself up for the second time and put on a fresh gown, I was more than ready for bed. Clinton, on the other hand, looked agitated, pacing back and forth, darting glances at me.

"You need anything?" he asked. I shook my head and climbed under the covers, making sure the small wastebasket was nearby. "I'll be in the living room. Call me if you get sick again." He left the room without closing the door.

I lay there waiting for the room to stop spinning so I could fall asleep. I wondered if there would be anything left of our relationship by the time we caught this madman.

I awoke to a hangover. An amused Clinton came into the room shortly after my alarm went off, bearing tomato juice and aspirin. "This and twenty-four hours should get rid of it," he said.

"Just what I needed to hear," I answered glumly.

Two cups of coffee and a hot shower later, I was feeling a bit better. "You don't have to drive me to school today," I told Clinton. "I'm going to need my car."

"You're meeting DeWayne?" He sounded disapproving.

"That's right."

"I can take you to a firing range," he said. "And if you're convinced that you need a gun, I know the place to go. You can pick out something small and easy to handle. You don't need a thirty-eight."

"I've already set this up."

He cocked his head to the side. "Are you still mad at me?"

"No."

"Then why are you acting so cool toward me?"

I looked at him. "It's just—" I paused, not knowing how to say it, not knowing whether I *should* say it. How did I tell him the way I was beginning to feel about him when I had no idea whether he planned to stick around? No, I wouldn't humiliate myself any more than I already had. And I wouldn't do or say anything that would make him feel obligated to me.

"I just have a lot on my mind, Clinton," I said after a minute. "That shouldn't be difficult for you to understand."

He looked like he had something to say, but he seemed to think better of it once he checked his watch. He followed me out of the house and waited while I locked up. "See you later," he said, squeezing my hand before making his way to his car.

"Yeah, see you," I muttered, already feeling depressed.

The morning passed swiftly, and I was so busy with my class that I completely forgot about my headache. Still, I couldn't keep my mind off Molly, and I decided I should probably be at Cordia's for her session. That meant I would have to cancel with DeWayne.

Once break time rolled around, I hurried to the office and asked to use the phone. I dialed the Orange Grove

Motel. A sluggish-sounding desk clerk answered and informed me that DeWayne Tompkins had moved. I fumbled in my purse for DeWayne's business card and called the main office in Columbia. I knew DeWayne checked his messages frequently, so I could cancel our lesson and be relatively certain he'd get it before driving out to our practice spot.

"Acme Medical Supplies," a woman answered, sounding brisk and professional.

"Yes, I'd like to leave a message for DeWayne Tompkins."

There was a slight pause. "I'm sorry, but Mr. Tompkins is no longer with our company."

I didn't quite know what to say. DeWayne had been with Acme forever. "Are you sure?" I asked.

"Yes, ma'am. Could someone else help you?"

"Do you have any idea where I can reach him?" I asked.

"No, I don't."

Her tone was impersonal; she reminded me of an automated answering machine. "Thanks." I hung up and just stood there, then realized that another teacher was waiting to use the phone. "Sorry," I said, moving out of her way. I walked back to my classroom feeling perplexed.

I arrived at Cordia's office right on time and found Molly and Susan sharing the waiting room with an elderly gentleman and a young couple. The room had been decorated in restful blues and mauves, no doubt to make clients feel soothed and relaxed. It didn't help me in the least. "Hi, Molly," I said.

She didn't so much as look at me. "Why is *she* here?" she hissed at Susan.

"Because she loves you and wants to see you get better," the social worker replied.

"I don't *want* her here. She's the reason all these bad things are happening to begin with."

I saw the couple look up. I reached for my niece's hand. "Molly, I—"

"Leave me alone!" she cried, snatching her hand away

as though she'd been burned. "Don't touch me! I hate
you!" She burst into tears.

"It's okay, Molly," Susan said, trying to comfort her.

"Make her go away!" my niece shrieked.

Her sobs got louder. I shot a frantic look at Susan, who
seemed beside herself as to what to do next. "Should I
leave?" I asked, unable to think.

"Maybe it'd be better if you did," she whispered. "I'll
call you later."

Tears smarted in my eyes as I literally ran out of the
waiting room. They blurred my vision as I raced to my car
and got in, trembling from head to foot. I locked the door
and sat there, dazed and pained. The tears came in a torrent,
so violent that they racked my body. Why did Molly hate
me so? my mind screamed. What had I ever done to her?
What the hell was going on?

Time passed. Once I'd collected myself, I started my car
and pulled away. I drove for a long time, not really paying
attention to where I was going. Suddenly, I found myself
pulling into the driveway of DeWayne's old house, the one
he'd shared with Lurlene.

I parked and got out, then rang the doorbell. No answer.
I walked around back to a detached garage. He and Lurlene
had never gotten around to painting it. I cleared a grimy
window with the heel of my hand and peered inside, where
I saw DeWayne's Town Car. I turned for the house and
saw him standing at the back door, watching me. He was
holding a pint-size bottle of whiskey. He raised it to his
lips and took a swig as I crossed the yard toward him.

I came to a halt at the bottom of the steps. "I thought
you gave that up," I said, nodding at the bottle.

He eyed me steadily. "Why are you here?"

He seemed different somehow, colder. I suspected it had
to do with Clinton. But why? DeWayne and I had never
been more than friends. "I was worried about you. I called
the Orange Grove, and they said you were no longer there.
I even called your job."

"So you know I've been fired." He gave a disgusted

grunt. "After all I've done for those bastards."

"Why did they . . . dismiss you?"

He held up the bottle. "You really have to ask?"

"Do you need any money?"

He shook his head. "I've got enough to keep me going for a while."

I stepped closer. "Listen, DeWayne, why don't you take this opportunity to go into treatment?"

He gave a snort. "Why don't you take this opportunity to go fuck yourself?"

I was too stunned to say anything at first. "Why are you mad at me?"

"I'm not mad, I'm fed up. Every time you need something, you come running to poor, stupid DeWayne."

"I don't think you're stupid."

"But when you want to get laid, you call Clinton Ward. You're as bad as your sister."

He was the second person who'd compared me to Lurlene. "Think what you want, DeWayne, but I happen to care a great deal about Clinton."

He turned for the door. "I don't want to hear this."

"I've got something to tell you," I said. "Bad news." He paused and turned. I could see the anguish in his eyes. "DSS took Molly away from me."

"I guess you fucked up."

I thought I had suffered as much pain as I could for one day. I was wrong. "Thanks for your support," I mumbled, turning away.

"What d'you expect me to say? You were probably screwing Ward's brains out right under the kid's nose. What do you *expect* DSS to do?"

I didn't need this, at least not right now, when the pain of my niece's rejection was still so raw and piercing. "Good-bye, DeWayne. Maybe we can talk some time when you're sober." I wondered when that would be as I rounded the house toward my car.

Clinton was not yet home when I returned. I changed into jeans and a sweater and went next door to talk to Mrs.

Hamilton, another widow who lived alone. Unlike Iris Ramsey, who had a busy social life, Mrs. Hamilton seldom left the house. As I followed the frail woman into her cozy den, I explained the reason for my visit and asked her to join us in the watch program.

She patted her white hair anxiously as I talked. Her hands were bony, with protruding blue veins running beneath the papery skin. "I suspected something was amiss when I saw that police car in front of your place," she said. "The detective who questioned me said someone killed Molly's dog. I was just heartsick over it. Please tell Molly how sorry I am."

Once again I was curious about the man who'd talked with my neighbors. "Do you remember the detective's name?" I asked.

She looked thoughtful. "Now that you mention it, I don't know that he actually gave me his name. He just flashed a badge and started asking questions."

"What sort of questions?"

"He wanted to know if I'd seen or heard anything suspicious going on at your place. He also asked a few personal questions about you."

"Personal questions?"

"Like, did I think you were a good parent to Molly. He wanted to know if you had any men friends. Frankly, I thought the questions a bit strange, and I told him so."

"Do you remember what he looked like or what color hair he had?"

"Oh, he was handsome enough. I didn't get a look at his hair on account of he was wearing a baseball cap. He didn't look like any detective I'd ever seen, but the badge was the real thing, so I figured he was okay."

I decided I was going to have to find out who the man was, but I didn't want to act too concerned about it in front of Mrs. Hamilton and have her worry. "So do you want to join our group?" I asked. "I'd like to schedule our meeting for Sunday night."

She nodded. "Count me in. I'll even call a couple of the neighbors, if you like."

I told her to call Iris Ramsey, who had offered to help as well. I thanked her and left, promising to call in a day or two so we could set a time for the meeting.

On the other side of my house, Bob and Marilyn Frazier sat on their front porch, sipping iced tea. Bob had been a builder before his retirement a few years ago; he now spent his days working on his own house. He'd widened the front porch, added a screened porch on the back and built a ga-zebo.

"Sit down," he said. "Marilyn, get Emily a glass of tea."

"No, thank you," I said, wanting to get right to the point, which was not always possible since Southerners often exchanged a good half hour of pleasantries first. Finally I told them what was up.

"We heard all about it," Bob said. "I would have invited you and Molly to stay with us, but I noticed you had a young man staying there, so I figured you were in good hands."

I felt my cheeks burn as I explained the part about Clinton being an ex-cop who'd been deputized by Chief Hix and had offered to stay at my place until we caught the intruder.

"Ah, yes," they said in unison, nodding their heads.

I went on to tell them about the program I wanted to start and when the meeting would be held.

"By all means, add us to the list," Marilyn said. "I refuse to let some sicko make me a prisoner in my own home."

"Ain't nobody going to bother you, hon," Bob told her. "Don't forget I got a twenty-two in the closet."

It was getting dark by the time I left, but I decided to try one more house. I didn't know the Platovsky couple very well, other than to nod in passing, but they were more than interested in the program.

"We tried to start something like this five or six years

ago,'' Mrs. Platovsky said, ''but nobody seemed to think
it was necessary. Shows you how the crime rate has grown
since then. I read about the poor girl that was just murdered,
and I cried myself to sleep. And now this one in Evansville—'' She shuddered. ''You just tell me how I can
help.''

I told her to call Iris, then thanked them both and started
home just as Clinton's car rounded the corner and parked
out front. I stopped by my mailbox, where I found several
bills and a plain white envelope. There was no return address. I didn't give it a second thought as I crossed the yard
and joined Clinton on the metal glider on the porch. Right
now, I wanted to make peace.

''Trying to line people up for the watch program?'' he
asked, having seen me make my way back from the Pla-
tovskys'.

I nodded and sat beside him. ''So far everybody seems
to think it's a great idea. I told them Sunday night, if that's
okay with you.''

''Sure. Did you talk to Molly today?''

''I showed up for the appointment with her therapist, and
the girl freaked out and demanded that I leave.''

''She'll come around, Emily,'' he said. ''Just give her
time.'' He paused. ''Did you have your shooting lesson?''

''No.'' I told him about calling the Orange Grove and
DeWayne's job, and what I'd learned. Then I told him
about driving out to DeWayne's house and finding him
drunk. I saw his jaw tense. ''What?''

''You could have put yourself in danger,'' he said.

''Don't be ridiculous. DeWayne would never hurt me.
But he made it plain he didn't want to see me anymore.''
I added, feeling a sting at the back of my eyes as I remembered how cold he'd been toward me. I reasoned with myself that DeWayne had lashed out at me because he was
upset over losing his job and the fact he'd been drinking.
Of all times for his company to fire him—just when he'd
decided to give up the booze.

''I don't know what I've done to become so popular

lately," I said, feeling very sorry for myself at the moment.

"Well, I still want to see you," he said, leaning over to plant a kiss on my cheek.

"You may not feel that way when I tell you what your share of the power bill is." I opened the envelope and looked. "Not too bad," I mumbled, then tore open my water bill.

"Why don't we go out for dinner tonight?" he asked.

I tore open the white envelope. "Where?"

"Someplace dark and intimate, where I can whisper sweet nothings into your ear."

I reached into the envelope, pulled out a photo. I felt everything in my body shut down.

"I'll have you home early," he promised. "What do you say?" He glanced at me. "Emily?"

I couldn't speak. Actually, I felt like someone had knocked the breath out of me.

"What's the matter?"

"This picture. It's . . . it's—"

"What is it?"

I handed it to him and watched the changes that came over his face. His body tensed; his eyes glittered with rage.

"Is that her?" I managed to ask.

"Yes. It's Cindy Brown in her bathtub with her wrists slit."

27

Chief Hix was out to dinner when we pulled into the station, but the dispatcher assured us that he would be back at any minute. We sat in the waiting room. I was still terribly shaken by what I'd seen; I couldn't get the image of the dead woman out of my mind.

"Who do you think sent it to me?" I asked Clinton.

He looked preoccupied. "Obviously the killer."

"Then this *does* have something to do with what's been going on at my place." He didn't answer. "Don't lie to me, Clinton."

He opened his mouth to answer but was interrupted when Chief Hix walked through the door. The look on our faces must've told him that something was terribly wrong.

"What's happened?"

Clinton handed him the envelope. "Be careful, in case there are fingerprints." The chief reached inside and pulled out the photo, holding it by the very tip. He glanced at it, looked up abruptly. "Where'd you get this?"

"It came in the mail today," I said.

Hix turned the envelope over, obviously looking for a return address. He sat down in one of the chairs across from us and fixed his gaze on Clinton. "What do you suppose this means?"

Clinton shrugged. "I've no idea."

"Don't play dumb with me," I said sharply, causing the dispatcher to look up from his work. "You know damn good and well what it means. It means I'm next."

"You're jumping to conclusions," Hix said.

"I think I have a right to."

"Settle down," the chief said. He turned to Clinton. "I called the pathologist this afternoon, but he was tied up. He got back to me right before I went to dinner."

"And?"

"He said he saw something fishy when he opened up Cindy Brown's stomach; figures she was full of barbiturates. Course, we won't know till the lab runs some tests on her liver. They haven't even had a chance to look at the girl from Evansville. I didn't figure that would surprise you any. Things move a little slow down here."

"What about Frank Gillespie?" I asked.

"Frank's sick," Hix said. "Got a chest cold last week that turned into full-blown bronchitis. He ain't been anywhere, ain't going anywhere."

"Do we know for sure that he's sick, or did Augustus just tell you that?"

"I talked to Frank's doctor personally. I even asked what prescriptions he'd written." He looked at Clinton. "Did I tell you Conner's mother-in-law took a turn for the worse? He's going to be in Atlanta a few more days."

"He seems like an okay guy," Clinton said.

"Yeah, but he's got his head set on going with the FBI. Wants to train at Quantico with the big boys. I have a hard time keeping good men, always get stuck with guys like Duffy. Thank goodness you came along when you did. Did you find out anything at PJ's Lounge?"

"I managed to get the names of a few of the regular customers. If anybody saw anything, they're not saying. I'm also trying to find out if she was seeing someone on a regular basis. I've gone through her address book and phone records, anything I can think of to pick up a name. I'm willing to bet Cindy's best friend knows if there was a man in her life, but I can't seem to locate the woman. She's been out of town since before Cindy was killed."

"Could she be visiting relatives?" Hix asked.

"Maybe. But the owner of PJ's couldn't find her application. At least that's what he said. All he had was her W-two form. I'm running a check on her Social Security number, but who knows what'll come of it. I checked with her landlord, and he couldn't help me either. I'll just have to keep looking." In a softer voice, Clinton added, "Chief, you know damn well Randy Dempsey didn't kill these women. You're going to have to let him go."

Hix seemed to ponder it. "If I let him go, folks'll go into a statewide panic. Until I have something else, I'm going to have to hold him. Besides, he gets three squares a day, and our cells are a lot cleaner than that rattrap he was living in."

"You're going to have a lot of explaining to do if he hires a lawyer and sues for false arrest."

Hix suddenly looked angry. "I reckon I'll have to face it when the time comes, won't I? Right now I'm more concerned with keeping peace in this town." Finally, he sighed and glanced down at the photo once more. "This guy's a real squirrel, if you ask me. Taking pictures of his own work. I'll check for fingerprints right away."

"You and I both know it's going to be clean," Clinton replied.

"We can always hope." Hix regarded him. "You ain't planning on moving out of Emily's guest room for a while, are you?"

Clinton shook his head. "I'm not going anywhere."

I thanked him. "By the way," I said, "someone's been questioning my neighbors."

"I sent Duffy out to talk to them," Hix replied. "That's about all he's good for."

"This guy wasn't wearing a uniform."

Hix shook his head. "He didn't come from this office. Maybe DSS?"

"I'm going to ask them," I said, feeling more hostile toward Susan.

"I've been updating the sheriff on this case; he's offered

to help in any way he can. If you like, I can put a patrolman on Emily's street.''

Clinton shook his head. ''That'll scare the guy away. We want him to come after her. When he does, I'm going to have a surprise waiting for him.''

''If something happens, call dispatch, and you'll have an officer on the scene within a few minutes.'' He glanced at me, then back at Clinton. ''Why don't you take her home? She looks beat.''

I noted the concern in Hix's eyes, and I remembered how I'd looked up to him as a child. Now he looked old and beaten down, and perhaps a bit frightened that the citizens of his town were in danger. I suspected that he wished he'd retired before any of this had occurred, but there was no way he could bow out gracefully with all that was going on now.

Clinton stood and reached for my hand, then pulled me up. He looked at Hix. ''Don't you ever go home?''

The chief shrugged. ''I can shower here in the locker room and sleep on the cot in my office. No need to go home. No need a-tall.''

We left the building a few minutes later, stepping into the nippy night air. The sky was clear and star-studded. Clinton unlocked the door of his car and held it open for me, then climbed in the other side to join me.

We barely talked on the way home. Soon Clinton pulled into my driveway and parked. He glanced at me. ''You're frowning. What's wrong?''

''I don't want to go in.''

''You're afraid he's been here?''

''Yes.''

He leaned back in the seat and put his arms around me. ''Tell you what. I'll check it out first.''

''Who's going to sit in the car with me while you do that?'' I asked, feeling like the biggest coward who ever drew breath.

''Then we'll go in together. You can wait in the living room or kitchen while I search the rest of the house.''

"Why do you suppose he sent me that picture?"

"He's trying to scare you."

"And doing a very good job of it, I might add. For once, I'm almost thankful Molly's not here; otherwise I'd be out of my mind worrying about her."

We entered the house, both noting that the living area and kitchen looked the same as we'd left them. Clinton checked bedrooms while I listened to my telephone messages. My mother called asking if we had any news, and Lilly called saying she was going to call the police if I didn't start explaining things soon. I picked up the phone and dialed her number.

"I hope you're sober tonight," she muttered.

"You caught me at a good time," I said. "Just got back from my AA meeting."

"So what the hell is going on?"

"Can you meet me for breakfast Friday, say, ten o'clock?"

"You're not working?"

"I took the day off. I have to see a lawyer." I winced the moment I said it.

"I'm not going to ask *why* you need a lawyer," she said. "I trust you'll fill me in on Friday."

We worked out the details, and I hung up. I turned and found Clinton standing in the doorway. "Well?"

"You'll be relieved to know that he didn't make your bed or pick up your dirty laundry."

I cocked my head to the side. "Why do you suppose he does that? He tries to take care of me on one hand; then, on the other hand, he's out to kill me. Why?"

"He's sick; what can I say?" Clinton offered me a sad smile. "He's not really trying to help you, Emily. When he made up your bed, he was just trying to prove that he can come in whenever he likes."

"So far he's succeeded." I pressed my fingertips to my temples, where I could feel the beginnings of a headache. "We forgot to eat dinner."

He shrugged. "Are you hungry?"

"Not really. Besides, I can't sleep on a full stomach. I'll have nightmares all night." I rolled my eyes. "What am I talking about? My whole life is a nightmare."

"I know."

"Clinton?"

"Yeah?"

"I can't get over seeing that woman's body."

He closed the distance between us and took me in his arms. "It'll go away in time. If it doesn't, at least you'll learn to live with it."

"How do *you* live with those images? How do you close your eyes at night?"

He sighed. "If it was easy, we wouldn't have so many cops drinking and killing themselves. It's *not* easy."

"You don't have a drinking problem, and you haven't killed yourself."

He looked thoughtful. "I try my best not to let it in where it counts, Emily," he said, placing his hand over his heart, "but I'm not always successful. Sooner or later the walls come tumbling down, and I have to deal with it the best I can."

"Molly builds walls, too. I think she's paying for it now."

"What do you mean?"

"When you build a wall, nothing gets in. Not even the love."

We were quiet for a moment. Finally, he smiled. "I didn't say it was a *good* plan."

I laughed and realized how good it felt.

I got ready for bed and waited for Clinton to join me. It would have seemed so normal, so perfect, if he hadn't still been half dressed, if he hadn't placed his gun on the table before he joined me. I'd seen his weapon before, but I had no idea what it was.

"What are you packing these days?" I asked.

This seemed to amuse him. "A thirty-eight. Same as you."

I rose up on one elbow and looked at him. "Chief Hix

once shot himself in the foot while cleaning his gun. Has anything like that ever happened to you?''

"I pinched my finger with the hammer once—bled like a sonofabitch."

"You ever been shot?"

"I've been shot *at* a couple of times. Luckily I wasn't hit."

"You ever shot and killed anybody?" When he didn't answer right away, I hurried on. "I'm sorry. I shouldn't have asked that. It's none of my business."

He reached for my hand and squeezed it. "Yeah, I killed a man once. After he pumped half a dozen bullets into my partner. The shooter was high on PCP at the time. I had no choice. It bothered me for a while. Contrary to popular belief, cops don't like drawing their weapons."

"Did your partner die?"

Clinton nodded. "Yeah. Left a wife, kids, dogs, the whole shebang. I'd heard of guys riding together so long they knew one another better than their wives knew them. That was the case with me and Davis."

I was about to respond when a noise from the backyard startled us both. "What the heck was that?"

Clinton bolted off the bed, grabbing his gun from the night table and turning off the lamp. "Stay here." He walked through the dark house while I waited in bed, shivering and suddenly having to pee. I wished I could be brave just once.

I heard Clinton go out the back door and into the yard. It seemed like forever before he returned and switched on the lamp. He grinned. "Man, are you going to have a mess in the morning."

"What?"

"Somebody's dog just turned over your trash can. Don't worry; I chased him out."

I sighed and lay back on my pillow. Thank goodness that's all it was. Then I began to wonder. "What kind of dog?"

"Just some mutt."

"How do you suppose he got over the fence? I keep the gate closed."

"I knew you were going to ask that question. Some dogs can climb fences, you know."

"Maybe someone dropped him over the fence, hoping he'd make noise and scare me."

"Or maybe he dug a hole under the fence and got in that way." He climbed into bed. "Let's get some sleep."

It was a long night, and I was too anxious to fall into a deep sleep. I was aware of Clinton leaving the bed several times, strolling through the dark house. I could hear the wood floors creak beneath his feet. I waited for the night to end, waited for the sky outside to lighten and for the alarm clock to sound.

I didn't know how many more nights I could endure.

I awoke the next morning to the sound of Clinton taking a shower. I quickly donned my robe and slippers and let myself out the back door. I entered my backyard through the gate and sighed my relief when I noted that the garbage had already been picked up. Clinton must've gotten up early to clean up the mess, which explained why he was already in the shower.

I followed the fence and told myself that one day I'd have to buy a weed eater so I could cut the grass that couldn't be reached with my lawn mower. I circled the yard and found no dug-out places or other openings large enough to let a dog through the aluminum mesh. I reached the house as Clinton, cup of coffee in hand, stepped out, wearing only his jeans.

"What are you doing?" he asked curiously.

"I was going to pick up the trash."

"I've already done that."

"So I noticed. Thanks." I reached for his coffee and took a sip. It seemed quite natural to share the same cup. "Actually, I was looking for a hole under the fence."

"There isn't one."

"I noticed that, too."

"My mother used to have a poodle who could climb a

six-foot privacy fence in three point five seconds.''

I offered him a sad smile. ''You're lying. I can always tell.''

He looked hurt. ''Always?''

''That dog didn't climb my fence last night, Clinton. Someone dropped him over, knowing he'd go straight for the garbage can and make a racket. Just another scare tactic to keep me on edge.''

He reached for his cup. I could see by the look on his face that he shared my belief. He simply didn't want to frighten me more than I'd already been. It didn't help. I was scared to death.

28

It was decided that I could go to my appointments alone as long as I stayed in public places and carried Clinton's personal phone with me wherever I went. Also, I was to call Clinton often and advise him of my whereabouts so that he or Hix could put their finger on me at all times.

I felt like a sixteen-year-old who'd just been allowed to use the family car, as I pulled out of my driveway with a concerned-looking Clinton watching as he got into his own car. I decided it was a small price to pay in order to enjoy a little freedom. I'd come and gone as I'd pleased for years, and it annoyed the heck out of me to have to worry about checking in. I despised the creep that had put me in such a position.

The town of Mossy Oaks looked much the same as it always had, except that they'd already started putting up Christmas decorations, despite the fact, that Thanksgiving was still two weeks away. Taking in the quaint surroundings, no one ever would've guessed that we had a killer on the loose. It was still early, not quite nine o'clock, and the sky had that leaden look it often takes on before the sun comes out. The air was cold, but I was warm in my wool slacks and matching jacket. As I drove down Main Street, following a sluggish garbage truck, I noticed a patrol car following close behind and decided Clinton wasn't taking any chances.

I tried to imagine the type of individual who'd go to so much trouble to terrify me. As always, Frank Gillespie's name popped into my head. Who else could be doing these things? Who hated me that much? I had no clue.

Several minutes later, I parked in front of a vintage Victorian-style house that had been renovated to accommodate several lawyers. The house was beige, with dark green shutters and ornate fretwork. As I parked, I saw the patrolman park just across the street. I climbed out of the car and made my way up a short walk to the front porch of the house. The beveled glass door squeaked like an injured bird when I opened it.

Attorney Ronnie Patterson—real name: Rondell—was a petite bleached blonde who'd attended Mossy Oaks High one year ahead of me before going off to college and law school. Although a bad case of teenage acne had left her scarred, she had a nice figure and showed it off by dressing in smart but snug-fitting business suits. She took notes and chain-smoked from a box of Kools as I explained my reason for being there.

Finally, she looked up. "So DSS has not charged you personally with anything," she said after I gave her the sorry state of my affairs.

"No." I reached into my purse for the hearing notice. "They said Molly's removal was temporary. As soon as the person responsible for these acts is caught, she's free to return home."

"Do you think your niece would be safe living with you at the moment?" she asked.

I hesitated. As much as I wanted Molly with me, I had to be honest with myself—for her sake.

"Let me answer that question for you," Ronnie said. "You say you've got a deputy with a loaded weapon staying at your place to protect you. Not only that, you're practically tripping over dead animals. Lastly, you tell about a photo of the murdered woman, which you received in the mail. Frankly, I'd say DSS was smart to move on this so quickly. If something happened to your niece, God forbid, this town would probably torch their offices for not removing her from a dangerous situation."

I felt a dull throb at the back of my head. My eye

twitched, and my bladder felt full. And we hadn't even gotten around to discussing her fee. "You're saying I don't have much of a case."

"I'm saying you'd be foolish to bicker with DSS at the moment. Their quarrel isn't with you; it's with the circumstances surrounding you. I've read the stories in the paper myself, and I'm horrified. I'm sure that as soon as this madman is caught, they'll be only too glad to give the girl back."

"Molly thinks I've abandoned her."

"She'll get over it."

I shot her a dark look. "She lost her mother to suicide nine months ago. I don't think she's going to *get over it* as easily as you think."

"I'm sorry if I sounded flippant, Emily, but I'm going to have to side with DSS on this." She leaned closer. "Look, as soon as this guy is caught, we'll petition the court to get her back. I don't care what it takes, but for now I think you'd best leave her where she is."

The phone rang. Ronnie snatched it up and listened to the person on the other end. "Give me two minutes," she said.

I took it as my cue to leave. I stood. "What do I owe you?"

"Nothing for now. Think about what I said." She reached for her briefcase on the floor, opened it and rifled through a stack of papers, probably pertaining to her next appointment. "If you decide you want me to go to court with you next Friday, I will, but I think it's in your niece's best interests for you to comply with their decision. This thing can't go on forever."

I thanked her and left, then drove to Mazel's Restaurant with the patrolman several cars behind. Once I'd parked, I called the police department and learned from Myrtle that Clinton had stepped out. "Please just tell him I called," I said. "If he needs to reach me, I'll be at Mazel's for the next hour or so." The woman promised to do so, and we hung up.

Mazel's had looked the same for as long as I could remember: dull wood floors, square tables draped in cheap plastic cloths and vases of fake carnations sharing space

----

with metal napkin holders, cylinder-shaped sugar containers and salt and pepper shakers. I chose a table near a window, ordered a cup of coffee and waited for Lilly. I was glad to have a moment to myself; I was still trying to come to terms with Ronnie Patterson's advice.

What would Molly think if she found out I'd agreed to let her stay in foster care, even temporarily? She already hated me for reasons I didn't understand; she might never forgive me if she thought I was not putting up a fight with DSS over her. And who could blame her for not feeling rejected after the way life had treated her thus far?

I could feel myself growing agitated, and I turned my attention to a wall where old black-and-white pictures of Mossy Oaks hung. I wondered if life had been as complicated back then as it was now. Surely not. Even without the conveniences we had today, the people that stared back at me seemed at peace with themselves.

Lilly arrived ten minutes later, wearing a baggy dress and looking near exhaustion. She took a seat across from me and said in a matter-of-fact tone, "I know I look like shit. I'm fat and tired and having a serious case of postpartum depression. Other than that, everything is just *dandy*."

"You look fine," I said, realizing she'd somehow put me on the defensive. "But you *do* look tired. How many times are you getting up during the night?"

"The little angel is waking me up every two hours."

I was tempted to tell her to bring the baby to my house. We weren't getting much sleep there, either. "Is Stoney's mother helping?"

She sighed. "Yes, bless her heart, she's doing all she can. You know, I snapped right back to my old self when the girls were born. I'm afraid it's going to take longer this time. I just don't have the get-up-and-go that I had before. I suppose it comes with having a baby at thirty."

I gave a grunt. Just what I wanted to hear, since I was already thirty and had no idea when I might conceive my first child. Our waitress appeared, and we quickly glanced at our menus before choosing the Daily Special: a cheese omelet with home fries and biscuits.

I waited until we were alone before offering advice to my friend. "Lilly, I know what a perfectionist you are. Everything has to be just so. I wish you'd just let the house-work slide for a while. Let Mrs. Dunseath do what she can, and forget the rest."

"I'm afraid I have no other choice. I'm too tired to care. But that's not why I wanted to see you. I want to know what's going on at your place."

"The truth?" She nodded, and I began. It felt I'd told the story a million times, but I knew Lilly wouldn't be satisfied unless she had all the facts. By the time I finished, our food had arrived, and Lilly looked near tears. I suddenly remembered that she was suffering postpartum depression and wished I'd left out some of the more gruesome details.

"Was it really awful?" she asked.

I nodded. "I see the photo every time I close my eyes."

"Why do you suppose he sent it to you?"

I met her gaze. "To tell me I'm next."

"This is absolute bullshit," Lilly said, mopping her eyes with her napkin. "Who could possibly do such a thing?"

I didn't want to share my suspicions about Frank Gillespie, because I had no proof and because I'd have to explain *why* I was suspicious of him. And the longer this thing went on, the more I was beginning to think that I suspected the wrong man. "I haven't a clue," I said.

She was quiet for a moment. "I'm sorry they took Molly," she said. "I know that must've broken your heart."

I nodded, not trusting myself to speak because of the lump in my throat. Once again I stared at the pictures on the wall. "I thought I'd die," I whispered. "I met with a lawyer this morning, and she doesn't think I should fight DSS. She advised me to let them keep Molly until this is over."

Lilly touched my hand. "That's probably a good idea, Emily. You don't want to have to worry about Molly's safety on top of everything else." She paused. "Look, you know we've got plenty of room at our place. Why don't you stay with us for a couple of weeks? Surely they'll catch him by then.''

She didn't know how tempting it sounded. My place had begun to feel so gloomy; I dreaded coming home at the end of the day. Had Clinton not moved in temporarily, I would have jumped at the chance to leave. But I knew I could tolerate just about anything as long as he was beside me.

I explained why I couldn't leave. ''It's okay, really. I feel safe having Clinton with me. He knows what he's doing.''

We sat there for a moment, picking at our food, lost in our own thoughts.

''What do you know about this Clinton fellow?''

''He just moved here, works in the probation and parole office. He was on the Chicago police force for fifteen years.'' I didn't want to go into the part about Clinton beating up the repeat child molester. Lilly had heard enough bad stuff for one morning. ''Why do you ask?''

''Well, doesn't it seem strange that none of this happened until he moved here?'' she asked. ''Have you checked out his story?''

''I never really felt the need.''

''Are you sleeping with him?''

''Define sleeping with him,'' I muttered. She gave me a funny look. ''We sometimes share the same bed, but there's nothing sexual going on. It's hard to get in the mood with a killer lurking nearby.''

''Are you in love with him?''

I sighed heavily. ''I think so. But I don't know how long he's going to hang around. I think he might eventually go back to Chicago.''

''You want to know what I think?'' She didn't wait for me to answer. ''I think you ought to have Chief Hix check him out.''

I shook my head. ''You're wrong, Lilly. Clinton is doing everything possible to help catch this nut. Chief Hix consults with him on his every move. He even deputized him.''

"Exactly. These people try to get close to those working on the crime. That's part of the excitement."

"What do you mean, *these people*? Are you suggesting that Clinton is a murderer?" I stared at her—gawked, actually—unable to believe my ears. "What's the matter, Lilly? Don't you want to see me happy?"

She looked hurt. "Of course I want to see you happy," she said. "But, more important, I want to see you stay alive. You don't know the first thing about this man. Other than what little *he's* told you. Dammit, Emily, you're so gullible sometimes."

"How can you say that? I've lived on my own for years now. I'm raising my sister's child. You've always had Stoney to lean on. You of all people should not be calling *me* gullible."

"Okay, let's just drop it," she said. "You're obviously so crazy about the man that you can't even begin to look at the situation realistically. And I'm so scared for you that I'm going to see everyone as a suspect." She looked like she might cry. "Just be careful. If something happened to you—"

"Nothing is going to happen," I said, covering her hand with mine. "If you met Clinton, you would see that he's on the up-and-up."

"Oh, I have all intentions of meeting him," she said. "I want the two of you to come to dinner tomorrow night."

"Lilly, you're not up to this," I protested. "Why don't you give it a few weeks? You just had a baby, remember?"

"It won't be anything fancy," she said. "I just want to meet him for my own peace of mind."

"I'll have to talk to Clinton and get back to you."

She pushed her plate away. "I've got to get home; my boobs are killing me."

I gave her a blank look.

"It's feeding time," she said.

"Oh." I motioned for the check, and we left our money lying on the table. I walked Lilly to her minivan. "Try to get a nap in today, if you can," I said.

"Look who's talking. When was the last time you had a good night's sleep?" She didn't wait for me to answer as she opened the door and climbed in. "I'll be waiting for your call. If you don't call me, you can bet I'll call you."

I walked to my own car and climbed in, then sat there wondering what to do next. I had the day off, and it was still early. I decided it was time to pay Susan Blake a visit at DSS.

The Department of Social Services shared an antiquated building with the Social Security office, Drug and Alcohol and the Mossy Oaks Housing Authority, among others. Susan Blake's office was on the top floor. Suspecting that the elevators would take forever, I used the stairs. I ran into Susan in the hall.

"Can we talk?" I asked, noting that she looked stressed. "It won't take long. I just want to apologize for coming down on you so hard. I know now that you were only trying to protect Molly."

"Emily—"

"I want to see her, Susan. You told me I could visit. Please don't try to keep me away from her." I knew I sounded like I was begging, but I didn't care. This was Molly we were talking about.

"Maybe you'd better come into my office," she said.

I wondered at her tone, at the almost bleak expression on her face. "What is it? Has something happened?"

Her eyes filled with sudden tears. "Molly was hospitalized this morning, Emily. She's in the psychiatric unit at Mossy Oaks Memorial. I was just on my way there now."

29

I rode to the hospital in Susan's car, since she insisted that I was in no condition to drive. "I tried to reach you at school this morning," she said, "but they said you took the day off. There was no answer at your house."

"I had to attend to business," I mumbled, wishing she would drive faster. "Who put her in the hospital?"

"The psychiatrist at mental health. Mrs. Burke, her foster parent, called, said Molly was in some sort of stupor. She wouldn't talk or get out of bed when Mrs. Burke went in to wake her this morning." She paused. "Did Molly's mother suffer from depression before she killed herself?"

"My sister never had a depressed day in her life. She was a party girl. And I've since learned that she didn't kill herself." Susan gave me a look of outright shock. "That's confidential information, since the case is being reopened," I added. "Tell me something: Is Molly allowed to make phone calls from the foster home?"

Susan hesitated. "Because we suspect that she might be in danger, we've restricted her calls to family members only. We've told the school she's got a bad case of the flu. I personally go by each day and pick up her work so she won't get behind. So far, the only person she has asked to call is you."

I looked at her. "Molly hasn't called me."

Susan looked surprised. "Not even once?"

"You saw how she acted when I came near her the day before yesterday. She was hysterical."

Susan looked thoughtful. "Well, she asked Mrs. Burke twice yesterday if she could call you and was given permission."

"Did Mrs. Burke check to see who was on the other end of the line?"

Susan hesitated. "I doubt it. The last thing we want to do is make Molly feel like she's being punished. We took her out of your home because we thought she was in danger, not because she did anything wrong."

I could hear the defensiveness in her voice, but I knew it was not the time to start placing blame.

We arrived at the hospital and searched for a parking place. The construction work seemed louder than usual as we hurried to the main entrance, and it grated on my already-tense nerves.

The psychiatric unit was located on the top floor of the hospital. We took an elevator up, got off and made our way down a short hallway to a set of metal doors. Susan pushed a button and spoke into an intercom. The doors buzzed, and we entered.

We stopped by the nurses' station, where a bearded man in a dark suit introduced himself as Dr. Greenburg, Molly's psychiatrist. He led us into a small conference room and closed the door, then waited until we were seated before he spoke.

"You're Molly's mother?" he asked.

I shook my head. "I'm her aunt and legal guardian. Molly's mother is deceased."

He opened a file and pulled out a slip of paper. "I need your signature on this release form so I can take a look at Cordia Bower's file on the youngster. I understand she's been treating Molly for some time now."

"That's right." I signed the paper and returned it to him.

He tucked it inside the file, studying me as he did so. "I've spoken with Cordia only briefly about your niece, but why don't you tell me what's been going on at home."

I filled him in quickly, from the first minute I noticed my jewelry missing to the latest incident, which was, of course, the photo of the dead woman. "For some reason Molly blames *me* for everything that's happened."

"I hope the police are actively involved," he said.

"Oh, yes. I actually have a detective staying with me."

He nodded and made more notes. "How long ago did the girl's mother die?"

"It's been close to ten months now." I couldn't believe I'd lost track. At one time, I had it down to the day and hour. "We originally thought that her mother had taken her own life, but the police now have reason to believe that's not the case. Nevertheless, Molly discovered the body."

"What exactly did she see?"

"Her mother hanging from a rafter."

He winced. "What a wonderful image for a child to have to live with," he said, sarcasm ringing loud in his voice.

"Has she told you anything?" I asked.

"She's not talking. She's in what we call a catatonic stupor. She's aware of her surroundings, but she's not responding."

I could feel my mind shutting down; I didn't want to believe this about my niece. Tears smarted in my eyes. "Is she eating?"

"We're feeding her." He paused as though he suspected that I needed time to grasp the situation. "When did you first notice the changes in her?"

I tried to think. My mind was fogged. "Well, considering her past, Molly hasn't been what you'd call a perfectly normal teenager."

He smiled. "I have teenagers of my own. None of them are perfectly normal."

I was relieved to hear it. "She's been withdrawn and frightened since her mother died. Then she got worse when someone killed her dog. She taped handmade crucifixes around her window and started talking about Judgment Day. At first she said it was her fault that all these bad things were happening. Now she blames me."

"Has she ever mentioned hearing voices?"

"No."

"Ever suffered hallucinations?"

"Not that I'm aware of."

He clasped his hands together in front of him. They were big and hairy. Capable hands, I thought. "I suspect Molly is suffering from what the textbooks refer to as brief reactive psychosis. We sometimes see these symptoms if the patient has been through an extremely stressful event, such as the loss of a loved one."

"But why would she break down like this over a dog," I asked, "when she never shed a tear over her mother's death?"

"Maybe she's been in denial, and the dog brought it all back to her. I'll know more after I go through her file. Anyway, the symptoms seldom last more than a few days and never more than a month. I can treat her with antipsychotic drugs, but I'll have to start with low dosages due to her age and size. Once she's released, you'll have to see that she stays on medication and continues her sessions with Cordia."

"Of course," I said, thinking that he looked kind. I trusted him, and that was important with all that I was going through. "May I see her now?"

Dr. Greenburg led us to Molly's room. A young nurse, in the process of feeding her, saw us and smiled. "Molly was just finishing her lunch," she announced in a cheerful voice. She wiped the girl's chin. "Look, Molly, you have company."

I walked to the bed. Molly lay perfectly still on her back, staring straight ahead. She was strapped to the bed. "Hi, sweetie," I said. "How're you doing?" There was no response, not even a flicker of interest. I glanced at the doctor.

"Go ahead and talk to her," he said. "She can hear you."

"I've brought Susan with me, Molly."

"Hi, kiddo," Susan said, coming up to the bed. "I

thought you and I might play some poker while I'm here. As long as you don't cheat.''

If the girl recognized either of us, she didn't give any indication.

"I have to go," Dr. Greenburg said. "Call the Mental Health Center or check with the nurses' station if you have any questions. One of them usually knows where to find me." The nurse excused herself as well, saying that she needed to check on another patient.

I stood there, feeling totally helpless. I touched Molly's hand, her arm. She didn't so much as flinch. "I thought that maybe, when you get out of here, we could go back to Savannah for a few days," I said. "Remember how much fun we had last time?" My eyes misted as I spoke, and I felt a lump the size of a goose egg at the back of my throat.

"You're going to have to come out of this, Molly," I added with a sob. "I can't stand seeing you this way." I remembered how scared she'd been before Susan took her, and I knew a moment of intense rage. I would find whoever was responsible and see that he was punished. With that in mind, I knew I could go on for a while longer.

I leaned close and pressed my lips against her forehead. "Molly, if only you could tell me who has been scaring you," I whispered, "I'll see that he never does it again. I'll—" My voice cracked. "I'll see to it that he never bothers you again." I didn't realize I was close to falling apart until Susan touched my arm.

"Let's go," she whispered, nudging me toward the door.

I shook free. "I can't leave her."

"You have to. For your own good. For *her* own good." We exited just as the nurse returned.

"Are you okay?" she asked me.

"She'll be fine," Susan assured her, dragging me toward the metal doors that led out. The nurse at the front desk must've sensed that I was near tears. She hit the buzzer, and the doors swung free.

I vaguely remembered making the walk to Susan's car

but didn't remember getting in. I must've cried for a long time; when I'd finished, I had a wad of tissue the size of a baseball in my lap. Finally, I felt my control return.

"Are you going to be okay?"

I nodded. "Just take me to my car."

Susan started her engine and pulled out of the hospital parking lot. "I don't think you're in any condition to drive."

"I'm okay now. Really."

She stopped at a red light. "You heard what Dr. Greenburg said, Emily. This condition seldom lasts more than two or three days. Molly's a fighter. She'll come out sooner than that."

"Somebody is scaring her, Susan, I just know it. I don't know who or why, but somebody is filling Molly's head with terrible thoughts." I gritted my teeth. "I have to find out who."

She glanced at me, then turned her attention back to the road. The light turned green and she went on. "What sort of thoughts?"

"Have you ever read the Book of Revelations from the Bible?"

Susan shook her head. "No, I try to stay away from stuff like that."

"It's pretty heavy reading, even for a stable adult who is able to understand portions of it. If someone wanted to scare a child, they wouldn't have much trouble. My mother used to threaten my sister and me with what was going to happen to us if we didn't toe the line. I had terrible nightmares as a child. So did Lurlene."

Susan looked furious. "If she's telling Molly these things, then you have to stop her immediately," she said. "That, combined with what Molly has already been through, could push the girl over the edge. If it hasn't already," she added on a sour note.

"My mother claims she hasn't said a word to Molly."

"What about your father?"

"He doesn't discuss religion. He's very private about his beliefs."

Susan drove for a moment in silence. Finally she asked, "Who else does Molly talk to?"

"She talks to DeWayne once in a while. But DeWayne would never try to scare her like that. He saw firsthand the damage it did to my sister. I recently learned that Molly was hanging out with a boy who has been in and out of trouble since he was ten years old. Serious trouble," I added.

Susan turned into the parking lot of the DSS building. "And you let her associate with him?" She frowned. "I don't like it."

"Wait just a minute, Susan," I said, annoyed with her for being so quick to judge me. "What do you think Molly would do if I flat out told her not to have anything to do with this boy?"

She nodded. "She'd probably see him anyway, even if she had to sneak around to do it."

"Right." Once again I remembered my suspicions on that issue but decided not to say anything, since that's all they were. "Molly led me to believe that they were just studying together, and that she was trying to help him after all the trouble he'd been in. I had to trust her."

"Do you think he's behind the break-ins and killing Molly's dog?" she asked.

"At first, I considered it. Now, I know he's not the one."

"How do you know?" she asked, parking beside my car and cutting her engine.

I told her about the photo I'd received in the mail and watched her expression turn to outright fear. "Why didn't you tell me?"

"The police are handling it, Susan. Besides, Molly was out of the house, so there was no reason for you to know."

"You're such an idiot," she said, her eyes watering. "It would never occur to you that I'm scared for you as well."

I was genuinely touched by the concern on her face. I took her hand and squeezed it. "I'm going to be okay," I

----

told her. "I have every confidence in the man who is staying with me."

Susan looked thoughtful. "So what we have here is some
nut who's scaring the hell out of Molly and who could also
be the same person who killed her dog and these women."
She looked at me. "Is that what it boils down to?"

"I wish I could answer that," I said. "But I don't even
think the police have figured it out yet. In my gut, I'd have
to say yes; I believe the incidences are related." I opened
the door and stepped out.

"You could stay with me," she said. "Nobody would
have to know."

I went through my spiel about why I had to remain at
home. Only then did I remember what I needed to ask her.
"Have you had someone checking on me? Asking questions?"

"I called a couple of people right before we picked up
Molly. It's standard procedure."

"Have you sent a man out to question my neighbors
about my lifestyle?"

"Of course not. Why do you ask?"

"It's a long story, and I'm too tired to go into it right
now. I'll talk to you later." I closed the door of her car
and walked to my own.

I pulled out of the parking place a few minutes later. It
was only one-thirty, but I was dragging. I dialed Clinton's
office, and his secretary put him on the line immediately.

"Where the hell are you?" he demanded. "Duffy lost
you in traffic—something I figured would be impossible to
do in this town, I might add."

"That was Duffy following me?" I asked in disbelief.
"Jeeze, if I'd known that, I'd have been scared to death."

"We had a deal, Emily. You were supposed to—"

"Save it, Clinton," I said. "I can't take any more right
now. Molly's in the hospital." He was quiet as I went on
to explain everything in a trembling voice.

"Tell me where you are, babe. I'll come get you."

"No, you have work to do."

"I don't want you to be alone."

"I'm driving out to my parents' house. Maybe I'll take a nap before going back to the hospital. I'll meet up with you later."

We worked out the details. Once Clinton was convinced I'd be safe, we hung up.

I drove straight to my parents' house without making any stops along the way. I glanced at my reflection in my rearview mirror and was shocked at the woman who looked back at me. My eyes were swollen from crying and ringed with dark circles from my missing so much sleep the night before. I'd lost weight, and my face seemed to consist of angles. No wonder Susan had looked worried.

I pulled into the driveway of the small country house I'd grown up in, and I leaned back against the headrest and closed my eyes. I couldn't remember ever feeling so tired. I heard a noise, opened my eyes and found my mother and father standing there, looking gravely concerned.

"Open the door, hon," my father told me.

I unlocked the door and opened it, then forced a smile. "Mind some company?" I asked.

"Clinton has already called," my mother said. "Come into the house where it's warm. You look terrible."

30

They led me inside, where they insisted that I lie down on the sofa immediately. I didn't realize how badly I was shaking until my mother covered me with a blanket. Still, I couldn't seem to get warm, couldn't seem to get a grip on my nerves.

"Where's that bottle of rock'n'rye?" my father asked. "That stuff I drank to clear up my chest cold last winter."

"I'll get it." My mother hurried into the kitchen. I heard her going through cabinets. She returned with a pint-size bottle and a juice glass. She handed it to my father, and he poured a hefty amount into the glass.

"Drink this."

I took the glass and downed the liquid in one clean gulp. Tears sprang to my eyes, and fire scorched a path from my throat to my belly. "Jeeze!" I cried, giving one great shudder. I would have dropped the glass had my father not taken it from me. "What *was* that?"

"It'll help you relax," my father said. They both pulled their chairs closer, and I felt my mother's hand holding mine tightly. "Now then, Emily," my father said. "Why is Molly in the hospital?"

I filled them in on what had been happening since I'd last spoken with them. My mother cried softly into a tissue when I got to the part about receiving the photo of Cindy Brown's body in the mail; my father sat in utter disbelief. "Naturally, the only thing we can assume is that I'm to be his next victim," I added, my mind already taking on a dullness from the strong drink.

"I can't believe you kept this from us," my father said. "There's a maniac after you, and you don't think we have a right to know?" He stood and paced. "Isn't it enough that we've already buried one daughter?" he almost shouted, his eyes bright with tears.

"I'm sorry, Daddy," I said. "I kept hoping they'd catch him, and it would all be over with."

They were both quiet for a moment, as though trying to get a better grasp on the situation. "What does the doctor say about Molly?" my mother asked.

I repeated most of what Dr. Greenburg had told me, including the fact that he didn't expect the illness to last.

"We've got to go see her," my mother said. "Molly needs to know that her family is behind her."

"We can go after Emily rests," my father said. "I'd like to talk to this Dr. Green—"

"Greenburg," I supplied.

"I want to know exactly what it is he plans on giving my granddaughter," he went on. "I don't like the thought of him pumping her full of some mind-altering drug."

"Yes, but if it'll pull her out of this thing," my mother pointed out.

I felt my eyes close, and their voices suddenly sounded muted and disconnected. I heard my father on the old rotary-dial phone in the kitchen, heard him say Clinton's name. No doubt he was letting Clinton know that I had arrived safely. I also heard him mention that his .22 was loaded and within reach, and would remain that way for as long as necessary.

Finally I slept, too exhausted to do anything more.

I awoke some three hours later, feeling like a new person until I remembered everything. My parents, who had changed clothes in the meantime, told me that we were going to the hospital.

"You should eat something," my mother said to me.

"I don't think I could hold it down," I said. "Maybe

I'll grab something at the hospital.'' Finally, we were ready to go. "I want to drop by DeWayne's house," I said as we climbed into our respective cars, once I'd insisted I was okay to drive. "He has a right to know. Besides, Molly is crazy about him. He might be able to help.''

My parents looked skeptical but agreed to follow me. They waited in their car while I knocked on DeWayne's door. It took a moment for him to answer, and when he did, I almost didn't recognize him. He hadn't shaved in days, and his clothes were filthy. He stank of booze. He saw my parents' car in the driveway behind mine, and his jaw hardened. "What's this, a family reunion?''

"I have more bad news, DeWayne," I said quickly. "Molly's in the hospital." His eyes narrowed; for a moment it looked like he didn't believe me. "She's had some sort of breakdown," I said. "She's in the psychiatric ward.''

"What did you do to her?" he demanded.

I was stunned by the question. "I didn't do anything," I said defensively.

"You must've done something. She was perfectly fine last time I saw her." He looked angry. "You should never have been given the responsibility of a kid.''

I shook my head, unable to believe it was DeWayne I was talking to. "What's gotten into you?" I asked. "Why are you acting like this? Is it the booze?''

"I want you to go," he said. "Get the hell out of here, and don't come back." He slammed the door in my face.

I stood there, wondering what could have set him off. Was it because of my involvement with Clinton? That's the only thing I thought it could be. I climbed back into my car and followed my parents to the hospital.

Although I tried to prepare them as we took the elevator up to the third floor, my mother and father were plainly shaken at the sight of their granddaughter. Both seemed hesitant to go near her bed.

"It's okay," I said, trying to make my voice sound natural, as though finding my niece in a psychiatric ward were an everyday occurrence. I walked up to the bed and took Molly's hands in mine. They felt like cold bundles of bones, and I wondered how much weight she'd lost. "Hi, Molly," I said. "I brought Grandma and Grandpa to see you." Her eyes were closed, but she opened them at the sound of my voice. Nevertheless, there was no response.

My mother stepped closer and smoothed her thin arm. "Hello, dear," she said. "How are you feeling?" When Molly didn't answer, she exchanged nervous looks with my father.

The door opened, and a nurse walked in. "Sorry, I didn't know Molly had company," she said. "I was just going to take her vitals, but I can come back."

"Has there been any change?" I asked.

The nurse shook her head. "Dr. Greenburg has started her on medication, but we probably won't see anything right away. Her therapist was in earlier. She wants you to call her."

I had completely forgotten about Cordia, who would probably have a lot of questions to ask, none of which I thought I could answer. She would want to know what might have pushed Molly over the edge. That's the question I'd been asking myself all afternoon.

"Tell me something," my father asked. "What kind of drug is she on?"

The woman didn't hesitate. "Dr. Greenburg has her on a tranquilizer, sir."

"Why does she need a tranquilizer? Looks to me she's already *tranquil* enough."

"It's not meant only to induce tranquility. It's also an antipsychotic drug."

My father looked at me. "Is she making any sense to you?"

"The doctor thinks Molly is suffering from psychosis—"

"What in tarnation is that?"

"You might say it's disordered thinking," the nurse said. "Sometimes, like in Molly's case, the person becomes mute. This drug, Haldol, has shown much success in cases such as Molly's.''

My father nodded, although he still looked skeptical. ''So you feel certain she'll come out of it?''

''Dr. Greenburg is optimistic.''

''Will there be any lasting effects?'' I asked.

''She might be slightly depressed for a while. You really should take up these questions with her doctor.''

''Where is he?'' my father asked.

''Dr. Greenburg has already made his rounds for the day.''

''Figures,'' he said with a snort. ''Never around when you need 'em.'' The nurse smiled benignly and left us.

After spending close to an hour with Molly, during which time we didn't so much as get a flicker of recognition, my parents and I stepped out and made our way to a small lobby. My mother, who'd obviously been holding back tears the entire time, started crying.

My father took her hand. ''It's going to be okay, Claire,'' he said. ''She'll come around once that medicine gets into her system. You heard the nurse.''

My mother fumbled in her purse for a tissue. I remembered how hard I'd cried after Susan and I had visited Molly earlier. ''Did you see how skinny she is?'' my mother asked. ''Lordy, the girl's nothing but bones. Didn't they feed her in that foster home?''

''The foster parent told Susan that Molly refused to eat,'' I said. She cried some more.

''Why don't we go down to the cafeteria and grab a cup of coffee?'' my father suggested, looking lost at trying to deal with my mother's tears.

''Give me a minute to pull myself together,'' my mother told him, blowing her nose into a tissue. She pulled out her compact and tried to make repairs to her face, then applied fresh lipstick. We left the psychiatric unit and made for the elevators. The doors opened, and Clinton stepped off.

''Hi,'' he said, his gaze automatically meeting mine. ''Are you leaving?''

"We're on our way to the cafeteria for coffee," I told him. "Want to join us?"

"Sure." We got on the elevator and rode to the basement, then followed the smell of food. Inside, Clinton told us to find a table while he went for the coffee. I selected one in the corner, where we could talk privately. Clinton returned with a tray bearing four Styrofoam cups. He passed them out.

My mother had started to cry again, and I put my arms around her. She sniffed. "I thought that after Lurlene's death the Lord wouldn't give me anymore heartache. He must be testing me."

"Molly's going to come out of this, Mom," I told her. "You've got to believe that."

"You can't go back to that house," she said, her voice filled with conviction. "You have to come home *immediately*."

I took her hands in mine. "Listen to me," I said. "If I leave, he'll just find out where I am and follow me. I won't risk putting anyone else in danger. Besides, Clinton knows what he's doing, and he won't let anything happen to me."

She sipped her coffee in a thoughtful silence. "Why do you suppose it started all of a sudden?" she asked mournfully. "Everything was just about to return to normal." She looked at Clinton. Tears streamed down her cheeks. "Do you think Frank Gillespie is behind all this?"

"The sheriff put a tail on Frank several days ago, Claire," he said. "We have no reason to suspect him."

"Everybody knows he's a mental case," my father said. "Wouldn't surprise me to learn that he killed those two women."

Clinton looked at me, and I shook my head slightly. I had not yet told my parents of Clinton's suspicions that Lurlene's death had not been a suicide after all, that she could possibly have been killed by the same man who'd committed the recent murders, thereby clearing Frank. I felt I'd dumped enough information on them for one afternoon.

"Let the police worry about it for now," I said as gently

as I could. "I just want to concentrate on getting Molly better."

"Of course," my mother replied. "We all do." Then, just as it looked like she'd gotten herself under control, her face crumpled and she became tearful once more. Finally we ushered her out of the cafeteria and insisted that my father take her home.

"What time will you come to the hospital tomorrow?" my mother asked before they pulled away.

I was glad tomorrow was Saturday. "I'll come as early as they'll let me."

"Your father and I will be here after breakfast."

Clinton and I returned to the lobby, took the elevator to the third floor and went into Molly's room. Clinton was visibly shaken by the sight of her. As for me, I was numb. We stayed until visiting hours were officially over, then left after I'd hugged Molly and promised to return early the next morning. From the blank look she gave me, I wasn't sure she'd even heard.

At home, I checked my messages. Cordia had called and wanted me to call her at her home. I dialed her number. "How's Molly?" she asked, the minute I got her on the line.

"The same."

"I'm so sorry, Emily. I understand that Dr. Greenburg started her on Haldol. That's a powerful drug, and I've seen a lot of success with it."

"We can only hope," I said.

"How are you holding out?"

"Okay, I guess. I've cried a lot today."

"Is the situation at your place any better?"

"They haven't caught the guy, if that's what you mean."

"Aren't you scared there by yourself?"

"I have a deputy staying with me," I said. "I'll be okay."

"Listen, Emily, about this business with DSS—"

"I'm okay with it, Cordia. Susan Blake and I had a long talk, and she assured me that Molly can come home as soon as this is over." If she snaps out of whatever's happened to her, I thought. But I couldn't let myself continue along those lines right now, or they'd probably end up putting me in the bed next to my niece.

"I'll drop by to see Molly tomorrow," she said. "You take care of yourself."

After we hung up, I called Lilly, gave her the news and told her I'd have to get back to her on dinner the following night. Frankly, I was in no mood to socialize, not even with my best friend. Nevertheless, I was touched by the genuine concern in her voice and wished I could answer her questions regarding Molly's prognosis. "Why don't I call you from the hospital tomorrow?" I suggested. "Perhaps I'll know more then."

I hung up a few minutes later and found Clinton sitting in the living room watching the news, his gun on the coffee table. "This town is crawling with reporters over Cindy Brown's murder," he said. "It's the same in Evansville. The public already suspects that the murders are related. People aren't stupid; they'll figure it out soon."

I sat on the sofa beside him. "Anything new on either case?"

"I was able to locate the store where the washer and dryer unit came from, the one that Randy mentioned had been a gift. Nothing there. Cindy came in alone and paid cash for it."

"It's hard to imagine that someone living in your own town is capable of something like this," I said.

He nodded. "Yeah." Then he turned to me. "How're you holding out?"

"All right, I guess."

"You've been crying a lot today, haven't you? Your eyes are puffy."

I nodded.

"Come here." He put his arm around me and pulled me close, then held me for a long time. I felt comforted for the first time that day. "She's going to come out of it, Emily,"

he said. "I've seen people go through similar episodes.
They eventually got better."

"How long does it usually take?"

"It differs with everybody. Hopefully, that drug she's
taking will hurry the process along. Did the doctor give
you any idea?"

"Two or three days, in most cases. But they had to start
her out on such a low dosage. Did you see how tiny she
is?"

"She's lost weight. How long has she been starving herself?"

"She'd already lost much of her appetite before DSS
took her," I said. "Then the foster parent called Susan a
couple of times because Molly absolutely refused to eat.
Susan assumed she was just pouting, so she began to stop
by fast-food restaurants on her way home, trying to find
something to entice Molly to eat." I told him the rest: how
the foster parent had found her that morning. By the time
I finished, I had no strength left.

"I'm really scared, Clinton," I said.

He took my hand and squeezed it. "You have every right
to be."

31

There was no change in Molly when Clinton and I arrived at the hospital the next morning. I'd stopped by the gift shop downstairs and purchased a vase of yellow daisies with a tiny GET WELL SOON balloon tied to a dowel that was stuck into the vase. I sat them on her night table and regarded my niece. Her eyes were closed, and the blanket was pulled up to her chin. I wondered if she was cold or if she wanted to hide beneath the covers. I stepped closer, touched her forehead.

She opened her eyes. "Good morning," I said brightly. "How do you feel today?" There was no response. "I brought you flowers." She continued to stare straight ahead as if she hadn't heard me.

Clinton approached the other side of the bed. "Hiya, kid," he said. "Can you hear me?" When she didn't reply, he went on. "I know you can hear us, Molly, but if you don't want to talk right now, that's okay. You do what you have to do to feel better. We'll be here when you decide that you have something to say."

My parents arrived shortly thereafter, my mother carrying a worn teddy bear. "Here, sweetheart," she said, tucking it close to her granddaughter. "I thought this might make you feel better. It belonged to your mother, you know. I had Grandpa go up to the attic for it last night. I hope it doesn't smell too much like mothballs. We've been airing it out." She paused as if searching Molly's eyes for

311

signs of recognition. Finally, she turned to me. Her bottom lip quivered as our gazes met.

"What's the bear's name?" I asked gently.

She blinked. A tear clung precariously to her eyelashes. "His name? Oh, I believe Lurlene called him Fuzzy, or something or other." She reached into her purse for a tissue and dabbed at her moist eyes. "I can't begin to tell you how many times I've sewn the poor thing back together."

Dr. Greenburg came in. I introduced him to my parents while he examined Molly. He raised her arm straight out in front of her and stepped away. The arm stayed just as he'd positioned it. "I've increased her dosage of the Haldol," he said. "All we can do now is wait."

"Why is she doing that?" I asked, motioning toward her arm.

Dr. Greenburg glanced at me. "Some motor behaviors take on what we refer to as a waxy flexibility, meaning that a person can be fixed into a position, and he or she will remain that way indefinitely. I've also witnessed some catatonic posturing, though it's not as bad as I've seen in some of my patients." He lowered her arm and tucked it under her covers.

I asked questions. How long would it take for her to come out of the psychosis? What were Molly's chances of full recovery? Would she have problems in the future? Dr. Greenburg answered my questions the way all doctors answer questions: He talked around the subject as much as he could, then left us standing there, wondering what he'd said.

"I don't think he knows," my mother whispered.

The morning dragged on. Lilly and Stoney visited briefly, and I couldn't decide whether Lilly spent more time studying Molly or Clinton. She pulled me aside on her way out. "Why don't you guys just stop by for dessert and coffee tonight when visiting hours are over?" she suggested. "I'll feed the kids and put them to bed early, so we can relax."

"I haven't had a chance to ask Clinton," I told her.

"That's okay. Just wait and see how the day progresses. If you can't make it, I'll understand." They stayed and chatted for a while, both of them trying hard not to stare at the girl in the bed who now resembled a life-size doll. I noticed Lilly beginning to look uncomfortable, and I suspected that her breasts had become engorged. I pictured a frantic grandmother pacing the floor with an infant screaming for his next meal.

"Go home," I said. "I'll call if anything changes."

Cordia came in shortly before lunch, looking beefy in her blousy garb. I introduced her to my parents and Clinton, then watched her carry on a one-sided conversation with Molly. Finally she motioned for us to follow her out. "What did Dr. Greenburg say?" she asked when we'd reached the lobby.

I shrugged. "I'm not sure. I think we're just supposed to wait."

She studied my face. "Did you sleep last night?"

"Off and on. It was a quiet night. Maybe the guy knows I have my hands full and can't deal with anything else right now. Besides, what more can he do? My niece is locked away in a psychiatric ward, and I'm fresh out of animals for him to slaughter."

I heard a soft gasp and realized it had come from my mother. "I'm sorry," I said, knowing it had been a terrible thing to say. "I'm not thinking straight."

"I could ask Dr. Greenburg to give you a sleeping pill," Cordia suggested, "or something for anxiety."

"I'm okay for now."

Cordia looked doubtful but didn't push. Once she left, I returned to Molly's bedside and tried to brush her hair. I rubbed her arms and legs and her feet. I talked to her, cooing softly as one would to a new baby while my father and Clinton stood just outside the door looking uncomfortable. When a nurse came in with a lunch tray, I insisted on feeding her. She fell asleep afterward, and we slipped from the room.

In the cafeteria, we stood in line behind people wearing

----

green scrubs and white lab coats. My mother and I decided
to share a chicken sandwich, since neither of us had much
of an appetite, but we were both in dire need of a cup of
coffee. The men selected the special, which consisted of
sliced ham, macaroni and cheese and a vegetable.

"How about that table in the corner?" I said, wanting
to escape the chattering crowd. Nobody seemed to care one
way or the other, so I led the way.

We ate in silence for several minutes. Finally, my mother
looked up at me. "What are you going to do if she doesn't
wake up by Monday?"

"I'll have to take time off from work. I'm sure Mr. Higginbotham will understand."

She looked thoughtful. "Your Aunt Bessie used to get
like this. She'd be depressed for days. We couldn't get a
word out of her."

I felt my irritation flare. "Molly is nothing like Aunt
Bessie," I said sharply. "The kid hasn't even had a chance
to get over losing her mother, and now she's dealing with
a psychopath." I didn't realize how loudly I was speaking
until I saw a couple staring at us from the next table. Clinton covered my hand with his.

My mother looked near tears. "I wasn't trying to insin-
uate that there was something wrong with Molly, dear. I
was just trying to make you aware that I know what you're
going through."

I shoved my sandwich away and picked up my coffee
cup. Clinton shot me a disapproving look. "You have to
eat."

"I'll get sick if I do."

"You'll get sick if you don't."

I picked up my sandwich and took a big, unladylike bite.
I realized I was acting like a child, but I didn't care. I was
in pain. I was in so much pain that I wanted to die. I wondered suddenly if that's why Molly had stopped eating. Had
her life become so unbearable that she'd tried to kill herself
by starvation? The thought frightened me.

" 'Attagirl," Clinton said.

The stuff in my mouth tasted like shredded newspaper, but somehow I managed to swallow. "I have to get back," I said, sliding my chair away from the table. "I don't feel comfortable being away from her."

"I'll come with you," my mother said.

"No, please." I felt shaky all of a sudden. "I just want to be alone with her for a few minutes."

I left them, hurrying out of the cafeteria and toward the elevators. I took one up to the top floor, hit the intercom button and was buzzed through. At Molly's room, I paused in the doorway. DeWayne was sitting in a chair beside her bed, stroking her hair and talking to her softly. He must've sensed my presence; he looked up.

"Why didn't you tell me she was this bad?" he demanded.

I entered the room. "I tried. You were too busy telling me what a rotten person I was."

He glanced away. "What does the doctor say?"

I repeated my brief conversation with Dr. Greenburg, deciding to let DeWayne arrive at some sort of conclusion on his own. "Basically, we're waiting for the Haldol to kick in."

He looked at me. "Why is she so damn thin?"

"She'd stopped eating."

"Jesus Christ, Em!"

"Listen, DeWayne, don't come in here and start blaming *me* for everything that's happened. You of all people have no right to condemn me. At least I was there for Molly, which is more than I can say for you."

"I would have been there, too, had I felt welcomed."

"You would have been welcomed if you'd stayed sober long enough."

We were quiet for a moment. I heard someone clear their throat, and I realized that we had company. My parents and Clinton stood just outside the door.

"I can see this isn't a good time to talk," DeWayne said, his eyes darting to Clinton. He started out, then glanced at me, his eyes empty of the warmth I'd seen in the past.

"Call me if there's a change," he said. "You can get my new number from information." He left without another word, and I suddenly realized that our argument had taken place right in front of my niece.

"What was *that* all about?" my father asked as soon as he stepped into the room.

"Let's talk in the hall," I suggested, knowing that Molly didn't need to witness more problems. "DeWayne blames me for all of this," I told him.

"I could smell alcohol from across the room," my mother said.

"Try not to be too hard on him," I said. "I'm sure that seeing Molly like this was a big shock. He also lost his job recently, so he's under a lot of stress."

"We're all under a lot of stress," my father said. "That's no reason to act uncivilized."

"We have to be careful," I told them. "Molly may look like she's out of it, but she hears every word we're saying."

The day took its toll on all of us—even Clinton, who looked weary when it was time to leave. "Will you be joining us for church tomorrow?" my mother asked.

I shook my head. "I'll come here as soon as I get up."

"We'll be over as soon as services are finished."

We walked out to the parking lot together, then split up and made our way to our respective cars. "You want to grab a hamburger?" Clinton asked once we'd pulled onto the main road.

"I sort of promised Lilly we'd come by for coffee and dessert."

"Do you still want to go?"

"It beats the heck out of going home."

We arrived at Lilly's shortly before nine o'clock. The twins were in bed, but the baby was still up, bright-eyed and looking as though he had no intention of going to sleep anytime soon.

Stoney handed Clinton a beer while Mrs. Dunseath made several sandwiches and Lilly and I fussed with the baby. Finally, Stoney led Clinton out to the garage to show him the old Chevy he'd bought some time ago. He planned to restore it when the kids were older and he and Lilly had more time on their hands. Moving to the nursery, I rocked the baby and gave Lilly the latest news on Molly, which was absolutely nothing. I told her about DeWayne's brief visit.

"He has no right to criticize you," she said, trying to keep her voice low. "After all, what has *he* done for the girl?"

"He called her from time to time," I said, almost in a whisper. "I suppose I have to give him credit for that."

"Big deal. Has he ever offered to keep her so you could have some time to yourself? Has he ever given you one dime for her support?"

"He gives her birthday and Christmas gifts," I said, "but I've never asked him for money. He's not her real father, so I don't expect it."

"I remember a time when he wanted to adopt her."

"Everything changed when Lurlene died," I said.

The baby was nodding on my shoulder. I snuggled him close, taking great pleasure in the sweet smell of him and his warm little body. For a brief moment, I forgot everything else.

"I think Danny boy has finally had it," Lilly whispered. She lifted him gently from my arms and carried him to his crib. We slipped out of the room and made our way into the kitchen.

"You probably don't want any more coffee after being at the hospital all day," she said. "How about a glass of wine?"

I remembered the last time I drank wine and opted for a soft drink instead. She grabbed a couple of diet colas from the refrigerator, and we took a seat at the table, where her mother-in-law had left the plate of sandwiches. I took one.

"Clinton seems nice," Lilly said. "I haven't spent enough time with him to know for sure, but I get the impression that he truly cares about you. I'm sorry for having suspicions."

"He's been a big help. I would never have been able to stay alone after what's happened."

"Do the police think the guy who killed Cindy Brown is the same one who killed the girl in Evansville?" she asked.

"They're still looking into it," I said, knowing that I couldn't reveal what I'd learned. "Both the chief and Clinton are very hush-hush about it." I decided to change the subject. "You know, if Hix catches this guy, he'd retire a hero. We might even have to throw a parade on his behalf."

"Well, if he doesn't find a replacement fast, they're going to have to push him down Main Street in a wheelchair. Do you think Clinton's interested in the job?"

"Your guess is as good as mine."

"Talk in town has it that Clinton was *forced* to leave his job in Chicago."

"That's right."

She looked surprised that I would admit it so easily. "So he's told you about it?"

"No reason to keep it a secret." I told her all I knew about Clinton's resigning from the Chicago Police Department.

"Seems to me, they should have pinned a medal on him," Lilly said once I was finished. "I don't know how I'd live through it if someone raped my child."

I sighed. "The criminals seem to have all the rights these days."

Lilly reached across the table and took my hand. "I'm scared for you, Emily. I know Clinton's experienced with this sort of thing, but I still worry."

I gave her my best smile. "I'll be okay, Lilly. And so will Molly."

"You really believe that?"

"I have to. It's the only thing that keeps me going."

32

The next morning I awoke to the sound of the heat kicking on and realized that we were already into the third week of November. I glanced at the pillow next to me and saw that Clinton had already gotten up. The house was cold as I kicked off the covers and got out of bed.

I slipped on my robe, stepped into a pair of fuzzy bedroom slippers and made my way into the kitchen, where Clinton was already dressed and having coffee. He looked deep in thought but smiled the minute he saw me.

"Have a seat, and I'll pour you a cup," he said, getting up from the table.

"Thanks." I wondered if he knew how nice it was when he did things for me these days, even something as small as pouring my coffee. I wondered if he did them because he thought I needed the extra attention. I had been trying so hard to take care of Molly's needs these last ten months that I'd forgotten about my own.

Now I felt fragile, as though I might fly apart if something else happened, which is probably why I was content to let Clinton cuddle me like a child in his arms at night until I was finally able to close my eyes. Once or twice, I'd felt him become aroused, and I'd automatically tensed, holding my breath in anticipation. He must've felt the stiffening of my body; both times he'd gotten up to check the house and hadn't returned for a long time. I'd lain in bed

----

feeling guilty for wanting him when my world seemed to be collapsing around me.

He set the coffee cup in front of me, and I thanked him again. He patted my shoulder and reclaimed his seat. "I thought maybe we could go out to breakfast before we drive to the hospital."

"You don't have to go with me today," I said.

"Of course I'm going."

"It's boring just sitting there. Sometimes I don't think Molly even knows we're in the room."

"She knows."

The phone rang, and I checked the clock over the stove. Not quite eight. I sighed and got up. Chief Hix spoke from the other end. "Good morning, Emily. I hope I didn't wake you."

"No, I was up."

He paused. "Look, I heard about Molly, and I'm real sorry. I promise, I'm doing everything I can to put a stop to this business. Is Clinton around?"

"Just a minute." I held the phone out to Clinton. "It's for you."

He reluctantly got up from his seat and took the phone. "Hello?" He was quiet for a moment as he listened. "Well, that's good news." He looked at the clock over the stove. "Give me time to grab a shower. I'll be there as soon as I can."

I almost cringed at the thought of having to rush. I longed to drink my coffee and relax before hitting the road. Not only that, but I'd planned to straighten the house because my neighbors were coming that evening for the Neighborhood Watch meeting. I shot Clinton a questioning look as he hung up. "What?"

"Cindy's best friend got back into town late last night. She heard about the murder this morning, supposedly freaked out and called Hix. Claims she has information. Anyway, he's sending a car for her and wants me there on the double."

I tried not to get my hopes up, but I felt them soar anyway. "This could be the break you've been waiting for."

"We need to hurry. I'll drop you off at the hospital on my way to the station."

Clinton broke all the speed limits getting me to the hospital. He let me out at the entrance after promising to call the minute he knew something. When I entered Molly's room, I found a nurse tending to her. "I just bathed her," she said. "She's ready for visitors, right, Molly?"

I didn't expect my niece to respond to the woman's question, and she didn't. "Has there been any change?" I asked, walking over to the bed and laying my hand against the girl's cheek.

The nurse smiled on her way out. "Not yet, but we're hopeful."

I sat on the edge of the bed and carried on the usual one-sided conversation with Molly, telling her all about the newest Dunseath, about how things were going at school, anything I could think of. After about an hour of steady talk, I moved to the comfortable-looking recliner near the bed. Within no time, I drifted off to sleep. I didn't wake up until my parents came through the door.

"Oh, I'm sorry we woke you," my mother said. She and my father still wore their church clothes. "Has there been any change?"

I yawned wide and shook my head, glancing at Molly, who was sleeping.

"Where's Clinton?" my father asked.

"He had to run by headquarters. He shouldn't be long."

My mother went to the bed and gazed down at Molly, touching her cheek lightly, kissing her forehead. "Hi, sweetie. Grandma and Grandpa are here."

I got up from the recliner and offered it to my dad. "You look tired."

He nodded. "Your mother kept me up half the night with her tossing and turning."

"I couldn't sleep for worrying," she confessed.

A nurse came to the door. "Miss Wilkop?" she said. "You have a phone call."

"That's probably Clinton now," I told my parents. "I'll be right back."

The nurse led me to a wall phone, and I picked it up. "How's it going?" he asked as soon as I spoke.

"No change," I told him. "Did you find out anything from Cindy's friend?"

"Yeah. She not only had a boyfriend; he was her sugar daddy as well. Also, Hix called a friend of his who owns a jewelry store. He came by and looked at the tennis bracelet. Says it's worth about twelve hundred bucks."

"Wow. I don't know many men in this town who could afford to drop that kind of money on a girlfriend," I said.

"Only one that I can think of," Clinton said.

"Augustus Gillespie," I heard myself say. "Do you think he's capable of murder?"

"Murder, maybe. But I'm not so sure he'd cut up a woman and risk ruining a two-thousand-dollar suit. He'd hire someone to do it."

"Are you going to question him?" I asked.

"He's on his way here now. I need to hang around a while."

"I want to be there when you interview him."

"No way," Clinton said.

"He won't even know I'm there."

"Forget it."

"He may have killed my sister. I have a right to know."

"Augustus has rights, too, Emily. Besides, we don't know that he's guilty."

"You let me watch Randy Dempsey's interrogation."

"That was a mistake. I was just caught up in the murder and not thinking about the legalities. I've got to go now. I'll be at the hospital as soon as I can."

"Clinton, wait—" He'd already hung up.

I was tempted to bang the phone against the wall. Instead, I hurried into Molly's room. "I have to leave for a few minutes," I told my parents.

"Is something wrong, dear?" my mother asked.

"No, no, everything's fine. Just a couple of errands I need to run. I'll be back shortly." I grabbed my purse and raced out the door before they had a chance to ask any more questions.

I made it to the police station in record time and parked in back, away from Clinton's car and Chief Hix's patrol car. I hurried around front and found Myrtle. "Hi," I said, breezing past her. "Chief Hix is expecting me. Told me to wait in his office."

She opened her mouth to say something, but I didn't stop to listen. I hurried into the chief's office and paused long enough to catch my breath. It was located three doors down and across the hall from the break room. I started out, then almost bumped into a patrolman coming out of another office.

"Can I help you, ma'am?" he asked.

"No, thank you," I said. "Chief Hix asked me to wait for him here."

He nodded and made his way toward the lobby and dispatch area. Once the hall was clear, I eased down toward the break room, noting as I did that the door to the interrogation room was closed. As I passed, I heard voices and decided they'd already begun.

The door to the break room was closed as well. Hoping and praying it would be empty, I turned the handle and stepped inside. Duffy was sitting at the table, eating a sandwich. A shade had been pulled down over the window; obviously, he wasn't as curious as I to see what was going on.

He stood. "Miss Wilkop. What are you doing here?"

My brain scrambled for a reason. "Oh, Duffy," I said breathlessly. "You're just the man I'm looking for."

"I am?"

"Yes. On my way here from the hospital, I noticed a man following me. He could be the one we're looking for."

"Did you get a make on the car?" he asked, whipping out his notebook.

"Teal green Buick, I think it was. I couldn't get a license tag number, but if you hurry, he may still be out there or in the near vicinity."

Duffy was already on his way to the door. "Did you recognize the man driving the car?"

"I couldn't get a good look. But I'm willing to be he's still out there. Somewhere. Just waiting."

Duffy raced out. I closed the door behind him and locked it. Then I moved to the window and lifted the shade.

Augustus, wearing a dove-gray suit, salmon-colored shirt and charcoal and black striped tie, was standing near the same table Randy Dempsey had occupied only a few days earlier. If Randy had looked frightened at the time, Augustus looked anything but. In fact, I got the feeling that he was close to losing his temper as he surveyed the room.

"What is this?" he asked in a voice that suggested that someone was trying to pull something over on him. "Am I being interrogated? Should I have brought my lawyer?"

Hix patted him lightly on the arm. The chief looked exactly one half of Augustus's size. "Settle down, Augustus. We just want to ask you a few questions is all. And this is the only place where I know we won't be disturbed."

Augustus spotted the mirror, walked over and glared into it. He seemed to be looking directly at me. I shrank back, then reminded myself that he couldn't see me.

"Come, have a seat, Augustus," Hix said. "I want you to meet my new deputy." Augustus left the mirror and walked over to the table.

"I know you," Augustus said, staring down at Clinton, who was already seated. "Who's taking over your job in parole?"

"I've taken a brief leave of absence," Clinton said. "Chief Hix is short on staff right now, so I agreed to help him out. Sit down, Mr. Gillespie." He indicated the chair opposite him.

Augustus seemed to ponder it, then shrugged and sat down. He leaned back and crossed a leg over his knee, eyeing Clinton impatiently as he waited to see what this was all about. Hix pulled up another chair so that all three were sitting around the table.

"What's going on here, Hix?" Augustus asked. "What's so important you had to call my home on a Sunday afternoon when I should be spending time with my family? I'm tempted to file a harrassment suit."

"Now, don't go getting yourself riled over nothing," Hix said. "We just think you might be able to help us with a case we're working on. It'd look real good for you if you were instrumental in helping us solve it."

"What case?"

"The murder of Cindy Brown."

"Never heard of her," Augustus said, facing the mirror once more. He took a moment to straighten his tie.

"Take your time and think about it," Hix prodded gently.

"We understand that you were seeing Miss Brown," Clinton said.

Augustus shot him a dark look. "Who the hell told you that?"

Clinton leaned forward slightly. "If you don't mind, I'd like to ask the questions."

Augustus's eyes narrowed. "I don't like smart-asses, and if I'd known you were going to hit me with a bunch of questions about some murder, I'd have brought my lawyer."

"You're welcome to call him," Clinton pointed out.

Augustus turned to Hix. He suddenly looked amused. "Am I under arrest, Ben?"

"No Augustus," Hix said quickly. "We just wanted to ask you about Cindy, that's all. If you'll cooperate, this whole thing'll be over before you know it."

Augustus seemed to relax as he returned his attention to Clinton. "Yes, I knew Miss Brown," he said.

"So why'd you try to deny it?"

He shrugged. "Why should I try to make your job any easier?"

"In what capacity did you know her?"

The other man looked thoughtful. "She was my—uh—traveling companion, you might say."

"For how long?"

Augustus shrugged. "A few months. Four or five at the most. I'd recently dismissed her."

"Dismissed her?"

"Right. In other words, I was no longer in need of her services."

"How did she react to her dismissal?"

"She didn't like it, naturally, but what was she going to do?"

"Go to your wife, maybe?" Clinton suggested.

Augustus gazed back at him, his expression cool. "She may have threatened once or twice. Most of them do. They seldom follow through."

"How would your wife react to something like that, Mr. Gillespie?"

He shrugged. "I really don't know. You'd have to ask her."

As I listened, I wondered how the man could remain so confident in the midst of a murder interrogation. Had money made him cocky, or had he always been like that? I suspected that Augustus Gillespie had been a bully all his life.

"If you weren't concerned about your wife finding out, why'd you insist on taking Miss Brown to some of the sleazier motels in town?"

Augustus came close to smiling. "Maybe I like it that way. No law against that."

"So you're telling me that you preferred meeting in such places because it turned you on and not because you feared that your wife might find out."

Augustus leaned forward, eyes narrowed, mouth tight. "Let me tell you like I told Cindy," he said. "My wife would not have been surprised or upset to learn of my affairs, past or present. We've lived quite comfortably like this for a number of years. Any more questions?"

"Yeah. Where were you last Monday night between the hours of seven and nine?"

"I was coming back from Hilton Head, where I'd attended a dinner meeting with a number of contractors."

"Did you make the drive back alone?"

"My chauffeur drove me."

"And you can supply us with the names of those you dined with?"

"If I have to. But before you drag my good name into a murder investigation, you'd best come up with something better than this or I'll personally see to it that neither of you wears a badge for long."

He stood and smiled politely, as though he'd just made a social call. "Any more questions, gentlemen?"

"Only one," Clinton said, reaching into his pocket. He pulled out the diamond tennis bracelet and laid it on the table. "You recognize this?"

I froze as I waited for his answer.

Augustus picked it up and studied it. "How could I forget? I gave this to someone some months ago."

"Who?"

Augustus tossed the bracelet on the table. "Don't play games with me, Ward. You already know, or you wouldn't have brought it up."

"Don't you think it's strange that two of your ex-lovers are dead?" Clinton asked.

"I don't think about it, period."

"Twelve hundred bucks is a lot to spend on a woman who means nothing."

"I'm not working for cop's wages," Augustus replied. "I can afford it."

Clinton chuckled. "Very good, Mr. Gillespie. You're a real ball-buster. Tell me, did you know the woman from Evansville?"

"I've never even been to Evansville. Now, if you don't mind, they're holding Sunday dinner for me back at the house." He reached out and shook the chief's hand. "Ben, nice seein' you again. You'll have to come out for supper some night. Lula-Mae always makes plenty.''

Chief Hix promised to do just that as he opened the door for Augustus and thanked him for coming.

I waited until Augustus had had time to leave before I slipped out of the break room and made my way down the hall. Luck was with me; Myrtle was not at her desk. I let myself out the back door and hurried to my car.

Instead of going back to the hospital, I drove toward home but turned onto the street where I knew Henry Dean lived. I drove slowly, checking the mailboxes as I went, until I spotted the Dean residence. I parked beside the road and climbed out.

33

I didn't know the Deans personally, and when Henry's father answered the door, I had to explain who I was. He didn't look pleased to see me. "Chief Hix has already sent a patrolman by here, asking questions about Henry," he said. "Every time something bad happens in this town, Henry automatically gets blamed. I don't have nothing to say to you." He started to close the door.

"Mr. Dean, wait!" I said. "I'm not here to accuse Henry of anything. I just want to ask him a few questions. He and my niece, Molly, are close friends. She's seriously ill, and—" My eyes smarted with tears. "I just need to talk to him. Please."

He hesitated, running a hand over his thinning brown hair. He adjusted his glasses and studied me through thick lenses. "I reckon it won't do no harm," he said. "As long as you don't mind me sitting in on the conversation." He opened the door and motioned me through, then called Henry.

The boy looked surprised to see me.

"Hi, Miss Wilkop," he said.

I smiled. I hadn't been invited to sit down, so I stood. "Henry, Molly's very ill right now, and—"

"She's got the flu."

I paused, not knowing how to respond. While I didn't want the whole town knowing about Molly's breakdown, I had to convince Henry that her condition was serious. "It's

----

. . . it's worse than the flu, actually. She's been hospitalized. And the saddest part is, she doesn't seem to want to get well. I think she's either scared or depressed or both.''

He looked sad to hear it. "What can I do to help?''

I glanced at Mr. Dean, then back to his son. "I know this is going to sound weird, Henry, but I think somebody is scaring Molly.''

"You mean threatening her?'' he said, squaring his shoulders as if the mere thought made him want to go out and look for this person and beat him up.

"What makes you think my son is involved?'' his father asked.

"I don't think he's involved at all,'' I assured him quickly. "But he and Molly are so close, I was hoping she might have told him if something was bothering her.''

We both looked at the boy.

"Well, I noticed that Molly wasn't acting like herself this past week,'' Henry said. "I asked her what was wrong, but she got mad and told me to mind my own business. After that, she was too busy to take my calls.'' He glanced down at his feet. "Then I heard about Buster, and I was scared to call after that. I figured she'd need time. You know, to get over it. But I still planned to call her.''

Henry looked sincere, but I didn't know any more now than I had when I'd arrived. "Has she had problems at school that I should know about?'' I asked.

He shrugged. "Nothing I can think of.''

I thanked him and started for the door.

"Can I visit Molly in the hospital?'' he asked.

"It would be best if you waited until she came home,'' I told him. "I'll call you the minute she does. If you think of something that might help in the meantime—''

"I'll let you know right away,'' he promised.

I arrived at the hospital only minutes before Clinton. He found me sitting in Molly's room with my parents. "How's she doing?'' he asked me.

"Sleeping right now.''

"You feel like a cup of coffee?'' he asked.

"Sure." I turned to my parents.

"We're fine," my mother said. "You two go on."

Neither of us said anything until we'd bought our coffee and selected a table. "I hope you're proud of yourself," Clinton said.

"Excuse me?"

"Myrtle told me you came by and sent Duffy on some wild-goose chase. It doesn't take a genius to figure out why. You infringed on Gillespie's constitutional rights by watching the interview."

"To hell with his rights," I whispered. "What about mine and Molly's? What about my dead sister's rights? Our laws are designed to protect the criminals, not the victims."

"You don't have to remind me of the shortcomings of our judicial system, Emily. I know it sucks. But what good would it do us if I was able to prove that Augustus killed those women, and he got off on a technicality?"

I knew he was right. "I was hoping Augustus would confess, and I could have the satisfaction of watching him do so."

"People like Augustus don't confess. You have to paint them into a corner, so to speak, and you can only do that by piling so much evidence on them that they can't explain their way out of it."

"In the end, though, there's a good chance he'd walk," I said, "or his lawyer would tie up the case in appeals until he's too old to serve time. I know how the system works."

"It wouldn't hurt if you tried to be a little more optimistic. At least give me a chance."

"I'm sorry," I said. "I'm having a bad day. What do you plan to do next?"

"I'm going to take a few photos of Cindy Brown around to the motels in town, see if they remember seeing her or a man with her. Just in case Augustus wasn't the only one. Like he said, he really didn't have a reason to kill her."

"Well, we both know Augustus wasn't emotionally involved with Cindy. What if he asked her, as a personal favor, to go out with Frank a couple of times? After all,

Frank's been in prison all this time and hasn't been with a woman. And just suppose Frank doesn't know that Cindy's been seeing his daddy. Maybe he's falling for her. Then he finds out about Augustus and goes into a jealous rage and kills her.''

"Yes, but would Frank kill her if he knew there was a chance that his father would be charged with the crime?''

"If he was mad enough. And it would only make sense that he'd send the photo of the dead woman to me, since he feels I've been making trouble for him.''

"It sounds good, Emily, but you're forgetting. There are two other victims in this case, and one of them was killed while Frank was still incarcerated.''

"Maybe they're not related after all.''

"I find it hard to believe that three suicides-turned-murders within a hundred miles of one another is sheer coincidence.''

"And I find it hard to believe that the more questions I ask myself, the more confused I become.''

He covered my hand with his. "Try not to think about it for a while,'' he said. "You have Molly to worry about. I'll deal with this other.''

We finished our coffee and took the elevator back to the psychiatric ward. Once inside, we headed straight for Molly's room. I found my parents standing just outside the door. "What's wrong?'' I asked anxiously. "Has something happened?''

"Dr. Greenburg's in there with her now,'' my mother said. She looked excited, her face flushed with emotion. My father was smiling.

"Somebody tell me what's going on.'' I demanded.

"She's coming out of it,'' my mother said. "I told you she would.''

I felt faint with relief. "Oh, thank God.''

Dr. Greenburg stepped out a few minutes later and looked surprised to find us huddled around the door. "She's going to be fine,'' he said. "A little fuzzy-headed at first, but she'll pull out of it. We can release her as early as tomorrow if she continues to improve.''

"May we see her?" I asked.

He nodded. "As long as you keep it light and don't expect too much. She may be down in the dumps for a few days. That's normal.''

I entered the room a few minutes later, leaving my parents and Clinton at the door. I rounded the bed and found Molly staring out the window. Her eyes shifted and focused on me.

"Hi, sweetie. How're you feeling?''

A slight shrug. "Okay. My head feels funny. Do I look any different?''

"You look wonderful." I approached the bed. "We've been worried sick about you.''

"Why am I in the hospital?''

I hesitated. I groped for an explanation, then decided it was probably best not to go into details and risk upsetting her. "You weren't feeling well. You weren't yourself.''

She closed her eyes briefly, and the expression on her face was sad. When she didn't open them right away, I was afraid I'd lost her again. "Molly?''

She opened her eyes but didn't speak.

"I love you. Everything's going to be fine. Please trust me.''

My parents visited briefly before Cordia arrived with a gift and asked that she see Molly alone. After about fifteen minutes, she met with us in the lobby.

"Molly didn't do much talking, and I didn't delve too deeply," she said. "She claims that she doesn't remember what got her so upset. It may be that she doesn't *want* to remember right now. Once she's stronger, I'll try to learn more.''

We left the hospital before visiting hours were officially over, since my neighbors were coming at eight to discuss the watch program. Molly didn't seem to mind; in fact, she complained of being sleepy, and I suspected she'd drop off the moment we left.

"I never thought a person could become tired just sitting all day," Clinton said as he drove us home.

"Would you rather hold the meeting another night?" I asked.

"I'll be okay once I start moving around."

I was glad he didn't want to cancel. Once I'd told Iris Ramsey about Molly, she and Mrs. Hamilton had taken over the project, and I knew it would hurt their feelings if I canceled. Still, I had less than an hour to straighten the house and put coffee on—unless, of course, my intruder had cleaned the place while I was away.

"I'm surprised DeWayne didn't visit," Clinton said.

"He's probably embarrassed," I said. "Once he sobers up, he'll call and apologize."

"You sound pretty sure about that."

"I've known him a while. DeWayne doesn't cope well with problems, at least not since my sister's death. He hides out and drinks when something bothers him. Sooner or later, he comes to his senses and asks me to forgive him. I always do."

"You said he was abused while growing up?"

I nodded. "DeWayne never mentioned *how* his mother abused him, but I gather it was pretty bad. He wrote to his grandmother and asked for help, but the woman never wrote back. She was supposed to be this great Christian, but she wouldn't even help her own grandson. He never knew his father."

"Where's his mother now?"

"Dead. She overdosed on drugs when DeWayne was in high school. He's been on his own ever since."

Clinton shook his head. "I'm always amazed at the things some parents do to their children," he said.

We pulled up in front of my house and parked. Once again, I was hesitant to go in. "I wonder if we're going to have any surprises," I said.

"I'll go in first," Clinton said. He got out of the car, came around and opened my door. "Why don't you wait on the front porch?"

I did so, even though it was cold and I had things to do inside. I glanced down my street and was surprised to see it so well lit. My neighbors were obviously uneasy now that they knew about the break-ins at my place.

"Everything looks normal," Clinton said, coming to the front door.

I felt relieved—and tired. But I had too much to do to be tired.

"What can I do to help?" he asked the minute I stepped inside.

I glanced around the living room. "If you could dust and vacuum the area rug, that would be wonderful. I'm going to straighten the kitchen."

The house was in relatively good order when my neighbors started filing in through the front door at eight. Clinton had pulled several folding chairs from my hall closet and brought in those from my kitchen for extra seating. While I poured coffee, Mrs. Hamilton sliced the coffee cake she'd baked.

Once everybody was seated, Clinton stood and introduced himself, then quickly gave his background in law enforcement, including the fact that he'd been deputized by Chief Hix to assist in the recent murder. He promised that we could all make our neighborhood a safer place to live if we followed a few guidelines.

Next, he tossed out crime statistics that concentrated on the elderly, which was who the group was mostly composed of. He also listed some of the things that burglars looked for when casing a house—tall grass, newspapers lying on the driveway, mailboxes overflowing and other such giveaways.

As he spoke, several women took notes. I remained perched on the arm of the sofa, ready to jump up in case anyone wanted more coffee.

"Tonight we'll concentrate on the needs of your street and community," he said. "Then, once you've had a chance to think about it, we can meet again and outline our program." People nodded as he spoke. He sounded sure

----

and authoritative, and I was again thankful to have him staying with me in light of what'd been happening.

"First of all, I'm going to give everyone a little homework. I want to see what kind of detectives you'd make," he added with a smile. Several people chuckled. "You'll need to decide exactly how much area you wish to include in your Neighborhood Watch. Everyone should agree on this. Once you've done that, I want you to take a good look at your surroundings.

"Things I want you to look for are how many abandoned buildings you have in your area, if any. What is the lighting situation on your street? Are there rentals in your area that stay vacant for any length of time and might invite vagrancy? Are there juveniles in the area, and, if so, do they have problems with drugs or alcohol?"

"Slow down," one of the women grumbled, scribbling as fast as she could. She told him when he could proceed, and he listed the other items more slowly.

When Clinton was finished with that part of the meeting, he held a question and answer period. I slipped into the kitchen for the coffeepot and began warming everyone's cup. It was after nine-thirty by the time people started drifting out the door with Clinton's promise of a meeting the following Sunday night to finalize things. Clinton closed the door behind the last of them and locked it tight, and I sank onto the couch.

"I may never get up again," I said.

He looked at me. "You think it went okay?"

"I think they would have recommended you for knighthood, if they could have."

He gave me a weary smile, and I knew he was as tired as I was. "Why don't you take a shower?" he suggested. "I'll put things away out here."

I decided right then that I was in love with him.

Once I'd showered, I grabbed a book and climbed into bed. I realized then how my whole routine had been upset by the man who was after me. I actually missed the quiet nights when I sat in my bed reading or grading papers, missed hearing Molly on the phone across the hall.

I wondered if our lives would ever be normal again.

I could hear Clinton watching television in the living room. I was too tired to go in and try to make conversation. After reading less than a page of my novel, I could feel my eyes closing. I didn't even have the energy to turn off the lamp on my night table.

I awoke with a start some hours later, finding the place dark and Clinton's side of the bed empty. I don't know exactly what woke me, but I sensed that something wasn't right. I glanced at the alarm clock and saw that it was after midnight.

I rose and slipped from the bed as quietly as I could, then tiptoed toward the hall. At the door, I spied a shadow. "Clinton?" I whispered.

"Be quiet," he said. "Someone's out there."

34

I was used to the fear by now. I recognized the adrenaline rush that made my heart beat faster, and I was no stranger to the knot of terror in my stomach.

"Who is it?" I whispered.

"I don't know. Go back to the bedroom."

"No way," I said, grabbing hold of the waistband on his jeans.

He made a sound of irritation. "Stay behind me."

I followed him into the kitchen. The house was dark; Clinton insisted on cutting the lights as soon as night fell, so we wouldn't be moving targets if the killer approached the house undetected. Although the floodlights were left to burn, I noted that the one outside the kitchen door was out.

Clinton turned slightly so that his mouth was at my ear. "He unscrewed the bulb," he whispered, his voice so low that I wondered if I'd imagined it. "So we can't see him. Where's the flashlight?"

Actually, we had a flashlight in every room. "There's one on the counter beside the door. Right where you told me to keep it."

We crept toward the door, our bodies so close that we moved as one. Clinton groped for the flashlight in the dark, then noiselessly fitted the key into the lock. I heard a sound outside the door and thought my knees would give.

Suddenly, Clinton turned on the light and shined it through one of the glass panes. I did not recognize the man at first, but the mere sight of the grim-faced person staring back at us startled me so badly that I thought my bladder would give. A split second passed before I realized I was looking into the face of Frank Gillespie.

I screamed.

"You sonofabitch!" Clinton yelled, flipping the key in the dead bolt and jerking the door open so quickly that I barely had time to get out of his way. "Keep the light on him." He shoved the flashlight at me and took off.

I tried to shine the light on them, but my hands trembled so badly that I had difficulty holding it steady. I grasped the flashlight with two hands and pointed it toward them, thinking that Frank had surely gotten away by now.

I was wrong. He'd obviously stumbled over my lawn mower, giving Clinton ample time to reach him. They had not left the paved area between the house and garage, no more than fifteen to twenty feet from me. They struggled and something hit the pavement, followed immediately by an ear-splitting shot that sounded like a cannon in the covered walk-through. I screamed again and wondered where the bullet had gone.

"Let me go!" Frank cried, trying to pull free. "I ain't out to hurt anybody."

Clinton ignored him. They moved in my direction, and their struggles intensified, Clinton cussing and Frank trying to escape. I couldn't get to the gun without the risk of being trampled. Suddenly, Clinton's hands were around Frank's neck, and I saw the other man gasping for air. I pleaded with Clinton to release him, but his rage was too great. All at once, he rammed his fist into Frank's face. The other man staggered and tripped, landing ungracefully on the pavement against the corner of the steps that led into my kitchen. I heard his skull crack.

When I looked up, Clinton was holding the gun and breathing heavily. His face was slick with sweat. "Stand up, you sonofabitch," he said, his voice menacing. There was no movement.

Only then did I notice the box of candy with an envelope

taped to the front. I didn't have time to think about it as I watched Clinton walk over and nudge Frank with his foot. The other man rolled over on the concrete, leaving a small pool of blood on the step.

"Shit!" Clinton wiped his face.

"Is he dead?" I asked.

He knelt beside Frank, pointing the gun cautiously at him while he checked his pulse. "Call an ambulance."

Chief Hix arrived twenty minutes after Frank had been carried away in the ambulance, after I'd opened the envelope attached to the box of candy and read Frank's brief message.

You have no reason to be afraid of me, Emily. I'm just trying to be your friend.

None of it made sense, not a damn word of it.

Now Clinton glared at Hix as he stepped through my back door. "Sorry if I rushed you," he said.

Hix looked just as irritated. "I would have been here sooner, but—" He paused. "We have a situation."

"Ah. Somebody's prize bull break out of his pen?" Clinton asked, sarcasm ringing loud.

"No, smart-ass." Hix looked at me with sad eyes. "Emily, I hate to have to tell you this, but Molly's missing from the hospital."

There is a point at which you feel you can't take any more, and I must've reached it. "You're lying," I said.

He shook his head. "I wish I were."

"Where the hell is she?" Clinton demanded.

"Settle down," the chief said. "I've already got people out looking for her."

"How in Christ's name did she get out of a psychiatric ward?" Clinton asked.

"There was a bomb threat. They had to evacuate most of the patients. Hell, I even had to call in the bomb squad from Charleston. They flew out here in a chopper."

Clinton looked angry. "And you didn't call me?"

Hix glanced at me, then back at Clinton. "I was hoping that we'd find Molly, and I wouldn't have to put Emily through any more than she's already been through."

"We have to go to the hospital," I said quickly.

"We've searched the grounds; she's not there." The chief paused and looked uncomfortable. "With Frank in ER, I think it's best if you stay away. Augustus will start a ruckus if he sees either one of you."

Clinton gave a snort of disgust. "I don't give a shit—"

Hix interrupted "Look, there's no sense borrowing trouble. If Molly was still there, we'd have found her." He looked thoughtful. "By the way, do either of you know what Frank was doing here in the first place?"

I was only vaguely aware of Clinton telling Hix about the box of candy and the note we'd found. "This whole thing is screwy, if you ask me," the chief said. "None of it makes a damn bit of sense."

My mind was on my niece. Fear shimmied up my backbone as I thought of her being out on the streets this hour of the night when she was unstable to begin with. My only comfort was knowing Frank was finally out of the picture, and that Augustus was most likely by his side. Still, I was anxious. "We have to find her," I said. "She's only thirteen years old. We have to—"

"That's why I'm here," Hix said, looking at Clinton. "I need all the help I can get."

I turned for my bedroom. "I can be dressed in two minutes."

"Wait!" Hix said. He paused as I turned around. "Somebody needs to stay here in case this is where she's headed."

"I don't know, Chief," Clinton said. "I don't like the idea of Emily being here by herself."

I tried to get control. "The chief is right," I said. "If Molly has run away, it's only natural that she'd come home. I want to be here for her. Besides, I've got a gun."

The chief gave me a speculative glance but didn't ask

where I'd managed to come up with a weapon. "We can check back with you every fifteen minutes or so to see if you've heard from her," he said. He hurried out.

"Try not to use the gun unless you absolutely have to," Clinton said, tucking his own gun into the waistband of his jeans and grabbing his jacket. "Cut the lights and stay near the phone so one of us can reach you at all times. And don't unlock the door for anybody except Molly." He kissed me hard on the mouth and hurried out the door.

I immediately locked up behind him, then went for my gun. I cut the lights and knelt on the floor beside the front window so I would see anyone crossing my front yard. I was aware of the surrounding darkness, the ominous shadows. The house creaked as old houses tend to, and I jumped at every sound.

After five minutes I realized that I had to pee, and I cussed my bladder for all it was worth as I hurried to the bathroom, gun in one hand, flashlight in the other. I was just in the process of relieving myself when the phone rang. I cussed again and tried to halt the flow of urine, then discovered that some things in life just can't be stopped so easily.

Finally, I managed to cut it off and drag my sweats up. Grabbing the gun and the light, I hurried into the living room and yanked the phone from its cradle just as my recorded message began.

You have reached the home of Emily Wilkop. I can't come to the phone at the moment, but if you'll leave a message at the tone, I'll be glad to call you . . .

"Hello?" I said, trying to talk over my own voice.

"Aunt Em?"

I had never been so happy to hear her voice. "Molly, is that you? Honey, where *are* you?"

"Are you alone?" she asked.

"Yes, why?"

"I need to know if you're alone."

There was a loud beep. "Yes, sweetie, I'm alone. Clinton is out looking for you right now."

"Hold on," she said. There was a muffled sound, and I realized that she was talking to someone. "Can you come get me, Aunt Em?" she asked anxiously.

"Of course I will, Molly. Just tell me where you are."

"You have to promise not to say anything to anybody."

I could tell she was frightened. "I swear, Molly."

She hesitated. "I'm at DeWayne's house. Come alone. And make sure you're not followed."

I wasn't surprised that she'd turned to DeWayne, nor that she'd asked me to come alone. She was probably terrified of being sent back to the foster home or hospital. I decided then and there to leave town if I had to, in order to keep her from having to do either. Perhaps with Frank out of circulation . . . But there was still the problem of his father. I felt certain Augustus was behind my sister's murder.

"I'll be there in ten minutes," I said. I hung up the phone, grabbed my coat and gun and raced out. I didn't even bother to lock up.

The drive seemed to take forever. I passed very few cars along the way. Not that I was surprised to find it so quiet; it *was* the middle of the night, and those who weren't chasing murderers or looking for runaway teenagers were probably in bed. As I drove my mind played out the scenario of how Molly had managed to end up at DeWayne's house.

The bomb threat must've appeared very real for the hospital staff to evacuate. I could imagine Molly, scared and confused, slipping away from her group and disappearing. She would have called DeWayne and asked him to come get her instead of coming home and risking another run-in with DSS.

But where would she have called from? I asked myself. It wasn't likely that she'd knocked on someone's door; they would have taken one look at her hospital gown and called the police. Perhaps she'd had time to throw on some clothes. Her jacket, maybe. The staff wouldn't have sent their patients out into the cold night air without coats and shoes.

I was only a few minutes away from DeWayne's house. I remembered Molly's frantic voice.

Are you alone? I need to know if you're alone. Make sure you aren't followed.

I suddenly felt uncomfortable. Actually, I'd felt that way from the moment Clinton had mentioned the elderly woman who'd died from strychnine poisoning so long ago. Why did it continue to nag at me?

I searched my memory, and it came to me in bits and pieces.

I vaguely remembered the conversation DeWayne and I'd had the night of Lurlene's funeral. As tipsy as I'd been at the time, I seemed to remember him mentioning something about his grandmother having been poisoned some years back, for no apparent reason.

Not that I blamed anybody for killing the old goat. A religious fanatic, that's what she was. A fucking pillar of the community who thought her shit didn't stink. She turned her back on me when I asked for help.

Dr. Hislop had referred to the victim as a pillar of the community; that must've been what'd jogged my brain. She was married to a minister, he'd said. Had DeWayne's grandmother been a minister's wife? I wondered. Had she tried to instill the fear of the Lord into her grandson, at the same time ignoring his cries for help from an abusive mother? Could it be coincidence? I remembered Clinton's words about strychnine poisoning.

In all my years as a detective, I've never come across one. . . . And what makes this coincidence even more baffling, is that it happened twice in a town of less than six thousand.

I shook my head. I couldn't believe the direction my thoughts were taking. If DeWayne had been brought up with a fanatical grandmother he'd despised, why would he use those same techniques on Molly?

The answer was simple, I realized. Mind control. What better way to manipulate a child than to scare her to death?

As vulnerable as Molly was, she would have been an easy target.

I gripped the steering wheel tighter and told myself I had to be crazy to think that DeWayne was capable of such madness. He had seen firsthand the damage it had done to my sister, the damage it had done to him. And if DeWayne was guilty of the crimes that had taken place in my house, it meant he was probably guilty of murder, too.

Would he have been capable of putting a noose around my sister's neck?

I was new in town and didn't know what she was.

"No." I said the word aloud. At the same time, I scrambled to remember the name of the town DeWayne said he'd been born in. He'd claimed it was a small Southern town, much the size of Mossy Oaks. Was it Barnesville? Abbeville? *Evansville?* It sounded familiar. "Damn," I muttered, wishing I'd stayed sober that night instead of sucking down all those margaritas.

I spotted the turn and left the main road. No matter what my suspicions against DeWayne—and that's all they were—I had to get Molly out of there. Later, I'd tell Clinton what I knew, but for now all I wanted to do was get to my niece.

There was no reason to be afraid, I told myself. Even if DeWayne *was* guilty of killing my sister, he had absolutely no reason to hurt Molly or me. I would just pretend that everything was fine, thank him for his help and leave.

I pulled into the driveway and parked. For once I wished the house was not hidden from the road by tall shrubs. During the day it looked quite lovely; at night, the place looked menacing.

As I climbed out of my car, I noticed that there wasn't a light on in the house, nor was the porch light burning. I picked my way carefully up the short walk. I raised my hand to knock and saw that the door was cracked open a bit.

DeWayne was expecting me.

I took a shaky breath and stepped inside. The wood floor

creaked. I waited, trying to adjust my eyes to the darkness.

"Anybody home?" I asked, my voice wavering slightly.

"Are you alone?"

I jumped at the sound of DeWayne's voice, and I knew immediately that because I'd spent so many months feeling sorry for him, I hadn't seen him for what he was. "Y-yes. Everybody's out looking for Molly."

"Close the door, Em."

I did as he said, still waiting for my eyes to adjust. The room was as black as a tightly closed vault. No movement, no shadows, nothing. "Where's Molly?"

"She's here with us," he said, this time slurring his words. "Say hello to your aunt, Molly."

"Hi." Her voice trembled, even on that single syllable.

I took a step toward the voice. "Are you okay, honey?"

"Don't come any closer," DeWayne warned.

"What's going on, DeWayne?" I asked, trying to make my voice sound natural. "You're not still mad—"

I heard movement. A lamp came on, and I blinked several times at the brightness. I recoiled in horror at what I saw. "Oh, God, no," I moaned.

DeWayne sat on a straight-backed chair with Molly at his feet, a large butcher knife held to her throat. He gripped a whiskey bottle in his other hand.

"What are you *doing*?" I asked, panic-stricken.

"What I should have done a long time ago," he said calmly. He set the bottle on the floor beside Molly. I saw that it was almost empty. "Throw me your purse."

I hesitated. "Why?"

"Just throw it to me, goddammit!"

"The gun isn't in it, if that's what you're thinking," I said, grasping my purse tighter. "It never occurred to me that I might need it."

"I'm only going to ask you once more."

I tossed him the purse. He caught it in one hand and took a quick glance inside. He smiled. "Good girl." He tossed it back.

"You made me think I could trust you," I said.

He picked up the bottle, took a swig. "It was important that you trust me at the time," he said. "But that time has passed, and now I'm going to show you what happens to evil women."

"Evil women?" I repeated in a dazed fashion. He wasn't making sense. How drunk *was* he?

"I thought I'd gotten rid of the bad blood in your family, but it seems that I still have my work cut out for me."

"He killed Lurlene," Molly said. "And Buster, too."

"Shut up!" DeWayne hit Molly hard on the side of her head with the bottle. She winced in pain.

I made a move toward her, and he pulled the knife across her throat, slicing the delicate skin. She cried out as a thin red line appeared and started to run. She raised her hand protectively, and he cut her again. This time she yelped.

I felt my legs go rubbery. "For God's sake, DeWayne, please don't hurt her," I pleaded, hoping I could get through to his intoxicated brain. "She's only a child."

"Her mother was a slut, and she's going to grow up to be a slut," he replied. "I know about these things, Emily. I know what happens to children who are raised by whores. I've made it my mission in life to destroy these evil women."

He was growing agitated; I could see it by the spittle forming around his mouth. His eyes were wild. "DeWayne, certainly you don't think *I'm* a whore," I said, trying to reach him.

"You're fucking Clinton Ward."

I shook my head quickly. "No, no. That's not the way it is between us."

He laughed and took another swig from the bottle. "You wouldn't admit it if you were." He paused, and his voice sounded sad when he went on, "And to think, I once loved you. Why else would I have gone to so much trouble to scare you?"

"You were the one coming into my house?" I shuddered. "You put that rat on my table?"

He nodded. "It was much easier once I convinced Molly

----

to give me a spare key. I guess she just didn't trust you to take care of her after how her mother treated her. She came to me for protection."

I dropped my gaze to my niece, who looked ashamed. Instead of feeling betrayed, though, I felt sorry for her. "Okay, DeWayne," I said, trying to keep my voice calm, "if you're determined to protect her, then let her go. This is between you and me."

"Molly understands why I have to kill her," he said. "It's all your fault, Emily. When I tried to be there for you, you turned to another man. You forgot about me and Molly. I even offered you a second chance by calling DSS. I thought for sure you'd come to your senses."

I couldn't believe the things I was hearing. "*You* called DSS?"

"I didn't want my stepdaughter living in that kind of environment."

I didn't want to know the answer to my next question, but I had to ask. "You killed those women, too, didn't you? You mailed me that photo?"

"Whores. Luckily, I was able to find a number of them since I traveled so much."

The whole thing was a puzzle. "Your grandmother wasn't a whore."

He looked surprised. "You and Ward have been busy," he said. "I'm impressed." He glanced toward the ceiling, his bleary eyes trying to focus on something. "She refused to help me. I told her what my mother was doing to me, and she suggested that I spend more time reading Scripture.

"She turned her back on me." He sneered. "It would have created a scandal if my grandfather's congregation caught wind of it. But it no longer matters. I had the thrill of watching both women die a horrible death."

He was quiet for a moment. "There's some things a mother should not ask of her son, Em."

I glanced away, unable to bear the pain in his eyes any more than I could stand the stark pleading in Molly's. "I'm sorry, DeWayne. Truly sorry."

"Are you?"

"Of course I am," I said. "What do you take me for?" I asked, knowing I had to keep him talking. "I made a mistake, okay? But I'm not the monster your mother was."

He eyed me steadily. "There are different degrees of wickedness, but it exists just the same. Most women are basically evil, you know. My mother, Lurlene, you and Molly. The only thing that keeps you from living as barbarians is the threat of Judgment Day. And today I'm going to see that you keep that appointment. You're going to have to account for your sins."

He smiled, and I wondered how he'd been able to hide this side of himself from me. I remember the times he *had* said something weird or off-the-wall, and I'd blamed it on the booze.

"You've brought all this on yourself, Em. You with your sinful ways. I tried to warn Molly that judgment was at hand, tried to point out the many signs that signaled the approach of Armageddon, but she refused to listen."

I hated myself for being so naive, for not suspecting that he was the one frightening Molly. But neither of us deserved to die for my stupidity. "On the contrary, DeWayne," I said, feeling near tears. "I think Molly listened to every word you said." I glanced at my niece. I could sense her fear from across the room. "I'm so sorry," I said. "If only I had known."

She blinked, and I could tell she was doing her best to hold back the tears.

"Oh, how touching," DeWayne said, then gave such a frown that it looked more like a snarl. "We could have been together," he said. "You and I could have given Molly the loving home she deserved. Together, we could have prevented her from becoming like her mother."

"It's not too late," I said.

He gave a derisive snort. "I don't want Ward's leftovers. I had enough of that when I was married to your slutty sister." He paused. "She tried to pass herself off as a good woman. What a fool I was."

"I know you were hurt, DeWayne," I told him. "You had every right to be. But that's in the past. You and I could—"

"You're just like her. Oh, you pretend to be respectable and all, but you don't fool me for an instant. Won't be long before Molly'll be just like you."

"No, DeWayne, we're different."

"You're trash," he said, waving my statement aside. "Where's your car?" he asked, changing the subject abruptly.

"Out front." My mind raced, trying to get ahead of him.

"We're going for a little ride."

I felt hopeful for the first time. Locked inside DeWayne's house, we didn't have a prayer, but if I could get him outside and divert his attention, we might stand a chance. One chance. And with the knife pressed against Molly's throat, I couldn't afford to screw up. I tried to hide my excitement with a question. "Where are we going?"

He stood up. "Jones's Woods. But don't worry; you won't be alone. I'll lay out you and the kid right next to ol' Herschel."

"Oh, my God," I said, sudden tears stinging my eyes.

"He deserved to die, Emily. He suspected that somebody was after you when he saw how upset you were that night at the school. He almost caught me then."

I was sick at heart, so sick that I almost wanted to die right then and there. But I couldn't give up, couldn't dwell on Herschel's death. I had to save Molly.

"Herschel got in my way. I just planted that jewelry in his desk so folks would start asking questions when he disappeared."

I knew then that DeWayne had planned things very carefully and had every intention of killing Molly and me. There wasn't a damn thing I could say to convince him otherwise. Still, I had to try.

"You'll never get away with this."

DeWayne looked sad. "I don't much care. There's a time when you have to stop fighting, when you have to accept the inevitable." He turned off the lamp and shined the flashlight right in my face. "Now stop talking and let's go."

I knew that he was prepared to die with us, and it gave me little consolation. He had nothing to lose, had every intention of taking us out with him. The situation was even more dangerous than I'd suspected.

"Okay," I said slowly, so as not to excite him. I did not know how deeply Molly had been cut, but her collar was already blood-soaked. "I'm going to open the door now."

His flashlight was powerful and blinding. I stumbled out the door and onto the porch with him and Molly right behind. "I—I have to look for my keys. Do you think you could turn on the porch light for a second?" I asked, hoping to distract him.

He flipped the switch so quickly that I didn't have time to even think about making some sort of move. The floodlights bathed the yard in a yellow glow and brought the hedges into focus.

"I'll give you two seconds."

I found them right away and held them up for his inspection.

"Walk toward the car and get behind the wheel," he said. "I'll sit in the back with the kid. One word of warning, though. If you even look like you're going to try something, I'll cut this girl up so bad you'll beg me to kill her."

I swallowed hard. I had heard of DeWayne's handiwork, and I had no desire to watch him carve up my niece. I simply couldn't take a chance. All I could do was hope and pray for the right moment.

I started for the car. From the corner of my eye, I thought I saw a shadow pass behind one of the hedges. Clinton? My hopes soared. But how had he found me? My answering machine. I had picked up after it had started to record the call from Molly.

My niece choked back a sob. I glanced up sharply. "What are you doing to her?" I demanded.

"What's the matter with you?" DeWayne gave her a shake.

"I have to go to the bathroom," the girl replied. "I told you an hour ago."

"Stop acting like a baby and get into the car." DeWayne shoved her hard against the door, still grasping her collar with one hand. "Open it." She didn't budge. "Don't fuck with me, Molly, or I'll kill you right here."

"She can't help it, DeWayne," I said. "I have the same problem when I get nervous."

He wasn't listening. "Molly, I'm only going to say this one more time before I—"

"Hold it right there, you sonofabitch!" Clinton yelled, coming out of the hedges like an angry Doberman. He pointed the muzzle of the gun at DeWayne.

DeWayne almost smiled when he spied Clinton. "Isn't this sweet," he said. "Look, Em. Your knight in shining armor." The smile faded into a nasty grimace as he pulled Molly tighter against him, pressed the knife against her throat. "Don't come any closer, hero."

Clinton came to an abrupt halt. "What's the matter, DeWayne? You scared to take on a man?"

"Drop the gun, asshole. I'm just looking for a reason to slice this kid wide open."

"You're pretty good when it comes to defenseless women and animals. Why don't you let the girl go and take a shot at me?"

"Put the gun down, Clinton," I pleaded. "He's already cut her twice."

Another sob escaped Molly.

DeWayne glanced down. "What the—?" His face showed disgust. "She's pissing in her pants!" He backed away as though he couldn't stand the thought of her urine touching him.

Clinton rushed him, but he wasn't quite fast enough. DeWayne swiped at the hand holding the gun, and I knew Clinton had been cut from the menacing roar that left his throat. The wound must've been deep; blood gushed and ran down his fingers. He dropped the gun, and it landed in the grass. There was no way for him to reach it without risking another attack from DeWayne's knife.

"Come on, Ward," DeWayne said, crouching slightly and egging him on. "I'm just looking for the chance to cut your balls off and shove 'em up your ass."

Molly seemed to have been forgotten in the meantime. She stood there blinking, as though she wasn't sure what to do next.

"Run, Molly!" I cried. The girl shook herself and sprinted away. DeWayne glanced in her direction, and I threw my purse at his face as hard as I could. He ducked. Clinton lunged at him, and they fell to the ground.

The men rolled in the grass, struggling and grunting. DeWayne got control of the knife and slammed it down, missing Clinton's face by a fraction of an inch. I screamed as DeWayne raised the knife once more and aimed it at Clinton's chest. Clinton grabbed DeWayne's wrist with his good hand, holding it high, but he was no match for the other man, who was bearing down with all his weight.

I suddenly remembered the gun in my pocket and fumbled for it, my hand slick with sweat. Fear seemed to ooze from every pore, and my hand shook violently. "Drop the knife, DeWayne!" I shouted. "Drop it or I'll shoot."

His brief glance told me I was no threat. "You won't shoot me, Em," he taunted. "We've both known that all along."

"Drop it, DeWayne," I ordered in a voice that sounded nothing like my own. "Or I swear to God I'll blow your goddamn brains out."

The knife came down slowly, the point poised less than an inch from Clinton's throat. I knew I wouldn't get a second chance.

Are you going to be able to pull the trigger when the time comes?

Tears stung my eyes. I squeezed the trigger. Both men jumped, but I could see, even as close as I was to them, that I'd managed to miss DeWayne completely. I fired several more times, hoping and praying that I didn't hit Clinton. Suddenly DeWayne stiffened and fell away, and the knife slipped through his fingers.

Clinton rose slowly. I dropped the gun and covered my face. "Did I hit him?" I asked.

He was quiet. I chanced a look in his direction, saw him bending over DeWayne. "You did what you said you'd do, Emily. You blew his goddamn brains out."

35

It is not easy to kill a man, I discovered over the next few days, even when it's a matter of saving your own life and that of a loved one. Luckily, Molly's injuries were not as serious as I'd feared, and the doctor in the emergency room assured us that they would heal in no time. Clinton, too, would be fine. Once I was convinced she was okay physically, I began to worry about her emotional wounds. I took a week off and kept Molly out of school to give us time to recuperate. Susan and Henry took turns bringing her school assignments to the house.

I made DeWayne's funeral arrangements and saw that he was laid to rest in the plot next to my sister, which had already been paid for. Molly and I attended the private burial service, despite Clinton's grumblings and only after Cordia and Dr. Greenburg had said it would be okay for Molly to go. I knew I had no choice but to pay my last respects; after all, DeWayne had once been my closest friend.

"I'm sorry I gave him the keys," Molly said as we gazed down at his grave beneath a gray sky. "I thought he was trying to protect us. I didn't know he was the one coming into the house those nights."

I put one arm around her; she didn't try to pull away. "I know."

"He started saying awful things about you once Clinton was coming around, said you were doomed to burn in Hell for eternity. He said I could expect more bad things to happen as long as you lived like the wicked.'' She paused. ''And then, before I knew it, all these bad things started happening just like he said they would.

''But he promised to come for me before I had to suffer much longer. And he did come for me. I was standing outside the hospital the night of the bomb threat when I saw him waiting for me in the parking lot. I just slipped away from the crowd and climbed into his car. I didn't know he planned to . . . to kill me.''

It didn't take a genius to figure out DeWayne had been behind the bomb scare. ''You don't have to talk about it right now, if you don't want to.''

''Grandma said he brainwashed me.''

I put my arm around her. I still found it hard to believe that DeWayne had used those tactics on my fragile niece. ''DeWayne was sick, Molly.''

''I can't believe you're taking up for him.''

''I'm not. What he did—killing those women and all— was terrible.'' I suspected that we would learn of more killings once the FBI's VICAP system started processing the information Chief Hix and Clinton had compiled. As DeWayne himself had told me, he'd had the opportunity to kill when he traveled so much for his job.

''I guess what I'm trying to say is that people don't just start out being bad,'' I continued. ''Things happen in their lives that make them the way they are.''

Molly and I were the only ones to put flowers on DeWayne's grave—yellow tea roses, which I remembered he'd placed on Lurlene's and were his favorite. We checked them over the next couple of days. They hadn't even begun to turn brown when a search party discovered Herschel Buckmeyer's body in a shallow grave in Jones's Woods. His throat had been cut. I mourned his death in the privacy of my bedroom, knowing that Molly didn't need to see any more tears.

Less than a week after DeWayne's death, Molly broke down in front of Cordia and me and cried over her mother's death. Cordia asked the question I'd been dreading for so long—whether or not Lurlene's boyfriends had ever touched her in a bad way. Molly assured her that they hadn't. We considered the session a major victory. Later that same day, I drove out to my parents' house and told them the truth about how Lurlene had died. Although they cried, I felt that they were both relieved that my sister hadn't ended her own life.

Despite it all, I missed Clinton something fierce.

I had not seen or heard from him since before De-Wayne's funeral; he didn't even call when the *Gazette* carried a front-page story about why he'd left Chicago. Clinton had been portrayed as a bad cop with a hair-trigger temper who'd almost killed a man with his bare hands. I still don't know why I didn't call.

I knew that Augustus was behind the article; it was his way of getting even with Clinton for putting his son in the hospital with a serious brain injury. Frank had been moved to a hospital in Charleston but was not expected to recover fully. Augustus was also furious about having his affair with Cindy Brown and my sister dragged out into the open, but there was no way around it. DeWayne had obviously planned Cindy's death when he'd seen the two of them sneaking into the Orange Grove Motel one night.

I had to let it go, I thought. It was time to go on with my life. But the future looked bleak without Clinton beside me. I called Chief Hix and learned that he'd gone back to Chicago.

"That's what you get for playing hard to get," Hix said, chuckling, although I didn't see anything funny about it. "He'd have stayed if you had asked him to."

Two days before Thanksgiving, I arrived home to find Clinton and Molly sitting on the metal glider on my front porch with what appeared to be a golden retriever puppy. My heart soared. Both of them offered me a sheepish smile.

"I told him I couldn't accept the dog unless you said it was okay," my niece said.

Clinton nodded soberly. "And I told her I couldn't give her the dog unless you approved."

I had to force myself to look at the puppy when all I wanted to do was gaze at the man before me. I studied the animal. He had big feet. Big feet, big dog. He would eat a lot. I saw dollar signs in his luminous brown eyes.

"What's his name?" I asked.

"Bubba."

"Oh, jeeze."

"Can I keep him?" Molly asked, giving me the same melting look as the pup.

"He's had all his shots," Clinton said. "I just got back from the vet. And there's a fifty-pound sack of food in the trunk of my car."

"That ought to hold him till supper," I muttered.

"I'll take care of him," Molly said. "You won't have to do a thing."

I pinched the bridge of my nose to keep my eye from twitching. "How big will he get?"

"Not big," Clinton said innocently. "No more than ... say, twenty pounds."

I knew he was lying, and I told him as much.

"Pleeeze, Aunt Em," Molly said.

I gazed down at my niece and knew there wasn't anything I'd deny her at this point. Besides, a pet would go a long way in mending the hurts she'd suffered. "I'm not shoveling doggie doo out of the backyard," I said.

She took that as approval and gave a gleeful yelp. "I told you she'd say yes. I'm going to call Henry and tell him." She rushed inside the house with Bubba on her heels.

"That was a rotten thing to do," I told Clinton as I joined him on the glider. The sunlight was slowly fading, and the air was nippy. I huddled in my coat. "You knew I couldn't say no with the girl standing there looking at me like that."

He nodded. "You're right; I *did* know."

As I gazed at him, it was all I could do to keep from

touching him. I hadn't realized just how much I'd missed him until now. Why had he stayed away?

"You okay?" he said.

"Some days are harder than others."

"You saved three lives, Emily."

"I wish I could have saved Herschel's," I said sadly.

He took my hand and squeezed it. We were both silent for a moment. "You've probably been wondering why I stayed away."

I offered him a blank look. "Oh? Were you away?"

He grinned. "I had to go back to Chicago. To get my things out of storage."

I was determined not to act curious. I merely nodded.

"Chief Hix has finally decided to do some traveling in his RV after all, so he's retiring. The mayor offered me his job. Actually, they offered it to Conners first, but Conners has been accepted into the FBI, so I was their second choice. I wasn't real flattered at first, but Hix reminded me that Conners had been here a while, so it was only fitting they approach him first. Even if I do decide to take the job, I might make them sweat it out for a while."

"Aren't you afraid you'll get bored working in a small town?"

He studied me. "Boredom is the last thing I'm worried about."

I didn't know how to respond. "So what's the first thing you're worried about?"

"Losing you. I think I would have seen DeWayne for the killer he was, if I hadn't been personally involved. All the clues were there: Who else but DeWayne, with all his contacts, would have managed to get his hands on strychnine? But I kept telling myself that my suspicions were based on jealousy and nothing more. After all, he'd done so much to help you and Molly; he seemed genuinely concerned about your welfare."

"So you're blaming me because you're a lousy cop?"

He laughed, then sobered instantly. "When I listened to Molly on your answering machine that night, I knew

DeWayne was the one, and I wanted to kick myself for ignoring the facts. You told me that DeWayne was abused by his mother, and I knew the killer hated women.'' He shook his head. ''I was so blind. Just goes to show you what happens when a cop lets his heart do his thinking.''

''A few days ago, you told me you were able to remain somewhat detached.''

He shook his head. ''Not when it comes to you, babe.''

The look in his eyes almost curled my toes. ''It's over now,'' I said.

''Not quite. It looks like Augustus Gillespie is going to do everything possible to hurt me. Not that I blame him after what I did to his son.''

''It was an accident, Clinton. Frank tripped.''

''I'm still reponsible for the fact an innocent man is suffering from a brain injury and might not recover.''

''Frank wasn't so innocent.'' I saw him frown. ''There's something I've been meaning to tell you,'' I said. ''Something I should have told you a long time ago.''

I told him about that night fifteen years ago and the murder I'd witnessed at the hands of Frank Gillespie. As I relived the details I watched Clinton's expression change from disbelief to horror and finally pity. ''I could never be sure if Frank saw me, but he threatened to come after me if I told what I'd seen.''

''And you stayed quiet all these years?'' Clinton said.

''I told DeWayne about it the night of my sister's funeral. When Frank was paroled, DeWayne used it to scare me, hoping I would turn to him. He'd already been filling Molly's head with doubts and fears. He imagined us as one big happy family. Until you came on the scene, and he figured we were sleeping together. I suddenly became no better in his eyes than my sister. Or those other women,'' I added.

''That's why you were so sure Frank was the culprit,'' he said. ''My God, Emily, why didn't you say something? How did you manage to live with this all those years?''

I realized I was crying. "I was so scared. If you'd seen what Frank did to poor Daryl. I suppose you think I'm a big coward."

He put his arms around me. "Not in the least, babe. I think you're one of the bravest people I know. We're going to get through this, Emily. Nobody's going to bother you or Molly again. Not as long as there's breath in my body. I love you, sweetheart."

In an instant things suddenly felt brighter, as though the sun had come out after days and days of gloom. "Are you sure?" I asked.

Clinton took my hand and raised it to his lips. The look in his eyes was tender. "You've restored my faith, Emily. For that, I'd like to thank you." He paused. "Would you marry me if I asked you?"

I think my heart stopped beating. Did he say "marry"?

I probably shouldn't have accepted his proposal so eagerly and had him think I was overly anxious, but that's exactly what I did, literally pouncing on the poor man, kissing his face and making an absolute fool of myself. But I knew a good thing when I saw it, and I wasn't about to let this one get away from me, even if it meant breaking both of his legs. He laughed at my show of exuberance and pulled me into his arms for a long kiss.

Afterward, I snuggled against him, only vaguely aware of the chill in the air. Inside, it felt as though my heart were on fire.